CURSED CITY

Other great stories from Warhammer Age of Sigmar

CURSED CITY

C L WERNER

BLACK LIBRARY

A BLACK LIBRARY PUBLICATION

First published in 2021.
This edition published in Great Britain in 2022 by
Black Library, Games Workshop Ltd., Willow Road,
Nottingham, NG7 2WS, UK.

Represented by: Games Workshop Limited – Irish branch,
Unit 3, Lower Liffey Street, Dublin 1,
D01 K199, Ireland.

10 9 8 7 6 5 4 3 2 1

Produced by Games Workshop in Nottingham.
Cover illustration by Kevin Chin.

A CIP record for this book is available from the British Library.

ISBN 13: 978-1-78999-947-1

See Black Library on the internet at

blacklibrary.com

Find out more about Games Workshop
and the worlds of Warhammer at

games-workshop.com

Printed and bound by CPI Group (UK) Ltd, Croydon, CR0 4YY

The Mortal Realms have been despoiled. Ravaged by the followers of the Chaos Gods, they stand on the brink of utter destruction.

The fortress-cities of Sigmar are islands of light in a sea of darkness. Constantly besieged, their walls are assailed by maniacal hordes and monstrous beasts. The bones of good men are littered thick outside the gates. These bulwarks of Order are embattled within as well as without, for the lure of Chaos beguiles the citizens with promises of power.

Still the champions of Order fight on. At the break of dawn, the Crusader's Bell rings and a new expedition departs. Storm-forged knights march shoulder to shoulder with resolute militia, stoic duardin and slender aelves. Bedecked in the splendour of war, the Dawnbringer Crusades venture out to found civilisations anew. These grim pioneers take with them the fires of hope. Yet they go forth into a hellish wasteland.

Out in the wilds, hardy colonists restore order to a crumbling world. Haunted eyes scan the horizon for tyrannical reavers as they build upon the bones of ancient empires, eking out a meagre existence from cursed soil and ice-cold seas. By their valour, the fate of the Mortal Realms will be decided.

The ravening terrors that prey upon these settlers take a thousand forms. Cannibal barbarians and deranged murderers crawl from hidden lairs. Martial hosts clad in black steel march from skull-strewn castles. The savage hordes of Destruction batter the frontier towns until no stone stands atop another. In the dead of night come howling throngs of the undead, hungry to feast upon the living.

Against such foes, courage is the truest defence and the most effective weapon. It is something that Sigmar's chosen do not lack. But they are not always strong enough to prevail, and even in victory, each new battle saps their souls a little more.

This is the time of turmoil. This is the era of war.

This is the Age of Sigmar.

PROLOGUE

A heavy fog rolled over the waterfront and into crooked streets and alleyways. The greasy tang of the Cor Mortifus percolated through the air, redolent of the grisly creatures that swam and crawled in its murky sea. Blackened beads of condensation dripped down crumbling walls and sagging roofs to gather in shadowy puddles amid the cobblestones. The sharp chirps of bats and the flutter of leathery wings drifted down from the night sky. From a distance, wolf-like howls and ghostly shrieks sent their macabre echoes down into the city.

Ulfenkarn. Perched on cliffs overlooking Banshee's Bay, the great city on the island of Szargorond had stood proud and defiant, a bastion of mankind in the unforgiving chill of Shyish. Long had it stood as a light amid the darkness. But no light burns forever in the realm of Nagash. When the shadows finally came for the city once known as Mournhold, they did so with a vengeance.

Once the sun had set and night ruled the streets, only desperation could make the mortal inhabitants of the city stray abroad.

For they were no longer alone. The old nobility had been cast down and new masters now ruled over them. An aristocracy of the night.

Annika Haustel was desperate. The last two years had been harder on her than the twenty before them. Her parents were dead. Her husband was missing, his ship lost at sea so long ago it was delusion to think he was alive. For a time, she'd enjoyed the support of a middle-aged chandler, but he'd been crippled fighting off a hungry blood-bat one night and could no longer earn enough to feed himself, much less anyone else. A younger brother was the only family she had left, aside from her child, Milja. Her brother had taken him in, but only so long as Annika could pay for the extra food. As he put it, he wasn't going to starve his own family to feed his sister's brat.

Thieving came easily to Annika. The short stature and slight build that came from a starveling existence all her life suited the trade. Her reflexes were keen, her fingers deft, and her eyes sharp. She could see in the dark almost like a cat and was able to evaluate the contents of a purse from ten yards away. It was natural for her to put these talents to use. The problem for Annika was that most of the people in Ulfenkarn were as poor as she was. Seldom did she find a good prospect.

Tonight, Annika was feeling pleased with herself as she stole through the dark alleyways between the rotting buildings of the Ostvein district. She'd found a black-market dealer hurrying away from a rendezvous with a customer, and the purse hanging from his belt had been deliciously heavy. A flash of her knife and she had her prize and was darting into a side street. Perhaps once the man realised it was gone he'd recall the woman who'd brushed so close to him. Then he'd raise the alarm. Or perhaps not. The Volk-shaufen would be apt to ask questions about where he'd got his wealth to begin with.

Annika stopped in the shadow of an archway beside a rope-maker's shop and jiggled the purse in her hand. It felt heavier than she'd expected. She pulled the bag open and teased a piece of its contents out into her palm. Her eyes widened with wonder. It wasn't a bit of whalebone she held, but something much smoother. Her breath caught in her throat and she rushed to a spot of moon-light that had fought its way down through the fog. Even in such feeble illumination, she knew what she held was pearl.

Pearl! Annika's heart thundered with the promise of what this wealth would mean for her. She could rent a room of her own instead of sleeping under a table in Baoban's beerhall. Milja could live with her too. Yes, there'd be enough for that. Even after she had a fence change the pearl to ten-weight ivory, there'd be enough money to do that!

The promise of almost forgotten dreams sent fear flaring through Annika as nothing before ever had. So close to having everything she wanted, now she was terrified it could all be taken away. The man she'd robbed, certainly he would be looking for her. He was sure to have noticed by now that the pearl discs were gone. He'd scour the Ostvein looking for her. When he caught her, Annika would be left with nothing! No real home to offer Milja, just that spot in the sawdust under Baoban's table.

Annika's fingers curled around the purse in a steely grip. She hurried away from the moonlight, shunning its revealing rays as she rushed through the frigid darkness. She ran and ran, dart-ing down alleys and across streets to confuse the pursuers she was certain were after her. The turns she took were seized upon at random. Up one lane, down another. In her haste she didn't even notice the gibbet swinging from a lamp post, its occupant bled white by the bats that infested the city. Fright and fog soon had Annika uncertain of where she was. All she knew was that someone was following her.

Perhaps if Annika Haustel had paid more attention to what was ahead of her than what was behind, she wouldn't have died.

The first Annika was aware of the dark figure that met her in the courtyard was when she felt a burning pain in her abdomen. She gasped and dropped the purse to the ground. Dimly she heard the sound of pearl discs scattering across the cobblestones. She registered faintly the presence of someone standing in front of her. The only thing that was distinct was the sharp pain in her stomach and the blood that rushed over her hand.

'It's… mine…' Annika groaned. She was still thinking of the money and the dreams it would buy.

The gleam of the knife in the stranger's hand was the last thing she saw.

Her killer had no interest in the money at all. Though Annika Haustel would never know it, she'd just become the first victim of a monster the people of Ulfenkarn would soon call Baron Grin.

CHAPTER ONE

Though the shutters were barred, and the doors bolted, the Black Ship was more alive in the long hours of the night than it had been during the dreary grey day. The tavern was ablaze with the light of whale-oil lamps and its common room rumbled with the clamour of a hundred raucous conversations, people huddling together in the warmth that was absent in the cold streets. Flagons of ale, steins of beer, bottles of pungent vodka and glasses of dark wine were carried to patrons throughout the building's three levels, borne upon wide copper trays by the buxom, strong-armed beer maidens employed by Effrim Karzah, the establishment's roguish proprietor. Notes of music crawled through the rooms as a rotund performer worked a hurdy-gurdy and bellowed salacious sea shanties.

A long casketwood bar dominated one side of the common room. Patrons flocked to the counter, loudly shouting for more drink. Whalers with salt-encrusted slickers would brush shoulders with crookbacked lobstermen, their fingers and hands scarred from the claws of their catch. Stokers who worked the immense try pots to render blubber into oil sought to cool their hot work with cold ales. Drovers and stevedores propped their boots on the copper rail that ran along the base of the bar and swapped lies about the day's custom. Among those seeking to retreat from their labours mixed those whose vocation catered to such relaxation. Gamblers and panderers, sellers of wares and seekers of services all ventured to the counter to engage those gathered there.

Only at one spot was the bar not crowded. Towards the back of the common room, for a radius of a dozen feet, there was an open space. Within that space only two people stood. The two men had been there for some time now, yet none of the carousing inmates of the tavern intruded on their privacy. From the guarded looks that sometimes were directed their way, it wasn't courtesy that provoked such distance, but fear.

One was tall with a light complexion and locks of fair hair spilling out from beneath his wide-brimmed hat. His features had a rugged handsomeness about them, with a hawkish nose and piercing blue eyes. A long coat encompassed his figure, but around the waist it was bound by a wide belt from which hung a rakish sword and a big horse pistol. It was not the open display of weapons that so unsettled the occupants of the Black Ship, however. Hanging about the man's neck was a pendant, a little silver talisman cast in a symbol long taboo in Ulfenkarn. The hammer of Sigmar. To openly display veneration of the God-King in the city was to invite swift and terrible destruction. Had night not already fallen, were the doors not already barred, there were many who would have slunk back to their slovenly hovels. As things stood, they tried their best to keep apart from the stranger. When doom came for him, nobody wanted to share in it.

Except perhaps the man who was with him. He was thin with short black hair and a trim moustache beneath his knife-sharp nose. Though he wore clothes that were rich by the standards of Ulfenkarn, his skin had the grey pallor of those who toiled away in the mushroom plantations beneath the streets. His eyes looked as though they were caught in a perpetual scowl, disdainfully appraising everything and everyone they gazed on. From his haughty demeanour and sinister appearance, there were many in the Black Ship who marked him as an agent of Ulfenkarn's rulers, one who'd been promised the Blood Kiss by his masters. Why a spy for the vampires was sharing a drink with a Sigmarite was a mystery none felt inclined to explore.

Gustaf Voss pushed back the brim of his hat so he could better see the bottles arrayed on the rack behind the bar. 'They've a nice vintage from Carstinia there,' he commented to his companion. 'That is if you don't think it would be too strong for you?'

The other man gave him a stern look. 'That's an old Belvegrodian fable, you know. That *they* don't drink wine.' He frowned at his glass and tapped a finger against its stem. 'I don't like drinking in public. It dulls the senses and you never know what might be watching, waiting to exploit the first hint of weakness. If you're going to have libations, it's better to indulge when you're alone.'

Gustaf cast his eyes at the empty space around them. 'We're as good as alone right now, Vladrik,' he said.

'All it takes is wealth to be popular in places like this,' he replied. 'Though I don't know if there's enough money to make them friendly while you're wearing that.' He gestured to the hammer around Gustaf's neck.

Gustaf took a pull from his beer stein and wiped away the residue of foam from his mouth. 'There was a saying, something along the lines of "Let them hate as long as they also fear." That wisdom has served me well until now.' He gave Vladrik a more serious look. 'If I make myself conspicuous then the man I'm looking for might find me, instead of making me find him.'

'Or you might draw attention from those you don't want to see,' Vladrik cautioned. 'I've told you I'll find Jelsen Darrock for you.'

'It's been two weeks that I've been hearing that,' Gustaf said. 'You haven't given me any results.'

Vladrik swallowed some of his wine and dabbed a monogrammed handkerchief against his lips. 'Better than anyone, you should know that those who serve the Order of Azyr can be very hard to find when they want to be. I think Darrock has been keeping himself under cover right now. He's been busy. Only two days ago someone broken into Count Vorkov's coffin and put a stake through his heart. Aqshian fyrewood. Very rare. Very dangerous. The kind of thing even a vampire doesn't recover from.'

Vladrik leaned closer and laid his hand on Gustaf's arm.

'That's one thing I'm still unsure of. Did the Order of Azyr send you to Ulfenkarn to help Darrock or to stop him? You've never told me which.'

'No, I didn't,' Gustaf said. 'If you expect an answer, find Darrock for me.'

Gustaf spun around suddenly, one hand dropping to the big horse pistol on his belt. Someone had entered the circle of privacy that surrounded them. A haggard stevedore, the quality of his tunic and the polish of his boots indicating him to be a mark above the labourers who crowded behind him, marched towards the shunned pair. He threw back his head and gave Gustaf a sneering study.

'You make sport of us, do you, outlander?' He gestured at the talisman hanging from Gustaf's neck. 'Even a fool fresh off the boat knows better than to wear that openly. So, if you aren't a fool, you must be an idiot.'

Drink slurred the man's words, but Gustaf wasn't one to allow even a tipsy antagonist to challenge him.

'Where I come from, men are still men. They don't hide their faith and cower in the shadows like vermin. They don't bow and scrape to the monsters that prey on them.'

The stevedore's face turned red. His hands curled into fists at his sides.

'He's got a gun, Loew,' one of the other labourers warned.

Gustaf fixed his steely gaze on Loew. 'I don't need gun or sword to settle accounts with cowards,' he said, moving his hands away from the weapons hanging from his belt. For a moment, the tableau held, the two men glaring into one another's eyes, each ready for his foe to make the first move.

Loud pounding against the Black Ship's door interrupted the brewing fight. Silence descended on the tavern. Most of the patrons turned to look towards the barred entrance while others retreated into the nearest shadow. From outside, an imperious voice demanded entry.

'The Volkshaufen,' Vladrik hissed. He quickly bolted what was left of his wine.

'Maybe,' Gustaf said. It was rare for the watchmen to be abroad at night. Ulfenkarn had other guards who patrolled the city when the sun set… but not the sort to ask admittance.

'Make yourself scarce until we know who it is,' Gustaf told Vladrik. He didn't watch his companion withdraw and climb the back stairs to the Black Ship's upper floor. His attention was fixed on the barred door and whoever was demanding entry.

Perched on a stool near the entrance was a short, scrawny creature with long ears and scabby green skin. The grot looked across the room to where Karzah sat at one of the gambling tables. The Black Ship's proprietor nodded reluctantly. The grot jabbed the hulking brute that stood beside it with a sharp stick. The square-jawed orruk roused itself from its fungus-addled lethargy and drew back the bar on the door. Karzah preferred to use the greenskins as his establishment's first line of defence because their blood wasn't appetising to the things that prowled the city.

Instead of the Volkshaufen, it was a trio of men in finely cut sealskin coats who sauntered past the orruk. Gustaf noticed the mirror discreetly placed on the ceiling above the door. All three men were reflected in it, but that meant nothing. If one of them was a vampire and was aware of the mirror's presence, he could project an image into the glass and thereby conceal his nature.

Of course, in Ulfenkarn, a vampire had little reason to hide what he was. At least from people who weren't Jelsen Darrock. Or Gustaf Voss.

'Looks like it's already too late to teach you anything,' Loew told Gustaf, a trace of regret in his voice. 'May the soil rest easy on your grave,' he added, withdrawing back among the labourers. They retreated while the three men walked straight towards Gustaf.

'Now there's a peculiar sight,' one of the men quipped as he approached. He turned his ferret-face and glanced about the tavern. 'It seems no one wants to drink with you. Don't you have any friends?' The question brought a cruel laugh from one of his associates, a bull-necked ruffian who looked more like a shaved bear than anything human.

'No company is better than poor company,' Gustaf replied. He raised his beer stein and took a quick drink.

Ferret looked at his associates. 'Bravado,' he said. 'I like that. I tell you what, I don't like to see someone drink alone.' He walked to the counter and snapped his fingers at one of the barkeepers. 'Bring me ale,' he demanded.

While Ferret waited for his flagon, the men with him circled around Gustaf. Bear took position to his left while the other, a nasty specimen Gustaf decided to think of as 'Cur', sidled towards his right.

'We'll have a drink and then we'll leave,' Ferret said, a sneer on his face as he regarded Gustaf. 'No smart words for me now?' He glanced at his associates. 'Notice how the banter falls off when they feel the noose get tight?'

Bear laughed at the remark. Cur just closed his fingers around the grip of his sword.

'To your health, as long as it holds out,' Ferret toasted Gustaf, raising his flagon.

At that moment the subject of his mockery exploded into action. To onlookers, it all seemed to happen simultaneously, so quickly did the outlander move. A boot kicked out and struck the flagon, bathing Ferret's face in ale. Gustaf threw the beer in his stein into Cur's face, blinding him. Bear sprang forwards, but as he did the stein came smashing down onto his head and dropped him to the floor.

Gustaf dashed away from his reeling foes and hurried across the common room. Before he reached the door, the orruk had once more drawn the bar away. He lunged past the greenskin and out into the darkened street. He could hear angry oaths and the stamp of running feet from the building behind him.

Of more immediate concern were the men who'd been waiting outside.

The ruffians converged on Gustaf the moment he stepped from the Black Ship. In their eagerness to seize their victim, they made a costly mistake. Like Ferret and his associates inside, these men discovered that their enemy was far from helpless. Steel flashed in the light escaping from the tavern as Gustaf whipped the sword from his belt. Its keen edge slashed across the face of the closest ruffian. He reeled away across the icy ground and pitched backwards into the arms of his comrades, screaming and clutching at the gory wreckage left by the blade.

Shocked by the abrupt violence, the ruffians were slow to react when Gustaf turned from them and ran down the darkened street.

It was only when Ferret appeared in the Black Ship's doorway and cursed at them that they remembered their task. Leaving their maimed companion to writhe in the dirt, the thugs set off in pursuit of their quarry.

'You can't escape, outlander!' Ferret shouted as he led the mob. 'I'll carve your face worse than you did Karl's before I turn you over to the boss!'

Gustaf risked a glance over his shoulder as the threats reached his ears. There were nine men chasing after him, each brandishing a sword as they ran. A single adversary, even two, and he'd have stood his ground and crossed blades with them. These, however, were odds that surpassed even his confidence.

He saw the dark mouth of an alleyway ahead of him on his left, just beyond the shadowy hulk of a broken wagon. Gustaf feinted a sideways lunge to the right, then pivoted and threw himself to the left.

'He's ducked under that wagon!' one of the thugs shouted.

Gustaf grinned and hurried down the alleyway. He'd soon put distance between himself and the ruffians.

At least that was the hope, but after only a few steps into the narrow alley Gustaf was betrayed. Trying to keep tabs on his pursuers, he didn't see the pillory until he blundered into it. The prisoner, some manner of thief to judge by the marks branded into his cheeks, had been left out to give back to the community what he'd stolen in the only way the poor could make recompense. Locked in the pillory, the prisoner's blood could be drained by anyone who wished to offer it in place of their own as their blood tithe. Usually a prisoner didn't live long enough exposed in the cold to see the sun set, much less to last after nightfall. By some perverse chance, there was just enough life left in the thief to cry out when Gustaf stumbled against him.

The cry carried out into the street.

'He's not here, you idiots!' Ferret roared. 'He's down there!'

Gustaf ran as his pursuers picked up his trail. His lead was less than a dozen feet. The slightest setback would see him fall into the clutches of his enemies. When he dashed out the other side of the alley, he found that setback. The narrow pathway opened into a small courtyard bounded on all sides by dilapidated buildings. He was trapped.

Vicious laughter rang out behind him. Gustaf spun around to see Ferret and his men slowly emerging from the alley.

'Outsmarted yourself, didn't you?' Ferret grinned. He waved for the thugs to spread out and encircle Gustaf. 'Remember, the Elder said he wants him alive. Whatever else happens' – he made a dismissive shrug – 'happens.'

'I can promise a few of you won't have an easy time of it,' Gustaf swore, punctuating his words with a flourish of his sword. His other hand pulled the horse pistol from its holster.

'Good.' Ferret laughed. 'If you kill a few that just means more pay for the rest of us.' He gestured with his hand, motioning his confederates to close in.

Before they could, Ferret barked in alarm. His sword clattered against the cobblestones as he raised his arms in surrender.

Standing behind Ferret, the edge of her sword pressed against his throat, was a woman wearing a long black cloak. Gustaf could only see clearly the hand gripping the sword. The skin was coarse and deeply tanned, the fingers calloused from rugged employment. The face was largely hidden by the shadow of a hood, but he could feel the intensity of her gaze as she looked at him.

'You seem to be the leader,' she snarled at Ferret, pressing the sword closer so it drew a bead of blood from his neck. 'Call your dogs off.'

'Do as she says,' Ferret called to his men. None of them moved in response to his plea. 'I'm the only one who knows the Elder.

If I die, nobody gets paid.' The last bit of logic swayed the ruffians. Sullenly they backed away from Gustaf and shuffled towards the edges of the close.

Gustaf peered suspiciously at the woman behind Ferret. He kept a firm grip on his weapons, but didn't move.

'What are you waiting for?' the woman snapped at him.

'I've been in Ulfenkarn long enough to know better than to trust anything,' Gustaf replied. He glanced around at the thugs and the narrow confines of the close. 'Nobody does anything in this city unless it is to benefit themselves.'

Ferret laughed. 'Is that what you want? A cut of the reward?'

The woman responded by whipping her sword away from Ferret's neck and smashing the hilt against his ear. He crumpled at her feet, staggered by the blow. 'Get moving or stay here with your playmates,' she shouted at Gustaf. 'I've done my part.'

She turned and ran into the dark alley.

Gustaf lost all hesitation. He sprang forwards and dashed into the alleyway, mashing Ferret's face with his sword's guard as he passed.

'After them!' Ferret shrieked, one hand trying to staunch the flow of blood from his broken nose. 'I want them! I want both of them!'

Gustaf reached the street and caught sight of his rescuer's cloak whipping around a corner on the other side. With the sound of pursuing thugs behind him, he raced after the mysterious woman. He still had no idea who she was or what her motives might be, but at least it was certain she wasn't in league with Ferret and his mob. For the moment that was enough to sway Gustaf.

When he reached the next street, Gustaf glimpsed her dashing into a narrow gap between a half-ruined net-maker's shop and a fishmonger's stall. He rushed after her, slipping into the shadows a moment after she vanished from sight. As the dark closed around him, he felt the point of a blade pressing against his ribs. Only faintly could he make out the outline of a hood in the feeble light seeping down through the fog.

'Easy,' he said. 'I'm Gustaf Voss. The man you rescued just now.'

'I know who you are,' the woman said. 'I've been observing you for a week now.'

The explanation escalated Gustaf's suspicions. 'So that swine was right. You are after my scalp. What are you? Bounty hunter? Assassin?'

The blade was withdrawn. The woman took a step forwards and drew back her hood.

'Neither. I've nothing to do with such scum.'

Gustaf could make out her face now. There was a loveliness there, but it was subdued, locked away beneath the resolute and uncompromising strength that dominated her visage. Her eyes were like flakes of steel and their gaze pierced him every bit as her blade had threatened to do.

'I'm Emelda Braskov.'

Her name made Gustaf's fingers tighten about his sword. 'Braskov!' he cried. He raised the pistol, pointing it at her face. She met the threat with a steely stare.

'The last of the Braskovs,' Emelda explained. 'The last that… that isn't one of *his* creatures. The last *living* Braskov. If you understand what that means, then you'll know why a man like you interests me.'

Gustaf peered keenly at the woman's face, searching for the least hint of deception. Long years training in the Order of Azyr had made him an expert in distinguishing truth from trickery.

'If you know who I am, then you know it is fatal to tell lies to a vampire hunter.'

By way of reply, Emelda pressed her hand to the amulet Gustaf wore. He felt her fingers against his chest as they curled tight around the icon.

'If I were one of *them* could I do this?' she challenged him. 'I tell you, I am Emelda Braskov. The last of my line.'

Gustaf turned to face the street. He could see two of the ruffians hurry around the corner. It was obvious to him that the thugs were following their trail through the snow.

'Braskov or no, right now we've other problems,' he said. 'Two against nine are still bad odds.'

'There's a back way out,' Emelda said.

The vampire hunter sheathed his sword and let her draw him down a darkened pathway. The buildings pressed close upon them so that Gustaf was compelled to remove his hat as they went. He could smell the chalky odour of a stone-cutter's shop as they progressed. At the end of the path he saw a small yard littered with unworked marble and granite. A few partly carved stones were leaning against a wooden framework. A sledge and a small cart peeked out from beneath the shadow of a wooden awning. A rusty iron fence circled two sides of the yard, while the others were bordered by the surrounding buildings.

'We can lose them in those streets.' Gustaf pointed to the dark lane outside the yard's gate. He started towards it, but Emelda held him back.

'We're not alone,' she told him. 'I've been around long enough to recognise an ambush.' She reached down and recovered a splinter of stone from the cracked cobbles. With a powerful throw she sent it flying against one of the half-finished memorials. The impact brought the heavy block tipping over. It crashed against the ground with a resounding boom.

All around the yard, figures sprang out of hiding. They started towards the fallen block, but quickly realised their mistake.

'They're over there,' Ferret snapped at the thugs as he emerged from beneath the awning's shadow. He glanced over at Bear and Cur, who'd likewise been hiding in the dark, beckoning them forwards. Another man kept to the shadows, only the outline of his head and shoulders visible. 'Get them before they get away again,' Ferret ordered the ruffians. 'They can't take all of us.'

'Maybe not, but you won't be spending any blood money!' Gustaf shouted. He raised his pistol and fired at Ferret. Flame exploded out the gun's barrel, briefly illuminating the yard. The bullet slammed into Ferret's chest, the impact hurling him back like a rag doll. He crashed against the sledge, then toppled forwards onto his face, a gory hole the size of a fist in his back where the shot had punched through his flesh.

For an instant, the remaining thugs stood in stunned silence. Then a raspy voice snarled at them from under the awning.

'There's still a fifty-weight of whalebone to share among you.'

The speaker stepped into the dim light. The 'Elder' of which Ferret had spoken. A gaunt shape dressed in crimson, heavy cape drawn about his shoulders, feathered hat poised above his predatory features. His was a face impossible to forget, lean to an improbable degree, the flesh drawn tight about the bones. There was a savage aspect to his visage that evoked the snarling wolf and the prowling jackal. His eyes were like firebrands, shining with wicked hunger. His ashy skin was drawn away from his mouth, exposing the long, jagged fangs.

'Vampire,' Emelda hissed when she beheld the creature.

'It calls itself Viscount Lupu,' Gustaf told her. He thought about what Vladrik had said. There could be only one reason the vampire had taken such pains to lure him out of the Black Ship. It was looking for Darrock and had mistaken Gustaf for the witch hunter. Gustaf decided not to disabuse Lupu of the error. 'It is a pity I didn't find your coffin when I was disposing of Count Vorkov.' He shifted his grip on the spent pistol, feeling the bite of its hot barrel through his glove. The heavy, studded butt of the gun would make a vicious cudgel. With his other hand he drew his sword. 'At least you've done me the courtesy of not forcing me to look for you.'

'You destroyed the master,' Lupu growled. 'Without him, I don't know what will become of me. But I know what will become of *you*.' The vampire pointed one of his clawed fingers. 'Kill them,' he commanded the ruffians. 'Kill them both.'

The thugs came at them in a rush. 'Guard my flank and I'll guard yours,' Gustaf told Emelda as he sprang forwards to meet the charge. He was startled to find that she'd lingered back in the alleyway, leaving him to face six killers on his own. There wasn't time to consider her unexpected timidity. He had trouble enough to match the surge of enemies. In a swirl of blades, he parried enemy weapons and slashed at unprotected shoulders and arms with his sword and tried to club them with his pistol. None of his strokes did more than nip the skin of the ruffians, but it served to make them draw back.

While grateful for the respite, Gustaf feared the consequences of giving his enemies time to think. If they came at him with any measure of coordination, he was finished.

'Lost your taste for blood?' Gustaf mocked the thugs. 'I can assure you your employer hasn't. Right now, it's probably lapping up whatever spilled out of your leader.'

Before he could gauge if his taunts were having any effect, a scream rose from the alleyway behind Gustaf. He turned his head to see Emelda come rushing out. She'd thrown aside her cloak, revealing a hauberk of boiled leather and studded steel. The sword in her hand was stained with blood.

'The two we saw in the street,' Emelda explained as she joined Gustaf. 'When the wolf is before you, you can't afford to forget the weasel at your back.'

Gustaf nodded and glared at the other ruffians. 'No more help,' he warned them. 'Just you and us. My only question is, who wants to die first?'

'Kill them or suffer,' Lupu threatened the thugs. The vampire's displeasure was more a menace in the minds of the ruffians than the swords of Gustaf and Emelda. Shouting fierce battle cries, they swarmed the two warriors.

Emelda's blade ripped open the leg of the first thug to get near to her. The man staggered back, wailing in agony. Two others closed with her, however, and gradually forced her back. Gustaf was left to contend with the remaining three. They fought with a sloppy, careless style, displaying the prowess of men unused to opponents who could fight back. To their slovenly technique, however, was added a frantic recklessness that made them attack with little regard for their own safety. Beset by such foes, Gustaf found he had to suppress his own instincts. If he capitalised on an enemy who blatantly left an opening for him, he would expose himself to the blades of the others. He was compelled to adopt a defensive approach and employ a caution he hadn't shown since he'd first learned to swing a sword.

At length, one of Gustaf's enemies exposed a weakness that he felt safe to capitalise on. He plunged forwards, stabbing his blade deep into the ruffian's chest when the man let down his guard. Blood spurted from the wound as the killer's body sagged at the end of Gustaf's sword.

Before he could wrench his blade free of the dying man, the vampire hunter was thrown onto the ground, his fingers ripped away from the weapon's grip. The pistol went skittering away from his other hand.

It wasn't a mortal thug who had knocked Gustaf to the ground. Viscount Lupu leaned over him, the vampire's rank breath blowing down into his face. The fiend had waited for his enemy to be disarmed before entering the fray. Now Lupu exulted in his supremacy.

'See to the woman,' Lupu snarled at the surviving ruffians. His claw-like hands pressed down on Gustaf's arms, pinning him to the ground. The vampire's fangs glistened in the moonlight. 'This one... This one is *mine*.'

Gustaf lifted his head and spat in the cadaverous face. Lupu hissed in rage, but then a wicked smile curled his withered face.

'Killing you will be thirsty work,' he promised.

Gustaf closed his eyes and whispered a prayer to Sigmar. He'd resigned himself to a death like this when first he took it upon himself to hunt vampires in Carstinia. Even so, now that the end was upon him, he was determined to resist it to the last.

A flash of spectral light caused Gustaf to open his eyes. The pressure against his arms lessened and he wrested himself free of Lupu's grip. He found the vampire writhing in agony. The ashy skin was blackened and crumbling, flakes falling away to disintegrate on the ground.

While Gustaf crawled away from the vampire, there came a second burst of spectral light. This time he saw the glow envelop Lupu, watched as the undead sizzled within the horrible luminescence. The vampire opened his mouth to scream, but as he did, teeth fell free from the jaw and the charred residue of his tongue fell back into his throat.

Across the yard Gustaf spotted a sinister shape draped in black robes. The man held a crooked staff topped by a scythe-like blade in the pale hand that he was pointing at Lupu. The interloper had a dark and morbid countenance, drawn and wasted in its expression. Gustaf could see the narrow slit of a mouth moving, whispering words he knew to be some manner of incantation. While he watched, an orb of ghostly energy flitted away from the staff and struck the vampire. This third blast of arcane power was too much for the undead. Lupu was bowled over by the assault and when his burnt body struck the ground, it disintegrated into a mound of ashes.

The vampire's destruction provoked screams of terror from the surviving ruffians. To a man they fled across the yard, leaping over the iron gate and scattering into the surrounding streets. Emelda leaned down and cleaned her blade with the shirt of a fallen enemy. Then, like Gustaf, her attention was fixed on the strange interloper.

'Your help was rather timely,' Emelda said, an edge of suspicion in her tone. Though she'd cleaned her sword, she made no move to return it to its scabbard.

The wizard brushed aside the complaint. 'No more so than your own, Emelda Braskov. Like yourself, I've taken an interest in our friend Gustaf Voss. It would have been inconvenient to me if he'd perished for the sake of that grave-leech's petty revenge.' He made a dismissive wave at Lupu's ashes.

Gustaf recovered his own weapons. He replaced the pistol in its holster but like Emelda, he kept hold of his sword. 'You'll be welcome to my thanks once I know your motives...'

'Morrvahl Olbrecht,' the wizard said, stroking the long black beard that hung from his chin. 'I see that name means little to either of you, but there are some in Ulfenkarn who have reason to tremble when it is invoked.' He nodded and wagged his finger at Gustaf. 'Yes, it would surprise you who *does* know me here. For the nonce, let us say I intervened because we share mutual enemies. That makes us friends, doesn't it? Or am I presumptuous?'

'It makes you hasty,' Gustaf said. 'At best. I know something of magic and its character. What you used to destroy Lupu... that was necromancy.'

'A necromancer,' Emelda growled, brandishing her sword.

Morrvahl shook his head. 'There isn't time for this,' he said. 'You picked a poor night to tussle with Lupu and his hirelings. This district will soon be crawling with patrols.'

'Because of Lupu?' Gustaf asked.

'No,' Morrvahl said. 'Because of the murder.'

A bitter laugh escaped Emelda. 'Murder? There are murders every night in Ulfenkarn!'

Morrvahl turned towards her. His eyes had an intense quality to them. 'Not like this one there aren't.' He glanced about the yard and swung around towards the gate. 'Come along with me. I know a safe place to hide that isn't far from here. You can lie low there until the hue and cry dies down.'

Emelda looked over at Gustaf. 'I don't trust him.'

'That's two of us,' the vampire hunter agreed. He glanced at the heap of ashes then back to the robed wizard waiting for them at the gate. 'I confess I am intrigued to know what kind of game he's playing.'

'So, what do we do?' Emelda asked.

'For now, we follow him,' Gustaf said. 'Just keep your eyes open.' He nodded at Emelda's blade. 'And keep your sword close. If Morrvahl is up to something, he won't give us much time to do anything about it.'

'Hurry along,' the wizard urged them. 'If we tarry too long the Ulfenwatch will decide one of us is the killer. Trust me, that's one death you don't want blamed on you.'

Dragomir was unique among the ranks of the Volkshaufen. He hadn't bought his captain's commission through either bribery or blackmail. He'd risen through the ranks by dint of his skill alone. He'd proven himself a keen investigator and a remorseless persecutor of the city's criminal elements. Whether uncovering the hiding spots of those who would defy the city's blood-tax or rooting out a nest of proscribed Sigmarites, his accomplishments had garnered him notice. Even the corrupt mortals who administered the slums of Ulfenkarn knew better than to defy the desires of the vampires who ruled the city.

In all his years patrolling the streets and back alleys, Dragomir couldn't remember a scene to equal the ghastliness of that within the courtyard. It was remarkable enough that even his commander had agreed with him that the nobles should be informed of what had been found. It still came as a shock to him when a troop of Ulfenwatch arrived to cordon off the courtyard while an emissary from the Ebon Citadel itself investigated the scene.

Dragomir had a twinge of envy as he watched Silentiary Arno. The man had a bloodless pallor to him, yet exuded a sense of strength and vivacity that was largely absent in the mortal denizens of Ulfenkarn. A gift from the vampires. Some small part of their own immense power bestowed on a favoured servant. Arno was bundled up in a fur-lined cloak, the jewelled pectoral of his station hanging loose against his chest. There was a hungry light in the silentiary's eyes as he crouched over the body, his gaze roving over every inch of the victim's butchered remains.

'It certainly wasn't robbery,' Arno said. He shook the purse of pearl discs that had been found alongside the corpse and nodded at the dead woman. 'One look at her could tell you that, though. No thief would be that depraved.'

Arno nodded and stepped away. As he did, Dragomir again was afforded a view of what had been done to her. There wasn't any face left. The murderer had carved away every shred of flesh and muscle until all that was left was a grinning skull. The face had been utterly obliterated, denuded by the killer's knife.

'We know who she was,' Dragomir explained. 'People recognised the clothes. She was a cutpurse named Annika. If the killer was trying to hide her identity, they did a bad job of it.'

'Yes,' Arno agreed, 'but it is the murderer's own identity that is of consequence here.' He frowned at the corpse. 'I've tried to call her spirit, but it won't respond to me.' He raised a finger to emphasise his point. 'That is unusual.' He pointed down at the bloodied cobblestones. 'That is also strange. The blood is discoloured. I've never seen blood look like that before.'

Dragomir realised the silentiary was speaking more to himself than the captain. Arno turned away and gestured to the closest of the Ulfenwatch. Silently the skeletal warriors marched over, their ancient glaives held at the ready. Arno plucked the weapons from their fleshless claws and dropped them on the ground, then waved at the murdered woman.

'Pick it up,' Arno commanded the skeletons. 'Take it back to the Ebon Citadel. Chamberlain Torgillius may be interested in it.'

The undead advanced and clumsily picked the corpse off the ground. One gripped her feet, another pulled her up by the shoulders. Together the skeletons carried her away.

Arno turned back to the bloodstains. He leaned down again and used a knife to scrape some of the residue into a glass vial. 'Very unusual,' he muttered as he walked away. The remaining Ulfenwatch fell in around the silentiary as he left the courtyard.

'Can you beat that?' one of his watchmen whispered to Dragomir when the undead were gone. 'Silentiary Arno is interested in this killing. Torgillius might even look into it. You'll have the notice of important people if you do things right.'

Dragomir shook his head. 'It's dangerous for small people to be noticed by their masters,' he told the watchman. He didn't like attention from the dreadful beings who ruled Ulfenkarn.

If there were more murders, Lord Radukar himself might notice them.

INTERLUDE 1

It was well past curfew when Kucharz slipped out of his dingy room in a dockside tenement. He winced as the sour smell from the nearby tannery hit his nose. He'd lived in this place for over a year and the stench of sealskin drying on the racks still turned his stomach. Every time he promised himself that his next job would get him into better lodgings. Up in Barrowhill, where the big merchant combines had their guildhouses. That was where he felt he really belonged, not down with the dregs along the Tannersweg.

Kucharz paused on the landing and fished a scrimshawed flask from beneath his coat. He took a long pull of *kvas* before putting it away. The drink sent a warm flush through his body. He needed fortification against the cold. Ulfenkarn was under a strict curfew and it was dangerous to move around on the streets. The bonies, the undead soldiers who took over from the Volkshaufen after sunset, couldn't be reasoned with or bribed. They arrested anyone they found, and the least resistance would see an old rusty glaive ripping into the offender's body. Of course, that was probably more merciful than the fate that awaited those taken prisoner. Exsanguination was the punishment for all crimes in the city, the only question being how long and brutal the method of bleeding would be. Kucharz had seen a few executions that made even his callous heart shudder.

There was little danger of running afoul of the Ulfenwatch though. Kucharz was too clever to risk the streets. He preferred to use the rooftops. Buildings were built so close together in the city that entire blocks could be traversed in such a manner without the least difficulty. Where the gaps were wider, strength and agility were called upon. Kucharz was unlovely to look at, but his body was well suited to these sorts of manoeuvres. His short legs were like coiled springs and his long arms were powerful. In those areas where these weren't enough, he had what he affectionately called his 'monkey tail' wrapped around his waist, a length of thin rope that was as durable as steel and to which he'd affixed a clawed grapple. Using it, he'd been able to pass unseen across the widest boulevards.

Kucharz reached up with his ape-like arms and pulled himself onto the roof of the tenement. His boots dug into the fog-slick shingles. He looked out across Banshee's Bay, at all the ships moored on the docks. Here and there he could see the glow of a whale-oil lamp or the ghostly luminance of the beacons out on the headlands. Down below he could see a troop of Ulfenwatch making their patrol along the waterfront, the rattle of their armour the only sound that rose from the skeletal warriors as they marched. Kucharz thrust his finger at the skeletons, but there was more bravado in the gesture than he really felt. Only a madman was ever comfortable in the presence of the undead.

The man reached into his threadbare coat once more and withdrew a small clay bottle. He frowned as he removed its stopper and splashed its contents liberally across his head and shoulders. Squid-spray, it was called, a venomous ink projected by the foul cryptkraken that sometimes rose from the depths to steal captured whales. The ink was expensive and Kucharz resented using it because of the cost and the fact he'd only have a few hours to wash it off before it did damage to his hair and skin. It was an essential tool of his trade, however. Without it, the blood-bats would swoop down and make a meal of him. The smell of the ink was all that would keep them off and let him cross the roofs at night.

And it was far easier for an assassin to do his work under cover of darkness than in the light of day.

Kucharz was a natural for his chosen profession. Those ape-like arms were fitted with enormous hands. He could crush clams in them, pulverising the shells as though they'd been smashed by a hammer. He'd been eight when he claimed his first victim, a boy three years older who made the mistake of bullying Kucharz about his ugly body. He regretted that killing now. It was Kucharz's motto that a tradesman should never practise his trade without making a profit. Murder, he'd found, was a very profitable trade. Its only hindrance was the irregularity of work. A fisherman could depend on the tides, but an assassin had to wait for a patron to decide to have someone removed.

Kucharz was thinking of tonight's work as he scrambled along the rooftops. His current employer was a ship captain who was in partnership with a merchant. An uneven partnership it seemed, since the mariner bore all the expenses of maintaining his ship while the merchant drew straight profit from his investment. Kucharz's strangling hands would terminate the deal and free the captain to enter a more reasonable one with another investor.

Money! Enough to finally get him out of the squalor he'd sunk into. Kucharz wouldn't squander his pay this time. He'd keep away from the taverns and gambling halls. No more frivolity. He needed to conserve his assets. Too many more years and he wouldn't be spry enough to keep plying his trade.

That last thought gave Kucharz pause. He stopped on the crest of a glass-blower's workshop and dug out the scrimshawed flask. He felt slightly better about his future prospects when he had a little liquor in his belly.

The assassin made a quick survey of his surroundings. He doubted if anyone but the blood-bats could navigate Ulfenkarn so easily from this vantage. Looking down across the city he picked out landmarks. He needed to work his way up to Barrowhill. That was where his quarry had his home. There were guards, of course. But they'd be down below, vigilant for an intruder who came by the door. They wouldn't be expecting one who slipped in from one of the upper windows. Kucharz anticipated it would be only a few minutes of work from that point. The merchant would be lying in his bed, the strangler would get his hands around his throat, and that would be that. The only hitch would be if the victim wasn't alone. Kucharz was quiet enough, but sometimes a victim would thrash about and wake someone. Then it would be two killings for the price of one. Kucharz hated that.

An unexpected complication arose when Kucharz swung his grapple and tried to take a shortcut across the Wurmplatz, where the weavers would hold their market days. The old iron statue of a dragon rusting away at its centre proved too tall to swing over, so he moved around to make his crossing closer to the edge of the square. He cast his hook easily enough, but the stone gargoyle it looped around wasn't as sturdy as he thought it was. The moment his full weight was on it, the sculpture broke free and Kucharz fell to the cobblestones forty feet below.

The assassin landed on his back. He bit down on the pain that shot through him. As he tried to roll onto his side, he felt even greater pain. He'd broken something. Kucharz ground his teeth together. Pain or no pain, he had to get moving. The Ulfenwatch might not find him, but there were many other things prowling the night. Things that would gleefully set upon a helpless man with long fangs and sharp claws.

Kucharz forced himself to rise. His legs wouldn't cooperate, but he was able to hold himself up with his powerful arms. Any reserve of courage crumbled into raw terror now. He couldn't move his legs! He'd have to drag himself to some kind of shelter before something found him! He glanced frantically at the dark buildings around him. He was only too aware that nobody would respond if he called for help. Nobody would take the gamble that what called to them was human.

Breathing heavily, Kucharz started to pull himself across the plaza. Perhaps there was an open cellar or a space under a stairway where he could conceal himself until morning. Anything that would give him some modicum of shelter. Anything that would hide him from the creatures of the night.

Suddenly the assassin froze. Instincts honed over his murderous career warned him that he was no longer alone. His every sense grew taut, straining against the dark silence, fumbling for the least hint of what was out there. Straining his ears, he caught the sound of breathing close by. That alone was enough to provoke a sense of relief. The things he most feared weren't living creatures.

Painfully, Kucharz turned himself around. He could make out a shadowy figure standing between him and the iron dragon.

'I've fallen,' he said. 'Help me and I'll pay you.'

Kucharz had no intention of paying his rescuer. There wasn't money for that. He wasn't sure just what he'd do, but as the figure came towards him his only concern was getting somewhere safe.

It was when he felt the knife sink into his body that Kucharz realised his assailant wasn't interested in being paid.

At least not in money.

CHAPTER TWO

Emelda leapt aside as the shabby figure shuffled towards her. She gave the wretch only the briefest scrutiny, unable to tell if it was even a human under the layers of dirt and rags that covered the hunched shape, though she guessed it must be alive since it had a sprig of wolfbane pinned to its hood as a guard against the feral vargskyr. Her focus was mainly upon the buckets gripped by those hairy hands. The pungent reek of nightsoil wafted from the containers and as the muckraker trudged down the street, filth sloshed onto the cobblestones.

Gustaf refused to give ground to the tatterdemalion, forcing him to shift his burden awkwardly to navigate around the vampire hunter. The muckraker stumbled, but recovered. Emelda watched as the ragged shape continued down the Koenigstrasse towards the miserable little grave-gardens clumped about the base of Ulfenkarn's southern wall.

'For a Braskov, you're strangely obliging to commoners,' Gustaf said.

Emelda gave him an acid look. 'For a cautious man, you don't seem to mind having shit spattered on your clothes.' She felt a twinge of amusement when Gustaf glanced down at the specks of filth the muckraker had splashed on him when shifting out of his way. The humour was tempered by a more serious concern. Calling Gustaf 'cautious' spoke more clearly of what really troubled the swordswoman.

Gustaf Voss was anything but cautious. Emelda wasn't sure if it was arrogance or zealotry, but the vampire hunter seemed to dare fate to do its worst to him. Openly wearing a Sigmarite medallion in Ulfenkarn was brazen defiance of the lord of the city, Radukar the Wolf. The people of the city had long ago learned better. Whatever their inner thoughts and beliefs, they kept them to themselves. The least provocation was all the excuse the vampires needed to condemn an entire household to death... and worse than death. Nor was there any shortage of human sycophants only too eager to ingratiate themselves to the monsters by betraying those around them. Gustaf's boldness was an invitation to disaster.

'I see what you mean,' Gustaf said with a frown. He stopped beside one of the many vendor carts that cluttered the street. The seller started to protest when he snatched an ear of black corn from the sorry display of vegetables. A glare from him killed the old woman's objection before she muttered more than a few words. Gustaf peeled away the husk and tossed the rest of the ear back onto the cart, then began wiping away the filth from his clothes.

Emelda was distracted by a group of street urchins who came rushing down the street throwing snowballs at each other. The sight and sounds of their frivolity warmed her against the chill in the air, but only for a moment. Only until she really paid attention to the ditty they were singing.

'When ye hear the scrape, scrape, scraping of Old
Gorslav on his walk,
    The only sound he ever makes, for he ain't one
for talk.
    Flee then, fool, and hide away, and hope he don't
come take,
    And bind your arms and drag ye off to bury ye
awake.'

The morbid song crushed that brief flicker of hope she'd felt, that idea that there was some corner of Ulfenkarn that wasn't yet corrupt. Even the songs and games of the children had darkened in Radukar's shadow. To her mind, Emelda thought there was no greater sign of a people's subjugation than to have their children tainted by the horrors they endured. She turned back to the old woman with the vegetable cart. She stepped over and threw a piece of whalebone to the woman as compensation.

Emelda scowled at Gustaf. 'You could show a bit of decency,' she said as they continued along the street.

'Not in my trade,' Gustaf replied. 'Courtesy breeds contempt. A vampire hunter can only accomplish his work if the people are more afraid of him than they are the evil that is preying on them.' He gave her a look that was almost regretful. 'If they think I'm meaner than the monsters, they might also think I can beat those monsters.'

'That's a cynical way to look at people,' Emelda said.

Gustaf tossed the soiled husk into the gutter. 'Not cynical. Pragmatic. Realistic.' He pointed at her cloak, or rather the sword concealed beneath it. 'You were a leader in Mournhold's army. You commanded soldiers in battle.'

'I led my men,' Emelda said. 'I rallied them by inspiring them to remember everything they were fighting for. I didn't sneer down at them like they were animals.'

'Didn't you?' Gustaf asked. 'When a battle was going poorly, when fear threatened to break your troops and send them fleeing the field? Did you use honeyed words and inspiring speeches? Or did you threaten and shame them until they did what you needed them to do?'

There was a bit too much truth in that challenge for Emelda's liking. 'That was different. They were soldiers and it was war.'

The vampire hunter waved his finger at the sinister ruins beyond the slums and the dark castle that rose above them. 'This *is* war,' he told her, 'and every one of these people is a soldier in that war. The tragedy is that so many of them don't realise it.'

Ahead of them, Emelda saw something that seemed to emphasise Gustaf's comparison of war and the state of the city. A big wagon slowly lumbered through the street, drawn by a gang of naked, rotten creatures with vacant, lifeless faces and green necrotic skin. Behind the zombies, seated on the wagon, was a man in a long coat and tall hat, the emblem of the Gravemasters' Guild emblazoned on both. Behind him, in the bed of the wagon, was a heap of corpses. As the wagon rolled through the street, a bell fastened to its side tolled its doleful note. A summons for all who heard it to bring out the bodies of those who'd died in their buildings during the night.

There were no funerals for Ulfenkarn's dead. The corpses were taken away into the haunted ruins at the centre of the city. Emelda had heard rumours of their eventual fate. Some would be fed to the ghoulish creatures kept by the vampires, others would be given over to necromancers for their black sorcery; many would be given to the horrifying Gorslav the Gravekeeper and surrendered to his hideous Corpse-Gardens to rise again as ghastly undead or to be eaten by the deadwalkers already prowling the graveyards. Yet such terrible things paled in comparison to the dangers faced by the grieving family who tried to hide their dead. The smell of rotting flesh brought ravening monsters out of the ruins to glut their foul hunger. Or the body itself might be corrupted by the dark energies that spilled down upon the city, reawakened as a murderous abomination. Many who tried to defy the call of the corpse-bell didn't live long enough to be punished for breaking the law.

Thoughts of the hidden dead turned Emelda's mind back to Morrvahl Olbrecht. He might have saved them from Viscount Lupu, but she didn't trust him. The hideout he'd taken them to was the cellar of an abandoned mill. What they found there was a chamber of horrors. Bits of bodies preserved in jars and bottles. Strange apparatus and equipment that seemed to merge the concepts of magic and science. And then there was the cube of dark glass that stood in a little alcove all of its own. Emelda was certain she'd seen something moving within that glass, something that groped at the walls of its prison with spectral claws.

'What will we do about Morrvahl?' Emelda asked Gustaf.

'He might call himself a scholar, but if his magic isn't outright necromancy, it's near enough to it.' Gustaf's face contorted in a grimace. 'It's clear he's no friend of the vampires, but that's no great recommendation.'

'How far can we trust him?'

'We don't,' Gustaf stated bluntly. 'Morrvahl hasn't any interest in redeeming this city or helping its people. If he's the enemy of Radukar, it's because he sees the Wolf as an obstacle. To him, we're nothing but pawns to exploit to his own ends.'

'So, what do we do?' Emelda said.

'We do the same thing to him he intends to do to us,' Gustaf replied. 'We make use of him. We exploit his animosity towards the vampires. We use his filthy magic against our common foe.'

Emelda was shocked to hear Gustaf speaking this way. 'You're a Sigmarite, a member of the Order of Azyr. How can you condone such a thing?'

'Even the God-King himself made use of Nagash against the abominations of Chaos,' Gustaf explained. 'Sometimes to kill the fox you make peace with the weasel.' He looked away and pointed to a building they were approaching. 'Since coming to Ulfenkarn, I've become resigned to choosing which evil I'm focusing my fight against.'

The building was a half-timber structure, its plaster painted a vivid red. A narrow balcony opened off its first floor and stretched out over the street. Emelda felt sickened when she saw the long pole that had been bolted to the structure, a length of bone painted white with a crimson stripe winding around it. Many horrible things had arisen in Mournhold since it became Ulfenkarn, but none were more loathsome than these leech-parlours.

'Blood-lenders? Really?' Emelda scowled.

'Lupu's thugs scared away my contact last night in the Black Ship,' the vampire hunter hurried to explain. 'I'm hoping he'll be here.' Gustaf's face grew flushed when Emelda just gave him a blank stare. 'You don't think anything but business would bring me to a place like this?'

Emelda gave him a cold look, and walked away before he had a chance to explain. She reached the entrance of the leech-parlour ahead of Gustaf. A young boy, no more than ten, was sweeping dirt from the doorway. He threw down his broom and scrambled inside when she came close. Emelda followed him through the heavy ironwood door.

Inside was a large room dominated by a broad stairway that curled its way up to the first floor. A menagerie of tables and chairs were arrayed all about. The stuffed head of a tide tiger stared down from the far wall. Along the wall to her right was a counter behind which stood several large casks and a rack of clay beer steins, all of them heavily caked in dust, relics of days when the custom of this building had been scandalous rather than sanguinary. To her left Emelda noted heavy curtains in an assortment of colours, each closing off a smaller room or alcove.

One of these was pushed aside and the boy reappeared. Behind him was a middle-aged woman, her blonde hair piled high atop her head in an elaborate coiffure, her face caked in powder. She wore an exaggerated blue gown that was simultaneously ostentatious and tawdry.

The woman gave Emelda an appraising look that set the swordswoman's blood boiling. 'You don't look rich enough to be buying, so I'll explain what I pay. The first pint gets you a cot for the night. The second earns you a meal. Porridge and bread. I only give goods for trade for the third pint. And mind, you're still responsible for your own blood-tithe as well. I'll not stick my neck out for anybody stupid enough to defy the Wolf.'

Emelda reached the powdered woman in a single step. She grabbed the front of her dress and pulled her close. 'Talk to me like that again, and there isn't enough powder in Szargorond that'll hide what I do to your face.'

The woman sputtered in horror at Emelda's threat. The outcry brought two men out from another of the alcoves. They were as brutish and ugly-looking a pair as she'd ever seen, but they seemed like they knew how to use the clubs they carried. Emelda returned their angry glower with an icy stare.

'Call your troggoths off,' she told the blood-seller. She tightened her grip, tearing the material as she drew the woman closer. 'I promise they won't get me before I get you.' The menace in her tone made her captive's eyes go wide with fear.

'Emelda!' Gustaf shouted across the scene. 'Name of a motherless spider, what's going on here!'

'Just having a discussion with the proprietress,' Emelda told him. She stared into the blood-seller's frightened eyes. 'I think we understand each other better now.'

The proprietress licked her lips nervously. 'Andrei, Serban, it's all right,' she called to the two brutes. The men looked unconvinced, but shrugged and retreated back into their alcove. When they were gone, Emelda released their boss.

Gustaf walked over to the two women. He gave Emelda a warning look, then fixed his attention on the blood-seller.

'We came here looking for Vladrik Brandt. Is he here?'

The woman glared sullenly at Gustaf. 'Why should I tell you anything?' Her fingers pulled at the torn neck of her gown. 'This will cost plenty to mend. Are you going to pay for it?'

Emelda bristled at the blood-seller's wheedling tone. She started forwards to give her something to really complain about, but Gustaf motioned her to keep back. His voice dropped to a grim whisper, slicing the air like a knife.

'I'm sure you're eager to have us leave,' he said. He turned in place and made a show of looking at the decayed finery with which the room was decorated. 'The way to make that happen is to tell me what I want to know. It would be a shame if something happened to all this.'

'Quite a shame,' Emelda quipped. She kicked one of the chairs over with her boot, sending it clattering against the base of the stairs. She stared daggers at the proprietress when the woman raised a protest. 'Of course, you could always call your goons back out. Then you could try to make a bit of money selling their blood.'

'The faster you two are gone, the better it suits me,' the proprietress snarled in defeat. 'You'll find Vladrik upstairs. Third room on the right.'

'Thank you,' Gustaf said. He hurried past Emelda and started up the stairs.

'When you leave, see that you stay gone,' the proprietress said.

Emelda turned as she climbed the stairs. 'That suits me fine.

The only reason I'd come back here is to burn this leech-parlour to the ground.'

The look of shock and outrage on the blood-seller's face was very satisfying to the swordswoman. She was tempted to linger a moment and truly savour the sight, but she didn't want Gustaf to get too big a lead on her. After the bother of finding someone in Ulfenkarn willing to stand up to the vampires, she didn't want to lose him now. She wanted to know everything about his contacts in the city, what kind of support structure he'd developed. They'd be potent resources to add to the few friends left over from before the army marched out to cleanse the countryside of Chaos. Before the nadir devastated the city and left Radukar to conquer what was left.

Gustaf was already in the room the blood-seller had directed them to. It was a small, shabby apartment, its walls dominated by crude bunks fashioned from old doors, shutters and whatever else could be salvaged from Mournhold's ruins. On each cot lay a wasted, almost insensible wretch. The clothes that covered their emaciated bodies were the roughest rags. There was a dead, apathetic glaze over the eyes of those who were awake, listlessly staring at the walls. Emelda felt her blood boil at this hellish sight. These were the most desperate of the city's inhabitants. Those who'd fallen into such poverty that the only thing they had left to sell was themselves. To be bled by the leeches who ran the place and have their blood sold to more prosperous citizens to substitute for their own when they paid their blood-tithe to the vampires at the marble fountains spread across Ulfenkarn. Emelda thought nothing was a clearer indication of how debased her city had become than this obscene exploitation.

A sealskin chair was in the middle of the room, and seated in it was a man who looked nearly as pale and sickly as Morrvahl. He was studying the occupants in the bunks with a rapt fascination that made Emelda think of a snake watching a bird. He turned and looked at them as they entered. He made a wave of his hand towards the bunks.

'Isn't it strange that it takes this for people to appreciate how valuable blood is? The blood is the very life. The ambrosia of gods and monsters.'

'This is Vladrik Brandt,' Gustaf said in introduction. He gestured towards Emelda. 'Vladrik, may I present–'

'Just Emelda,' she said, interrupting him. 'No offence, Vladrik, but until I'm more certain of you, I prefer to be cautious.'

The man in the chair smiled at her and a hint of a laugh left him. 'You've no need to tell me more than that. I recognised you the moment I saw you.' For just a moment the air of superiority left his eyes and his voice lost its haughty tone. 'In better times I was an expert heraldist and quite familiar with the noble families of Mournhold. I should recognise the features of a Braskov face as easily as my own.' An uneasy look came onto his face. 'You marched out with the army, but I understood all of our soldiers were killed fighting.'

'Not all of them,' Gustaf said.

Emelda shot the vampire hunter a warning look. 'This man might think he knows who I am, but let's leave it at that.'

'Vladrik has been helping me,' Gustaf told her. 'His knowledge of the city has allowed me to persist in my activities without being captured. He's been helping me to track down Jelsen Darrock. He's been invaluable to me.'

'I have been able to render some slight assistance,' Vladrik said, downplaying his role. 'Truthfully, I am something of a middleman. I have many contacts across Ulfenkarn who bring me scraps of information they hear. These in turn I pass along to those who most need to know about them.' He shrugged his shoulders. 'If you don't wish to disclose the nature of your miraculous return, Lady Braskov, then I will respect your discretion.'

Emelda looked away and stared at the wall while memories and images flashed through her mind. None of them were pleasant to recall. Even the hope that inspired them when they left Mournhold had become poisoned by the tragedy that followed. She'd spoken a little to Gustaf, but he was an outlander. She felt the need to unburden herself to a countryman. Someone who truly appreciated all that had been lost.

'We left our homes to crush the last vestiges of Chaos haunting the lands around the Cor Mortifus so that Szargorond might never be threatened by the followers of the Dark Gods again. Month after month, battle after battle we fought. Each victory was bittersweet, bleeding away the strength of our army. Always there was another enemy to march against. At last it was too much. We'd lost too many soldiers in our crusade to carry on. When the hordes of the Blood God came against us at the end, we were too weak to defeat them. Few of us survived to retreat back to Mournhold.' Emelda's voice quivered as guilt filled her heart. 'The perils of the journey claimed us, one after another, until I alone was left to bring word back to our people.'

Emelda turned back towards Vladrik.

'Everything we sacrificed. All those lives, and for what? To come back and find the heart of Mournhold in ruins. To find most of our people dead, and those left alive eking out an existence in these slums. To learn that Radukar had seized complete dominion and rules over what's left with an iron fist.'

'While there's life, there's still hope,' Gustaf said. 'You must believe that Sigmar watched over you and guided you back here for a purpose.'

'Must I?' Emelda retorted, wiping away the tears that had gathered in her eyes. 'I can name hundreds who marched out with that army who had just as much claim as I do for a god's protection. I knew several who were braver and more righteous than myself, soldiers whose faith in Sigmar never wavered even when they lay dying from a bestigor's axe. Why were they not spared?'

'Because none of them were named Braskov,' Vladrik said, leaning forwards in the chair. 'That makes you special. Unique even. The Wolf was most thorough when he turned against the noble houses. The families were massacred, the only survivors those who submitted to Radukar and became as he is, a creature of the night. You, Emelda, are the last of your line. The living embodiment of Mournhold's glorious past. The only one who can present to the people the hope of restoring that past. From anyone else, such a dream would sound shallow, but from the last of the Braskovs, it could rekindle the flame of defiance.' Vladrik slumped back and laughed. 'Forgive me. Before I was a heraldist, but now I fear I've taken on the mantle of poet.'

Emelda shook her head. 'I'm just a soldier,' she said. 'I'm not a leader to rally the people. I've had enough of watching people die because of my orders.' Her hand closed around the grip of her sword. 'I'm done with all that. All I want now is a chance to get at Radukar and put an end to him.'

'The Wolf's tyranny can't last,' Vladrik declared, his lips pulling back in an almost feral snarl. 'Whatever it takes, the vampire will pay for his crimes.'

Gustaf shot a worried glance at the bunks and the wasted shapes lying in them. 'You've warned me to be careful, and you speak like this?'

'These poor souls are at the end,' Vladrik told him. He nodded at a crude plaque nailed to each bunk. 'They've been drained three times today. Perhaps they'll recover enough to pay their blood-tithe tonight, perhaps they won't and Ilona will toss them into the street for the deadwalkers and blood-bats to find.' He sighed and shook his head. 'I come in here to look at them because somebody should notice their passing. They're a metaphor for

Ulfenkarn, on the verge of death but trying desperately to cling to life.' He looked back at Gustaf. 'Of course, there are other reasons. Ilona the blood-seller hears things and has a wonderful penchant for gossip. In fact, she might have learned where Jelsen Darrock is.'

The poet curbed Gustaf's visible excitement.

'It's too dangerous to follow that lead right now, however.'

'Why?' Emelda asked. From what little Gustaf had told her about Darrock, she was eager to meet him. The witch hunter would make a potent ally against Radukar.

Vladrik's expression became solemn. 'There's been a murder. The second of its sort, actually. The Volkshaufen and Ulfenwatch have cordoned off the entire area. We'll have to bide our time until things calm down. If Darrock has any sense, he'll do the same.'

Gustaf was puzzled. 'What is it that makes these murders so damn interesting to the vampires? Is someone going around killing their spies?'

'Suppose we sneak over there and have a look,' Emelda suggested. 'The best way to learn anything is to see for ourselves.' She smiled at Vladrik. 'Don't worry, we'll be careful. I might have no interest in leading some kind of rebellion, but I'm also not in any hurry to donate my blood to a vampire.'

There was a sick feeling in the pit of Gustaf's stomach while he followed Emelda down back alleys and gaps between buildings that didn't look wide enough for a cat to navigate. He was thinking about how Vladrik had described the first murder and the mutilations inflicted on the victim. Even if she'd been a spy for the vampires, it had been a savage thing. Witch hunters were no strangers to the art of torture, but it revolted him to think Darrock might be responsible. He couldn't see any reason to disfigure a body in such a manner. Even the more extreme methods of preventing a corpse from rising as one of the undead he'd been instructed in by the

Order of Azyr didn't call for peeling away a person's face to expose the grinning skull beneath.

If Darrock was responsible, then Gustaf feared it was too late to find the witch hunter. The evil of Ulfenkarn had already driven the man mad.

Emelda stopped suddenly. She reached back and grabbed his shoulder. 'This is as close as we get,' she told him.

Gustaf leaned to one side so he could see past the swordswoman. The other end of the narrow passageway opened out into what looked like a plaza of some kind. He could see the half-timber buildings on the other side with their tile roofs and stone chimneys. He could also see men watching those houses, spears and halberds in their hands. Though there was no uniformity in their garb beyond a general trend towards dark colours, each of them had a grey band of cloth wound around their right arms, a badge that marked them as the Volkshaufen.

'They're keeping guard over the square,' Gustaf said. 'Even the people who live here aren't allowed to see what's going on.'

'Only the dead keep a secret,' Emelda commented. 'By tonight at least one of these watchmen will have blabbed about what he saw. Then the rumours will spread until they get back to your friend Vladrik. Or Morrvahl.'

'I don't think so,' Gustaf said. 'Morrvahl has other ways of finding out what happens in Ulfenkarn. Methods it's better not to think about.'

They both fell silent when they heard voices nearby. Their side of the plaza was also being watched by the Volkshaufen and at least two of them were close to the opening of the gap. Their proximity was such that Gustaf feared even a soft whisper might be heard by the guards.

'...as bad as the one yesterday,' they heard one of the watchmen say. 'Captain Dragomir lost no time sending word to the castle.'

'He's trying to get noticed,' a second guard said. 'Sick of being just a captain, I suppose.'

'Dragomir better be careful,' the first responded. 'Silentiary Arno's sending this body back to the castle too.'

The voices faded away as the watchmen continued their patrol. Gustaf started forwards, trying to hear more of their conversation, but Emelda held him back. She shook her head and pointed. There was a puddle of icy water inside the passageway. Gustaf could see tiny ripples rushing across it.

It was a few moments before he felt the heavy impacts agitating the puddle. A little later and the sound of ponderous footfalls reached them. Out in the square a ghastly figure lumbered into view. Ten feet tall, six feet across at the shoulder, the thing's hulking body was draped in the rotten remnant of a fur cloak. Rotten too was the monstrosity's flesh, necrotic skin peeling away to expose blackened bones. Clumps of decayed meats and coarse hair clung to the abomination's skull while the dented remains of a spiked helm sagged against its scalp.

An undead ogor! Gustaf had heard such beasts served Radukar. They were called the Nightguard and were all that was left of the Kosargi, the monstrous army the Wolf had led into Mournhold centuries ago to save the city from the Chaos horde of Slaughn the Ravener. Then, Radukar had been the saviour of the people. That was before the vampire's thirst for power made him tyrant of Ulfenkarn. His faithful Kosargi were the first to be sacrificed for their master's ambition.

Gustaf drew Emelda's attention to the sack slung over the Nightguard's shoulder. It was the right size to accommodate a human corpse. He motioned for her to follow him back the way they'd come.

'Let's see where it's taking the body,' Gustaf told Emelda once they were far enough away from the square to speak. 'Those men spoke of Arno, that means the castle they were talking about could be the Ebon Citadel.'

'If they're sending the body there, it could mean the Wolf wants to know what's going on,' Emelda said. 'That would be useful to verify. We might be able to make use of it.' She scratched her eyebrow as she thought it over. 'Come on. If the Nightguard is headed to the Ebon Citadel, I know where we can pick up its trail and follow it.'

'Go into the ruins?' Gustaf asked. The prospect wasn't one he found appealing. He'd heard too much about what lurked in those ruins. The ravenous corpse-rats. The flesh-eating deadwalkers. The horrific vargskyr, capable of running a man down in a heartbeat and ripping him apart in another. These and a thousand other nightmares were spoken of in terrified whispers by the mortal inhabitants of Ulfenkarn. Gustaf wasn't timid, but he was wary.

'Until the High Star descends, most of the things that haunt the inner boroughs will be resting, waiting for true night before stirring from their lairs,' Emelda explained. 'Whatever is out and about will be chased off by that ogor. Living or dead, nothing wants to tangle with a Kosargi unless it has to.'

Emelda's reasoning impressed Gustaf. She knew the city better than he did. Both in terms of what it had been and what it had become.

They hurried through the slumland of Ulfenkarn's Neuesmarkt, dodging past the dilapidated carts from which street vendors tried to peddle their wares. Emelda led the way to the dried-out canal that snaked its way along the periphery of the district, its banks stained with dried blood. Gustaf kept his pistol in hand as they navigated their way through the thick layer of debris that littered the canal. He tried not to look too closely at the shattered bones he stepped on, or think about what might have been gnawing on them not so long ago.

'This way.'

Emelda preceded Gustaf into a culvert that opened into the canal. They climbed along its scum-slick darkness, pressing their hands against the clammy stonework to keep from sliding back. The channel proved to be a short one, their going slowed more by the steepness of the angle than by the length of the tunnel.

'If it was any longer, something would have picked this for a lair,' Emelda said, 'but with light at either end it makes for a bad place to hide if you're anaemic to the sun.'

The culvert led to what Gustaf imagined must have been a lush park once. Now it was overgrown with bone-coloured weeds that sported ugly, claw-like spurs. He started to brush them off his cloak, but Emelda grasped his hand and stopped him.

'You'll cut yourself if you do that,' she said. Emelda showed him her hand and the deep scratches on her fingers. 'Trust me, I know. It's dangerous to have the smell of blood in the air here. Trust me on that too.'

They picked their way cautiously through the park, avoiding the clusters of crimson bushes with thorny branches and bruise-coloured flowers. The stands of trees were shunned as well. It took Gustaf a moment to realise that the shapes hanging from the skeletal branches weren't rubbery leaves but the leathery wings of sleeping bats.

Past the broken park gates, they came upon a wide avenue. The buildings that faced the park were of much finer quality than those in the outer boroughs, but unlike in the slums there wasn't even an impoverished shadow of vitality here. The shops and the homes above them were dark and silent. As inviting as an open tomb.

'There it is.' Gustaf drew Emelda's attention to the lumbering Kosargi. The undead ogor was walking about one hundred yards ahead of them on the avenue, the bag swaying against its back with every step. Ahead of it, in the distance, were the grim towers of the noble estates.

'My home was there,' Emelda said, pointing towards one of the darkened castles. There was a forlorn look on her face as she continued. 'I tried to go there when I returned to Ulfenkarn. I wanted to see if anything... anyone... was left. I couldn't even make it as far as the grounds. The closer I got to it, the more it felt like my energy was seeping away. I seemed to hear a voice inside my head coaxing me to lie down and just let everything trickle away. That was when I gave up and went back.' She gave him a wary look. 'I haven't tried again.'

Gustaf could only nod in sympathy to Emelda's story. Words were a feeble thing to offer someone who'd lost so much. He couldn't imagine what it must be like, to be able to see your own home but to be incapable of going there. Of finding the answers hidden there.

'It isn't headed that way, at least,' Gustaf said. The Nightguard had turned and was marching into an even broader road.

'That's the Kriegstrasse,' Emelda said. 'It leads almost straight to the Ebon Citadel. When it was still used as a fortress, long before Radukar came to the city, catapults would be carted along the Kriegstrasse from the other forts to augment the weapons at the citadel if invaders tried to attack Mournhold from the sea.'

Gustaf lifted his gaze. The avenue they were on was wide enough that no buildings blocked their view of the gruesome fortress perched upon its spire of rock. It stood there, looming above the rest of the city like a ravenous beast ready to pounce. The many turrets were like so many jagged fangs, the sharp crenellations along its walls were like claws. The place exuded its own atmosphere of night and shadow, a perpetual darkness that wrapped itself around the spire like a shroud.

'Are there any other castles to which the Nightguard might be going?' Gustaf asked.

'No,' Emelda said. 'Only the Ebon Citadel is that way. Radukar was given the fortress by the nobles because it was as far from their own estates as possible.'

'Then we have our answer.' Gustaf shook his pistol at the fortress. 'The body's being taken to the Ebon Citadel.

'Now, the question is, why are these killings so interesting?'

A strange agitation vexed Radukar the Wolf. In all his centuries of unlife, the vampire lord had felt its like only a few times. Always it had presaged some great conflict, a preternatural omen forewarning him that a formidable foe was near. Far from being intimidated, Radukar savoured the prospect. Eternity became tedium without the occasional diversion.

Radukar stalked the dark halls of his castle, the sound of his boots echoing in the corridors. He passed mementos from across the span of his long existence. The oldest of these was a few strips of black cloth, all that remained of the standard he'd used when still mortal. Close beside it was a trophy claimed after receiving the Blood Kiss. It appeared to be the pelt of a great grey wolf, but Radukar knew better. It was the flayed hide of his progenitor in darkness, the last king of the vampiric Vyrkos tribe. Too late did the Vyrkos learn that they'd created a monster far worse than themselves.

The vampire lord passed by other curios as he made his way down through the halls. The dried heads of fallen enemies. The broken weapons of vanquished foes. Each and all spurred some fragment of memory. Radukar felt it important to keep track of such things. An exacting knowledge of where he'd been and what he'd already done was the best way to gauge what he could achieve in the future.

Radukar's cloak billowed around his muscular frame as he descended a flight of blood-coloured stairs. He was passing below the foundations of his citadel now, plunging into the spire on which it was built. Here he saw the remnants of a Kosargi barracks, the sea chests of the ogors caked in dust and slowly crumbling into splinters, the piled furs of their beds now a habitat for spiders and rats. The Kosargi had no need of sleep or plunder now. They were beyond the limitations of life and death. As Nightguard they would serve their master always.

The desolate barracks had once been a guardroom. Past it, down another flight of stairs, was what the ogors had been guarding. Great copper-lined doors of coffin-oak met Radukar at the bottom of the steps. He made a gesture and the portals swung open, moved by unseen hands.

The chamber within was vast and illuminated by spirit-globes that hung from the ceiling on chains of bone. The spectres imprisoned inside the crystal spheres emitted a soft wail along with their gibbous light, a macabre melody that suited the room well. The walls were lined with high shelves on which tomes bound in human skin reposed and bottles filled with such things as gheist ichor and grave-sand dominated. Bins full of mummified organs and limbs squatted next to barrels of necrotic unguents. Iron racks held skeletons in varied stages of deconstruction, their parts requisitioned for other purposes.

The lone denizen of this eerie hall stood beside a long table of polished stone. He looked like an impossibly old man, his skin drawn tight about his ancient bones. His withered frame was swathed in a heavy robe lined with batskin. Strips of scraggly, colourless hair drifted from his scalp and chin, flowing around him like strands of cobweb when the breeze caught them. It was only in his eyes that there was any vibrancy. They were aglow with a feverish intensity, greedy for each new sight they could glance upon.

'Torgillius, Arno tells me the second body has been brought to you,' Radukar said as he strode into the laboratory.

The necromancer laid his hand on the corpse before him on the table. 'It's just like the other one,' he stated.

Torgillius picked up a skeletal wand and passed it across the body. As he did so, he invoked an ancient formula. For an instant, a ghostly glow surrounded the dead man, but it faded away just as quickly.

'These bodies are unique,' Torgillius said. 'Neither of them respond to any spell I've used on them. Flesh or spirit, they refuse to obey my summons.'

'And what does that mean?' Radukar asked his chamberlain.

Torgillius set the wand down again. 'Some other force has corrupted these bodies. They don't respond because they can't respond.' He scowled at the dead man with his grinning skull exposed. 'There's something here stronger than my magic.'

Radukar pondered the chamberlain's assertion. 'Stronger than your magic, perhaps, but we'll see if it is stronger than me. Whoever or whatever is doing this made a mistake hunting in my city. Because now the hunter will become the hunted.'

INTERLUDE 2

Borek Komarek was as scared as he could ever remember being. There were enough reasons for the people of Ulfenkarn to hide behind locked doors and bolted shutters when night fell upon the city. His own brother had been run down and killed by deadwalkers when he'd been caught outside after sunset. Borek had every reason to fear the dark.

There was one thing the middle-aged man feared more than the perils of night. He feared for the little boy lying abed in his home. A strange cough had settled into his son and Borek suspected it was the dreaded chillblight. The malady wasn't uncommon for the whalers who plied the Cor Mortifus and in an adult it would pass after a few days. A child, however, was far more vulnerable to the sickness and could die from its ravages. That possibility sent terror rushing through Borek's heart. To his concern for the well-being of his son was added a punishing sense of guilt. Borek earned his living making canvas for the whaling ships. He wondered if when he brought the canvas to the docks he hadn't brought the disease back with him, to his home and his son.

Driven by urgency, Borek refused to wait for dawn to help his boy. Leaving the child in the care of his mother, he stole from their room above his workshop and slipped into the darkened streets. He knew of a toad doctor who prepared salves and unguents as well as curative potions. His shop was only a few streets away. This toad doctor had a reputation for always providing medicine to those who could pay his fee, no matter how late they called upon him. In his desperation, Borek was forced to put that reputation to the test.

The rattling of armour froze Borek where he stood. The canvas maker hurried to a pile of scrap wood standing beside a dilapidated building. For weeks the inhabitants of the neighbourhood had been scavenging the abandoned structure, plundering it for anything they could use and stacking the refuse outside. Now he found a different use for the scrap pile. Like some human gopher, he burrowed into the heap. He dug down until only his eyes were visible. He stared in the direction from which the sounds came. With his heart pounding like a steamhammer, Borek waited.

The wait wasn't a long one. Out of the darkness they appeared, a file of ghastly figures. The light of the High Star gleamed upon the fleshless bones of the marching patrol. Walking skeletons called forth from their graves by the power of Radukar, these were the custodians of Ulfenkarn's midnight streets. The Ulfenwatch. As they advanced, the only sound that rose from them was the clatter of rusted mail against bleached bones.

Though there were no eyes in their empty sockets and no ears on their bare skulls, Borek knew the Ulfenwatch could see and hear. The undead were as aware of their surroundings as any living patrol. Some whispered that the skeletons had some sixth sense that alerted them when a mortal was nearby. The canvas maker prayed to Nagash that was just gossip as the Ulfenwatch came still closer.

The spears and halberds the skeletons carried became a thing of horrified fascination for Borek as the patrol neared his hiding place. A mind accustomed to calculating the dimensions of a sail, and how much a yard of material should cost, now fixated on estimating how many people had died on those weapons. The Ulfenwatch were merciless when they found someone defying Radukar's laws. To that tally must be added those who'd fought the skeletons when they'd been truly alive, for the vampire lord had recruited his army from the tombs of Szargorond's ancient warriors.

Borek used his frantic calculations to keep from surrendering to his fear and screaming. The least sound now, and the Ulfenwatch would find him. Even the noise of his pounding heart must be too much. It was so loud in his ears! The skeletons must hear it! If not now, then surely when they advanced the next five feet.

Borek closed his eyes. He didn't want to see the end when it came. But he couldn't blot out the sound. The rattle of armour steadily drawing closer. The rumours! They didn't need to see him or hear him to know he was there. They'd find him, they'd add him to their gruesome tally, which he'd decided must be somewhere between twenty and a hundred for each of the monsters. His own death he could almost accept, but with his demise his son's fate would also be decided.

The rattle of armour came closer and closer. Then it began to grow less strident. It took Borek's terrified mind a moment to appreciate that the reason the sound was fading was because the Ulfenwatch were marching away. They hadn't found him!

Borek moved with exacting care when he crawled out of the heap. He turned his eyes towards the slowly fading sound. He couldn't see the skeletons in the darkness that had swallowed them, but he knew they were somewhere further down the street.

Between Borek and the toad doctor.

The canvas maker knew he'd had a lucky escape. To follow behind the Ulfenwatch was to test that luck. He'd need to take an another route to reach the toad doctor. It would mean circling around the area and coming in from the north, but to wait until he was sure the skeletons were gone might cost even more time. Borek had felt his courage pushed to the edge of breaking. If he was left idle too long, given the time to consider his peril, his determination might collapse completely.

Borek dashed off into an alleyway and circled around the decayed building. The remains of a woman who'd been exsanguinated, presumably for violating curfew, hung from a noose wound about a lamp post, a stark warning of the peril he courted. The sound of gnawing teeth drifted down from the body and he could see corpse-rats had burrowed their way into her flesh. Hurrying along he found a side street and crossed it, then hastened across what had once been a busy boulevard in better days. He turned into a little close. After his brush with the Ulfenwatch, he found the deep shadows almost comforting.

Even the shadows couldn't quite hide the gleam of white marble and ivory. Borek paused and stared in revulsion at the gruesome fountain. More than anything, it was a monument to the complete subjugation of Ulfenkarn's people. While so much of the city had fallen into decay, the fountains were new constructions. There were hundreds of them across the slums, each devoted to the same obscene purpose. It was here that the mortals paid tribute to Radukar. This was where the blood-tax was collected. Each evening, every man, woman and child walked to the fountain in their neighbourhood and cut their hand against one of the sharp ivory spikes. They clenched their fists over the basin and watched as their blood dripped down. Some said pipes carried the blood straight to the Ebon Citadel, others whispered that evil spells drained it away to feed the vampires; a few claimed that swarms of bats descended on the fountains and lapped up whatever was in the basin before flying away to spit the contents of their bellies into the fanged mouths of their masters.

Borek didn't know what was true, but as he ran a finger against the scars on his palm and the crusted blood on his hand, he knew it didn't really matter. They were a broken people, as much slaves to Radukar as his undead creatures. It was a life of fear and hardship, with only the most fleeting happiness. Yet he was just greedy enough to want his son to have the opportunity for such a life. He couldn't let him go, and he wouldn't rest while there was still any chance to save him.

Borek turned from the fountain. He was intent on crossing the close and making his way to the toad doctor. In the darkness, he never saw the shape that struck at him or the knife that ripped into his body.

The killer lingered over Borek, flaying away the anguished face. When the task was finished, the corpse was dragged back to the fountain. With a heave, the killer sent Borek toppling over into the residue of blood that lingered in the basin.

Borek's face, as fleshless as that of the Ulfenwatch, stared up from the fountain, but there were no eyes to watch the canvas maker's murderer as a gore-soaked hand began to write on the nearby wall.

CHAPTER THREE

The Ebon Citadel's grand hall echoed with anguished moans and debauched laughter. Upon luxuriously appointed couches well-dressed youths languished, pulling feebly at the golden chains that bound them to the furnishings. The lush finery of the carmine gown that enhanced a young woman's beauty was spoiled by the deathly pallor of her skin and the weary despair that clouded her visage. The richness of a young man's tunic, the boldness of the flared sleeves and padded shoulders, the extravagant epaulettes and jewelled accoutrements only emphasised the blood that trickled from his torn throat. After weeks of being pampered and preened, coaxed to the limit of their own physical perfection, now the captives were being destroyed. Drop by drop.

Arno could sense the despair each prisoner exuded as they felt their life ebbing away. They'd been seduced into believing themselves to be favoured by the new nobility, encouraged to think that the horrors of the slums were behind them now. A fool's hope had grown inside each of them, only to be brutally snuffed out by the master of Ulfenkarn. It was the belief that release was near that made the despair all the greater once the truth was revealed.

The silentiary kept to the periphery of the hall, careful to avoid the nobles as they strolled about the couches, sometimes pausing to admire the moans of a dying captive, occasionally lingering over them to draw off some more of their sanguinary fluid. Arno was no longer human, but neither was he fully vampire. He existed in the nebulous gap between the might of the undead and the fragility of the mortal. An overexcited or simply inattentive vampire might decide he looked appetising and put him on the menu.

The ring he wore on his finger offered protection. Formerly he was a thrall of Countess Zora, but now Arno served Radukar himself and it was the Wolf's ring he bore. Only a vampire out of their mind with bloodlust would dare to interfere with him now, but among the Vyrkos Blood-Born the threat of feral reversion was never to be discarded entirely.

The vampires of the Thirsting Court displayed the wealth they'd enjoyed in life. Many had belonged to Mournhold's oldest families. Ven Alten, Vossheim, Braskov, Gaunt and Olt, those who'd once been the great and grand of the city had sold their souls to retain their status under the Wolf. Now they aped the luxuries of life, drinking the blood of youth as though it were the finest wine, dancing to the hollow strains of a skeletal orchestra as though listening to an elegant waltz. They pretended to be oblivious to the changes that had come upon them, the savage and predatory cast that altered their faces into nightmarish masks, the hungry light that glowed in their eyes and was never satisfied. They had taken onto themselves the curse of the Vyrkos Blood-Born to retain their power, only to discover too late that all they had were shadows and echoes of what once was.

Arno had only contempt for them. They'd become what they were without understanding what the change meant. He was different. He'd sought the Blood Kiss eagerly, knowing both the price and the reward. He served Radukar not from some desperate attempt to hold onto the past, but from ambition for the future.

The silentiary looked away from the Thirsting Court and their morbid debauchery. He looked instead to the great throne that dominated the back of the hall. Carved from the obsidian beak of the greatest cryptkraken ever taken in the Cor Mortifus, long had it been the seat of Mournhold's Grand Prince. Now it was the seat of Ulfenkarn's tyrant. Radukar observed the activities of his entourage from the depths of his throne, the white wolf pelt he wore just visible in the shadows cast by the beak's upper jaw. The pelt, cut long ago from the hide of the two-headed wolf Vilnas, created a barbaric and primitive appearance. It was Radukar's customary affectation, something to emphasise his brutal power, and to make the arrogant underestimate the sophisticated mind which governed that power.

Even among his Vyrkos Blood-Born, Radukar sometimes found it useful to remind others he wasn't to be underestimated.

Arno saw the pale hand that held the crystal goblet slide out from the shadows of the throne an instant before the vessel was flung to the floor and shattered into a thousand shards. Radukar leaned out into the light, his lupine features eloquent in their disdain. At once, silence fell across the hall as skeletal musicians collapsed into piles of bones and dying moans faded into death rattles. The vampires of the Thirsting Court froze and turned slowly towards their master. In this moment, not even the proudest Ven Alten was more than a frightened mongrel.

'One of you has sought to betray me,' Radukar pronounced, lingering over every word. He reached to the side of the throne and picked up a sheathed sword. The scabbard was leathery and adorned with gore-gems that looked more like frozen beads of blood than stones.

Radukar let his gaze sweep across his now trembling entourage. 'There are those who know of whom I speak.'

Slowly he unsheathed the sword, an ancient blade that seemed to draw all light into itself. The barrow-blade of Emperor Morkan. Only too well did the Thirsting Court know what it could do in Radukar's hands.

'Expose the traitor and you will be rewarded.'

The silence that followed was filled with tension. Not one among the vampiric throng dared to move. Minutes passed as Radukar let his expectant gaze linger over the company. Finally, one of the nobles came forwards. Arno recognised the grotesque Duchess Sargozy. She'd taken the Blood Kiss after eighty years of decadent opulence, but no amount of fresh young blood could restore her long-vanished beauty. She fixed her one good eye on the sepulchral grace of Baroness Karlsson, a sneer curling her lip as she pointed at the other vampire.

'There,' Sargozy hissed. 'There's the one who thought to betray you!'

Somehow, Karlsson managed to become even paler, the flush from feeding on the captives draining from her cheeks. She shook her head in protest, little frightened gasps rising to her throat. She looked to the vampires who had only moments before been beside her, but all of them slowly backed away, unwilling to share in her fate.

Radukar turned his attention on Karlsson. 'What say you? Do you deny these accusations? Is the duchess wrong?'

Karlsson found her voice. 'Yes, my liege,' she said, dropping to her knees and bowing to the Wolf. 'I have only ever been loyal to you. I exist only to serve you.' She raised her head and darted a hateful glare at Sargozy. Arno had never seen a look filled with such malice. 'She's envious of me. That's why she makes such claims against me.'

A bark of fearsome laughter rang down from the throne. 'And now we know how far she will go to pursue her jealousies.' Radukar gestured with his sword at Sargozy. 'I expected better things of you when I let you share my blood. You were quite cunning in your prime, but it seems I was too late to harvest that brilliance.'

The Thirsting Court cast their eyes to the massive doors at the front of the hall. These were flung open and a pair of gigantic Kosargi Nightguard marched into the room. Sargozy didn't resist them when the ogors seized her. The panic that filled her was too great. Arno knew that she'd intended this scene to bring ruin to Karlsson. It hadn't taken much to unravel her attempt at manipulating Radukar. A mad thing for anyone in Ulfenkarn to attempt.

'Take her out onto the battlements,' Radukar told the Nightguard. 'Leave her there. I think it has been much too long since the duchess has felt the sun upon her fair skin.'

As Sargozy was dragged away, nervous laughter spread among the nobles. Each was horrified by the vampire's fate but relieved it wasn't one in which they would share. Arno suspected their relief wouldn't last long. He had other tidings to bring to the Wolf.

'Eminence,' Arno addressed the tyrant with a bow as he walked towards the throne. 'I bring a report from the slums. There has been a third killing.'

Radukar returned the barrow-blade to its scabbard. 'Like the others?' he asked, looking up from the weapon.

'So it would appear,' Arno replied. 'The Volkshaufen have left the corpse where it was found so that it can be...'

The Wolf stepped down from his throne. 'I would see it for myself,' he declared. The statement sent shocked murmurs through the Thirsting Court. It was seldom that Radukar left the Ebon Citadel, much less to inspect the carcass of a mortal killed in the slums.

Arno felt terror rush through him. Did this mean Radukar

didn't trust him to make an accurate report? With the recent example of Duchess Sargozy, earning the Wolf's disfavour was the last thing he wanted to risk.

'I will see that all is in readiness for your arrival, eminence.'

Radukar turned away from Arno and motioned for the nobles to be quiet. 'I will be gone some short time. In my absence I trust you will comport yourselves appropriately.' He lifted his eyes and stared meaningfully at the ceiling. 'After all, tomorrow is another day.'

Radukar could smell the close long before he entered the little square. Those who bore the Vyrkos strain of vampirism were even more attuned to the scent of blood than others of their kind. This scent had the peculiar foulness about it that the Wolf had smelled on the corpse in Torgillius' laboratory.

The men of the Volkshaufen standing guard over the place turned pale with horror when they saw a company of Ulfenwatch marching through the street. Though the day had grown dark and murky, blotting out the sun behind a stormy mantle, none of them had expected to see such a procession of the undead. The streets through which Radukar's entourage travelled had quickly become deserted, the mortals scurrying back to their homes like scared rabbits. The watchmen at least stood their ground, even if they were shivering in their boots.

When the heavily cloaked vampire lord emerged from the midst of his skeletal warriors, the mortal sentries struggled to salute the ruler of Ulfenkarn with trembling hands and eyes brimming with fear. Radukar's lip curled back in contempt, exposing one of his long, wolfish fangs. The pathetic weakness of mortals was something he'd cast aside centuries ago. He'd ascended far beyond those miserable limitations, beyond even the strength of other vampires. There was only one thing he'd yet to transcend, the craving that haunted all his kind. He still depended upon the blood of mortals to sustain himself. That dependency would one day be severed, when all of Ulfenkarn was sacrificed to the nadir and the Wolf assumed powers beyond even his imaginings.

'Where is Arno?' Radukar's eyes roved across the sentries. He could see the blood rushing through the veins beneath their skin, watched as their hearts pounded faster and faster. The first faint twinge of craving nagged at the back of his mind, but he was no feral abhorrant. There was a time for indulgence and a time for restraint.

The silentiary scrambled forwards, bowing to him. Radukar could see that his heart pounded with the same fear that dominated the mortals, but outwardly Arno gave no expression to his emotion. He maintained a veneer of professionalism. The Wolf gave that a modicum of respect.

'Lead me to the corpse,' Radukar told Arno. The silentiary bowed again and waved aside the sentries.

The Wolf followed Arno into the close. Guards positioned around the marble fountain withdrew as Radukar approached, not waiting for their captain to dismiss them. The vampire stared down at the corpse. Though the body lay in a mire of congealed blood, the sight revolted rather than enticed him. Dimly he could recall when he'd been merely mortal, starving for want of food. He'd stolen bread from the ship's larder, only to discover his prize was foul with worms. The dried blood evoked the same sort of disgust.

'Who has done this thing?' Radukar mused. He stared down at the head, at the face that had been cut away to expose the grinning skull beneath. 'Too precise to be without purpose. The culprit lingered over this deed. As with the others.'

'Eminence, there's more this time,' Arno stated. He gestured to the wall beside the fountain. A pair of guards stood there, and between them there was a sheet pinned to the plaster. A nod from the captain in charge of them and the watchmen drew back the covering.

'Amusing. "Blood is the path to redemption."' Radukar read the words that had been smeared on the wall. The letters were drawn in blood, the same corrupt filth that had dried around the body and polluted the fountain. The perpetrator hadn't been overly careful in the work, leaving the impression of a hand too large for that of either a woman or a child.

'I thought it best to cover it,' Arno said. 'It is a call to revolution. The killer is a fanatic trying to incite rebellion.'

Radukar's face spread in a lupine snarl. 'More than that,' he growled. 'This one seeks to mock me. An open challenge to me.' He fixed Arno with his fiery gaze. 'Do you fear me?'

The question broke the semblance of composure Arno had mustered. 'Yes… of course, eminence.' He glanced at the Volk-shaufen around them. 'Everyone here fears your displeasure.'

The vampire nodded. 'All mortals hate and fear me. That is of no importance so long as they obey.' He pointed at the graffiti and then at the body. 'This killer is trying to make these people fear him more than me. Not a call to revolution, but rather a threat of what will happen if there is no revolution.'

Radukar drew closer to Arno. 'If the people have something they fear more than me, it will, in its way, inspire them.' He studied the silentiary even more closely. 'Do you understand?' he hissed. 'It will give them hope that my dominion over them can be broken.'

He spun around and fixed his attention on the mortal captain in charge of the Volkshaufen.

'What is your thought on the subject?' he asked, watching as the officer struggled to control his fear.

'You are our sovereign and our protector,' Dragomir replied. 'Were it not for you, there would be no refuge for anyone in Ulfenkarn.'

Arno took up the conversation when Dragomir's speech faltered. 'These people would be lost to the wilderness with no place of safety at all.' For a moment he was able to hold Radukar's gaze. 'Without you, eminence, their situation would be far worse.'

'Remember that,' Radukar advised Dragomir. 'It is my power that holds back the things which haunt the ruins. My power that keeps the dangers of the wild away from the city. Should I withdraw that power, how long do you think any of you would endure?' He pointed at the graffiti. 'This call to revolution will not spread. I want those words washed away and that wall pulled down.'

'It will be done, eminence,' Arno assured him. He indicated several watchmen who were detaining a few dock labourers. 'I had the witnesses who reported the murder detained. Only those two and Dragomir's men know what happened here.'

Dragomir nodded, striving to maintain any measure of composure. 'My men can be depended on to keep silent about what they've seen.'

It was obvious to Radukar what the officer was worried about if he didn't explain their dependability.

'There's much talk already about these murders among the people,' Arno said. 'They're calling this killer "Baron Grin" after the way he leaves a skull instead of a face when he's finished. To tamp down the panic and keep it from growing into disorder, the Volkshaufen have been tasked with ending such talk, not adding to it.'

'Good,' Radukar said. He regarded the watchmen with a toothy smile. 'Emphasise that they're expected to stay quiet. Remind them of what will happen if they don't.'

'They'll need no reminder, eminence,' Arno said. 'That you've come here in person is something none of them will forget. That you should deign to notice…'

Radukar pounced upon the word. 'Yes, I have noticed. You are appointed Watchmaster. The entire Volkshaufen now answers to you.' He waved his hand at the corpse. 'These killings are your responsibility. You will suppress gossip about them and you will keep me informed of the smallest detail.' He tapped Arno's chest with one of his icy fingers. 'When the killer strikes again, you'll tell me at once.'

The vampire laughed at Arno's uneasiness. 'There will be more killings. There's nothing to stop another one from happening. Not yet, anyway.' Radukar turned his wolfish grin on Arno now. 'This is your opportunity. Don't squander it. Serve me well and you will be rewarded. Fail me… and you'll not have the chance to do so again.'

'I will not fail you, eminence,' Arno said. 'These men won't speak a word of what they've seen here. They'll swear the witnesses to silence…'

'No,' Radukar corrected him. His pale hands curled against one another, the fingers interlacing in a cabalistic sign. In response, the skeletal Ulfenwatch stirred into motion. 'The witnesses will be taken to my castle.'

As the skeletons marched forwards, the watchmen withdrew. A few of the guards shoved their charges towards the undead. The two labourers had no chance to run. Fleshless talons closed on their shoulders and dragged them into the centre of the formation. Surrounded on every side by the skeletal warriors, the captives were herded away from the close.

'They'll be allowed to speak all they want,' Radukar told Arno. 'But their words will never leave the Ebon Citadel. Neither will they.'

Radukar noted the shudder that passed through Arno's body as he spoke. It pleased the vampire. Fear was ever the surest way to guarantee obedience.

The cellar where Morrvahl Olbrecht had established his hideout was a place Emelda didn't want to see again. Gustaf's arguments had finally prevailed upon her, however. These Baron Grin murders had resulted in increased activity by the Volkshaufen and the Ulfenwatch, and with that activity had come the less conspicuous agents of authority, the spies and informants who'd betray their own families for a bowl of soup. For two people actively working against Radukar and his vampires, a secure refuge was essential. Whatever other faults he might have, Morrvahl had demonstrated in no uncertain terms that he was an enemy of the vampires.

There was something more, though. Something that occupied Emelda's mind as she lay back on a pallet of musty straw and stared at the brick ceiling of the small alcove she'd taken for herself at the far end of the cellar. They'd watched one of the Nightguard lug a body back to the Ebon Citadel itself. That meant the rulers of Ulfenkarn were interested in these murders. Interested enough that they might even stir from their benighted stronghold. The chance to strike at Radukar when he was away from his fortress was too important to jeopardise. Tolerating the wizard's macabre collection of 'oddities' and the equally outré apparatus he employed to conduct his experiments was a small thing to endure for the sake of revenge.

Emelda disliked that word. She wanted so desperately to believe what she held were positive motivations, to free the people from their vampiric tyrant and restore Mournhold to its former glory. Deep inside, though, she had to admit her ambitions weren't so pure. She wanted to see Radukar destroyed because of what he'd done. The ruination of the city she'd fought so hard to protect and for which so many warriors had died under her command. The annihilation of the Braskovs, scoured root and branch until she was the only one left alive. Truly alive. These were things she'd make the usurper pay for, whatever the cost. Nothing would stop her. Until the Wolf was destroyed there could be nothing except the lust for vengeance.

The rap of knuckles against masonry caused Emelda to turn her head. The end of the alcove was closed off by a hanging curtain, but she could see the shadow of a man standing just beyond the partition. She heard him knock against the stones again.

'Emelda, Morrvahl wants to see us,' Gustaf called to her from beyond the curtain. 'He says it's vital.'

The wizard's severity must've impressed Gustaf for him to relay the summons in such sombre fashion. Their methods might be at odds, but Emelda knew she was of one accord with the vampire hunter where Morrvahl was concerned. Both considered him a necessary evil, something to endure for the moment but never to trust fully.

She glanced over at her armour lying on the floor. She considered putting it on before meeting Morrvahl but discarded the notion. There'd been wizards with the army when they went crusading against the Chaos tribes. She'd seen how little value armour had against magic. She did buckle her sword belt around her waist, because she'd also seen that spells didn't always stop twenty inches of sharp steel.

When she pulled aside the curtain, she found that Gustaf was also armed with sword and pistol. Emelda noted the weapons and gave an approving nod.

'You think he means mischief?' she asked.

'No,' Gustaf said, 'but if I'm wrong it does no harm to be ready.'

The vampire hunter led the way as they crossed the dingy cellar. Candles of seal fat sputtered and spat from niches in the walls, creating little patches of light amidst the deep shadows. Stone arches supported the vaulted ceiling, masses of cobwebs drooping down from each. Emelda saw a bat caught in the strands, each struggle to free itself only wrapping it more tightly in the trap. Eight red eyes gleamed from the fanged head of a spider the size of her hand, its palps trembling hungrily as it waited for the bat to tire.

The vermin that haunted the cellar were pleasant beside the furnishings Morrvahl had introduced. Huge racks slapped together from panels and beams stripped from deserted houses held a ghastly variety of bottles and jars. Emelda recognised the pickled remnants of ravens and rats. One huge jar held the horribly man-like head of a selkigor. A wooden crate bulged with the dried legs of pelicans and cranes. There was a box simply labelled 'eyes' and from which a translucent slime dripped onto the shelves below.

Beyond the racks were the tables on which Morrvahl conducted his experiments. Emelda hadn't seen such an assortment of alembics and flasks even in an alchemist's workshop. Glass tubes connected many of the vessels so that when a powder set above a pan of burning embers changed into liquid it would then be borne onwards to a second container and subjected to a still greater heat. The resultant gas would then rise to join a different liquid, then flow down to a frost-coated jar to become solid once more. There were cauldrons and a tiny furnace away from the tables in which the wizard reduced larger materials down to their 'essential constituents'. Emelda could see the necrotic hand of one of those materials poking up from the boiling broth in one of the iron vats.

Morrvahl was seated in a high-backed chair, one of the few furnishings in his lair that didn't reek of salvage and decay. Across his lap he had a map, his finger tracing a path across its lines. He'd lift his head from time to time and mutter to the filthy thing perched on the back of the chair. It was a huge rat, but even by the low standards of its kind it was a horrible sight. Bone showed through its mangy fur and rotten flesh; its muzzle was entirely skeletal, with yellowed fangs exposed. Its red eyes glowed with unnatural brilliance. The mark of an obscene magic.

'Ah, so you've convinced the princess to join us, have you?' Morrvahl chuckled as he looked up from his map.

Emelda gave the wizard a grim look. 'I understood you had

something important to talk about,' she said. 'It seems Gustaf was mistaken.'

Morrvahl held up his hand when Emelda started to turn away. 'Wait. Voss didn't mislead you. I assure you what I have to say will be of interest. If my efforts at conviviality come across as brusque, do remember that I seldom have opportunity to practise social courtesies.'

'Say what you have to say and forget the courtesies,' Emelda told the wizard.

Morrvahl stroked his long tuft of beard, his eyes glittering with amusement. 'I think that is what I like most about you. Your ability to focus on what you want and ignore distractions. A most refreshing and capable mindset.'

'What do you have to tell us?' Gustaf demanded.

Morrvahl gave the vampire hunter an irritated glance. 'You could do well to follow her example,' he said. His face curled into a grimace. 'You risked everything for only the smallest gain. What would've happened had I not intervened and settled Lupu for you? You'd be dead, my young gallant, and no nearer to accomplishing anything of consequence in this city.' He waved his hand at Emelda. 'You might've got her killed too, in the bargain, and all of it for nothing.'

'I don't have to listen to this,' Gustaf snapped.

The mantle of amused disdain dropped from Morrvahl. His eyes blazed as he regarded Gustaf. 'But you *will* listen, both of you. I tell you that until now you've risked much with little promise of reward. You've been like two duardin scratching away at a mountainside, no nearer to the gold within than you were when you started. What've you managed to do except draw the notice of Radukar's spies and assassins? Are you any closer to striking at the Wolf and ending his reign of terror?'

Emelda glared at the wizard. 'And what have you done? Hide yourself away in a cellar and play with your potions?'

'I've been waiting,' Morrvahl said. 'Biding my time until opportunity presented itself.' He nodded his head and smiled. 'That opportunity may be close now. You're familiar with these murders? What the people are now blaming on someone they call Baron Grin?'

'Of course,' Gustaf scoffed. 'Everyone is talking about them, much as the Volkshaufen tries to get them to stop.'

'You also know these murders have come to the notice of the Ebon Citadel,' Morrvahl said. Though neither she nor Gustaf had told him about following the Nightguard, Emelda was convinced he was aware of what they'd seen.

'A moment ago you spoke of an opportunity,' Emelda reminded Morrvahl. 'What do you mean?'

'There's been another of these murders,' Morrvahl said. He raised a bony finger for emphasis. 'This incident has drawn the Wolf from his lair. He went to personally investigate the scene.'

Emelda shook her head. 'Radukar left the Ebon Citadel? Why would the murders of a few mortals interest him that much?'

Morrvahl sighed and looked up at the decayed rat. 'My... assets... see and hear much, but sadly they comprehend little. I know that Radukar was there, but I don't know why.' He pointed at the weapons Emelda and Gustaf wore. 'It's good that you're armed. We'll have need of your weapons.'

'To fight Radukar!' Gustaf exclaimed, both anticipation and anxiety in his tone.

'That would be a senseless waste,' Morrvahl said. 'We'd be fighting on his terms, against not only him but the Volkshaufen and Ulfenwatch and whatever less visible guardians are with him. It is doubtful we'd even get close enough to strike at the Wolf.'

'What then?' Emelda asked.

Morrvahl again indicated the rotting rat. 'These bestial minds have limitations. What we must do is access a more aware mind that was present. A troop of Ulfenwatch are even now marching back to the Ebon Citadel. In their charge are two men, witnesses who found the murder scene… and were still there when Radukar arrived.'

The wizard turned the map around and pointed to a particular intersection.

'The Ulfenwatch have certain advantages over the living, but swiftness isn't one of them. We can intercept them here and relieve them of their captives.' Morrvahl chuckled and stroked his beard. 'I think they'd be worth making the effort to talk to, don't you?'

Gustaf felt the hairs on the back of his neck prickle when he saw the column of armoured skeletons march into view. Morrvahl's rodent spies weren't very good at numbers and had offered the wizard little to estimate the size of the group escorting the witnesses. Emelda thought ten was a reasonable number to expect, typical of an Ulfenwatch patrol. What was coming up the road was twice that number.

'There's too many,' Gustaf whispered. He crouched down behind the fragments of the old wall they were hiding behind. He looked over at Emelda. 'We'll have to forget it.'

Emelda's fingers played with the grip of her sword. 'If we do, those men are lost,' she said, nodding at the captives. 'Whatever they know will be lost with them. We'll not have a chance like this again.'

'My magic will even things,' Morrvahl insisted. The wizard drew from beneath his robes a loathsome candle. To Gustaf it looked like the wax-covered hand of an infant. Scratched into its surface were all three of their names. The foul thing smacked of the vilest sorcery.

'You'd have us trust the very thing we're fighting,' Gustaf said, pointing at the candle.

'To fight fire, sometimes you must use fire,' Morrvahl replied.

'It is because of the similarity between my magic and that which lends the skeletons a parody of life that the spell can work at all.' He raked his nail against the wax, just below Gustaf's name. 'If it bothers you, know that the protection will last only until the candle burns to your inscription. After that, you must look to your own defences. You, gallant, will be the first exposed.'

'How long will we have?' Emelda asked. Her name was just below Gustaf's, with the wizard last of all.

Morrvahl frowned and tugged at his beard. 'Not long. The candle will burn quickly. This kind of magic will not go unnoticed. If it burned any longer, things far worse than the Ulfenwatch would be drawn here.' The wizard looked across his companions. 'We must be quick and we must wait until the last moment before we act.'

Gustaf drew his sword and peeked over the crumbling wall. They were inside the desolate ruins, beyond the ring of squalid life that characterised Ulfenkarn's outer districts. Decayed structures, withered by the dark energies of the nadir, leaned out over the streets like weary drunkards. Clumps of plaster and broken bricks lay strewn about the road along with fallen shingles and splintered shutters. The walking skeletons tromped through the debris with unerring steps. The men they guarded stumbled and staggered, goaded on by the spears of their captors.

'By Sigmar, your magic had better work,' Gustaf swore. He felt ashamed to be trusting in magic to aid him, certainly magic as dark as that practised by Morrvahl. In better circumstances, he'd be bringing the wizard before the Order of Azyr for judgement. Of course, in better circumstances he'd never have left Carstinia.

'If it doesn't, you'll be the first to know,' Morrvahl said. 'Tell me when they're close enough.'

In his estimation, the skeletons were already too close, but Gustaf held his peace. He knew what the wizard meant. They'd discussed the plan after leaving the cellar. To gain the maximum advantage they'd wait until the Ulfenwatch were aware of them. Only when they'd been discovered would Morrvahl light what he called 'the glorious candle'.

Nearer and nearer the skeletons marched. Gustaf couldn't get a good look at the prisoners at the middle of the formation, but if they were still able to move then they couldn't be hurt too badly. Whether they'd stay in that shape once the fighting started was a question Morrvahl couldn't answer. Gustaf thought it would depend on what sort of orders Radukar had given the undead. If they'd been told only to convey the captives to the Ebon Citadel they might not attack the men, but if they'd been commanded to guard them, then the skeletons would try to kill them rather than let them escape.

The skeletons were only twenty yards away now. Gustaf could make out the design etched into the breastplate of the foremost undead, a rampant griffon struggling under clumps of rust. The skeleton stopped abruptly and the rest of the Ulfenwatch halted a heartbeat later. The creature turned its skull to one side, its empty sockets staring at the wall Gustaf was peering over. The eerie senses of the undead had discovered them.

'Now!' Gustaf shouted. From the corner of his eye he saw a bright flash as Morrvahl lit the candle. He saw nothing more, for with one hand planted on the wall, he was vaulting the barrier and charging towards the Ulfenwatch. 'The wrath of Sigmar is upon you,' he cried as he rushed towards the undead.

A moment before, Gustaf was certain the skeletons had seen him, but now there was no reaction from them as he attacked the formation. A few even walked past him to advance towards the wall. He felt a thrill of exultation. The wizard's magic was working! The skeletons couldn't see him!

Gustaf struck one of the undead against its bony leg, splitting it at the knee and sending it crashing to the ground. He spun away from the fallen thing to whip his sword across the neck of another. Oblivious to his presence, the skeleton made no move to protect itself and its skull was knocked from its shoulders to go rolling away.

'Gustaf! Hurry!' Emelda shouted. She too had cleared the wall and was cutting a path through the skeletons.

The admonition sobered Gustaf instantly. The spell that allowed him to wreak such havoc unopposed wouldn't last long. Before it was spent they had to rescue the prisoners. In his excitement he'd let himself veer away from that goal, assaulting the side of the column rather than striking for its centre.

He turned and drove himself at the skeletons. His shoulder smashed into one, throwing it aside as he plunged deeper into their ranks. The hilt of his sword smashed the skull of another, shattering its jawbone and spilling teeth in the street. A third staggered away, one of its arms shorn through by his blade.

Two more stood between Gustaf and the prisoners, but as he rushed towards them he saw that they were no longer oblivious to him. One shifted so that its shield met his charge, and his shoulder crashed painfully against the corroded boss. The skeleton wasn't equal to the momentum of his attack and it collapsed with its rusted shield broken and its arm snapped. Gustaf almost followed it, barely managing to keep his feet. The other guard jabbed at him with its spear, the point grazing painfully across his ribs.

'Keep going!' Emelda yelled as she whipped her own sword across the skeleton's arm and sent it flying from its shoulder. Even when she struck it, the undead was incapable of registering her presence and didn't react to her. An instant later a second swing sent its head spinning into the road.

Gustaf knew Emelda's protection would last only a moment longer than his own had, but he couldn't linger to help her. He saw why she'd urged him to keep moving. The Ulfenwatch were turning against their charges, determined to keep the prisoners from escaping.

'Get away from him!' Gustaf roared as he lunged at the skeletons. His sword smashed down against an exposed shoulder-bone and sent the guard crashing into two of its comrades that were moving against one of the prisoners. All three of the undead staggered back, trying to regain their footing.

The man he'd rescued didn't linger, but hurried away at a run. Gustaf was surprised to recognise him as the rowdy youth from the Black Ship, the agitator Loew. A scream of pain from behind made him turn from the fleeing prisoner. The other captive was sprawled on the ground, his leg pierced by an undead spear. While the first skeleton held him pinned to the ground, a second angled around to stab its spear into the man's chest.

'In a pig's eye you will!' Emelda cursed, leaping at the skeleton with the upraised spear. Her sword came cleaving downwards, splitting the rusted helm and cracking the skull inside.

'The other one ran away,' Gustaf told her as he ploughed into the remaining skeleton. The guard was sent flying by the impact, the spear ripped from its bony grip.

'Then he's having better luck than we are,' Emelda said. She stood above the injured captive and nodded at the circle of Ulfenwatch that now closed in around them. Even with the protection of Morrvahl's spell, they'd destroyed less than half of the skeletons. Now the rest moved in for the kill.

'Dracothion swallow all wizards and their spells,' Gustaf grumbled. He drew his pistol and snapped off a shot that exploded a fleshless skull. The headless body took a final step, then crashed to the ground.

'One down, too many to go,' Emelda said. Gustaf nodded in agreement. They'd fought hard, but it wasn't enough.

'Stay where you are and don't look into the cloud!' Morrvahl's voice boomed across the battlefield. The wizard stood atop the crumbling wall, the blade of his scythe crackling with a nimbus of dark energy. His protection too had faded and a few of the skeletons turned to march towards the wall once more. He gave their advance little concern, but simply repeated his warning. 'Don't look into the cloud!'

Gustaf felt the icy chill of magic in the air. The energy swirling around Morrvahl's staff surged outwards, becoming a dark, roiling mass. It spilled down towards the advancing skeletons, swiftly engulfing them. The sound of cracking bones and shriven armour reached his ears.

'Whatever he's conjured, do as he says,' Gustaf told Emelda.

'See to your sword or it won't matter,' Emelda replied, fending away the thrusts of two skeletons.

Gustaf was quickly put to the test by three more of the undead warriors. More of the creatures joined the attack with each breath. It was only by the grace of Sigmar that they weren't already overwhelmed.

Then all light faded away and the surroundings were consumed by a black fog. Gustaf knew that the roiling mass had swept down, spilling across the street until it overtook them. There was something in that dark cloud. He could sense it. If he tried, he could almost see it, lurking there behind the skeletons.

'Don't look at it!' Emelda cried. Gustaf clenched his eyes tight. Even if the Ulfenwatch skewered him on their spears, he expected it to be a cleaner death than whatever horror Morrvahl had conjured. The sound of cracking bones and crumpled steel surrounded him now, grisly sounds of havoc that sought to coax him into opening his eyes. It took all of his self-control to resist that urge. Instead he turned his mind to Sigmar and recited the prayers taught to him by the Order of Azyr.

It seemed the terrifying darkness would never relent, but then Gustaf was aware that the sorcerous chill was gone. The next moment he heard Morrvahl's voice, strained with effort.

'It's over,' the wizard wheezed. 'You can open your eyes now.'

The sight that greeted Gustaf was one of absolute carnage. The Ulfenwatch had been annihilated, their armour and bones shattered by some tremendous force. It looked to him that the undead had been twisted apart. Some of the more intact bones were curled in a loathsome manner and he saw a shield that was so warped that it resembled a corkscrew.

'Emelda!' Gustaf cried, panic rushing through him. He spun around to find her crouched over the injured prisoner.

'I'm all right,' she said. 'But I don't think he is.'

The prisoner was curled into a ball, his arms wrapped around his head. The man's eyes were wide with horror and his mouth hung open in an idiot's grin. The soft moan that rattled past his lips was scarcely a human sound.

'I warned all of you not to look,' Morrvahl said. The wizard hobbled forwards, leaning on his staff for support. The pallor of his skin was even more sickly than before and there were streaks of white in his beard now. 'I fear he didn't heed my advice.'

'What, in Sigmar's name, was that?' Gustaf demanded.

Morrvahl's eyes had a blemish in them that hadn't been there before. 'Magic. Dark and terrible magic. A spell that manifests nightmares and makes them real.' He shuddered under his robes. 'A spell I wouldn't care to invoke again. A wizard's nightmares aren't things it's healthy to ponder.'

'The other man ran away,' Emelda said. She pointed at the moaning figure on the ground. 'This one has gone mad because of your spell.'

Anger boiled inside Gustaf when he looked at the insane wretch. 'What've we profited by listening to you?' he growled. 'Look at this man! It would have been more merciful to leave him to Radukar!'

The wizard's eyes returned Gustaf's anger. 'We'll leave him to no one,' Morrvahl said. 'Pick him up and bring him back to my sanctum.'

'Why? What use is he to you?' Emelda asked.

'I'll show you,' Morrvahl said. The wizard turned and started back the way they'd come. 'Bring him and you'll see what I mean.'

Morrvahl found the squeamishness of his new allies vexing. He'd expected them to be more pragmatic, to understand that to achieve anything sacrifices had to be made. Even when those sacrifices resisted the role chosen for them.

'That is no longer a man,' Morrvahl explained, gesturing to the table. Flasks and alembics had been cleared away so that the rescued prisoner could be laid across it. 'What makes a man is the mind, not the body,' he said, tapping his brow. 'This man's mind has been shattered. What's left is only a husk of flesh. Only sentimentality makes you regard it as any different from one of the undead.'

'Then what possible use is he to you?' Gustaf demanded. 'If that's what you thought, why didn't we just slit his throat instead of carrying him back here?' The vampire hunter gripped his bandaged side. His agitation had started his wound bleeding again. Morrvahl knew a spell that would close the wound, but just now he preferred the zealot weakened.

Emelda's tone was even colder than Gustaf's when she addressed the wizard. 'What are you planning to do?'

'What's necessary,' Morrvahl said. He waved his hand over the pitiful shape on the table. 'You'll concede that in this condition, this man is no use to himself or anyone else? You'll agree that there's nothing left of his mind?'

'He's still alive,' snarled Gustaf. 'His mind might be gone, but his soul remains.'

'We'll let Sigmar tend to his soul, shall we,' Morrvahl said. Fanatical adherence to the God-King's creed had its uses, but at the moment it was tiresome. 'What concerns us now is the body.' He pointed at the madman's head. 'More particularly, the brain.'

'What do you mean?' Emelda stared at the man, trying to perceive the distinction Morrvahl made.

'The mind is gone,' Morrvahl said. He smiled at Gustaf. 'On that point, at least, we're all agreed. But upon that brain is imprinted everything thought by that absent mind. Every dream. Every idea. Every memory.'

Emelda paced around the table. 'You're saying your magic can extract memories from his brain.'

Morrvahl proudly indicated the racks of shelves. 'A few of the proper ingredients, and all will be in readiness.'

Gustaf raised a protest. 'This stinks of blackest sorcery,' he swore. He stabbed a bloodied finger at Morrvahl. 'You're a necromancer.'

'I weary of that accusation, and I resent it,' Morrvahl retorted. 'The school of magic I've studied does harness the energies of Shyish, but in the service of life, not at its expense. We seek to employ these deathly forces for the betterment of civilisation, not in the obscene pursuits of the sepulchrists and death cults. Zealots such as yourself fail to make that distinction, to appreciate the restraint which governs we who study this arcane art.' The wizard turned to Emelda. 'With your indulgence, I'll begin.'

Morrvahl frowned at her hesitance.

'If I wasn't convinced this man had something important locked inside his brain, I wouldn't waste my time over him. It will demand great energy and concentration on my part.' He looked from Emelda to Gustaf. 'And a great deal of forbearance on yours. Once I start, the process cannot be stopped.'

'If there's a chance, we have to try,' Emelda said to Gustaf. Morrvahl wondered if maybe she was more pragmatic than he'd given her credit for.

The vampire hunter hung his head in defeat. 'Sigmar have mercy on us,' he said.

'Then I'll begin,' Morrvahl declared. He motioned to Emelda. 'First I need you to strap him down. I don't want him running away.'

The process took more than an hour. Several times during the ritual, Morrvahl worried that Gustaf would intervene. His estimation of Emelda's resolve served him true, however, and she prevented the vampire hunter from stopping him. The information being wrung from the madman's brain was too precious to lose. Even so, Morrvahl was thankful that what he wanted to know was among the subject's most recent memories and he didn't have to probe too deeply for them.

The subject screamed. Cries of agony and torment that apparently exceeded anything Gustaf and Emelda had heard before. Morrvahl could see the vampire hunter struggle to stay where he was.

'Stop it!' Emelda shouted at the wizard. 'This is too much!'

Morrvahl ignored her entreaties and continued the ritual. The madman contorted with such violence that he threatened to snap every bone in his body. His face was twisted and tortured, his eyes somehow more eloquent of his suffering than any sane eyes could have been. There was no restraint in them, no dignity or pride. Only the raw emotion. A fascinating study, a novel and unexpected by-product of the experiment. For the sake of his own edification, Morrvahl intensified the spell.

'This isn't necessary,' Emelda snarled at him. Almost she reached out to break his concentration, but she wasn't absolutely convinced of what she said.

While she hesitated, Morrvahl pressed on. He was teasing away strands of the subject's life force, drawing it into himself. This draining increased the madman's pain. Now the only interruption of his screams was when Morrvahl forced him to speak.

'You… you enjoy this! You scum, you enjoy this!' Emelda punctuated her accusation with a punch at his face. Morrvahl felt the blow, but the lack of surprise meant he didn't lose his focus. It was an unjust accusation anyway. Joy had nothing to do with what was happening. It was simply interesting.

'That's enough!'

Gustaf's assault did come as a surprise. Morrvahl was knocked to the floor by the vampire hunter. The sudden breaking of the spell sent the residual energies whipping about the cellar. Bottles burst and plaster fell from the ceiling as the magical forces went wild. If Gustaf had any notion of further prosecuting his attack on the wizard, the arcane discharge interfered.

While Gustaf and Emelda tried to defend themselves from the renegade energies, Morrvahl picked himself off the floor. He wasn't so much annoyed at them for hitting him as he was irked that he hadn't been able to press on with the experiment. Now he'd have to find a lunatic some other time and try to recreate these conditions. For now, though, he had other things to occupy himself with. The first of which was a minor counterspell to dissipate the arcane energies Gustaf had unleashed.

'There we have it,' Morrvahl said, stroking his long black beard as he faced Emelda and Gustaf. The white had darkened during the ritual, as had the wizard's complexion. The blemish too had faded from his eye. While extracting memories from the madman's brain, he'd also siphoned a bit of his life force. It wasn't as if the idiot would have much use for it, after all.

Emelda's expression was bitter. The grisliness of the rite had shaken her. It was an effort for her to even look at the wizard.

'So it's true. Radukar has involved himself personally in investigating these murders.'

'And we know that there's some kind of arcane force involved,' Morrvahl said. 'Something strong enough to render blood so corrupt even a vampire is sickened by it.' He looked over and smiled at Gustaf. 'It appears you're not the only enemy Radukar has in Ulfenkarn. Perhaps your friend Darrock has found other means to oppose the Wolf?'

Gustav bristled at the remark. 'Darrock is of the Order of Azyr! He'd not stoop to such foul measures.' He started towards the steps leading up from the cellar. 'Neither will I, Morrvahl.'

'Don't be rash, Gustaf.' Emelda hurried over to catch him. 'We've a real chance if we work together! We know that Radukar left the Ebon Citadel because of this murder.'

'And he'll leave again when there's another one,' Morrvahl said. 'Somewhere in Ulfenkarn there's a murderer trying to foment a rebellion.' The wizard noticed that Gustaf spun around when he mentioned that fact. There was a disturbed look in his eyes for a moment. 'If we can figure out a pattern to these murders, then we can anticipate the next one. Should we manage that...'

'Then we'll know where to wait for Radukar.' Emelda grasped Gustaf's arm. 'Don't you see? We'll have a real chance at the Wolf!'

'I see,' Gustaf said, drawing away from her. 'I see that you'll do anything to destroy Radukar.' The vampire hunter turned back and pointed to the table and the now silent madman. 'But I warn you, both of you, that I'll not stand for such obscenity again. If we lower ourselves to such deeds, how are we any better than Radukar?'

Morrvahl laid an obsidian knife on the table. 'Your compassion is commendable, Voss. So I leave the choice to you.' He pointed at the subject. The screams had fallen to a dull and inane mewing. 'Do we slit that mindless hulk's throat now, or do we simply dump him in the street like a slab of meat? Which is more sympathetic, do you think?'

'You go too far, wizard,' Gustaf snapped.

'No, I merely try to impress on you that if we're to succeed then there can be no room for compassion,' Morrvahl said. 'That is a luxury for the victorious. Until the Wolf is gone, it's simply something we can't afford. If we keep working together, then we have an opportunity to make that happen.'

INTERLUDE 3

By his own reckoning, Grau was entering his forty-seventh year and far too old to still be plying his morbid trade. For a time he'd been able to turn to respectable work, apprenticed to a bookbinder in old Waldweg. If he closed his eyes he could almost hear the bustle of liveried servants shopping the stalls and commissioning artists to illuminate the pages of some noble's family lineage. He could smell fresh ink and old paper again, see Otto behind his desk dickering over the price of vellum with an intransigent vendor.

The Waldweg was gone these many years, lost with so much else when ruin descended upon Mournhold. The street was now abandoned, surrendered to the deadwalkers that lurched through the rubble in search of prey. The shops were deserted, a shelter for degenerate wolfish things when there was too much sunlight for them to endure. All the books so many had laboured so hard to copy and transcribe lying forsaken in the dust of better days. Grau supposed it was just as well. The great and good who'd patronised the bookmongers were gone now, lost when the shadow fell upon the city. The new aristocracy had no interest. The appetites of vampires were for things other than reading.

Grau shifted the heavy burden slung across his back as he slipped down a winding alleyway. Again he bemoaned his age. There'd been a time when he'd have been able to carry such a weight with ease. Too many years plying a different trade had made him soft. At least in certain areas.

He froze when he heard movement in the street adjacent to the alley. By day this part of Ulfenkarn would be busy enough, but even before the arrival of Baron Grin there were few who dared defy the curfew and stir from their homes at night. Those who did were like Grau, people whose activities wouldn't bear the scrutiny of broad daylight. Or they were no longer people. Grau turned his head and looked at the bundle slung over his shoulders, its hands tied together and looped around his arm, its ankles likewise tied and thrown across the other arm.

Bodysnatching. It was a foul business to be in and always had been. The penalty for being caught in the old days was beheading. Now, like all other crimes, it was exsanguination, to have every drop rendered up to the vampires. Grau would have preferred the headsman. At least that would be over quickly.

The sound of movement in the street became more defined. Grau crouched down, using the bulk of the body he was carrying to mask his presence. In the dark, he hoped his outline would be indistinct and far from what would indicate the presence of a person. Of course the things he had to hide from now weren't entirely human and not all of them needed eyes to find you. The corpse might confuse such things as to whether what they sensed was alive or dead, but Grau well knew there were creatures in Ulfenkarn that didn't much care what state they found their prey in.

The rattle of armour made Grau cower a little closer to the slimy wall. He peeked out from under his grim burden to see the fleshless bones and rusty mail of the Ulfenwatch as the undead marched past. There was what looked like a living man with them, clearly uneasy with his companions but obviously not a captive either. He could see the armband of the Volkshaufen on his arm and a gruesome talisman fashioned from a crow's foot hanging from his neck. Grau had seen such talismans before. They were highly prized, for they indicated to the Ulfenwatch that those wearing them were free to move about during curfew. Some foul magic was in them, however, and they'd rot into mush after only a day or two, losing whatever truck they had with the skeleton guards.

'Looking for Baron Grin,' Grau muttered to himself. 'Need a living set of eyes to spot something the bones might miss.' He shuddered as he thought about the implications. Even the rulers of Ulfenkarn were rattled by these murders and were taking steps to bring them to an end. For the first time, he wished the undead luck.

Grau kept close to the wall, sticking to the deep shadows while he waited for the patrol to put distance between itself and him. It had occurred to him that if they caught him with a dead body, they might think that *he* was Baron Grin. He wasn't sure what would happen then, but he imagined it would be far worse than exsanguination.

'I should've listened to Miranda,' Grau said. His wife was disgusted by the work he did. He'd tried to do right by her, buying his apprenticeship so he'd have a respectable vocation, but when that disappeared he'd been pushed back into his old activities. Scandal and shame were things a family could survive, starvation wasn't. Miranda insisted there had to be another way, but until he found it he had to do what he did to put food on the table. Even her scruples faltered when the prospect of watching their children starve was put before her. She'd kept quiet while he smothered the drunken 'friend' he'd brought home that evening and helped him to convince their daughters that he was just 'helping the man get home' when he left with the corpse slung across his back.

'She'll need more,' Grau whispered, thinking of his client. He'd got the measure of her when he'd brought her the first one and discovered she wanted others. Like some grisly grocer, she'd laid a standing order with him. Well, she was going to find that his wares were becoming more expensive. All this Baron Grin business made it harder to sneak through the streets. She'd simply have to pay more, and Grau felt she was desperate enough to meet his price.

The sounds of the Ulfenwatch faded away and Grau decided it was time to get moving again. He braced his legs and slowly lifted himself back up. His body was stiff from the awkward position he'd been holding. He felt a sharp pain in his side and wobbled as he started to lose his balance.

As he fell, Grau saw the bloodied knife gripped by the figure that had silently snuck up behind him. He felt the wet warmth rushing from where he'd been stabbed. His eyes bulged with horror as the realisation exploded in his brain.

The Ulfenwatch were looking for Baron Grin, but it was a body-snatching bookbinder who'd found the killer!

CHAPTER FOUR

Emelda drew the cloak closer about her as she passed a pair of watchmen. The Volkshaufen were out in force on the streets, in such numbers as she couldn't recall seeing before. They were going from door to door, dragging the inhabitants out for public interrogation. The guards were brutal in their methods, making free use of their cudgels and whips. Often the bloodied occupants were left to crawl back into their homes. Those who were still coherent enough to speak sobbed in gratitude when they were released, for with each group of watchmen was the monstrous spectre of the Ulfenwatch, a skeleton ready to drag them away to the Ebon Citadel if their answers were unsatisfactory. Beside the threat of the black fortress, the viciousness of the Volkshaufen was a thing to be desired.

'I feel so powerless,' Emelda hissed, her hands curling into fists beneath the folds of her cloak. She felt the hot flush of anger rising to her cheeks and burning in her eyes. 'This is senseless. Nothing but brutality for its own sake.'

Walking beside her through the lane, Gustaf gave only the

slightest nod of his hooded head. 'It would've been best had we turned down another street, but we'll draw more notice if we turn back now. Be grateful they're only taking an interest in the people who live here.'

The vampire hunter paused and watched while the guards systematically broke the fingers of an old man before making him squirm in the gutter on his way back to his house.

'This isn't senseless, though. It's a performance, a show for all those walking the street. The watchmen know that word of what's going on here will spread. It'll be a reminder to everyone in Ulfenkarn that Radukar still controls this city and it's the Wolf they should fear, not Baron Grin.'

'Fear has ever been the only thing that monster understands,' Emelda said. 'Even before he usurped complete dominion, he maintained his authority through fear. The fear of what it would cost to remove him and how much weaker the city would be without him.'

She paused and turned her head in the direction of where the Ebon Citadel stood upon its spire of rock. Even when it was obstructed by the clustered buildings of Ulfenkarn's slums, the presence of the vampire's fortress could be felt.

'I've wondered if that wasn't the real purpose behind our crusade against the Chaos tribes, a way to draw out the city's strength and leave it that much easier for the Wolf to devour.'

Emelda looked away as they drew close to another scene of savagery. The unfortunate the Volkshaufen were abusing was so bloodied that it was impossible to tell if there was a man or woman under the gore.

'Radukar's corruption has ruined the people every bit as much as the city itself. He's turned everyone into either frightened sheep or vicious brutes.' A snort of bitter laughter rose up within her. 'And even the brutes do what they do out of fear. The fear their utility will no longer be recognised and they'll be cast down among the sheep. The Mournhold I left was a proud and noble place.' She gave Gustaf a solemn glance. 'Sometimes I despair. Sometimes I wonder if it really matters if Radukar is destroyed. Sometimes I question if there's any coming back from what he's done to us.'

'While there's life, there has to be hope,' Gustaf said. 'Hope is the gift Sigmar has given to the Mortal Realms. No matter how dark the shadows, you must remember that the light *is* out there and that before the light the darkness will be driven away.'

'Tell that to these people.' Emelda shook her head. 'Tell them to cherish hope while every day the claws of despair tighten around them.'

Gustaf reached to his neck. Emelda knew his fingers were closing around the Sigmarite hammer he wore. 'That,' he said, 'is the time when hope is the most precious thing of all. The enemy can break your flesh, but if you keep hope, your spirit can never be broken.'

'There is a limit past which hope isn't enough,' Emelda said. She pointed to a house across from them where the Volkshaufen had a man's foot in an iron vice and were slowly tightening it. Even from where they stood, the sound of cracking bones was audible. Anger welled up inside her. Anger at her helplessness to intervene. Anger at Sigmar's refusal to intercede. 'Pretty sermons won't change their suffering,' she said. She turned back to Gustaf. 'But destroying Radukar, that will. Whatever comes afterwards, it'll be better than living under the vampire's shadow.'

Emelda could tell from the vampire hunter's expression that he wanted to contest her impious words, but he decided now wasn't the time for that battle. Instead he indicated a tumbledown building farther along the street.

'Let's hasten then and see what Poznan has to tell us,' he suggested. 'I'd sooner collect information myself than resort to Morrvahl's spells again.'

In that sentiment they were both of one accord. Emelda felt sick at the core of her soul by what they'd permitted the wizard to do. The only salve to her conscience had been bringing Morrvahl's experiment to an early finish. The madman was beyond help. Once away from the wizard, there'd been nothing to do except to smother him quickly and bury his body where it might escape the attention of the things that prowled Ulfenkarn. Gustaf had taken steps to at least ensure there was no danger of the unfortunate coming back as one of the undead. The entire affair had exposed to her the lengths she'd go to to have her revenge. She now had to ask herself if there was anything she'd balk at if it meant destroying Radukar.

They soon reached the decayed house Gustaf was seeking. It took some little while after pounding on the door before it eased open. The whole while Emelda kept watching the street and the watchmen prowling up and down the road.

'Sigmar's grace, what's happened to you?' Gustaf gasped when he saw the man on the other side of the door. He was a short, heavy-faced individual with a bald head and big ears. He wore a leather apron over his woollen clothes, wood shavings still clinging to its surface. What provoked the outburst were the livid bruises that discoloured the man's face, the dried blood that was crusted around his nose, and the ugly slit where the lobe of his right ear had recently been cut.

'Voss,' the little man wheezed, his eyes seeming to struggle to focus on the vampire hunter. Emelda could hear the thump of Poznan setting his foot against the door so it couldn't be pushed open further. 'I've nothing to say.' He peered past Gustaf and out into the street. 'By Nagash's black bones, go away before they come back!'

'Who comes back?' Emelda asked.

Poznan looked over at her, his face dripping with terror. 'The

Volkshaufen,' he said. 'They've been here three times already. Different ones, but asking the same questions.' He lifted a trembling finger to his mangled ear. 'Asking them the same way. You see they don't leave any mark on the door to let the others know they've already been here. So they just keep coming… and coming.'

Emelda thought about what Gustaf had said regarding the interrogations being a performance rather than a serious investigation. A cold fury swelled inside her. She wanted nothing more than to turn around and meet the nearest watchmen with her sword, but she knew it would be a futile act. More would come until there were enough to overwhelm her. She'd change nothing. All she'd do would be to get herself killed. The last of the Braskovs lying dead in a gutter, her revenge unfulfilled.

'What's it all about?' Gustaf pressed Poznan. 'Why are they doing this?'

Poznan licked his lips nervously. He looked as though he'd slam the door in their faces rather than answer, but finally he did whisper a reply. 'While they were beating me, the guards let a few things slip. Baron Grin was in this area last night. There's been another murder.'

'Another murder,' Emelda muttered. 'Near here?' She looked to Gustaf. 'We could go where it happened. See if there's anything we could learn.'

'You'd be mad to try,' Poznan said, horror in his voice. 'The area's cordoned off. They say… they say the Wolf himself has gone there.'

'Radukar,' Emelda said, her face brightening with vicious excitement.

Colour drained from Poznan's visage when he understood the intentions of his visitors. 'Go away,' he demanded. 'Don't come here again! Get yourselves slaughtered, but leave me out of it!'

Gustaf was almost thrown down into the street, such was the

violence with which the door was shut. The sound of the slamming door drew curious looks from those in the lane. More troubling were the turned heads of the closest watchmen.

'We'd best slip away while we still can,' Gustaf told Emelda.

'But Radukar,' she protested. 'If he's really here, then this is our chance.'

'We have to find him first,' Gustaf said. His eyes darted to the patrols. 'And we won't find him if the Volkshaufen gets hold of us.'

Emelda curbed her excitement. Gustaf was right. The first thing they had to do was get away.

'Down there,' she told him, indicating a narrow passageway between two of the buildings. 'If the guards come after us, they'll have to do so one by one.'

'Unless they block off the other end,' Gustaf said, frowning.

'We'll have to move too fast for them to do that,' Emelda said, urging him on. They broke into a jog and ignored the commands for them to stop that were raised by the watchmen. Like rabbits darting into a burrow, they hastened into the cloying darkness of the passageway and rushed onwards. Emelda could hear the shouts of their pursuers, but didn't look back. Their only chance to get away was forwards.

Then, once they were free of the guards, they'd circle back. Emelda wasn't going to let this opportunity go to waste. Radukar had left his fortress and if it was in her power, she was determined he'd never return to the Ebon Citadel.

Gustaf followed Emelda down the winding passageway. He was very much in the same position as his first meeting with her, depending on her knowledge of the area to steer him out of danger. Unfortunately their pursuers weren't giving up and they appeared just as knowledgeable of each twist and turn.

'Not much farther now,' Emelda said, kicking over a rats' nest and sending rodents scampering in every direction. The bones the vermin had used to make their lair were clearly human.

'The guards are still following us,' Gustaf reminded her. 'They sound like they're gaining.'

'If it comes to a fight, don't use your pistol,' Emelda said. 'If they've sent anyone to try to surround us, the shot will tell them exactly where we are.'

'There's a happy thought,' Gustaf grumbled. He eased his hand away from the holstered pistol. In the narrow confines of the passageway, a shot from the gun would've been certain death to a watchman, and probably any comrade behind him as well. With swords and knives, there were no such guarantees. Without the room to move, skill with the blade would count for less than speed and luck.

Emelda motioned to him and took the turn ahead of them. Gustaf followed her down a litter-strewn corridor. The light was brighter at the other end, an indication that at the very least the passageway widened ahead of them.

The corridor opened onto a stockyard. Barrels and crates were stacked all around, their iron fittings corroded by rain and mist, their wooden panels gnawed by rats. That they hadn't been broken up for someone's hearth was proof to Gustaf that this place was either hidden or protected. He decided it must be the latter when a dozen armed men stepped out to greet them.

'This feels familiar,' Gustaf muttered, thinking of the ambush Lupu had laid for them.

'Don't depend on the wizard to show up this time,' Emelda said, drawing her sword.

Gustaf's eyes narrowed when one of the men stepped forwards. 'Whoever they are, they're not Volkshaufen,' he said, nodding at the advancing figure. 'That man's named Loew. He's the one who escaped from the Ulfenwatch.'

Loew stared at the two of them, suspicion in his eyes. Gustaf felt like a catch being inspected by a fisherman.

'Lay down your weapons,' Loew ordered them.

'What if we don't?' Emelda snarled back.

As though in answer, the sounds of battle rang out from the alleyway behind them. The crash of blades. The cries of dying men.

Loew threw back his head and fixed his cold gaze on the swords-woman. 'You were being followed. You're not being followed now.' He nodded at the group of men who came up the corridor. Like the men in the stockyard, they were a motley assortment of common-ers. Stevedores, sailors, scavengers, some of them carrying bloodied swords, others with awls and cudgels. All had an expression of smouldering hostility.

'They're all finished,' one of the newcomers said with a smile. 'One patrol that won't go talking to the bloodsuckers about us.'

'You're sure about who they were, Witalas?' Loew asked. 'No mistake they were Volkshaufen?'

'I'm certain of it,' Witalas replied.

'We were being pursued by the Volkshaufen,' Gustaf told Loew.

'Maybe,' Loew replied. 'Or maybe you were working with them.' He waved his hand and indicated the bowmen among his entourage. 'If you don't drop your weapons, this will be a short conversation.'

Gustaf looked over at Emelda. 'We gain nothing by fighting.' He looked at Loew. 'You fight the Volkshaufen. That means we're on the same side,' he said, unbuckling his belt. His pistol, sword and other weapons fell at his feet.

Glaring at Loew, Emelda sheathed her blade and followed the vampire hunter's example.

'You know we're not in league with them,' she told Loew. 'We rescued you from the Ulfenwatch.'

Loew motioned Witalas and another of the men behind them to come forwards and bring him the discarded weapons. 'I've worked against Radukar long enough to know better than to underestimate his cunning. Never trust how something looks. A vampire's had lifetimes to hone his deceptions.'

'We fight against the Wolf,' Gustaf said. Mindful of the bowmen, he pulled open his cloak and waved the Sigmarite amulet he wore.

Loew shook his head. 'I've seen that before. In the Black Ship, remember? You might wear such a token to gain the confidence of those you're trying to trick. A black goat sent to lead the herd to the slaughter.' He held out his hand and took the weapon belts from his men. 'Indeed, I think the brazenness you show is…'

Loew's words trailed away. He stared at the weapons taken from Gustaf. The sword and pistol didn't interest him, it was the carved cylinder of bone Witalas gave him that held his fascination. Carved with Sigmarite prayers, the cylinder had a heavy cap of steel on its top. Loew eased this away and teased the object inside the cylinder free. His eyes bulged when he saw the stake of scarlet-coloured wood, whorls of orange light shimmering beneath its surface.

'A stake of Aqshian fyrewood,' Loew whispered.

Gustaf seized on Loew's reaction. 'That's not the first time you've seen one.'

'No, it isn't,' Loew admitted. He quickly returned the stake to the cylinder and pressed the cap back into place. 'Radukar would never trust one of his minions with such a weapon.'

'Then you understand we're not in league with the Wolf?' Emelda snatched the weapon belt from Loew's hand. 'You'd do well to be careful who you accuse of such obscenity.'

Gustaf wasn't interested in mistakes or damaged egos. All he could think of was Loew's familiarity with the Order of Azyr's weapons. As far as he knew there was only one other man in Ulfenkarn who'd be carrying Aqshian fyrewood.

'You've seen Jelsen Darrock?' he asked. 'Is he alive? Where is he?'

'Darrock was alive the last time I saw him,' Loew said. 'He

sought my advice a month ago. Where he is now, I couldn't say. It probably depends if he took my advice or not.' It was his turn to ask a question, and when he did it was the one Gustaf had been dreading. 'What happened to Wagner, the other man the Ulfen-watch were guarding?'

Emelda answered before Gustaf had the chance. 'When we left him, he was in the Sea Vulture drinking and trying to forget what he'd been through.' She shot the vampire hunter a warning glance. 'Doing a good job of it too.'

Loew's expression became regretful. 'I should never have allowed him to join us.'

One of the men who'd ambushed the Volkshaufen tried to reassure Loew. 'It wasn't your fault. Everyone knew Wagner didn't have the heart for this sort of thing. We tried to convince him of that, but he wouldn't listen.'

'What "sort of thing"?' Gustaf asked.

Loew rallied from the guilt that gripped him. 'Vigilantes,' he declared proudly. 'We've taken it on ourselves to put an end to this Baron Grin business. It's bad enough the vampires feed off us, we don't need some maniac carving up our people like a butch-ered seal.'

Emelda gave Gustaf another anxious look. 'You saw the last body, didn't you?' she asked Loew, feigning ignorance of both the fourth murder and the information Morrvahl had dragged from the madman.

'Not the last one,' Loew said. 'Baron Grin struck again last night.' His expression darkened. 'As you well know.' He pointed to the ambushers in the corridor. 'Karlion heard you asking questions. That was why we decided to intercept you.'

Gustaf shook his head. 'Forgive us. We didn't know if you had heard and we were reluctant to tell you. Each of these killings compounds the horror of the previous ones.' The vampire hunter frowned and confessed to the vigilantes the matter that was most important to him. 'These murders have drawn Radukar away from his fortress. Down into the streets. At least, so we've heard.'

'They don't care about us, they only care about trying to get at the Wolf,' Karlion growled. The stocky vigilante glowered at Gustaf and patted the bloodied head of the steel mace he carried.

'Baron Grin's acts are ghastly,' Gustaf said, 'but for all their horror they're confined. Radukar's tyranny affects every single person in Ulfenkarn.'

Loew nodded. 'None will shed tears when the vampires are gone,' he said, looking around at his men. 'You've heard true,' he told Gustaf. 'Radukar was there to see what was done to the third victim. He's there now investigating what happened to the fourth. You see, Baron Grin is of a similar mind to you. He's trying to use these murders to push the people into rebellion.' He went on to describe for Gustaf the details of what he'd seen and the writing on the wall. Emelda and Gustaf acted as though it were the first time they'd heard any of it.

'It would take a considerable force to try to break through the Wolf's guards,' Emelda commented when she'd heard about the entourage Radukar had with him. Her eyes roved across the faces of Loew's vigilantes. 'But it could be done with enough men.'

Loew caught her meaning and scowled. 'We're not going to throw our lives away on some mad idea about destroying Radukar. What you intend is folly.'

'To break through his circle of guards, yes,' Gustaf agreed. 'But if we hid ourselves, if we were waiting for Radukar, then things would be different.'

'If we can find a pattern to these killings, we could predict when and where Baron Grin will strike next,' Emelda said. 'Then we'd know where to expect Radukar. We'd be able to anticipate him and be ready.'

Loew gave them both a look as cold as steel. 'Our purpose is to stop Baron Grin, not stand idle and try to exploit these murders.' He shook his head and laughed. 'Trying to fight Radukar is suicide. You'd have a better chance pulling a terrorgheist's fangs.'

'We've a chance to–' Emelda started to protest, but Gustaf cut her off.

'There's nothing else to be said then,' the vampire hunter stated. He glanced at the other vigilantes. 'I trust we'll each hold the other's confidence, both in terms of intentions and activities.'

'That I'll guarantee,' Loew said. He gestured to Karlion. 'I'll send some of my men to help you get around the patrols.'

Emelda was quick to reject the offer. 'We can find our own way back. Two will be less conspicuous than a whole gang.'

'I'll wish you luck then.' Loew nodded to the men in the stockyard. A few of them moved over to the plank fence that enclosed the space and teased a couple of the boards aside to open a gap to the street beyond.

'Sigmar protect you,' Gustaf told Loew, making the sign of the hammer. 'We may feel at cross purposes, but we share the same enemy.'

Loew's gaze remained cold. 'The same enemy, maybe, but I've not lost sight of why I fight and who I'm trying to protect. That's the difference between us, outlander.'

Watchmaster Arno stood aside in the gore-spattered alleyway while the lord of Ulfenkarn crouched over the two bodies. As a child he'd once watched a tide tiger stealing along the shore, creeping up on a nest of sea vultures. Observing Radukar provoked the same sensation, the sense that this was a predator stalking prey, ready to pounce the moment some secret signal goaded him into action.

'The bodies were discovered a little after dawn,' Arno said. 'We've retained the witness…'

'You can release him,' Radukar said, not looking up from the subject of his study. 'There's no traitorous scrawl this time. Besides, if everyone who reports these killings to the Volkshaufen disappears, soon no one will report them.'

Arno nodded at the cold logic of the statement. Fear was a thing that had to be carefully balanced. Of course, most mortals had an instinct that was even easier to manipulate. 'A reward could be offered for information,' he suggested.

'That would be useless,' Radukar told him. 'You'd spend most of your time sifting truth from dross and fabrication.' The vampire flipped back the coat of the ghastlier of the two corpses, the one whose face had been cut away. 'Besides, it looks as though your informant might have picked some pockets before telling you what he'd found.'

Arno decided he'd have a talk about that with the witness before releasing him. He turned and glanced at the other body slumped against the wall. Unlike the first, it had suffered no mutilation. Except for its coldness and pallor, it might even have been mistaken for a sleeping man.

'Why would the killer only disfigure the one and not the other?' Radukar mused.

'Only one of them was murdered,' Arno replied. 'At least by Baron Grin.' He pointed at the unmarked body. 'This one was smothered, not stabbed. Those cords around the wrists and ankles are too loose to restrain, they're meant only to hold. That one was dead and was being carried by the other when this happened.'

'Why?' Radukar pondered. 'Why would the fool be carrying a corpse at night when he knew the risks? Violating curfew, taking the chance the body might… become more than a body.'

Radukar's fangs gleamed in a confident smile. 'That is something that may prove of interest.' He passed his hand over the first body with its exposed skull. 'This one's blood is corrupted, like the others. It has been desecrated beyond my power to recall.' He shifted and pointed his finger at the other corpse. 'This one's different. It isn't beyond my reach. It may give me a path to follow.'

Radukar waved the silentiary back. Arno stepped away as the Wolf exerted his own dark power over the corpse.

The atmosphere in the alleyway was squalid and rank, but the foetid warmth evaporated as the chill of dark magic exuded from the vampire. Arno could see the slime dripping down the walls become brittle with frost when Radukar evoked the dread energies of necromancy. The Watchmaster tried to quiet the frightened beating of his heart, tried to maintain the stolid expression on his face. He knew he'd failed when he felt a cold sweat beading on his brow.

Radukar kept his finger pointed at the corpse. The body twitched and writhed, like a fish gasping out its last breath on a pier. The glazed eyes remained dull and unfocused, but the tight rictus of its mouth dropped open. A putrid smell rushed up the corpse's throat, overwhelming the rancid odour of the alley. Close upon the stench came a low, piteous groan.

'Speak,' Radukar commanded the corpse. 'Your master will know what has happened here.'

Arno shuddered as the groans rising from the corpse condensed into words, speech uttered without inflection or emotion, only a tortured weariness.

'It is dark and it is cold,' the dead declared. 'Grau carries my body through the dark. There is sound ahead. A patrol. Grau hides in the alley and waits for them to pass. While he waits, someone comes. He's unaware of them until the knife stabs into him. I smell his blood, I hear it draining out of him. We fall. My body is shoved aside, pushed against the wall. I hear the scrape of steel against flesh.'

'Who was the killer?' Radukar demanded. 'What did they look like?'

'My eyes are turned to the wall,' the corpse answered. 'I do not see. I only hear.'

Mustering his resolve, Arno stepped towards the talking carcass and posed his own question to it. 'This man, Grau, why was he carrying you? Where was he taking you?'

Radukar leaned over the body. 'Answer him.'

'Grau killed me,' the corpse groaned. 'I listened as he told his wife he would take me to Frau Heimmer in Muellerstrasse. She would pay him twenty-weight in ivory for my body.'

'Of what use were you to her? Speak!' Radukar gripped the corpse's tunic and dragged it upwards. Arno could see now that the spell the vampire had conjured was consuming the dead man. The skin was sloughing away into a rotten mush, rapidly disintegrating before them.

'More,' the corpse wailed. 'Grau said she needed more. More and more... and she'd pay.'

'Pay for what?' the Wolf snarled. The corpse tried to reply, but all that rose now from its collapsing frame was an inarticulate moan. Radukar dropped the foul carrion and turned to Arno. 'Do you know this woman who hired the bodysnatcher?'

Arno nodded. 'Gertha Heimmer's a wealthy widow, owns several shops and ships.'

'I care nothing for that,' Radukar snapped. 'I want to know if you can find her.'

'She rarely leaves her home,' Arno said. 'On Muellerstrasse, just as your... witness stated.'

'Take me there,' the vampire ordered. 'Without delay.'

Arno saw the hungry light in Radukar's eyes, a look more ravenous than anything he'd seen before. The Wolf was roused to the likeness of his namesake, eager with the thrill of the hunt. The Volkshaufen and Ulfenwatch were left behind, too cumbersome to keep up with the vampire as he pursued his quarry.

The squalor of the district where the corpses were found was soon behind them as Arno led the lord of Ulfenkarn through the streets. People scrambled for shelter when they saw the ferocious presence that followed the Watchmaster. Even those who'd never set eyes on Radukar before could sense the vampire's malignant power. None were bold enough to cross his path.

The Heimmer residence was a tall structure that dominated the corner of Muellerstrasse where it joined with Baumweg. In better times it had been an opulent mansion, dozens of rooms filled with luxury and decadence. Arno had heard tales of the gala balls and parties held by the family. Gertha's daughter Rahel had been esteemed one of the great beauties of Mournhold, at least by those who didn't deem noble blood an essential for such judgement. All of that, of course, was in the past. Now the once grand house, like all those around it, was fallen into disrepair and neglect, its inhabitants without the means or will to maintain the pretensions of the past.

'This is the one,' Arno said as he pointed at the mansion.

Radukar sprang ahead like a hound that has reached the end of a trail. He was across the street in a heartbeat and climbed the steps leading to the door in a bound. The vampire didn't wait for admission to the home; he exerted his dominion over all Ulfenkarn. A single blow from his hand sent the heavy bronze doors crashing inwards. Arno ran to keep up as Radukar marched into the building.

The entry hall was a shambles when Arno reached it. He saw a liveried servant lying amid the wreckage of a table, his head turned about on his broken neck. Another servant was sprawled in a pool of blood, his skull shattered by a tremendous force. A third was cowering in a doorway, crying like a child and hugging a mangled arm to his chest. There was a fourth servant, his eyes bulging in terror, his throat caught in the vampire's hand. Radukar lifted the man off the floor, his hungry glare transfixing him like a lance.

'Where?' Radukar growled.

'Up… upstairs…' the servant said, struggling to answer. 'Her room… third on… the left.'

Radukar tossed the man aside, the force of his throw smashing the plaster on the wall and exposing the stone beneath. The servant crumpled in an unmoving heap. Radukar gave him no further notice as he mounted the stairway and ascended to the upper floor.

Arno hurried after his master, drawing his sword in case Gertha had any more servants and any of them were insane enough to confront Radukar after the carnage in the hall below. He reached the landing just as Radukar broke open the third door on the left. He heard a woman's scream and raced into the room.

Gertha cowered before Radukar, her arms wrapped about one of the posts at the foot of her bed. Every inch of her being squirmed in fear as the vampire glowered at her.

'The man you hired, Grau, is dead,' Radukar told her. 'I want to know why.'

Arno saw something more than terror enter the woman's face. When she heard Radukar speak, something of despair rushed into her visage.

'No! He can't be dead! I need him!'

'He's dead,' the Wolf snarled. 'Murdered. Another trophy for Baron Grin.' Radukar's eyes blazed. 'But perhaps you already knew this. Perhaps you know a great deal about this Baron Grin.'

Gertha dropped to her knees. 'No… I needed Grau. I needed him to help me.'

For just an instant Gertha's eyes darted to a connecting door. Arno spotted the glance. So too did Radukar. The vampire turned and marched to the door. Arno restrained Gertha when she would have charged after the Wolf. She struggled in his grip, fighting like a tigress to break free.

'Don't! Please!' Gertha screamed. 'Leave her alone!'

The vampire wasn't swayed by Gertha's pleas. He struck the heavy door, just as he had the others. It resisted, reinforced as it was by wooden bars and heavy chains. A second blow had it crashing inwards, however. Arno could almost feel the charnel stench that spilled into the room on his skin. He could see that the chamber behind the locked door was a shambles, littered with cracked bones. He'd no time for further observation, however, as a feral shape leaped from the chamber and flung itself at Radukar.

For an instant the vampire staggered back, arms raised to fend off the long talons and snapping teeth of his attacker. Then Radukar's hand tightened about the creature's arm and pulled it away. With an overhanded fling, he dashed the frenzied thing against the floor. Arno heard the crack of breaking bones as the violent impact reverberated through the house. The emaciated creature struggled to rise, but a second strike from Radukar's hand smashed it down again with a crushed spine.

'Rahel!' Gertha cried. The outburst so shocked Arno that for an instant he relaxed his grip. The woman broke free. For a second she moved towards the gangrel thing that lay dead at Radukar's feet. Then she turned and ran to the window. Her momentum carried her through the closed shutters. Arno scowled when he heard the dull crunch of her body crashing to the street below. It would mean the annoyance of another exertion of necromantic power to get her to reveal her secrets now.

'This was a fruitless pursuit,' Radukar said, his gaze shifting from the creature on the floor to the room it had inhabited. 'There's nothing here to lead me to Baron Grin.'

Arno stared at the horrible body on the floor. It bore only the remotest semblance of humanity, its face distorted by jutting fangs, its limbs withered until they were almost spidery in their appearance. The skin was grey and covered in scabs and sores, a few last scraps of hair still clinging to the thing's scalp. He noted with some alarm that these retained a golden colour. He recalled Gertha's final cry, the name of her beautiful daughter, and likewise remembered that Rahel's hair had been likened to the first rays of the rising sun. He turned away, still mortal enough to be sickened to think it might be true, that the corpse-eating ghoul might once have been Rahel.

'Stir yourself, Watchmaster,' Radukar admonished Arno. 'We've followed the trail forwards, now we'll follow it back. Find Grau's house. We'll see if there's anything to be learned there.'

The vampire's face curled into a contemptuous sneer as he gazed about the room.

'It is certain that this trail has gone dead.'

INTERLUDE 4

Horacy Sirak was well aware of the dangers of being abroad at night, but he was also aware of what would happen if he didn't take the risk. The people back home, his elderly parents and his young wife, were depending on him. Without something to trade, they'd starve. What little Horacy had been able to save was rapidly disappearing. An apprentice saltboiler, his wages had been meagre, but after cracking one of the big cauldrons, his master had dismissed him and even that revenue was no more. He was desperate now. He knew his former employer had just received a big payment from one of the whaling combines to provide salt for their ships. He knew where the box of ambergris had been secreted in Irwin Anders' shop.

Desperate enough to brave the dangers of both violating the curfew and the knife of Baron Grin, Horacy didn't balk at theft. He was able to slip into Anders' darkened shop through a window he'd left unbarred. Cautiously he picked his way through the now silent hall where the big cauldrons stood ready to reduce seawater to a salty residue. He saw the one that had been cracked and scowled at the injustice of Anders' decision. The pot was probably old enough to have been forged in his grandfather's day. It should've been replaced long ago.

Horacy made less noise than a mouse as he stole through the building. He was keenly aware that his old employer kept a room at the back of the shop. Miserly to a fault, Anders didn't give himself the luxury of better accommodations, but kept to the same shabby residence he'd had when it was he who'd been an apprentice saltboiler. His stinginess and paranoia actually served Horacy now. Anders had never invested in a strongbox, insisting that concealment was a better safeguard for his wealth. Nor did he keep his goods near him in that back room, reasoning that it would be the first place a thief would look. There was a craftiness in the saltboiler's reasoning, but he'd forgotten one thing – that an apprentice who was around long enough would inevitably stumble onto his master's secrets.

It was all Horacy could do to keep from laughing in triumph when he pulled aside the loose plank in the floor and teased the box from its hiding spot. The ambergris he now held in his hands would keep his family fed through the winter and beyond. More than enough time for him to find a new position somewhere.

The thief's nerves were on edge as he retraced his steps and slipped out of the saltboiler's shop. His spoils secured, Horacy was frantic to get back home and erase the worry that gripped his family. They didn't need to know how he'd got the ambergris. All they needed to know was that he had it now.

Focused on relieving his family's troubled minds, Horacy's thoughts strayed from the many hazards that haunted Ulfenkarn's darkness. Only when he crossed a seldom used side street did his danger announce itself. A knife flashed out from the shadows, plunging deep into his side. He stumbled onwards for a few steps, struggling to suck breath down into his punctured lung. When he finally fell, the stolen box split open and sent ambergris spilling out over the cobblestones.

Horacy was dead when excited hands flipped him onto his back. A vicious countenance glared down at the corpse. Sadistic glee blazed in the killer's eyes. The bloodied knife flashed again and again, slashing away at the thief's head. A maniacal titter rose from the murderer as he descended into a frenzy of mutilation. Ribbons of flesh were sent flying in every direction as the blade slashed down over and over.

The berserk action went on and on. Tattered strips of scalp were carved away, hurled aside by the killer as he dug his fingers into the gory mush that had once been a man. Steel scraped against bone, grinding away as the murderer inflicted still further desecration on the corpse. A hiss of warning reached his ears, but the sadist was too lost in his brutal work to be swayed from it now.

Again the gleaming edge of a knife whispered in the night. The murderer slumped over his mangled victim, blood pouring from the wound in his back. His hand tightened about the blade he yet gripped. He strove to rally, to rise to his feet and confront the interloper. The effort was thwarted when the knife plunged down into his back a second time. His attempt to rise turned into a head-first sprawl. The maniac's knife rolled free from his hand and clattered across the cobblestones.

The interloper stared down at the slain killer. A kick to ensure the murderer was dead provoked no response. A moment of silent contemplation, then the figure turned towards the atrocity scattered about the street. Cold eyes stared down at the butchered remains, fixating on the denuded skull with its bony grin.

The interloper crouched and used the knife to prise free a loose paving stone. Heaving it upwards in both hands, the figure stepped over to Horacy's body. Lifting the stone overhead, the shape dropped it onto the skull with such force that it was shattered into fragments.

For a moment, the sound of boots scraping against the cobblestones echoed in the street. The interloper kicked away the broken pieces of Horacy's skull. Only when they'd been scattered across the lane did the figure turn away from the scene of murder and retreat back into the darkness.

CHAPTER FIVE

The street was cordoned off by ranks of fleshless skeletons. People had started to gather once rumour spread that Baron Grin had struck again. Arno withdrew his watchmen and replaced them with the undead. Typically the same crowds that were bold enough to defy the Volkshaufen would wither away when confronted by the Ulfenwatch. This time, however, they lingered and tried to peer past the skeletons to see what was happening.

Dragomir watched Arno anxiously as the vampire inspected the scene. All it needed was an order from him and the Ulfenwatch would disperse the crowd in the most vicious manner. For now, at least, Arno was indifferent to the crowd, intent only on the bodies. Just as had happened the last time, there were two, but it was obvious to Dragomir that they'd both been killed here rather than elsewhere. The savagery of the murders convinced him this was the work of Baron Grin.

Arno confirmed that notion, pointing at the blood splashed

across the cobblestones. 'Corrupt. Befouled by an obscene power,' the vampire declared. 'Just as with the others.'

'What causes it, Watchmaster?' Dragomir dared to ask. 'Does the killer use some poisoned blade or' – he hesitated to make the suggestion – 'is it some kind of sorcery?'

'A power,' Arno said. 'A force that is invoked and which seeps into the blood to befoul it.'

Dragomir circled around the bodies. He considered the more mutilated of the pair. It was a hideous sight, with deep slashes about the shoulders, neck and chest. The head had been shattered, smashed to bits with a heavy stone. Fragments of flesh and scalp were strewn all around. 'Baron Grin wasn't satisfied to simply flay the face away. This time he obliterated the head entirely.'

'Does that not suggest something to you?' Arno asked. He drifted over to the body, his cloak billowing across the carnage. A pale finger probed at the deep slashes on the shoulder. 'No careful flaying as before. These marks indicate wild hacking, the abandoned violence of someone stripped of all restraint and caution.' His hand tightened into a claw and made raking motions over the crushed head. 'Someone consumed by the power he invoked.'

'Baron Grin went amok,' Dragomir said, considering the details Arno indicated. 'Went so far that he didn't just peel the skin away, but destroyed the skull entirely.' He nodded at the other body. 'Some sense must've returned to him though. This corpse isn't nearly as mangled as the other one. Baron Grin must've been scared off by something, or else was afraid he'd lose control again. So he left this body alone.' Dragomir nodded, trying to picture what had happened. 'He was looking for a victim and found these two on the street. In a rush he attacked them both and brought them down. Then he started carving away on the one body but went completely crazy.'

'Perhaps,' Arno said. The vampire reached down and plucked

a fragment of skull off the ground. 'Perhaps,' he repeated as he studied it. As he turned it over in his fingers, Arno could see a deep gash in the bone.

'Baron Grin was so frenzied he cut down into the bone itself,' Dragomir observed.

A cold smile curled onto Arno's face, a look of wicked triumph. He held the fragment in his fingers and shook it. 'Have the guards gather up every piece of the skull. Search the whole of the street. If they miss so much as a sliver they'll be given to the deadwalkers and their gnawed bones recruited into the Ulfenwatch.' As he spoke, his voice rose to a threatening snarl loud enough for all the watchmen to hear.

Dragomir gave the trembling men their orders and they scoured the carnage for the scattered fragments.

'What importance does the skull have?' Dragomir wondered after he'd got the guards searching.

'The killer lost control,' Arno said. 'He went beyond what he intended to do and by doing so, revealed too much.' He gestured at the men collecting the splinters of bone. 'When that skull is put back together, it may tell Radukar a great deal.' The vampire turned and looked again at the other body. 'This one is just as corrupt as the others, but it hasn't been defiled in a bloody ceremony. No, this is a body that was corrupt before it was killed.'

Dragomir's brow wrinkled in confusion. 'I don't understand.'

'We're hunting Baron Grin,' Arno said. 'There he lies. Struck from behind while he mutilated his last victim.'

'Can this be?' Dragomir gasped. His eyes gaped wide as he considered the possibility. The killer caught in his gruesome work by some avenger. Struck down and left in the street beside his victim. 'Is this the end of it?'

Arno watched the guards collecting the fragments, depositing them inside an upturned helmet. 'That depends on who killed him... and why. Was it to stop the murders, or was it to conceal their purpose?'

'But if Baron Grin's dead, then it's over, Watchmaster,' Dragomir said. 'The threat is over. The people will quiet down again.'

Arno looked away, the vampire's face becoming tense, a trace of fear entering his eyes. His heightened senses must have detected the approach of an armed company before Dragomir saw the file of Nightguard lumber into view. The captain trembled when he realised who it was the undead ogors were escorting to the scene. Once more, the Wolf had come to look into the murder. The crowd of spectators fled when they saw the Nightguard, scattering into the snowy streets with all the speed they could muster.

'You mean they'll remember who their master is,' Arno corrected Dragomir as the ogors drew nearer. 'They'll remember who it is they fear. Who it is they must obey.' The vampire waved his hand at the people fleeing down the streets. 'They've started to let their fear make them forget that each dawn they see is only because Radukar allows it.'

'Yes, Watchmaster,' Dragomir replied. The merciless tone in the vampire's words sent a cold shiver down his spine. He was grateful to withdraw and let Arno greet Radukar when the Wolf emerged from the company of Nightguard. In rapid fashion, the vampiric thrall explained everything that had happened to the lord of Ulfenkarn.

'Collect the pieces of that skull,' Radukar said. 'I will take them back to the Ebon Citadel.' His eyes gleamed as he stared at a few infirm stragglers from the crowd, still retreating down the street. 'This attitude of defiance will end.'

Arno was quick to agree. 'The mortals will quickly fall in line with Baron Grin gone.' Dragomir was struck by the undercurrent of fear that gripped the Watchmaster's voice. Even a vampire like Arno regarded Radukar with terror.

Radukar gave Arno an indulgent glance. 'Not too soon,' the Wolf said. 'This whiff of rebellion is useful to me. It emboldens my enemies. Gives them strange ideas.' His fangs gleamed as his face spread in a hungry smile. 'It may make them reckless. Make them reveal themselves.' He held out his hand, the fingers splayed wide. 'Put them within my grasp,' he said as he clenched his fist.

Whoever these enemies of the Wolf were, Dragomir suspected they'd have been better off running into Baron Grin than falling into the clutches of Radukar.

Vladrik was waiting for them at a table in a shadowy corner of the Black Ship's main hall. A jug of cheap dark wine sat before him, which he used to refill the pewter mug he had his hand wrapped around.

Gustaf sat down on the bench across from the scholar. He glanced over at Emelda, but the swordswoman preferred to remain standing, one eye watching the tavern's other patrons. There were only a few right now, but all it needed was for one to be a spy to bring them trouble.

'Any news of Darrock?' Gustaf asked. The whereabouts of the witch hunter remained foremost on his mind. If he could just find Jelsen and combine forces, he was certain their chances of destroying the Wolf would be vastly improved. Much as he admired Emelda's martial abilities, she wasn't trained to fight enemies like Radukar. Not the way those taught by the Order of Azyr were. They knew the tricks of witches and vampires… and how to overcome them. It was true she'd held her own in the fight with Lupu, but then the enemy's attention had been focused on him alone. Besides, fighting a thrall like Lupu was much different to going up against a creature as powerful as Radukar.

'None, I fear,' Vladrik answered, taking a slow sip of his wine. He leaned forwards and glanced over at the two hunters. 'It may be easier to locate him now, though.' He smiled at the perplexed looks they gave him. 'Then you haven't heard? The story's spreading throughout the city. Baron Grin's dead.'

The news was shocking to Gustaf. He leaned back, pressing against the wall behind him as he tried to digest what he'd just been told. 'Dead? How can they be sure?'

'My source had it direct from a watchman,' Vladrik said. 'A guard who was there when the bodies were examined. One was another victim of Baron Grin. The other… no less than Radukar himself deemed it to be the killer.'

Emelda stepped towards the scholar. 'The Wolf himself was there?' The question almost sounded like a groan of pain. Gustaf could see the intense frustration on her face. Even more than him, she'd seized on the idea of the murders drawing Radukar away from the Ebon Citadel and giving them a real chance to strike at the vampire lord. With Baron Grin dead, that chance was also dead.

'There's some peculiarity about these bodies,' Vladrik explained. 'Something that sets them apart from a normal murder.' He gave them both an awkward smile. 'I mean beyond the mutilations. There's something about them the vampires can sense. That's how Radukar was able to determine that one body was the victim, and the other was the killer.'

'But what happened?' Emelda persisted, unwilling to concede the field. 'Did one of the patrols catch Baron Grin there?'

Vladrik took another sip of wine. 'They're not entirely sure. But it wasn't a patrol. The Volkshaufen believe someone was out past curfew and chanced upon Baron Grin while he was mutilating his last victim. While he was distracted they came up behind him with a blade and…' He slammed his hand down on the table. 'Ulfenkarn is short one monster.'

'Things will go back to normal then,' Gustaf said. He was sympathetic with how Emelda felt, but at the same time he couldn't shake a sense of relief. As much as it interfered with their own plans, at least the people would be spared some suffering.

'The double patrols the Volkshaufen have been doing are already being called off,' Vladrik said. 'You'll probably see fewer Ulfenwatch around too. Yes, things will return to what passes for normality here.'

'That means the Wolf will keep to his lair,' Emelda snapped. Gustaf gripped her hand, trying to reassure her.

'There'll be other chances,' he said. 'Sigmar won't allow this evil to endure.'

Vladrik sat back, observing them over his mug of wine. 'Look to the brighter side. People will be able to move about more freely than they have been. Some folks who've been keeping themselves hidden might start stirring again.' He pointed at Gustaf. 'I'd expect to get some sort of information about your friend Darrock soon. So at least there's that.'

Gustaf knew finding Jelsen Darrock wouldn't be of particular interest to Emelda. She had no connection to the witch hunter except through him. However there was something else that the lessening of the patrols made possible.

'Emelda, we can find another place to stay,' Gustaf told her. 'We don't have to worry so much about being spied on.' He saw that he'd judged aright. She stirred from her disappointment to pay close attention to what he was saying. 'With Baron Grin gone we won't be watched so closely. As Vladrik says, we'll be able to move around more easily without drawing attention from Radukar's minions or Loew's vigilantes.'

'We can be quit of *him*,' Emelda said, a slight shudder passing through her.

Gustaf nodded. 'We'll both of us feel cleaner once we're no longer Morrvahl's guests. Whatever help he's given us, I don't trust him. Most wizards are peculiar, but Morrvahl... If we were in Carstinia, I'd have no hesitation condemning him to the stake.'

'And I'd help you light the pyre,' Emelda said.

'I don't know the man you're speaking of,' Vladrik said, 'but I'm minded of an old Belvegrodian proverb. "The evil of today can uproot the evil of tomorrow." Just something to bear in mind.'

Gustaf scowled, thinking back to the madman and the callous way Morrvahl had made use of him. The way the wizard's magic might so easily have overcome them all in the fight with the Ulfenwatch.

'You're right, Vladrik,' Gustaf said. 'You don't know the man we're speaking of.'

Morrvahl studied the grains that dripped through the hourglass, watching as each mote shifted between colours as it moved. The grains were beads of condensed magic, power trapped in physical form. That bound energy was contained by the glazed essence of ectoplasm, the residue of gheists and wraiths. The whole served the wizard as a gauge, a thing to determine the strength of an enchantment or dweomer. The shifting colours told of the nature of that enchantment, proclaiming from which of the Mortal Realms the attendant winds were drawn.

The same divinations could be applied to a place as well as an object, and it was with such readings that Morrvahl was concerned. Ulfenkarn lay under the influence of the Shyish Nadir, inundated with the very power of the realm. This was the core essence of amethyst magic, dark and sinister in its character yet still a thing connected to life. But the grains in the hourglass didn't keep the deep purple of Shyishian energy. They continually blackened, assuming the insidious traits of an even more grim breed of magic. A brand of wizardry that took the energies of Shyish and changed them, turned them to purposes no longer connected to life, but rather a profanation of it. The black art of necromancy.

Nagash, the Lord of Undeath, was credited as the first to practise necromancy, developing it in a time before the Age of Myth. Even today one of his titles was the Great Necromancer. Those who devoted themselves to necromancy were ever in the shadow of Nagash, whether in adulation of the god or envy of him, and they drew upon the forbidden secrets of their macabre master. The promise of power and longevity was too much for many to resist, and far too often those who studied the harnessing of amethyst magic were easily seduced. Morrvahl was somewhat grateful now that his own mentor had fallen to the lure of necromancy, for by doing so he'd given his apprentice a fearsome example of what could happen when a wizard pursued his studies too far.

No, Morrvahl wouldn't let himself be drawn into such madness. He knew precisely where the line was between the lore of death and that of undeath. He knew how close he could tread without crossing that line and damning himself as his old mentor had.

The great energy emanating from the nadir was what had drawn him to Ulfenkarn. To study it, find a way to harness it for the betterment of mankind, these were the lofty goals that made Morrvahl press on. Too many even among the wise distrusted the study of amethyst magic because it drew upon the same forces that had been turned towards necromancy. Perhaps in other realms wizards could shun the lore of death, but to do so in Shyish was foolhardy. Those arcane energies were too prevalent to ignore. Only by understanding and utilising them could the undead be kept at bay and any place be held for civilisation to flourish. The efforts of warriors from the Order of Azyr, even the mighty Stormcasts themselves, were too focused to do what needed to be done. These fighters could only fight back the darkness for a moment, could strike down only the smallest part of the evil that dominated the land. It was only through employing the power of Shyish itself that any meaningful progress could be made, a lasting rather than fleeting accomplishment.

The key, Morrvahl was certain, lay in the Shyish Nadir. In the past, these incredible arcane forces had existed at the fringes of the realm. Now, by some cataclysmic process that could only have been conjured by Nagash himself, they had shifted to the centre of the realm, concentrating in the nadir. Even those ignorant of these magical energies could sense the power that hovered over Ulfenkarn. To Morrvahl, it was a great nimbus of power filling the sky above, an omnipresent storm waiting to unleash its might.

How much time there was before that happened, Morrvahl had to concede that he didn't know. Not knowing instilled in him a sense of urgency. He had to remove the obstacles that interfered with his research. That meant eliminating Radukar. The vampire's tyrannical grip over the city was too firm, his agents too many. For Morrvahl to have a freer hand to conduct his studies, the Wolf's reign had to end.

Emelda Braskov and Gustaf Voss were useful in that regard. Their commitment to destroying Radukar was complete. Morrvahl could depend on them to do whatever they could to work the vampire's ruin. More, in their zeal they'd take risks the wizard wasn't prepared to take. Their focus was on destroying their enemy – he was concerned with what came afterwards. It mattered little to him how his allies fared so long as Radukar was eliminated.

The wizard stroked his black beard, teasing the tangles from the hair. His eyes narrowed as he sensed someone climbing down into the cellar. He reached over and picked up his staff, Gravebloom, feeling its gnarled wood dig into his palm, hungry for his life force. If it was intruders he heard on the stairs, the staff would have ample opportunity to ease its appetite.

A smile crawled onto Morrvahl's face when he saw Emelda and Gustaf enter the cellar. His humour darkened when he noted the intensity of their expressions.

'Another murder or two?' the wizard suggested as the reason

for their distemper. Though he was long past such vulnerability, he knew more sensitive minds suffered an excess of sympathy when dealing with matters of violent death.

'Did your "assets" already tell you?' Emelda said, her voice brimming with disgust.

'We've already discussed their capabilities,' Morrvahl returned, annoyed by the swordswoman's judgement.

'Yes, and you've said there's only so much you're able to learn from a rat,' Gustaf told the wizard. 'What was it you said? That they see much but comprehend little?' He pointed at the table where Morrvahl had drawn information from the madman. 'Wasn't that why you put that poor wretch–'

'And what charming lengths will the Order of Azyr go to in order to learn what they wish to learn?' Morrvahl shot back. 'Do not think to lecture me on the sanctity of compassion. Even were I receptive to such an argument, you aren't the one to be making it.'

'Making common cause with the likes of you was a mistake,' Gustaf declared. He looked over at Emelda. 'Fortunately it isn't one we have to live with.'

Morrvahl was surprised by the triumphant tone in the vampire hunter's voice.

'You look confused, wizard,' Emelda said. She too had an air of superiority about her. 'Your spies told you there were two killings, but they didn't tell you more than that. One of them was murdered by Baron Grin. The other *was* Baron Grin.'

'What?' Morrvahl hissed.

'It's true,' Gustaf said. 'Radukar was there to inspect the scene. He's satisfied that Baron Grin's been killed. The extra patrols have been called off.'

Emelda frowned and shook her head. 'It means we've lost the chance to get ahead of him and lie in wait for the Wolf.'

'There are other ways–' Morrvahl started to say.

'I don't want to hear about them,' Emelda cut him off. 'We've seen for ourselves how ruthless you are. I don't want to know what villainy you'd stoop to.'

'Because you'd oppose it, or be tempted by it?' Morrvahl challenged her. 'You know as well as I that sacrifices must be made for any great cause.'

'Forget it,' Gustaf snapped. 'We're not interested. This association is over. Whatever arrangement we had is finished. That's one good thing that's come from this. We might have lost a chance at Radukar, but at least we're rid of your company.'

'We'll collect our gear and be gone,' Emelda said. 'With the patrols lessened, we'll be able to find some place less odious to stage from.'

Morrvahl glowered at his erstwhile allies. 'As you like,' he said thinly. 'Should things change, you know where to find me.' His hand curled about the haft of Gravebloom and a bead of blood dripped from his hand as he cut his palm. 'Don't leave it too long,' he added mockingly. 'It would be a tragedy if you surrendered your lives to no good purpose.'

CHAPTER SIX

The corpses lay on stone slabs in one of the chill vaults beneath the Ebon Citadel, their dead flesh turned a ghastly green by the spectral wisp-lights imprisoned in the crystal globes on the walls. The havoc of gory wounds stood stark on the denuded bodies, dried blood turned black under the ghostly glow. The face of the ambushed killer was set, jaws clenched in a final snarl. That of his victim was obliterated, only a grotesque shambles left behind.

Away from the slabs, seated behind a desk of charnel-wood, the lord of Ulfenkarn manipulated fragments of bone to reassemble something of the annihilated face. Radukar was certain now that the more intact body was that of Baron Grin. It was every bit as corrupt as that of the victims, rejecting even the most potent of Torgillius' efforts to revive it. Though the body had been largely left free of mutilation, he noted that there was a part of the shoulder that had been carved away, stripped down to the bone. He suspected the reason the supposed avenger had done that, and the motive had nothing to do with vengeance.

Despite his threats, the Volkshaufen had recovered barely more than half the smashed skull. Still, Radukar thought this would be enough to confirm his belief. Several of the fragments bore the deep cuts of a blade. Not the wild slashes of unfocused violence. These were slow and deliberate, caused by stabbing the blade deep into the bone and carving across it. The whole of what had been carved there was impossible to recreate from the materials he had at hand, but there was enough. Enough for the vampire to recognise the sort of enemy with which he had to contend.

'So that was why they had to kill you,' Radukar addressed the dead murderer. 'You gave away the game.' His lip curled back and he swept his hand across the desk. The bone fragments went flying about the vault. 'Fool! I've prevailed against the champions of your foul god! You dare think you and your rotten cult can oppose me?'

Radukar stepped away from the desk and marched down the vault, his steps echoing through the halls. The bodies were no longer of interest to him. He'd learned all he needed from them. A ritual sacrifice. All of the victims had been sacrifices, all except the fanatic who'd gone too far in his devotions and been struck down by his companion. There wasn't one Baron Grin, but at least two. Probably more in the cult that was preying on Ulfenkarn's rabble. A cult devoted to the abomination that had nearly overwhelmed Szargorond not so long ago. The Blood God. The Skull Lord. Khorne, Chaos God of Slaughter.

The vampire's Kosargi ogors had fought the marauding horde of Slaughn the Ravener when they laid siege to Mournhold. Radukar himself had skewered the daemon prince's heart on his barrow-blade and felt the fiend's corrupt blood as it gushed from his writhing body. The Wolf was the city's saviour that day, rescuing it from certain doom. He'd claimed the Ebon Citadel and a place among the city's Grand Princes as a reward for his feat.

Now someone was invoking the Dark Gods again, offering them tribute. The malice of the Blood God invoked to oppose Radukar's rule.

The Wolf slammed his fist against the wall, cracking the stone. 'Pray to your filthy gods,' he hissed. 'They won't protect you. I'll find you. Wherever you're hiding, I'll hunt you down. Corrupt or not, I'll see your blood running in the gutters!'

Taking the stairs so quickly that his feet merely brushed the steps, Radukar withdrew from the vault and returned to the fortress above. There were plans he intended to formulate and set into motion. Arno and his Volkshaufen would need to be extra vigilant now. It was no longer a lone killer, but a society of Baron Grins they were looking for.

And they would find them. They would find them and send word back to Radukar, because each night they failed to do so another of them would be thrown alive into the hungry grave-pits and consumed by the ravenous soil.

Radukar found that fear of a horrible death never failed to inspire mortals to exert themselves to the utmost.

The stink of blood was everywhere. Emelda thought she'd have to cut off all her hair to rid it of the stench and take a whetstone to her skin to make it feel clean again. Only the gravest necessity could compel someone to live so near to the malodorous blood farms, and even in Ulfenkarn's slums there were few so desperate as to make that choice. Aside from the cries of the creatures slaughtered to sustain the loathsome thralls of Radukar's Thirsting Court – usually animals, thankfully – and the fug in the air, there was the menace of the monsters drawn by the gory reek. Flocks of blood-bats hung from the decaying rooftops around the stock pens and from the crenellations of the abattoir itself, their eyes staring hungrily. Sometimes a careless guard would leave a barn undefended and the leather-winged vermin would swoop in to suck the livestock dry. The penalty for such laxity was for the guard to be staked out and left for the bats, an example that encouraged vigilance in the others, no matter how sick or fatigued.

Emelda had also seen things much worse than blood-bats and corpse-rats slinking about the blood farms looking for a chance to satiate their ghoulish hunger. Every night the guards had to fend off rotting deadwalkers as the zombies tried to smash a way through the barricades. Usually they came singly and were quickly destroyed, but sometimes whole mobs would appear and force the blood farmers to get help from the Ulfenwatch before the morbid ranch was overrun.

More fearsome still were the lupine hunters that occasionally appeared, the dreaded vargskyr. Against these enormous wolf-like horrors the guards had no defence. When one of the powerful and cunning beasts slipped past the barricades, the blood farmers simply let it drag off whichever of their comrades the vargskyr had marked for its prey. A hideous compact that sickened Emelda, for it displayed how greatly the city's spirit had been broken. So long as death spared them personally, few in Ulfenkarn would lift a finger to help someone else.

In a twisted way, the very proximity of the blood farm served to obscure the shelter Emelda and Gustaf had taken. With such a smell of death in the air, the predators of Ulfenkarn were fixated on the abattoir and the stockyards. As long as they were careful and didn't expose themselves directly, there was only a small chance that they'd draw the notice of a prowling ghoul or a starving corpse-rat. Except for those who worked the blood farms or had been condemned to supplement the supply of livestock, none of the city's mortal inhabitants came this way. The Volkshaufen and Radukar's spies were unlikely to come snooping around, though the undead Ulfenwatch still made regular patrols.

Avoiding the skeletons, however, was something that had become second nature to both of them.

'It is a strange thing to sleep more soundly within earshot of a blood farm than I did in Morrvahl's cellar,' Gustaf quipped, sitting on the floor cleaning his horse pistol. He looked about at their ramshackle surroundings. The house they'd appropriated was abandoned, but looters had picked it clean of anything that was remotely portable. No one had lingered to prise panelling from the walls or steal tiles off the roof, so at least structurally it was more sound than other derelict buildings in the vicinity.

'Must be something about lying down above ground rather than below it,' Gustaf elaborated, his gaze straying to the boarded-up window that looked in on the first-floor sitting room they were in.

Emelda shook her head. 'It's the change in company,' she said. She pointed at the window. 'Here we know the monsters are outside. With Morrvahl around, I'm not sure you could say that.'

'War may make monsters of us all,' Gustaf said, his fingers straying to the Sigmarite talisman he wore. His expression turned solemn. 'The Order of Azyr always cautioned us to do what needed to be done, but never to revel in it. To take pleasure in bringing justice to evil is in itself an evil. Rather there should be a sense of regret, not satisfaction. Regret that there's any need for justice to be meted out at all.'

'Are you trying to say you regret it when you destroy a vampire?' Emelda asked, puzzled by Gustaf's tone.

'I can't pretend to be so holy as to claim that kind of calm,' Gustaf confessed. 'When I end the existence of a vampire, my heart thrills with the act. Instead I should lament that a mortal soul was befouled by the sorcery of Nagash and reduced to such a ghastly state. What good might they have accomplished if they'd been allowed to live out a natural life?'

Emelda turned from the window. 'Vampires warrant no sympathy.

They were monsters in life as they are in death. Radukar was a pirate and marauder long before he sought out the Blood Kiss. The creatures that infest his Thirsting Court were power-hungry, conspiring scum who surrendered their families to prolong their own existence.' Her voice rose into an angry snarl as she thought of those who still called themselves Braskovs, things that had once been part of her own family but were now only bloodsucking fiends. 'Save your pity for their victims.'

Gustaf inspected the barrel of his pistol, checking there wasn't any residual powder left after swabbing it. 'I'm not talking about sympathising with them. What I'm talking about is not allowing hate to control you. Calm, calculated measures, not those governed by emotion.' The vampire hunter returned his pistol to the holster lying on the floor beside him. 'We were told of a witch hunter captain who was determined to rid the town of Garnhoff of the witch hiding in their community. Hate made him ruthless and provoked him to torture and condemn dozens of the citizens. His search became a reign of terror that ended only when a retinue of Sigmar's Stormcast Eternals arrived to restore order. By that time, fifty-four people had been executed. It was later learned that the witch was among the first to be caught but in his fury the captain didn't realise he'd already found his quarry.'

'One doesn't mistake the innocent for a vampire,' Emelda retorted.

'No, but it might apply to Morrvahl,' Gustaf said, though there was a note of reluctance in his tone. 'I've heard before the argument that amethyst magic can be turned to a good purpose. Some of those who make the effort are sincere in that belief.'

'I know what I saw,' Emelda said. 'I watched him rip thoughts from a man's mind and then leech his life force to replenish his own. I'm ashamed that I stood by and didn't stop him, because I wonder if he's any different from the vampires themselves.'

'And the argument comes back to where it started,' Gustaf said.

'War may make monsters of us all. Winning the fight may demand dark deeds. It is our cause and our motives that justify us.' He pointed a finger in warning to Emelda. 'But only so long as our motives remain pure.'

Emelda glared back at the vampire hunter. 'Why does it matter? As long as Radukar is destroyed, what difference does it make?'

'Because that same logic would justify Morrvahl... even Baron Grin,' Gustaf said. 'What does it matter what methods they use if it means an end to Ulfenkarn's tyrant?'

Before Emelda could reply, a crash sounded from the floor below. In a flash she had her sword drawn. Gustaf looked longingly at the horse pistol, but there was no time to load the weapon. Whatever had found their refuge, they could hear the stairs creak as the intruder slowly climbed up.

Emelda motioned to Gustaf, telling him she'd take the lead. She was willing to bet she had more experience with close-quarters fighting, and even if she hadn't, her armour would be the deciding factor. Her steel breastplate would resist the swipe of a ghoul's claw. The same couldn't be said for Gustaf's coat and tunic.

'Now,' Emelda said. At her command, Gustaf threw back the door and she sprang through the opening into the hall beyond. She saw a figure in the darkness at the top of the stairs. With drawn sword, she stalked towards the indistinct shape.

'A rather fierce reception,' Loew called out as he stepped into the light. The vigilante held his hands up, well away from the cutlass and hatchet hanging from his belt. 'If I meant any mischief, I assure you I'd have brought more men with me.'

Emelda gave Loew a steely stare. 'How'd you find us?' she demanded.

'One of the members of my group, Karlion, is very good at keeping tabs on people,' Loew said. 'After our last meeting, I felt you were people worth keeping an eye on.'

'What do you want?' Gustaf asked. He had the empty horse pistol in his hand, pointing its muzzle at Loew. The vigilante's confidence wavered to see the gun aimed at him, unaware of its condition.

Loew pointed at the floor below. 'My people know I'm here,' he warned. 'So don't think you can act heavy-handed.'

'You were the one who came looking for us,' Emelda reminded him.

'Quite so,' Loew said. He glanced down the stairs behind him, then took a step forwards. He lowered his voice. 'You've no doubt heard the rumours? That Baron Grin's dead?'

'That should make your vigilantes happy,' Emelda said.

'That's exactly what I don't want,' Loew countered. 'Baron Grin was nothing beside Radukar's tyranny. I cared more about uniting the people against the vampires than I did about Baron Grin. But opposing Radukar is no small thing. My people have to be eased into doing it. Drawn into a rebellion without realising it. Most struggle enough merely to survive, they can't afford to think of anything bigger than that. They can't look farther than today.'

'So you hoped to use fear of Baron Grin to motivate your people.' Emelda didn't bother to hide the contempt in her tone.

'Whatever it takes,' Loew shot back. 'Whatever was needed to stir the people against their oppressors. If that meant a fiendish killer butchering them in the streets, so be it.' He looked from Emelda to Gustaf. 'There's something in your eyes that makes you different from us. There's still a flicker of hope there. Neither of you were here when the city was ravaged by disaster and horror, nor were you here when Radukar swept down from his Ebon Citadel to lay claim to what was left. Those of us who went through that, we've lost hope. But we still have fear, and fear can drive someone when nothing else will. Push a rat into a corner and it will fight a wolf. Baron Grin was pushing my people into that corner. In their minds, the choice between a life of subjugated squalor and hopeless battle was being pruned away. With no other option, they'd fight.'

'So when you lost Baron Grin, you lost your best recruiter,' Gustaf said.

Loew nodded and again cast a cautious look at the stairs behind him, watching to ensure none of his men were close enough to hear. 'These murders have let me plant a seed of defiance in my people. With each killing that seed grew a little more. Now I fear it will wither and die.'

'Why tell us this?' Emelda asked.

'We share a cause,' Loew said. 'In our own ways, we seek to destroy Radukar. Because you come from outside the city–'

Emelda cut him off. 'I'm not a stranger to Mournhold,' she said. 'I'm Emelda Braskov.'

Shock shone in Loew's eyes. 'Emelda Braskov,' he said. 'We thought all the Braskovs were dead.'

'There's one who yet lives, and Radukar will regret that fact before I send his foul spirit to the underworld.' Emelda touched her finger to her lips, the customary method for a Szargorondian to pledge a vow.

'There are people who would rally to you for that reason alone,' Loew said, a hint of bitterness in his voice. 'To me your family name counts for little, but I've seen your sword in action and know your courage will stand the test. Those are what matter to me. Both of you are capable fighters. Too many of my people aren't. You could change that.'

Gustaf frowned at the suggestion. 'It'd take a long time to turn fishermen and labourers into warriors. You say it's fear alone that drives them. Will their fear of what's behind them push them onwards against the fear before them? Do you think they'll stand and fight when they're pitted against the Ulfenwatch or the

Nightguard? Your intentions are admirable, Loew, but your ambition is beyond your reach.'

'At least it is an ambition,' Emelda said. Gustaf was truly an outlander, owing no kinship to the people of Ulfenkarn. She was different. She'd been born here, fought in the city's army, led its troops in battle. As much as the fall of the Braskovs weighed upon her, it was seeing the spirit of the survivors so utterly crushed that tormented her. 'Loew is trying to make the people of Ulfenkarn remember who they are.'

'All I ask of you is to come and meet with us,' Loew declared. 'My vigilantes are meeting tomorrow. They intend to discuss disbanding now that Baron Grin is gone. I want to give them another reason to stay united. You can help me plead my cause to them. Make them listen.'

Emelda looked over at Gustaf. The vampire hunter's expression was uncertain. Emelda spoke before he could, voicing her decision. The only choice she felt she could make.

'We'll be there,' she assured Loew.

Loew smiled. 'I'll send Karlion to lead you to our meeting place. I was able to stir my people against Baron Grin. Together we'll rally them against the Wolf.'

Arno turned the key and reached into the iron coffer. His fingers closed around the coins inside, feeling the coolness of the metal. No whalebone and ivory here, but silver and gold from abroad and all the more valuable for it. There was a small ransom under his hand.

The Watchmaster stared across the desk at the man who'd been brought to see him. He was mousy and weak-chinned, his eyes darting anxiously into every corner of the room. From his salt-ravaged garb, Arno took him for a fisherman – he lacked the robustness to be a whaler or the patience to be a lobsterman.

'I'm told you have information to sell.' Arno studied the man's visage, observing the gleam in his eyes and the flicker of a smile when he mentioned money. 'Tell me what you have to say and I'll decide what it's worth.' He took pleasure in the way the man's smile fell away. 'Mind, now that you're here I'll have the story from you. One way or another.' He bared his fangs to impress on the man the price of reticence.

The informant shifted uneasily. 'It isn't that, excellency. It's just there's some risk and I need compensation for that risk.' His tone was unctuous, only furthering Arno's contempt for him.

'This isn't a tradesman's shop,' Arno stated. 'There's no haggling here. Speak and you'll be rewarded.' He let a few coins fall from his hand into the bottom of the coffer. The clink of metal restored that greedy glint to the man's eyes.

'I've come to tell you about the vigilante society,' he said.

Arno nodded his head. He had a vague understanding that some sort of group had been assembling to protect themselves from Baron Grin. Until now he hadn't met anyone who could give him specifics. 'Why do you come to tell me this?'

The man blinked in surprise. 'Well, I thought you'd want to know. I mean we… they… are breaking laws. They've been out in the streets after curfew and stockpiling weapons.'

'Why now?' Arno asked. 'Surely these vigilantes have been organising for a while. Why bring this to me now?'

'Baron Grin's dead,' the traitor stated. 'The vigilantes will be breaking up. This might be your last chance to get at them.'

'And your last chance to sell them out,' Arno commented. He leaned back in his chair and gave the informant a closer scrutiny. What was standing in his office right now was exactly the kind of weasel who'd betray comrades for his own benefit. 'Where are they meeting and when?'

'Now, I'm taking a great risk…' the informant whined.

'You'll be paid well if your information is useful,' Arno promised. He turned the coffer around so that the man could see its gleaming contents. The way the traitor's eyes bulged from their sockets at the sight, he was sure it made the right impression.

'The chief of the vigilantes is named Loew,' he said. 'He's called a meeting tomorrow night at the old Kaldgrief refinery.'

Arno stared past the informant, his mind picturing the derelict building where, in better days, whale oil had been processed to light the castles of Ulfenkarn's nobility. The place had a reputation for being haunted and was shunned by the inhabitants of its district to such a degree that it had been spared the wholesale looting of most abandoned buildings. The stink of rotting casks of whale oil and decaying blubber was the most vivid impression he'd had of it on the few times he'd been in the area when he was still mortal. If the vigilantes were seeking a rendezvous where they'd be undisturbed, the refinery made an excellent choice.

'If this information is true, then it's worth ten pieces of silver,' Arno said. He removed the coins from the coffer and laid them on the desk in front of him. The traitor started forwards to collect them, but Arno laid his hand across the money. 'This is what will be waiting for you. After.'

'After?' the informant muttered.

One by one, Arno dropped the coins back into the coffer. 'After we've dealt with these vigilantes. After they've been taught what it means to defy Radukar's decrees.' When the last coin fell into the box, he slammed the lid shut and pointed his finger at the man. 'You'll be there, of course.' He saw the tremor of fear that rushed through the traitor. 'You'll have to be there. If you aren't, the others might be suspicious.'

He made a dismissive wave of his hand when the informant started to protest.

'See Captain Dragomir. He'll give you something to wear so the

Volkshaufen will recognise you when we make our raid. That way nobody will hurt you by accident.'

Arno made another gesture of dismissal and the traitor slowly withdrew.

When he was alone again, Arno removed a sheet of vellum from the desk and began to write his report. Radukar would want to know about this development because of its connection to the Baron Grin murders. How much interest the Wolf would have in a ragged group of vigilantes, Arno didn't know. It wasn't his job to know.

Once the report was complete, Arno took it with him to the basement where the Volkshaufen kept a cage of messenger bats. The leather-winged beast would fly over the monstrous waste-land at the city's heart and bear his words to the Ebon Citadel and the Wolf.

The members of Loew's vigilante group were gathered in the storage room above the main floor of what had been the Kald-grief refinery. Sentinels had been posted both outside the building and at the bottom of the stairs that offered the only entry to the room. Except for the iron hoops and decayed planks of unassembled casks, and the boxes of rusted tools, the vigilantes were alone in their hidden sanctum.

Alone except for the people Loew had brought to speak to them. There'd been no small amount of grumbling when Emelda and Gustaf were introduced. Several of the vigilantes were already aware of them and considered the pair reckless meddlers. With the death of Baron Grin, attitudes towards Radukar were quickly fading back to that of frightened servitude – the idea that by placating the vampires they might at least preserve their own lives and those of their families.

Gustaf's career as a vampire hunter in the Order of Azyr failed to make much impact with the vigilantes, far less than Loew had hoped. Emelda, however, as the last of the Braskovs not under Radukar's spell, did.

'It could be just as it was before,' a burly, raven-haired vigilante declared. 'With a Braskov to lead us, Mournhold can be what it once was.' Loew knew the man's background. Before the catastrophe he'd been an armourer, crafting suits of mail for the nobles.

'The "good old days" might've been good for you, but not for all of us,' another man said. He held his hand out so those nearby could see his missing fingers. 'The major-domo of the Ven Altens took those off me because I pruned her ladyship's rose bushes too far. I've no love for what this city was.'

'Do you have any love for it the way it is?' Emelda challenged him. 'Fighting for whatever scraps Radukar leaves you? Offend the vampires and they'll not stop at a few fingers.' She made a wringing motion with her hands. 'They'll squeeze every drop of blood out of you and toss your body to the rats.'

'Friends,' Loew addressed the vigilantes. 'We came together to protect our people from Baron Grin. We risked ourselves to guard against a marauding murderer because our rulers wouldn't. If we could muster the courage to do that, surely we won't slip back and meekly accept the whims of an inhuman tyrant?'

A squat, broad-shouldered woman with a leather patch over one eye stepped forwards and shook her finger at Loew. 'But the authorities did stop Baron Grin,' she contested. 'He's dead and we've naught to fear from him now.'

'Do you believe the stories the Volkshaufen tell?' Loew asked. 'They're nothing but slaves and stooges of the vampires. They'll say whatever Radukar commands them to say.'

Emelda stared into the woman's remaining eye. 'The killer might just as easily have been stopped by someone else and the militia is simply taking credit.' Her voice dropped to a low hiss. 'That is, if he's actually dead.'

The last point proved a bridge too far for the argument as far as many of the vigilantes were concerned. Grumbled protests rippled through the room. 'There haven't been any more murders. Of course he's dead.'

Loew raised his arms, appealing to his followers for calm. 'You all know that Baron Grin didn't claim a victim every night. It's too soon to tell if he's been stopped or not. Or if Radukar's minions are lying to us again.'

The one-eyed woman shook her head. 'I know what you're about,' she claimed. 'You're just trying to keep this group together so you can feel important. So you can think you're better than the rest of us.' She smirked as she glanced over at Emelda and Gustaf. 'That's why you brought them here, so you could show off your fancy friends.'

'Marda,' Loew said, addressing the woman, 'my only intention was to explain to you… to all of you… that whether or not Baron Grin is gone, the real threat remains. None of us, none of our families, are truly safe while Radukar rules this city.'

'To the vampires, none of you are more than cattle,' Gustaf said. 'Cower before them all you like, one day they *will* come for you.'

As though conjured by the vampire hunter's words, the vigilante posted at the bottom of the stairs stumbled into the room, his garments dripping blood. Loew rushed towards him, catching the man as he collapsed.

'The Volkshaufen…' the sentinel gasped as the last of his energy drained out of him. He'd been dealt a savage slash across his chest. More than that, Loew had no time to determine. Close behind the vigilante came his killers.

The first militiaman to reach the storeroom went hurtling back down the stairs, his face a red ruin. The one behind him dodged the body of his comrade only to have Loew's sword stab down between his ribs. The wounded man sagged against the steps, gasping like a fish as he tried to suck air into his punctured lung.

'A patrol! A patrol's found us!' Loew shouted to his followers. A mob of vigilantes hurried to join him at the stairs. Armed with clubs and torches, hatchets and knives, they fought back the first wave of Volkshaufen. Loew drew away from the steps, a note of warning ringing inside him. There were too many of the militia to be a simple patrol. This was something else.

One of the vigilantes shrieked in horror. Loew looked on in amazement as a heavy sword stabbed up at the man from below and skewered the vigilante. He felt his blood run cold when the stricken man was lifted off his feet by the superhuman strength of his foe. Loew gaped in shock as the vigilante's killer climbed the steps into the storeroom.

'Radukar,' Loew gasped.

The vampire lord of Ulfenkarn in all his terrible majesty. The other vigilantes fell back, fear tightening around their hearts. Radukar's eyes blazed as he regarded them with cold contempt. A sweep of his sword sent the man spitted on the barrow-blade hurtling across the room to crash against the far wall in an unmoving heap.

'You have defied my laws,' the vampire snarled, fangs glistening in the torchlight. 'Your lives are forfeit. Submit now, and perhaps I'll spare your households the fate that awaits you.'

The vigilantes continued to retreat before Radukar. A few weapons clattered to the floor as their owners were overwhelmed with fear. Slowly the vampire stalked towards them.

'Radukar!' This time the name was invoked not in a frightened gasp, but in a vengeful howl. Loew turned his head to see Emelda rush at the vampire from the side, her sword clenched in both hands. The monster turned to meet her attack, a bemused look on his face.

His expression turned to one of surprise when they closed and, instead of meeting him head-on, she twisted about and struck at his flank. It was a remarkable feint, but Radukar's inhuman reflexes met the challenge. His sword intercepted her strike, the strength behind his parry almost ripping the weapon from her hands.

Before the vampire could capitalise on his advantage there was a thunderous roar. Radukar was spun around as Gustaf's horse pistol sent a ball of lead slamming into his torso. Smoke billowed from the rent in the vampire's armour, only a finger's length from his heart. Gustaf's visage contorted in an agony of frustration.

'Help them!' Loew shouted at his followers. 'The Wolf won't punish anyone if he's destroyed!' Loew didn't wait to see if anyone was running beside him when he rushed at Radukar, a battle cry flying from his lips. The cutlass in his right hand chopped at the vampire's chest while the hatchet in his left swung for his head. The sharp ring of metal striking metal sounded as his sword crashed against Radukar's armour, scarring its baroque ornamentation. The vampire twisted aside to avoid the hatchet and struck at Loew with his free hand. The blow threw him back into a stack of wooden planks that disintegrated under the impact.

Loew peered out from the cloud of dust and detritus to see his people swarming the vampire. Pride swelled up inside him and for an instant hope rose in his heart. Then he saw Radukar's barrow-blade carve the leg from the burly armourer and send him crashing down. A glancing blow from the flat of the same sword knocked Emelda to her knees, blood spilling from her torn scalp. Gustaf started towards the vampire, now with the Aqshian stake clenched in his hand. Before he could close with the monster, however, militiamen led by a second vampire were charging into the storeroom to support the undead tyrant.

Hands gripped Loew and lifted him from the wreckage. He looked up into the concerned face of Karlion.

'This is hopeless,' he said. 'We can't win this fight!'

Loew shrugged free of Karlion's grip. 'We've got to try,' he said, wincing as he moved his bruised body. He glanced around for his weapons. 'This is what I've dreamed of. A chance at the Wolf! This might never happen again!'

Loew didn't see his weapons. What he did see were the Volks-shaufen confronting his vigilantes. The militiamen had no surfeit of quality over Loew's people, but they had better equipment. Few of his fighters could boast proper swords, and the only one among them with real armour was Emelda. Irregular though they were, the guards each had a sword or spear and many had at least a steel cap to protect them.

More than that, they had Radukar.

The Wolf was a whirlwind of death. At every turn his sword delivered another butchering stroke and left a screaming pile of human debris at his feet. Radukar exulted in the slaughter, his bestial laughter echoing through the storeroom. With the inter-vention of the militia, Gustaf abandoned trying to come to grips with the tyrant, and instead dragged the stunned Emelda away from the conflict.

'We've got to try,' Loew cursed. He caught up a splintered board, his mind racing with childhood fables about brave heroes who'd killed vampires with such a simple implement. Karlion caught hold of him and once more held him back. Marda rushed over to help him restrain their leader.

'You'll just get yourself killed,' she told him. She plucked the board from his grasp and tossed it aside. 'You think that's enough to stop Radukar? The vampire hunter shot him and he didn't even slow down!'

Loew's eyes narrowed, his mind racing now. Had Gustaf charged his pistol with a bullet blessed against the undead, or had it been a mere ball of mundane lead? Special weapons were needed to fight a vampire. In the old stories, a stake through the heart had been one, but another had been fire.

He pointed at the torches still on the walls. 'Fire!' he told the vigilantes around him, those who'd either been forced from the fray or hadn't entered at all. 'A vampire can't withstand the purifying flames! We can fight Radukar with fire!'

Whether motivated by Loew's words or simply desperate to help their comrades, several of the vigilantes armed themselves with torches and charged back into the combat. Loew was ready to fight with them, but Marda took the last torch off the wall. Grabbing up a rusty hammer, he started after her to lend what aid he could to his fellows.

At that instant, Loew was struck from behind. He crashed to the floor, felt his nose break as he struck the boards. 'He's here! Loew's here!' a voice was shouting. Through his bleary vision he could see one of the vigilantes, an eggler named Witalas, standing over him waving a red vest and with a look of diabolic glee on his face.

Loew understood at once what had happened, how the Volkshaufen and Radukar had found them. Witalas had betrayed them! He glared at the traitor and tried to rise, but the eggler struck him again with the bludgeon he held. Loew slumped against the floor, his senses reeling from the blow.

'Stay down,' Witalas snarled at him. 'They might pay me more if I give you to them alive.'

Gustaf dragged Emelda away from the fighting. Her injury had dazed her. She offered no resistance as he pulled her across the storeroom. From the unfocused look in her eyes, he wondered if she even knew where she was. He doubted it, because if she did even Nagash himself wouldn't keep her from attacking Radukar again. Never mind that the vampire would slaughter her out of hand the way she was now.

The vigilantes were charging Radukar and the militia now. Many of them bore torches, trying to attack the vampires with their firebrands. Gustaf winced to see their desperate, unorganised effort. He clenched his teeth as Radukar picked them off one after another, chopping them down with his flashing blade. Another vigilante fell to the brutal sweep of the other vampire's sword, his blood spraying over the creature's fanged visage.

He set Emelda down on the floor and clenched his fingers tight around the Aqshian stake he carried. If he could just get close enough, if the vigilantes could only distract the Wolf long enough, he might be able to deal their enemy a wound he wouldn't easily shrug off. It was the only thing he could do to help the brave rebels dying around him.

Gustaf heard someone cry out from deeper in the storeroom. He turned to see a small, pasty-faced vigilante waving a vest in the air. On the ground beside him was Loew. The vigilante's head was bloody, but he was making feeble motions with his arms. Gustaf listened for a moment and through the clamour of fighting, he picked out the meaning of the little vigilante's shouts. The man was a traitor!

Gustaf drew Emelda behind a stack of wooden planks, then turned and sprinted towards Loew and his betrayer. He noted the bludgeon the little man held, blood dripping from its end. As he closed upon the weasel, he drew his empty pistol and aimed it at the man's face. He was counting on the same bluff that had fooled Loew working on the traitor.

'Get away from him, you Sigmar-cursed swine!' Gustaf roared at the villain, his thumb drawing back the pistol's hammer. The ferocious performance broke the traitor's fragile resolve. He yelped like a whipped cur and took off running. Waving his red vest as though it were a battle flag, he rushed back towards the fray. Gustaf could hear the traitor screaming that he was on Radukar's side.

Whether the Wolf heard him, or cared, the end was the same.

As he came close to Radukar, the tyrant's gore-coated blade licked out. The top of the traitor's head and the arm waving the vest were shorn away, sent dancing into the air by the Wolf's strike.

Close upon the traitor's slaughter, Gustaf saw Marda rush at the vampire with a blazing torch. Radukar caught her by the throat as she struck at him with the firebrand. Smoke steamed off his pallid flesh as the flames scorched him. With a brutal overarm move and an animalistic howl, he slammed her against the floor. The boards shattered under the impact and the woman was sent hurtling into the refinery below. Gustaf heard her anguished scream, but close behind it came a still more awful sound. A whooshing roar that shook the derelict building.

The abandoned refinery, its last supplies left to rot in the darkness, was riddled with pockets of incendiary fumes. In her downward plunge, Marda's torch had ignited the vapours seeping from neglected casks of oil. A great plume of fire boiled up from the hole Radukar's violence had created. Gustaf shielded his eyes as the mephitic flare snarled upwards and licked the roof with burning talons.

Radukar reeled away from the conflagration, blinded for the instant by the explosion. The vigilantes that had been fighting the vampires and the militia were thrown down, as were their foes. Only the tyrant remained on his feet, his lips curled back to expose his long fangs as he glared at the spreading flames. A few of the Volkshaufen staggered to their feet and scurried for the stairs, abandoning their comrades caught between the steps and the flames. Some of the trapped guards tried to leap through the spreading fire. Several went hurtling down through the weakened floor. Many of the vigilantes suffered the same fate as they tried to retreat deeper into the storeroom.

'Eminence, don't risk yourself!' Gustaf heard the other vampire yell. 'Leave them to the flames!'

The vampire hunter saw Radukar's expression change into one

of sneering contempt. His malevolent gaze met Gustaf's for an instant; then he turned and withdrew with the Watchmaster down the stairs.

'Better to have died fighting Radukar than in the fire,' Gustaf cursed. Less than a dozen of the vigilantes remained, all of them creeping back to the farthest corner of the room as the flames continued to spread. He gave them only a brief glance, enough to see that Emelda wasn't with them. His eyes darted to where he'd left her behind the planks. The piles were alight now and he could see that her cloak was starting to burn.

Gustaf wasn't certain whether she was still alive when he raced over to her; all he knew was he wouldn't sit aside while he watched the fire consume her. 'Praise Sigmar,' he whispered when she moaned as he pulled her up off the floor. He ripped the smouldering cloak from her shoulders and sent it spinning back into the flames. Then he was dragging her back to the momentary refuge where the last vigilantes were gathered. There might be only a few moments left, but their very brevity made them precious.

Loew was stirring now. The vigilante leader shook off Karlion's grip and waved frantically towards a stack of empty casks. 'Move them!' he shouted at his men. 'Behind... a secret door!'

The vigilantes seized on his words like a drowning man upon a spit of land. The casks were flung aside with wild abandon. Concealed behind them was Loew's hidden door. Half a dozen boots kicked at it until the splintered panel swung open.

'Out!' Loew shouted. Gustaf thought it a needless command. The panicked vigilantes wouldn't have done anything else. They streamed out from the storeroom and onto the crumbling roof of the refinery. By the time Gustaf helped Emelda out onto the shingles, the survivors had already found the ladders attached to the side of the building and were scurrying down them to the street far below.

'If the fire's made them pull back their cordon, we can still escape,' Loew declared as Karlion helped him to one of the ladders. 'We might make Radukar regret leaving us to the flames.'

Emelda stirred in Gustaf's arms, the shock of the cold night air reviving her. He led her to one of the ladders.

'We have to hurry. The building's on fire.'

'Radukar...' she growled back at him, her dazed expression sharpening into a bitter snarl.

'Later,' Gustaf told her. 'Right now we have to escape.' He helped her out to the ladder, dismayed by the clumsy way she gripped the rungs. 'Be careful,' he said, trying to hide the alarm he felt. If they went too slowly, the walls might cave in and drag them back into the inferno. But if she went too fast he was sure she'd fall.

Emelda gave him a sullen look, but she offered no more objections. Gustaf kept one eye on her as she descended, afraid she'd lose her hold at any moment. He didn't breathe easy until they were both down on the street and hurrying away from the Kaldgrief refinery. The whole structure was burning now, and embers thrown off by the fire had ignited surrounding buildings. Curfew or not, hundreds of people were spilling into the streets to flee.

'Hurry,' Gustaf said, turning and following the vigilantes as they fled into the network of alleyways around the refinery. They jogged past houses that were already in flames and dodged smouldering debris that fell from the roofs. All around them were screams of panic and despair. The cries of the frantic and the doomed.

'The people's misery is again our benefactor,' Emelda said. 'In all the confusion, we'll be able to sneak away.'

Most of the vigilantes had already melted into the crowds, hurrying to lose themselves in the streets. Loew and Karlion were still near enough to meet Gustaf and Emelda as they reached the ground. The vigilante chief scowled when he heard her remark.

'Perhaps you're right, noble,' Loew said, his eyes gleaming in the glow of the refinery. 'Maybe the misery of the people is our benefactor.' Gustaf heard the fury in his voice. 'Maybe right now Baron Grin is the hero Ulfenkarn needs.'

CHAPTER SEVEN

Arno stood in the debris-strewn street and watched the smoke rising from the Kaldgrief refinery. The imposing structure had been reduced to a heap of rubble and blackened chimneys. Much of the surrounding neighbourhood had been burned by the fire, entire blocks of houses consumed in the conflagration. Charred timbers and collapsed walls choked many of the lanes and alleyways, creating a smouldering wasteland.

Scores had died in the fires, caught in their homes before they could flee or else trapped when a pile of burning debris spilled down to seal their avenue of escape. More had perished inside the refinery itself. Arno didn't know how many vigilantes were killed, but he knew that ten of the militiamen had been lost.

No, he corrected himself, the final tally would be thirteen. Two of the guards and Captain Dragomir had suffered such grievous wounds that they'd been relieved of duty. They were to be exsanguinated and their skeletons reanimated to serve again in the Ulfenwatch. Radukar had claimed it was a mark of distinction to honour their bravery. But the way the Wolf grinned when he made the statement made his true meaning clear. He was warning the Volkshaufen what they could expect if they failed their master again.

Arno was perhaps still too close to his former mortality not to see the ghastliness of such a fate. He focused on the skeletal figures moving through the ruined refinery, probing its smouldering debris with their spears, indifferent to the heat and smoke. The Ulfenwatch had been tasked with searching the ruins, a duty they performed with the same unwavering fidelity as any other demanded of them. The skeletons were incapable of questioning the commands of Radukar.

Arno glanced at his master, who stood with him in the street. Radukar was wrapped in his fur cloak, its snowy folds enclosing him like the hide of his namesake. The light and warmth of morning were diminished in his vicinity, the air about him chill and dark. Arno could remember the folk tales he'd been told as a child, of how a vampire couldn't endure the light of day. He'd seen for himself that the rule didn't hold true. Thralls like himself found daylight unpleasant, but not destructive. It was more powerful vampires like Duchess Sargozy who had to shun sunlight, but even then Radukar had found ways to defy such vulnerabilities and make a mockery of them.

'Can you feel the difference?' Radukar suddenly asked.

'Eminence?' Arno fought to keep his voice composed, to keep his manner deferential rather than terrified. It was no easy thing to be in the Wolf's presence for a prolonged period. He'd been in Radukar's company almost the entire night.

Radukar extended one of his pale hands and gestured at the empty streets and blackened rubble. 'The mortals, Watchmaster. Those gawking crowds who gathered to look and listen, trying to dredge up some speck of courage from their being. To cling to some unguessed ember of hope.' The vampire turned the last word into a contemptuous sneer. 'Where are they now?'

Arno followed the sweep of the pale hand with his eyes. Except for the militia and more Ulfenwatch, the area was deserted. He didn't even see a stray dog or a slinking corpse-rat scavenging in the rubble.

'Perhaps the fire...' he started to suggest.

'No,' Radukar stated, turning to hold Arno with his intense gaze. 'Not the fire. They keep from here out of fear. The rumours your guards have spread have done their work. The people have heard that Baron Grin is dead. So now the fear that was forcing them to boldness is draining out of them. They remember that it is I who rule over them. That their lives and deaths are *mine* to command.'

'Only a fool would think to defy you,' Arno said.

The Wolf's face twisted into a feral smile. 'Then it was fools we fought in there so recently,' he said, pointing at the Kald-grief refinery. 'Or did you fail to notice the weapon one of them brandished?'

'Weapon, eminence?' In the crush of the fray, Arno couldn't recall the detail Radukar spoke of.

'One of the rabble had an instrument I've not seen in a long time,' the Wolf growled. 'A tool of the Sigmarite fanatics who presume they can oppose the dominion of the undead in these lands.'

He whipped back his cloak and displayed the bullet hole in his armour. In a living man it would have been a fatal wound, but for the vampire it was merely an inconvenience.

'The same man who did this carried a stake of Aqshian fyre-wood. A profane weapon that could only have been brought into Shyish for one purpose.'

'They would dare seek your destruction?' Arno shuddered at the insane audacity of such a thing. He'd seen with his own eyes Radukar's might. Any mortal who thought they could fight against the Wolf was mad. Yet hadn't Ulfenkarn already been ravaged by a madman? 'The rebels! The graffiti on the wall! These weren't vigilantes, but a conspiracy against you. They weren't hunting Baron Grin because they *were* Baron Grin.'

'Perhaps,' Radukar said. He turned and looked back at the smoking ruins. 'I will know for certain when the Ulfenwatch find what they need to find.'

The skeletons continued to pick and probe the rubble. Arno could hear a bell ringing from one of the city's remaining clock towers. The distant notes told him that another hour had passed. After the long night, he felt drained, the thirst for blood rising into a torturous urgency. The Ulfenwatch, however, pressed on with their task, unwavering in their labour. Such was the toil of the undead.

At last one of the skeletons found something beneath a jumble of charred timbers. Its spear hooked into a blackened mass and dragged it free. The skeleton brought its find out from the rubble and set it at Radukar's feet.

Arno had seen much of death, but few sights as revolting as this burnt husk that had once been human. One arm was curled against the chest, the other outflung as though to ward off the consuming flames. The legs and pelvis were gone entirely. He could discern no features in the charred crust of its head.

Radukar loomed above this human debris, his cloak flaring like the pinions of a vulture. The vampire's eyes blazed with unholy power. He scratched his palm with one of his talon-like fingers. Blood dribbled from the cut and dripped down upon the fire-ruined face.

'Awake,' Radukar hissed.

A tremor of motion stirred the charred wreckage. The black crust pulled itself apart to expose the congealed residue of eyes. A grisly crackling reached Arno's ears as the burned flesh stretched and tore, and the corpse opened its mouth.

'You see?' Radukar said. 'The husk responds. It lacks the corruption found in Baron Grin's victims... and in the murdered murderer.'

'Then... these rebels aren't responsible for the killings?' Arno wondered.

'Even if they aren't, they were prepared to fight me,' Radukar growled. 'Three lesser members of my court have been assassinated. These wretches might be behind such defiance.'

The vampire turned his imperious gaze on the burned corpse.

'Speak,' he commanded. 'You were a part of this secret group?'

'I followed Loew,' the corpse responded, its voice a dry rattle that rasped across its burnt lips. 'We were united to hunt Baron Grin.'

'But tonight you gathered for another purpose?' Radukar pressed. 'Baron Grin is dead and you sought a new cause.'

'Loew brought people to speak to us,' the corpse said. 'They wanted us to fight against Radukar and the vampires.'

Anger flared across Radukar's face. 'Who were these people? One of them carried a stake of fyrewood, did he not?'

'The man with the stake was Gustaf Voss, from the Order of Azyr. With him was a noblewoman. Emelda Braskov.' The corpse writhed and gnashed its teeth in pain.

The last name stunned Arno. 'A Braskov? But the family was wiped out.'

'Apparently not as completely as I'd intended,' Radukar snarled.

'If there's a Braskov trying to stir up revolution, it could be a serious threat,' Arno advised. There was no denying the fear that kept the people of Ulfenkarn in line, but with that fear went a smouldering resentment. It needed only the right touch to fan those embers into a fire fiercer than that which had destroyed the refinery. This Emelda Braskov was someone who could provide that touch, simply because of who she was.

The Wolf shook his head. 'She may be nothing but a pretender exploiting the name. Real or false, she will be attended to. This Sigmarite Voss, too.' Radukar leaned down and continued his interrogation of the corpse. 'These people, did they perish in the fire?'

'Release me,' the corpse moaned. 'Let this torment end.'

'There will be no end to your torment unless you answer me,' Radukar said. 'Did anyone escape the flames? What happened to these people, Braskov and Voss?'

The burnt head lolled from side to side. 'The roof,' it said. 'They made it onto the roof through a hidden door.'

'Then they might have climbed down to the street,' Arno mused. 'The door would have been small use to them without a way down from the roof.'

Radukar stamped his boot on the corpse's chest, cracking ribs beneath his heel. 'If they did survive, do you know where they would go? Answer me, or I'll leave your spirit in this ruined carcass forever.'

'I was with Loew when he sought them out,' the corpse answered. 'They were living in a house near the blood farms, a building on the Immerplatz.'

'You know this place?' Radukar said, turning to Arno.

'I do,' Arno replied. 'But I don't think they'd be there. If they did escape the fire, they'd have to worry that their hideout was compromised.'

Radukar nodded. 'They'd be eager to be shot of the place, but they'd be loath to abandon whatever supplies are there.' He bared his fangs in a predatory smile. 'I think they'd seek a new hiding place, then go back to collect whatever they left behind in the old one.'

'If we're careful, we might catch them,' Arno said. 'I'll set guards–'

'No,' Radukar told him. There was a vicious eagerness in his tone. 'I'll see to things. There will be no measure allowed for mistakes.

These people presume to threaten me. They'll learn the idiocy of such bravado.' His eyes bored into Arno's. 'You will show me the place. That is all I require of you.'

The Wolf started to walk away. As he did, the charred husk wailed in anguish. Arno stared down at the corpse in disgust.

'Eminence, what about this?' he asked, pointing at the crying body.

'Leave it,' Radukar said. 'It's of no further use. Leave it to rot. Its moans will be a reminder to others that for those who defy me, even the grave is no refuge from my vengeance.'

Gustaf crouched beside the marble fountain with its ivory spikes, using the morbid receptacle of the vampires' blood tithe to hide while he watched the house across the street. With the air already rank with the sanguinary smell of the blood farms, at least the stench rising from the basin didn't add to his discomfort. It was bad enough being in such close proximity to a thing so saturated in the necromantic energies of Radukar's infernal regime. The Order of Azyr's training had made him much more sensitive to the aura of black magic than most people, the better to track down and destroy his quarry. In a place as rife with these enchantments as Ulfenkarn, however, he found himself surrounded. It wasn't a question of discerning the stigma of evil, it was trying to pick out greater concentrations from lesser ones.

'Do you think it's safe?' Emelda whispered. She stood a few feet away, keeping to the shadow of the wall behind the fountain, stamping her boots in the snow to put some measure of warmth in her body. The swordswoman had her blade drawn, braced for sudden conflict. In creeping back to their former refuge, they'd narrowly avoided two patrols of Ulfenwatch. She'd been of the opinion that the skeletons were just following their normal routine, but Gustaf wasn't so certain.

'I'm not sure,' Gustaf said. He turned and solemnly shook his head. 'One of Loew's people betrayed him before the fire. Maybe the man was just trying to save his own skin. Or maybe he was a spy before that meeting. There's no telling what he knew and what he told before the raid.'

'Then you think Radukar knows about this place?' Emelda asked.

'It's possible. We can't depend on Radukar believing we died in the fire.' Gustaf closed his hand on the Sigmarite icon around his neck. 'In matters of death, the most powerful vampires easily divine the truth and Radukar is the greatest of that foul breed I've ever encountered.'

Gustaf heard Emelda strike her fist against the wall. 'We had him,' she snarled. 'He was there. He was within our grasp.' She gnashed her teeth in frustration.

'We had nothing,' Gustaf corrected her. 'It isn't enough to fight against Radukar. We have to be in a position to win. We weren't. He caught us unprepared. All of the advantages were with him.' He gave Emelda a stern look. 'It doesn't do any good to throw your life away needlessly. A blood-crazed disciple of Khorne does that, not somebody trying to liberate her people.'

Emelda's eyes were as cold as steel. 'There can be no liberation until the Wolf is destroyed.' Her face took on a pensive quality and a low sigh left her. 'But you're right in one thing. We've got to be in a position to win. It does no good to simply add to Radukar's list of victims.' She nodded at the decrepit house. 'Maybe we should forget about getting what we left behind. We can recover what we need.'

'By accepting help from Loew,' Gustaf said. 'I don't know if that would be wise. We've already seen what happens when you trust too freely. It's a paradox. There's strength in numbers, but the more people you gather together, the greater the chance one will betray you. Our vigilante friend found that out at great cost.'

The vampire hunter shook his head. 'No, Emelda, I think it would be best to do for ourselves as much as we can.' He thought of Vladrik and his other contacts trying to find Darrock. They too were vulnerabilities, yet he wasn't sure he could bring himself to cut them loose. Finding the witch hunter, the only other initiate of the Order of Azyr he knew to be in Ulfenkarn, remained a priority for him. He needed his contacts to keep him apprised of where Darrock might be.

'Then, if it looks safe, we should move quick,' Emelda told Gustaf. 'It could be that Radukar does know of this place but hasn't had time to act. The longer we tarry, the worse our chances grow.'

Gustaf studied the house again. Something felt wrong to him, but then the whole of Ulfenkarn felt wrong to a greater or lesser degree. He couldn't be sure this was really any worse than it had been. He softly offered a prayer to Sigmar that his concern was unfounded.

'All right,' he decided. 'Let's go. In and out. We take what we can carry easily and abandon the rest.'

'Weapons and food take priority,' Emelda added.

Gustaf nodded. Tools and supplies for casting bullets for his pistol were irreplaceable, or effectively so, in the oppressed city. Food, at least anything of dependable quality, was another rarity. The slums teemed with people too hungry to care overmuch what they put in their bellies.

The vampire hunter led the way. A quick sprint brought him away from the fountain and across the street. He reached the doorway and ducked into the threshold. Every sense was alert for the least sound, the faintest blur of motion. He counted to ten, then looked back outside. When he saw no one on the street, he gave Emelda the signal to come over. The swordswoman was soon beside him.

'So far, so good,' she said.

'Pray to Sigmar that our luck holds,' Gustaf replied.

They started up the stairs to the rooms on the upper floor. It was only when they reached the landing that they saw their luck had deserted them. Further down the hall, standing in its flesh-less horror, was an armoured skeleton. The skull's empty sockets stared at them with a presence that could only be described as malign.

'Ulfenwatch,' Emelda growled. She glanced at the doorways around them. Gustaf shared her fear, expecting the doors to be flung open and more of the skeletons to come spilling from the rooms.

Instead, the skeleton down the hall turned its back to them. Gustaf drew his pistol to end whatever ploy the creature was plotting, but stopped himself. The shot would be heard for several blocks and alert any enemies in the vicinity.

The alert was given just the same. Before either of them could charge the skeleton, the undead was in motion. It moved with a speed that Gustaf knew could only have been poured into its bones by dark magic, a speed a living man would have struggled to match. The undead didn't try to charge past them down the stairs, but kept running down the hall. Its momentum and the bulk of its armour were enough to accomplish its purpose when it crashed into the wall. The decayed wood splintered and the skeleton smashed through the barrier to hurtle down into the street below.

Gustaf rushed to the ragged hole and peered down. The skeleton had been crushed in the fall, several of its bones scattered across the street. But the creature had fulfilled its duty. It had been set as a sentry, not to stop Gustaf and Emelda when they returned but to alert the ones who would.

Sure enough, as the vampire hunter watched, the nearest of the neighbouring houses disgorged a fearsome sight. Two hulking ogors burst from the front of the building, plaster and wood bouncing into the street as they violently forced their way outwards. More sounds of destruction drew his eyes to the building on the other side of them. There too he saw a pair of the monstrous Nightguard, their flesh rotten with the foul energies of necromancy, their bodies draped in rancid furs and rusted armour.

Another figure swept into view along with the Nightguard, a being Gustaf had contended against only hours before. Radukar lifted his head and stared up at the hole. A predatory smile pulled at the Wolf's face. Gustaf knew that look. It was the look of a hunter closing a trap on his prey.

'Radukar!' Gustaf shouted as he turned back into the hall. 'He's set a trap for us!'

For just an instant the thirst for vengeance coloured Emelda's face, but reason quickly subdued reckless emotion. She spun around, ready to make a dash back down the stairs. The sound of splintering wood drew her back.

'The Kosargi!' she shouted. 'They're breaking in!'

Gustaf reached the head of the stairs just as the first of the ogors battered its way inside. He aimed the pistol he held at the brute. Despite the heft of the weapon and the havoc it could make of a man, it felt an ineffectual tool against the enormous Nightguard. Still, it was the only thing at hand with which to fight, to delay the enemy by even a few heartbeats.

A strange sensation swept through Gustaf as he took aim. A sickening chill that crawled through his body. He knew it was the touch of magic. He thought of Radukar's profane powers and tried to resist the enchantment stealing over him, but his defiance came too late. His arm grew cold, the pistol in his hand shone with an eerie green light. Below he could see the ogor lumbering towards the stairs, a massive axe clenched in its necrotic hands.

Gustaf snarled in defiance and pulled the trigger.

The pistol roared like an enraged dragon. The tongue of flame that exploded from the barrel had a sinister glow about it. Gustaf's shot struck true, boring into the ogor's thick skull. He was shocked when the Nightguard's head disintegrated under the impact, shards of bone and rotten flesh thrown in every direction. The huge body swayed for a moment, as though it might struggle onwards. Then it collapsed in a heap at the base of the stairs.

'Great shot!' Emelda cried out.

Gustaf stared in amazement at his pistol. The glow and the chill were gone now, but he knew what they'd meant. 'That wasn't me,' he said, unable to repress a shiver.

In the room below, more of the Nightguard lurched into view. One of them shoved the carcass of their destroyed comrade out of the way. Another stomped towards the stairs and leered up at them with a toothy snarl. Behind the Nightguard, Radukar stalked into view. The vampire stared at the dead ogor then lifted his eyes and looked up at the two heroes, his lips curled in a snarl of fury.

'Defiant to the end,' Radukar growled. 'You've proven more trouble than I expected. I'll savour your blood as I draw it drop by drop from your veins.'

'Just try and get it,' Emelda spat, brandishing her sword.

Radukar laughed at her. 'When I do, I'll learn if you're truly a Braskov or merely an imposter exploiting gullible peasants.' His eyes gleamed with an unholy radiance. 'I've sampled enough Braskov blood to recognise the unsavoury taste.'

Gustaf was forced to grab hold of Emelda and keep her from plunging down the stairs to attack the jeering vampire. 'That's what he wants! To draw you down there so his ogors can butcher you!' He nodded at the stairs. 'They can only come at us one by one. Up here we have some kind of chance. Down there we have none at all.'

The Wolf barked again with venomous laughter. 'Whatever you

do, your doom is at hand. Your choice is simply that of how you die.'

Gustaf turned Emelda around. 'Get to the ladder. Try to make it to the roof.' When they'd made the house their base, the roof had presented an alternate way out.

Emelda shook her head. 'Either we fight together or we run together,' she said.

'I can delay them,' Gustaf protested. 'At least one of us can get away. That has to be you. You're the one who can rally the people.' He knew the last point would sway Emelda. If her people were to be liberated, they needed a liberator to lead them.

'None of you will get away,' Radukar snarled. Despite their hushed voices, the vampire had caught every word. He raised a clawed finger and pointed at the ceiling. 'Once before you escaped me. That trickery is over. Listen, fools!'

From overhead, the flutter of wings could be heard. The shrill cries of bats. Gustaf felt his stomach turn as he remembered the swarms of thirsty scavengers that flocked to the blood farms eager to feed. He could imagine the leather-winged vermin now summoned by Radukar's power, circling above. Waiting for them to emerge onto the roof.

'A choice of death. Do you feed the blood-bats or do you come down to face my Nightguard?' Radukar smiled maliciously, a predator toying with his prey, delighting in their despair. 'Either way, know that you won't rest easy in your graves. Sigmar will never find your spirit, vampire hunter. Nor will your husk enter the family vault, maybe-Braskov. You will die a miserable death, but that will only be the beginning.' The gloating vampire gestured to his ogors. One of the brutes marched to the stairs and started to ascend.

Suddenly a cloud of darkness swirled into being, erupting amidst the Kosargi. Gustaf was reminded of the nightmare force that had overwhelmed the Ulfenwatch. The similarity was driven home an instant later when he heard Morrvahl's voice cry out.

'Stay where you are! It would inconvenience me if you were to die today!'

Now Gustaf understood the enchantment that had stolen upon him and heightened the force of his bullet. It had been Morrvahl's doing. Whatever spell the wizard now conjured, its power couldn't be denied. The black mist whipped around the ogors, slicing at their necrotic flesh like so many knives. A keening wail swept through the house, a cacophony of tormented souls. Their pain was echoed on the rotten faces of the Nightguard. Gustaf was stunned to see the undead grimace in agony, even their uncanny frames unable to deny the magnitude of suffering that now assailed them.

'Get them! Kill them!' Radukar howled at his monsters. What had been but a sadistic game to the vampire a moment before was now a desperate struggle. Rage as he might, however, the damage was done.

The black mist wrought little physical damage upon the ogors, not enough to demolish them. But the spectral pain that wracked them was something different. Glottal bellows of anguish slobbered up from their decayed throats. Maddened by their torment, the Nightguard thrashed about in wild confusion. Their huge bodies slammed into the walls around them. The whole house shook from the impacts. The ogor on the stairs crashed through the balustrade and smashed into another of the undead below.

'Move!' Morrvahl shouted. The wizard appeared suddenly, dashing out from the black mist he'd conjured. He waved Gravebloom at the hole the armoured skeleton had made. 'Out that way!'

'But the bats...' Gustaf objected.

'Remember the limitations of such creatures,' Morrvahl said. 'They watch the roof, not the walls!'

Emelda started for the stairs instead. 'Radukar! This is our chance!'

Before she could start down the steps, Morrvahl blocked her path. 'Not now. Not here,' he snapped. The wizard's argument was augmented by the loud crack that rumbled through the house. A mighty crash sounded as a section of the ceiling collapsed and sent beams smashing downwards. In their agonised rampage, the ogors were demolishing the building from the inside.

'Hurry!' Gustaf yelled. He put action to words as he sprinted down the hallway. For an instant he wondered if Morrvahl was wrong, if the bats would swoop down on anything leaving the house rather than only watching the roof. He knew there was no time to hesitate, however. Gritting his jaw, he swung himself out through the opening. Hanging by his fingers, he let himself drop to the ground below.

Gustaf felt the impact groan through his legs, but there was too much adrenaline in his blood now to appreciate any injury from his fall. He turned back instead and offered his support to Emelda as she followed his example and hung from the opening. With his help to brace her, the swordswoman managed a less painful descent.

The house now trembled as though rocked by an earthquake. Gustaf could hear things collapsing inside. It might be only a matter of moments before the whole structure came down. He looked up as Morrvahl scrambled from the hole. The wizard held his bladed staff out to them.

'Someone take Gravebloom,' he ordered. Gustaf was loath to touch the grisly thing, but he knew there was no time for such qualms. Catching it in his hand, he dragged it down and swung it onto the ground. An instant later, he and Emelda were doing the same with Morrvahl.

'Away from here,' the wizard said.

Gustaf and Emelda offered no argument. Their late refuge was coming apart before their very eyes. Plaster and shingles pelted the ground around them. A section of wall collapsed inwards. Groans and tremors shook the structure. Gustaf could only imagine the destruction inside. It was too much to hope that Radukar would be lost in the wreck, but at least the vampire might be stopped long enough for them to get away.

Emelda gave a lingering look at the building. She glanced at her companions and turned away. Gustaf knew what she was thinking. She was evaluating the risk of going back in and trying to come to grips with Radukar. Again, it was consideration for others that made her reject the idea. She didn't want to jeopardise them to sate her own urge for revenge.

'Let's get out of here before the Ulfenwatch shows up,' Emelda told them. They hurried into the maze of alleyways and side streets that burrowed their way into the more populated slums.

'It's fortunate for you that I kept tabs on you,' Morrvahl said as they moved through the squalor. 'My... agents saw what was happening and I was able to make preparations to save you.'

Gustaf didn't like Morrvahl's tone. 'You could have warned us before we went in. Before Radukar closed his trap on us.'

'Yes, I could have,' Morrvahl admitted. 'But doing so wasn't to my advantage. You needed a reminder of my powers. A demonstration of how much you need me.'

Emelda scowled at the wizard. 'For all your vaunted magic, you didn't destroy Radukar. You ran away, just like the rest of us.'

'It is a sign of intelligence to know one's limitations,' Morrvahl said. 'I know I'm no match for the Wolf by myself. That's why I need you two. The right plan, the right preparations, and we could destroy our mutual adversary.'

'If you didn't need us, you'd have let Radukar do what he wanted,' Gustaf accused. 'You don't care a damn about anybody else.'

Morrvahl's fingers ran through his beard. There was a grey

streak in it now that hadn't been there the last time Gustaf had seen the wizard. 'Compassion is an indulgence I can't afford. My goal is too important to concern myself with what it costs to achieve it.' He wagged his finger at each of them. 'If I succeed, all civilisation will benefit. The power of Shyish will be harnessed to the betterment of mankind. That is something greater than any of us.'

'We've heard that justification before,' Emelda said.

'You don't have to like me or my motives,' Morrvahl replied. 'But at least have sense enough to realise there's much to be gained by working together.' The wizard smiled at the two of them. 'At the moment, you need a secure place to stay. Why not accept my hospitality once more?'

Gustaf shivered at the prospect, remembering the foul atmosphere in the wizard's lair... and what had happened there. At the same time, he grudgingly admitted the sense in Morrvahl's logic.

'All right,' he decided. 'We'll accept your help, but know that I don't trust you. If I even suspect you're dealing falsely with us, I won't hesitate to kill you.'

'A suspicious mind is a twisted thing,' Morrvahl said. 'But at least it is an active mind. You'll need all your wits about you when we confront the Wolf.' He gave Gustaf a mocking smile. 'Until then, you might consider what you stand to lose by acting too hastily.'

The timber that lay across Radukar's body weighed as much as one of his Kosargi, yet the vampire threw it off with little visible effort. He rose to his feet amidst the rubble of the house and surveyed the destruction. Dust covered everything and already there were rats prowling about the debris, gnawing morsels from the corpses of the destroyed Nightguard. An exertion of his power revived the failing energies of the ogors. All rallied except the one decapitated by the vampire hunter's bullet. They strained to extract themselves from the wreckage caused by their rampage. The hungry rats fled, terrified by the reanimated corpses.

Radukar glared up at the swarms of bats still circling the isolated sections of roof that hadn't caved in. The nearly mindless vermin flew off with agitated shrieks as he angrily dismissed them. The creatures had slavishly obeyed his commands, but only too well. He knew the enemies he sought hadn't been killed. He would sense their bodies lying in the rubble if it were so. That meant they'd escaped somehow, and in such a manner that the bats hadn't pursued them.

A vampire hunter from the Order of Azyr and a warrior who claimed to be the last of the Braskovs. The two had proven themselves an annoyance. Now Radukar had to add another factor, the strange wizard who'd rescued them with his spells. The advantage of surprise had been with the mummer this time. If he were so foolish as to cross paths with the Wolf again, things would be much different.

Radukar left his Nightguard to extract themselves from the rubble. He strode back into the street. He could sense mortals approaching. When he was clear of the ruins, he saw Arno and a company of Volkshaufen hurrying towards him. The Watchmaster, of course, knew where Radukar had gone. For a moment he entertained the idea that Arno had advised the wizard of the trap and sent him to rescue the others. The vampire rejected the notion. Arno's fear of Radukar bound him to his master like a chain. A loyal dog too frightened of the hand that fed it to dare show its teeth.

Arno gawked at the collapsed house when the militia drew abreast of it. He stared with awe at Radukar while the Wolf brushed dust from his cloak.

'Eminence, are you all right?'

'No,' Radukar stated. 'My prey escaped. They had unexpected

help and they escaped.' His eyes gleamed with fury. 'Next time they won't have that advantage.' He arched his eyebrow and glowered at Arno. 'You were told to keep clear of here. It is too much to hope that in your disobedience you captured my enemies?'

'I… we followed your orders, eminence,' Arno sputtered, colour draining from his face. 'None of my guards were close enough to interfere.'

'Yet here you are,' Radukar said, baring his fangs.

'But not to…' Arno shook his head. 'Eminence, I came here to report to you.'

'What was so important that you disobeyed me?' the vampire asked, taking a step towards Arno.

Arno said the only thing in that moment that could make Radukar reconsider destroying him. 'Eminence, there's been another murder. Another body has been found. Baron Grin is back!'

CHAPTER EIGHT

Blood continued to drip down the cobblestone steps outside the quayside office. The body lay crumpled against the closed door, its coat stained with gore. The head was turned, staring out towards the docks. There was no face, only a leering skull. The hallmark of Baron Grin's crimes.

Radukar's lips curled back in a sneer as he looked at the body. The militia were guarding the area, but even keeping them away from the scene couldn't curb mortal curiosity. He could hear people creeping about, lingering at the periphery. Someone had seen the body before the Volkshaufen could keep others away, or one of the guards had been loquacious. Whatever had happened, Radukar knew the rumours were already spreading, racing through the slums more quickly than the refinery fire. Baron Grin wasn't dead and he'd killed again.

This time the victim had been an exciseman. The killer had taken an extra moment to rip apart the ledger that was the tool of that profession. Nor had that been the only token of rebellion.

Across the walls had been written revolutionary screeds. Calls to rise up and depose Radukar's Thirsting Court.

The Wolf studied the carnage and felt his ire rising. The murders indeed had caused the cattle to become bold and to forget whose hand held the whip. They were seeking to force his hand before he was ready. Radukar still needed the misery of these people to feed his effort to harness the power of the Shyish Nadir. The flame of hope was one that would interfere with his plans, but he wasn't completely confident he could exterminate the slums with impunity. He had to remember that there were others in Nagash's realm interested in the power he sought. Any act on his part that smacked of weakness and those rivals might challenge him. Yes, the mortals would need a reminder of who was their master.

'You see, eminence?' Arno pointed at the corpse. 'Baron Grin again. The other body wasn't him. Or else he had an accomplice.'

'This was done to frighten people,' Radukar reminded Arno. 'So the mortals need to be taught *who* they should fear most.' He pointed to the surrounding buildings. 'I want two hundred of this scum gathered up by the Volkshaufen. They will be marched to the docks and they will be scourged until the skin has been flayed from their bodies. Their blood will be collected then their flesh will be flensed from their bones and thrown into the bay for the sharks. Leave the bones in the street.' The Wolf's face spread in a grim smile 'Perhaps the whelps of this filth could use some new playthings. A reminder that I can be magnanimous.'

'It will be done,' Arno assured his master. 'I will ensure that the execution is well attended,' he added, anticipating Radukar's wishes. 'They'll be reminded of your authority.'

The Wolf nodded and looked back at the corpse. Radukar drew a deep breath, his body thrilling to the smell he drew into his nose. 'This wasn't the work of Baron Grin, though we are meant to think so.' He gestured to the sky above and the leather-winged shapes flitting through the air. 'The guards had to chase the bats away from the body when they found it. Now they circle, hoping to swoop down and drink their fill the instant they're given the least opportunity.' He indicated the slashed leggings on the corpse and the mutilated flesh beneath. 'Rats have been at the carcass.'

Arno nodded his understanding. 'Nothing would touch any of the other bodies.'

'The corruption of the blood, the defilement of the dead, these are absent here,' Radukar said. 'The character is different, but one look at that bare skull is meant to deceive us.' A grim laugh rose from the vampire. 'As though such a crude effort could deceive me.'

'Perhaps this accomplice lacks the knowledge...' Arno started to suggest.

Radukar brushed aside Arno's thought. 'The wolf doesn't change his tracks. The other murders were not done for the sake of killing alone, nor even for the sake of rebellion.'

He was silent a moment as he considered what he'd learned. The other murders were the work of someone devoted to Khorne, with at least one other devotee still unaccounted for. No cultist of Chaos would fail to render an offering to the Dark Gods. What made this killing different wasn't a lack of knowledge but an absence of profane devotion.

Chaos and the Blood God were unfit topics to discuss with underlings, however. It was enough for Arno to understand this murder wasn't connected to the others except in the matter of mimicry. Radukar would provide a demonstration that would leave no room for doubt on that matter.

'The real killer... and any accomplice... took measures to conceal the crimes from my power,' Radukar told Arno. He brought his talon-like nail slicing across his palm. Radukar's blood dripped down onto the vacant, staring skull. The mutilated corpse twitched as he whispered an invocation above it. The shudders increased until a suggestion of motion rolled through its chest and shoulders. The denuded head tilted back, fixing its empty sockets on the one who'd summoned its spirit back into its violated husk.

'See?' Radukar smiled. 'This carcass responds to my command.' He fixed his gaze upon the skull. 'Speak,' he ordered. 'Tell me who it was that killed you.'

A raspy moan grated from the body, wheezing past its exposed teeth. 'A man... a man came upon me... struck me down from behind... the knife! The knife!'

'Your spirit left when your body died,' Radukar informed the corpse. 'But the spirit is slow to withdraw from its flesh. You lingered. You saw. You watched.'

A tortured wail escaped the corpse. 'I saw! I watched!'

'The man who did this, tell me who he was,' Radukar snarled, irked by the dead thing's shriek. Arno stood beside him, eager to hear what the corpse might reveal. The guards had withdrawn several feet, putting distance between themselves and the arcane rite unfolding before their eyes.

'I knew the man...' the corpse moaned. 'His name... is Karlion...'

Radukar listened while the spirit went on to describe Karlion. The Wolf smiled as he recognised who the man must be and why he'd committed the murder. 'This Karlion sounds like one of the group we caught in the refinery,' he informed Arno. At a gesture, he dismissed the power binding the spirit to its body. A scream of abject despair rang out. For just an instant the glowing outline of the disembodied soul was visible; then it evaporated into motes of ghostly luminance that went speeding upwards. The body it left fell down the steps, its flesh bubbling away into a necrotic sludge.

The Wolf pointed at the graffiti on the walls. 'Scrub away that filth,' he ordered Arno. 'There's the motive for this murder. Rebels trying to incite the rabble against me. Others must have escaped with Braskov and Voss.' His eyes bored into Arno's, imprisoning them with his savage gaze. 'Find them, Watchmaster, or I'll find someone who can.'

Arno nodded his head in submission. 'I'll find them, eminence. Loew assembled his people as vigilantes against Baron Grin. Now they're using the fear of Baron Grin for their own purposes.' He shrugged. 'Perhaps they always have.'

'No,' Radukar said. 'The sloppiness of this killing is too different. Someone else committed the other killings. More than one murderer. But I will find them, as I will find Braskov and Voss and their wizard friend.'

He drew his cloak about him and stalked away from the dissolving corpse.

'I will attend to them,' Radukar told Arno. 'To you I leave the lesser annoyances unworthy of my attention. I anticipate results. See that I'm not kept waiting.'

Morrvahl's sanctum was one of the last places Emelda wanted to see again. Yet here she was. The tang of the wizard's dark magic permeated the air, a foulness that slithered across her skin. She tried to quell her imagination as her mind raced with visions of the vile rites he'd performed here. Her eyes kept straying back to the table where a man had been reduced to an idiot shell by Morrvahl's spell.

'You appear upset, Lady Braskov,' Morrvahl said as he led his companions into the cellar. He favoured her with a reptilian smile, his eyes glittering with a hint of mockery. 'I can assure you my humble refuge is better than the Wolf's dungeons.'

'The cockatrice and the basilisk can both turn your flesh into stone,' Emelda told him. 'That's a Szargorondian proverb. It means just because something's bad doesn't make something else good.'

The wizard's fingers teased at the black thorns curling around his staff. 'You're alive,' he stated. 'I don't expect gratitude, but I'd appreciate pragmatism.'

Gustaf came between Emelda and Morrvahl before her temper could rise again. She hated to concede a point to the wizard, even if deep down she knew he was right. It was an ugly thing to admit they needed his powers, ruthless and macabre as they were. She could tell from Gustaf's strained expression that the vampire hunter had the same repugnance, he was just more able to suppress it.

'You've made your point, magister,' Gustaf said. 'Even the Order of Azyr admits there's utility to employing magic – your brand of dark magic – but appreciation doesn't mean approval. Your art taps into the same energies that empower Radukar. You claim it is essential for ways to be found to safely utilise the magic of Shyish in order to defend civilisation, but I remain dubious. Emelda recited an old proverb, I'll give you a more recent bit of wisdom shared among the witch hunters. "Scratch an amethyst wizard and you'll find a necromancer."'

For just a moment anger flashed across Morrvahl's face. Then the oily smile was back.

'I'll chalk that insult down to being a product of ignorance, and as with all ignorant things, pay it no further notice.' He turned and ambled back to his chair. 'You've done quite a few ignorant things since we parted ways. Joining with Loew's society was an especially reckless choice, as you've learned.'

'We were trying to recruit allies against Radukar,' Emelda snapped at the wizard. 'People who would fight against this tyranny. The vigilantes had already proven their bravery–'

Morrvahl cut her off with a derisive laugh. 'Because they were willing to look for Baron Grin you think them brave? It isn't bravery when you feel you've no choice in the matter. The killer was murdering their people. None knew whether they would be next to have their face peeled away. Self-preservation isn't courage, only a poor cousin.' The wizard stroked his long beard, smoothing it until the faint streaks of grey became lost in the darker hairs.

'Loew came to us,' Emelda said. 'He is an enemy of Radukar just like we are. With Baron Grin dead, he knew the vigilantes would break up. He wanted us to speak to them, to turn them to the fight against Radukar.'

'But look how it turned out,' Morrvahl said. 'Whether you reached too far or too fast is a matter of debate, but what is inarguable is that even if Loew wanted to, his people weren't ready for this fight. They live in slums, forced to fight for their day's bread, commanded to make profane tribute to Radukar, but there is still *life* in such degradation. That's the difference between acting against Baron Grin and Radukar. The murderer offers no choice but death. Radukar permits a chance for life as long as his authority isn't defied. The very suggestion that they should fight the Wolf is enough to turn that instinct of self-preservation against you.'

Gustaf pressed his fingers against the Sigmarite hammer he wore. 'There's little faith and little hope left in Ulfenkarn,' he murmured. 'Too little to rally the people.'

Emelda rounded on him. 'I know these people better than you. I've seen them fight and die. I've seen them struggle and overcome. You don't know what you're talking about.'

'The soldiers in your army fought for something greater than themselves,' Gustaf pointed out. 'They were defending a living city, a light shining in the darkness. That's all gone now. The shifting of the nadir destroyed it, and what was left has been ground into the dirt under Radukar's heel. There's no great purpose left to these people. Their vision has been rendered so small that they can't see beyond what they need to sustain themselves until tomorrow. To be certain there are a few who still have some capacity in them, but most are little different from the cattle at the blood farms.'

'If you'd seen the way we fought across the wilderness, you'd know better,' Emelda retorted. 'Warriors who stood fast before the most monstrous of the Blood God's abominations.'

'And if you hadn't seen those things, you'd have a clearer view of what's happened to Mournhold,' Gustaf said. 'The city that sent its army on crusade all those years ago is gone. What's left is just a shadow. A shadow of the city and its people.' Sympathy worked its way into his tone as he added a fact with which Emelda couldn't argue. 'Loew's meeting was betrayed to Radukar. So was our hideout. We know the first was by a traitor in his group. I suspect the latter was too.'

'One must be certain of one's allies,' Morrvahl declared. 'Study them carefully and choose them wisely.' He shook his head. 'Even if they'd proven true and brave, Loew's group ill suits our needs. The vigilantes were a reactive force, seeking to catch Baron Grin after he'd committed one of his crimes. That approach does us no good.' He raised his finger for emphasis as he added, 'To prevail against Radukar, everything must be planned. To fight the Wolf – and win – he must be drawn out at the right time and the right place. Both must be of our choosing, not his.'

'Your spells weren't enough to destroy Radukar before, why should they be now?' Emelda asked.

'Rescuing the two of you from the Wolf's jaws was my purpose,' Morrvahl said. 'In that you'll agree I succeeded. There was no time to prepare for that confrontation. It was a conflict of Radukar's choosing. Which again is why it is vital that when we engage him, it is under conditions that favour us.'

'Before, your plan was to figure out when and where Baron Grin would kill again,' Gustaf said. 'Then we would wait there to ambush Radukar. But with Baron Grin gone…'

Morrvahl brought the end of his staff cracking against the floor. The sound of the impact echoed through the cellar. 'Baron Grin isn't finished. That's only what the vampires and their minions want you to believe. The pattern is not yet finished. There will be more murders.'

Emelda felt a chill run through her when she looked at the intensity in the wizard's eyes. 'You say that with a note of certainty.'

'Because I am certain,' Morrvahl said. 'I've discerned the occult aspect of these crimes. There is one, I can assure you.' He nodded, more to himself than them. 'That's why Radukar has taken such personal interest. He knows someone is invoking magic even more monstrous than his own.'

'If you know so much, then you know how to stop the killings,' Emelda said.

'Stop the killings and we lose our chance at Radukar,' Morrvahl replied. 'In any great enterprise, sacrifices must be made.'

'Then the next victim will be the last,' Gustaf said. 'If you know as much as you claim to know, we can wait there. Deal with Baron Grin and Radukar when he arrives.'

Morrvahl demurred. 'I know both when and where the killer must strike to keep the pattern. I could tell you, but I won't. It would avail us nothing. We aren't ready yet. We have to let this opportunity pass. Baron Grin must be left to ply his terrible trade a little longer.'

The callousness of the wizard's remark sent a cold fury racing through Emelda's veins. 'People are going to die and you say we must do nothing to stop it. How long? How long must we do nothing?'

'Until I say we're ready to fight the Wolf,' Morrvahl said. 'Until I say that the time is right to act.' He sank back in his chair and closed his eyes. 'Now you must let me rest. I expended quite a bit of my resources rescuing you. I must replenish my energies.' He waved his hand dismissively and was soon in a somnolent trance.

'I understand better why there are some witch hunters who

think there are no good wizards,' Gustaf told Emelda. She followed him away towards the alcoves at the back of the cellar. Even asleep, Morrvahl's presence was unsettling.

No. More than unsettling. Threatening.

It was then that a horrible connection occurred to Emelda.

Gustaf was surprised by the strange look that came over Emelda. It was an expression of sudden horror that gave her a haunted appearance. She turned her frightened gaze back towards the sleeping wizard. A shiver ran through her, a gesture of physical revulsion.

'What is it?' Gustaf asked her, unsure if he really wanted to know what could provoke such a reaction in the swordswoman.

Emelda slowly met his gaze. 'Morrvahl,' she said. 'I think he's Baron Grin.'

'That's not poss–'

Gustaf stopped himself as he tried to reject the idea out of hand. What did they really know about Morrvahl, after all? They'd seen ample evidence of his ruthlessness. Was it really such a stretch to believe him responsible for the string of ghastly murders?

'Consider his reaction when we told him Baron Grin was dead,' Emelda reminded him. 'Morrvahl didn't even try to think about how that would affect our plans. It seemed to me he just wanted to stay the course. Go on as though nothing had changed.'

Gustaf nodded. 'Which would be true if he knew for certain that Baron Grin was still alive.' He nodded again as he turned over the thought in his mind. 'Letting word get around to the people would lessen their unrest. We saw that with Loew's group. It would've suited Radukar to let that story spread, whether it was true or not.'

'Morrvahl knew it wasn't true because he's behind the murders,' Emelda said, her mouth curled with disgust. 'He's butchering people to draw Radukar into a trap. Using them like bait.'

'A ruthless monster,' Gustaf said, but with no conviction in his tone. He was thinking of how often the Order of Azyr was forced to weigh the good they hoped to achieve against the suffering they must inflict to reach their goal. Was what Morrvahl was doing so very different? The sacrifice of the few for the benefit of the many. 'No,' he corrected himself. 'You must be wrong, Emelda. This is too awful to contemplate. Morrvahl can't be Baron Grin.'

'Think about it, Gustaf,' she said, highlighting each point with a raised finger. 'We know there's an occult factor to the killings, otherwise the vampires would already have tracked down the murderer. We've already seen that Morrvahl's magic can hide him from Radukar. We know the wizard has his own foul spies to watch what goes on in Ulfenkarn. It would be easy for him to find victims for Baron Grin's knife. Then there's the barbaric nature of the murders themselves. Morrvahl spoke of a pattern and a purpose to the crimes, veiled details about designated times and places... and arcane rites more debased than necromancy. That was what set my mind on edge. His words reminded me of things I've seen before.'

'What things?' Gustaf asked. His voice was uneasy. He had a suspicion as to what connection it was that Emelda had drawn.

'I saw much of the handiwork of the marauder tribes when I was on campaign,' Emelda said. 'The filthy offerings they rendered up to Khorne.' She invoked the obscene name with a low hiss. 'The slaves of Chaos revere that fiend as not only the Blood God, but also the Skull Lord.'

'The flayed faces,' Gustaf whispered. 'All the flesh peeled away to expose the skull beneath.'

'An offering to the Skull Lord,' Emelda affirmed. 'A sacrifice to Khorne. Baron Grin fights against Radukar by invoking an even greater evil.'

Gustaf closed his hand tight about the hammer icon he wore, drawing strength from that symbol of Sigmar against the horror of Emelda's words. 'In the Realm of Azyr those who study magic are carefully supervised and mentored lest their minds wander into wicked places, but such structure isn't possible in places like Shyish. There are few to monitor what roads a wizard might travel in his researches. It's possible Morrvahl has learned the blood rites of Khorne, and in his obsession to harness the energies of the nadir he's convinced himself that even the obscenity of Chaos is a tool he can use.' Gustaf stamped his boot against the floor. 'The fool!' he cursed. 'As though anything but corruption can emerge from Chaos.'

'It leaves us with the problem of what to do about him,' Emelda said. 'Even if we were resigned to letting Baron Grin persist so that we could trap Radukar, we can't let him render sacrifices to Khorne.'

Gustaf took his pistol from his belt and started to load it. His eyes strayed back to the sleeping wizard. 'We know he's tired now. Fatigued from the magic he expended rescuing us from Radukar. If we're to act against him, now is the time.' He made a warning gesture to Emelda. 'Before we move, we must be certain. Are we sure of this, or is it our prejudice against Morrvahl colouring our judgement? Making us draw connections that we otherwise wouldn't see? We have to be sure, because there's no going back. Once we move, we have to see it through.'

Before Emelda could proffer an answer they both heard a subdued murmur percolate down into the cellar. It was the muffled growl of angry voices from the building above them. Gustaf motioned for silence and the two of them strained their ears to make sense of the distorted sounds. While the voices remained the most predominant, Gustaf could discern other noises. Hurried footsteps. The crash of heavy objects being pushed over. Combined, they formed a familiar whole to the vampire hunter's ears.

'A mob's searching the building above,' he whispered to Emelda.

'The Volkshaufen?' she asked.

Gustaf finished charging his pistol, ramming the cloth wadding down the barrel to keep the ball in place. 'I don't know,' he confessed. The militia were little more than a rabble themselves, but the sounds he was hearing struck him as too disorganised even for them. One thing was certain: whoever was up there was looking for something, and he could easily guess what. Morrvahl's lair had been discovered and they were looking for a way down into the wizard's sanctum.

'One thing we can be certain of,' Emelda said, pointing at the ceiling. 'That means trouble.'

A grimace worked itself onto Gustaf's face as he realised something. 'The only way out of here is up there. Through them.' His gaze drifted back to Morrvahl. The clamour from above hadn't disturbed the wizard's trance and he continued to sleep. 'At least the only way out that we know of.'

'You think he has some secret way out?' Emelda wondered. The noise from above was growing more violent as the mob's search intensified.

'We made sure to have a back way out,' Gustaf reminded her. 'Even if Radukar outguessed us, it was still there. But there's one quick way to find out. We wake Morrvahl up and ask him.'

Gustaf was starting back across the cellar when a tremulous groan shook through the chamber. Light poured down as the hidden door above the stairs was pulled open. Excited voices shouted in triumph and men rushed down the steps. They were a motley assortment, a mixture of stevedores and whalers, muckrakers and fishermen. A few carried whale-oil lanterns, but most bore crude torches fashioned from sticks and rags. Cudgels were the mainstay of their arms, but here and there Gustaf spotted a hatchet or a dirk, even a few swords. In one respect, however, the mob had uniformity, and that was in the raw hate on their faces.

Gustaf and Emelda turned to face the mob as they rushed down the stairs. The vampire hunter was surprised to recognise the man leading them. He was Karlion, one of Loew's vigilantes.

'Hold, Karlion!' he called out. 'What's this about?'

Karlion answered Gustaf's hail by spitting on the floor. 'There they are!' he shouted to the mob behind him. He pointed at Morrvahl in his chair. 'Baron Grin!' he denounced the sleeping wizard. Then his finger swung around and gestured to Gustaf and Emelda. 'And his accomplices!'

Emelda whipped her sword from its sheath. Gustaf took aim with his horse pistol.

'Get back!' he shouted. He didn't know what Karlion had told these people to bring them here, but he knew there was no reasoning with an enraged mob. Only a show of force could keep them back. 'You'll not take us without a fight!' He wagged the pistol at Karlion. 'You'll be the first to die,' he warned.

Karlion started forwards in defiance of Gustaf's warning. He took only a few steps before the vampire hunter pulled the trigger. Smoke and flame erupted from the mouth of his pistol. The agitator was still standing when the smoke cleared away. His face was pale and for a moment he bore a stunned expression. But there was no mark from a bullet on his chest where Gustaf had aimed his shot.

'Misfire,' Karlion growled. He waved his mob forwards. In a fierce snarl he gave his men their command. 'Kill the butchering scum!'

CHAPTER NINE

Night spread its ebon wings across Ulfenkarn. From forgotten crypts and hidden lairs obscene things stirred, goaded into motion by a remorseless hunger. The living cowered behind locked doors and shuttered windows, trembling at every sound that penetrated to their refuges, wondering if this would be the night when the barriers failed and they would fall victim to the horrors of their haunted city.

Only the most desperate dared to defy the curfew imposed on them by their rulers and brave the manifold terrors of the darkness. In the squalor of the slums there were always those whose existence was so tenuous, so fragile, that the hazards of the night weren't any worse than the dangers that threatened them by day. Even the rumours that Baron Grin wasn't dead and had returned to his gory trade weren't enough to keep them at home. In each there was the reassuring whisper, the rationalisation that it would always be someone else who paid the price.

Radukar well knew that dulling cadence, that urge to pacified complacency. It was the indifference of the herd to a stalking predator, the appreciation that only one would be needed to feed the hunter and that it was no great gamble to play the odds. He'd seen that mindset in many places before he brought the *Impaler's Gift* to Ulfenkarn. Villages and towns across Shyish where mortals eked out an existence in the very shadow of a vampire's castle, content that when the undead grew hungry some neighbour would be the one to die in the night. It was his experience that such snivelling apathy came normally to humans. It took a remarkable individual to inspire them to greatness, to instil in them the hope that could lead them to better things.

As he looked across the slumland of Ulfenkarn, Radukar reflected upon his success in rooting out such people. The old leadership had been obliterated after the Shyish Nadir opened above the city and wrought disaster upon it. Those not killed outright existed now as his minions. It would need new leaders to stir the populace, champions he'd always been able to hunt down before they could become any real threat to his dominion.

At least until now. Radukar brooded upon the many enemies that had arisen to challenge him of late. Emelda Braskov and her allies were an irritation that had the potential at least to become a menace. The swordswoman was a living link to Ulfenkarn's past and as such could become a symbol of the city's vanished glory. A symbol was even more effective at instilling hope than a person was. By her mere existence, Emelda could chip away at the chains of despair Radukar had cast around the mortals. Conversely, the more hope she inspired, the more devastating would be the effect once she did fall prey to the Wolf.

The others posed a more direct threat. Gustaf Voss, the Sigmarite crusader. Radukar had dealt with that kind before. Zealots who stubbornly persisted when a reasonable mind would accept defeat. Loew, the rabble-rouser with his proto-rebels. There too was an enemy that allowed tenacity to overwhelm prudence. Finally he considered the mysterious wizard who'd snatched away Emelda and Gustaf even as he closed his trap around them. There was a troublesome enigma. Radukar wondered what the mystic's motivations were.

Tonight's problem, however, lay in a different quarter. The killer the mortals had named Baron Grin. It was that scent the Wolf followed now. Perhaps the trail would cross that of his other foes or maybe it would lead him farther afield. Radukar knew only that the stink of Khorne was heavy about the murderer. A conspiracy of slaughter and profane sacrifice. At least one more devotee of Chaos was abroad in Ulfenkarn, of this he was certain. Soon that acolyte of evil must act. Like a vampire's thirst, the bloodlust of Khorne's disciples couldn't be denied for long. The urge to kill was so strong in those who venerated the Skull Lord that if they found no other victims they would turn on themselves in their madness. It had been several nights since the double killing. By now the compulsion to kill must be consuming Baron Grin's last vestiges of restraint.

This night, the vampire was certain, Baron Grin would try to kill again.

Radukar drew his fur cloak close about him, drawing himself into the shadows within the cupola. The vantage he'd chosen for himself was high atop a crumbling manse, an old widow's tower rising from the roof to overlook Banshee's Bay so that those left ashore might keep watch for their loved one's ship returning from a voyage. His eyes were turned not towards the sea, but inland. He watched the darkened streets and the deserted avenues, vigilant for the least sign of disturbance. He knew it would be something subtle, something easily missed, that would betray the killer. He had to watch for that little mistake, that error which would put Baron Grin within his reach.

Ugly flocks of bats flittered through the darkened sky. Radukar's keen eyes could pick out their wizened bodies and leathery wings easily, but he knew that to mortals they'd be all but invisible in the night. Only a whisper of motion and perhaps the gleam of bared fangs and crimson eyes. The hungry clouds of flying rodents could smell the slightest drop of blood from half a mile away. The fountains in which the mortals paid their tithe to Radukar's court were especially designed to ward off the bats, but those who foolishly defied the curfew had no such protection. The merest scratch might send a storm of ravenous fiends descending upon the victim.

While he watched, Radukar saw some of the bats wheel about in their flight and dart downwards. He knew the diversion meant some creature had drawn their notice. Human or otherwise, something was calling to them with its blood. These incidents attracted his notice only as far as they might be the prelude to what he was waiting for.

The expected moment came during the desolate hours beyond midnight. A cloud of bats started downwards to attack wounded prey. As suddenly as their dive began the animals were speeding upwards again, frightened chirps echoing about the rooftops as they scattered and fled. Radukar knew what had driven them away. The blood they'd thought to feed upon was corrupt, infected with the evil of Chaos. Baron Grin had set upon this night's victim.

The Wolf sprang into motion. A leap brought him hurtling from the widow's tower, his cloak billowing about him like great wings. He dropped down to the tile roof of a former guild hall, but only for the briefest instant did he linger there. Exhibiting a speed unmatched by mortal man, the vampire dashed across the roof. When he reached its edge he flung himself across the breadth of the intervening street to gain the top of the building opposite. From roof to roof Radukar ran, a predator on the hunt. Always he kept his eyes upon the distant spot from which the hungry bats had fled. It wasn't long before his goal was at hand.

Below Radukar was the residue of an old garden. Dead trees and ragged bushes sprouted from the grey earth, weeds choked stone benches and marble statues. Amid the desolation, a figure was sprawled across the ground. Above the prostrate man, a dark shape was crouched. The vampire could see the wicked knife clenched in the hand that sank against the victim's head. He could smell the filth that now tainted the blood seeping from the murdered wretch.

Without the least sound to betray him, Radukar dropped down into the garden. He could see the killer's hand playing the cruel edge of the knife across the murdered man, flaying the flesh from his face. Anger flared within him as he stalked towards the cloaked shape.

'You presume to destroy my property,' Radukar snarled. 'Such presumption ends now.'

As he spoke, the vampire lunged forwards, intent on seizing the killer in his iron grip. Radukar was surprised to find his enemy quick enough to defy him. The murderer spun around as he closed in and the bloodstained knife licked out. He turned his lunge into a sideways twist and the gory blade ripped across his arm. Pain surged through him, hot and sizzling. There was an obscene energy in the assassin's steel, a power profane enough to defile even a vampire's flesh.

Radukar reeled back, growling in pain. He readied himself for the murderer's next attack, but instead of rushing at him, the hooded killer ran across the garden and rapidly scrambled up into the branches of a dead tree. Again the vampire was stunned by the speed of his foe. The bestial kurnothi or the verminous skaven might move with such haste, but it wasn't a thing to be expected of a human, at least not a mortal one. Radukar's senses told him it was human blood that rushed through his enemy's veins, albeit with a tainted quality that set it apart. He knew there were certain herbs and potions that could excite a mortal's vigour in such a manner, but he suspected a far darker reason behind the assassin's swiftness.

The murderer reached the top of the tree and from that perch threw himself at the nearest building. His hands caught the edge of the roof. For an instant he clung there, feet kicking against the wall until he secured his grip and lifted himself upwards.

Radukar pursued the fleeing killer. A single leap carried the vampire from the floor of the garden to the rooftop. He glared at the hooded shape as it raced across the shingle.

'There is no escape,' Radukar jeered at the assassin. The vampire charged after his quarry, but they maintained an incredible pace, jumping from roof to roof with the agility of a cat. Radukar stayed close behind, gradually lessening the distance between them. When he could hear the agitated breathing of his prey, he knew the hunt was as good as over.

The killer reached the same realisation at almost the same time. Ahead was a gap between buildings, much as others the murderer had leapt before. This time, however, the assassin didn't jump forwards but instead swung back around. The gruesome knife flashed out once again, slashing across Radukar's cloak and striking sparks as it scraped his steel breastplate. The vampire struck out with his clawed hand, ripping the hood and slashing the scalp beneath.

He gazed in astonishment at the face revealed by the torn hood.

The murderer was a young woman, scarcely more than a girl. She might have been pretty once, Radukar thought, but any alluring quality was eradicated by the corrupt tang of the blood flowing from her torn scalp and the foul emblem that had been carved into her forehead. It was a symbol Radukar knew only too well. The Skull Rune, the profane sign of Khorne.

The knife ripped out at Radukar, flashing down across his arm and biting into his leg. Stolen blood bubbled from his cuts as searing agony raced through him. He could smell the vile corruption seeking to seep into his body.

'Khorne cares not whence the blood flows!' the woman screamed, her eyes blazing with fanaticism. She slashed at Radukar again with her blade.

'The blood of Ulfenkarn belongs to me!' the vampire snarled.

Radukar pivoted away from the murderer's attack and brought his hand cracking against her arm. The bone shattered beneath the superhuman might of the undead. The knife flew free from her grip and skittered across the shingles. The woman shrieked, more in outrage than pain, and plunged after the fallen weapon.

Radukar's fingers caught the killer's cloak in a steely grip and arrested her dive from the roof. Ignoring the pain surging through his own body, he lifted her towards him. She writhed and twisted, kicking at him with her feet.

'You've defied the Blood God too long, defiler!' the murderer raged. 'Your hour is over! You are finished, grave-worm!'

Radukar's hand smacked across the killer's face. The blow was sharp enough to stagger an ogor. Whether enhanced by potions or spells, her stamina now wilted. Her eyes rolled back in her head and she sagged limp in his grip.

'It is you who are finished,' Radukar hissed through clenched fangs. He felt his body slowly expelling the blood corrupted by the tainted blade. Unlike a mortal, he could get more to replace it. But it wouldn't be from the murdering filth he held in his hand. He had other plans for her.

'You will have much to tell me before I settle with you,' Radukar promised. 'Perhaps, if your answers satisfy me, there will be an end to the torture. But I'd not trust too keenly on my mercy.'

Radukar slung the senseless body across his shoulder and turned back towards the Ebon Citadel. His suspicions about Baron Grin had been proven. There'd been more than one killer and they were devotees of Chaos. Now there remained another factor to determine.

How many others belonged to this Khornate cult and was there some greater objective behind these profane sacrifices?

Emelda had faced many enemies in battle, but never before had she felt as sickened by the prospect of bloodshed as she did now. The mob that had penetrated into Morrvahl's sanctum weren't Chaos-worshipping barbarians or Radukar's treacherous thralls. These were people of Ulfenkarn, her people, those who yet had the spine to rise up and fight. The thought of crossing swords with them was repugnant. They should be allies, as they had been before.

She was even more disgusted because she couldn't discount Karlion's outcry. He might be right. Morrvahl *could* be Baron Grin. If anyone was callous enough to murder innocents to further his own ends, it was the wizard.

Whatever agreement she might feel, Emelda knew it would do no good. The mob wouldn't be swayed by words now. Karlion had whipped them into a frenzy. All that would satisfy them was the death of Baron Grin – and anyone associated with him. Repellent though the prospect was, she had no choice but to fight.

The mob surged forwards when Gustaf's pistol misfired. Both because of Karlion's command and the antagonism of that wasted shot, they rushed towards the vampire hunter rather than Emelda. Had they been a coordinated and disciplined force, the mob would've made certain to divert some of their number against her. As it stood, she was for the instant unopposed.

Trained or not, Emelda knew the numbers of the mob must overwhelm her own skills in any prolonged fight. She'd have to strike the head from the serpent if they were to have any chance at all.

She felt guilty leaving Gustaf to his own devices as she skirted around the crowd and darted past their advance. The vampire hunter met the rush with his sword, gashing one ruffian's shoulder. The butt of his pistol cracked the nose of a second man and spilled the stunned antagonist to the floor, tripping those who followed after him.

Emelda noted the initial part of the fight only with her peripheral vision. She focused instead on her immediate objective. Karlion was leading this mob, and with the assumption of command he was keeping himself clear of the fray. When he directed his men to charge ahead, he stayed back. By fixating on Gustaf, they'd left an opening for Emelda to reach the vigilante, a gap in their lines she hurried to exploit.

One ruffian swung around as Emelda ran past him. She drove the pommel of her sword into his throat and left him gasping on the ground. Karlion spotted the disturbance and realised his peril. He shouted to his followers and turned to meet Emelda. Her sword licked out, slashing his hand and sending his weapon clattering across the floor. She sprang forwards and caught hold of him. The point of her blade was at his neck.

'Call them off or I'll stick you like a pig,' Emelda threatened. The vigilante gaped at her, his eyes round with fright.

'You'll be lowering your sword,' a gruff voice snarled.

Emelda turned about, keeping her blade against Karlion. The speaker was one of the ruffians, a bloodied club clenched in his fist. Slumped down on his knees before the man was Gustaf, a crimson stream flowing down his face from under the brim of his hat. The thug who'd struck him had one hand locked about the collar of his coat. He jerked back on the garment and forced a groan from his captive.

'Surrender, or I'll brain your friend.'

Emelda met the ruffian's challenge with a cold glare. 'You intend to kill us all anyway, so what's the difference?' she snapped. When some of the mob moved towards her, she pressed her sword closer to Karlion's neck and sent a trickle of blood running down it.

An ugly laugh rose from Karlion. 'You overplayed your hand, Braskov. I led them here, but you're a fool if you think they value me enough to let Baron Grin escape.'

Karlion's prompting caused Emelda to glance away from Gustaf's plight. She'd been mistaken thinking the mob was focused solely on the vampire hunter. Four men had rushed across the cellar to Morrvahl's seat. Whether from fear of the wizard or their horror of Baron Grin, they remained a few feet away from the chair, but each of them had a weapon in his hands. They needed only the slightest push to overcome their trepidation. As great as her animosity towards Morrvahl, she didn't want to see him butchered while he slept.

Emelda's mind raced, trying to find a way clear of the impasse. Before she could, Karlion shouted to the men surrounding Morrvahl.

'Kill him! Kill Baron Grin!'

The command nerved the ruffians for what they'd hesitated to do. A man dashed in with a knife, driving it towards Morrvahl's belly.

Before the blow could land, however, the thorns wound about Gravebloom flared into sinister motion. They crackled around the man's arm, biting into his flesh. The knife fell from his fingers as the panicked ruffian tried to pull away. The thorns held fast, digging themselves deeper. A horrible pallor crept over him and he twisted around, imploring his comrades for help. The other men retreated in horror, unwilling to risk themselves to save their companion.

Emelda knew the wizard's scythe was leeching vitality from the ruffian, feeding his energy back into Morrvahl. She'd seen it once before... and the awful aftermath when it was left unchecked. She actually felt a sense of relief when Morrvahl opened his eyes and the thorns released their victim. The man crumpled to the floor, pale and withered, while the wizard's face was flushed with the glow of stolen life. He scowled down at the man who'd tried to kill him then turned his fierce gaze on the rest of the mob. A sardonic smile spread across his visage.

'About now, you're realising how stupid this was,' Morrvahl jeered.

'He's Baron Grin! Think of your families!' Karlion's shouts sputtered into a moan of pain when Emelda cracked his head with her sword's pommel. The vigilante wilted to the floor, but his cries had already done their damage. A moment before the mob had been ready to rout. Now they rallied once more to their purpose.

'Death! Death to the murderer!' the crowd roared.

Emelda shoved Karlion into the midst of the ruffians who charged towards her. While they floundered under his weight, she dashed past them and attacked the man holding Gustaf. The edge of her sword raked across the hand gripping the cudgel and sent fingers bouncing across the floor. The enemy shrieked and hugged his mangled hand against his chest. Emelda brought her boot kicking into his knee and sent him crashing to the floor. She made a grab for Gustaf, but as she did she felt the air within the cellar turn cold. A chill she knew was the sign of magic being invoked.

Emelda's eyes were drawn back to Morrvahl. The mockery of a moment before was gone, blotted out by an expression of severity. The flush of health that had been drawn into him by Gravebloom's thorns was ebbing away. The dark lustre of his beard was again streaked with grey. The swordswoman shuddered, wondering what terrible spell he was conjuring that would demand such energy from him.

The mob was starting towards Morrvahl, but their drive had faltered. Before they could regain their fury, the wizard unleashed his magic. A familiar black mist swirled through the cellar, bringing with it the anguished wail of tormented souls. Cold fear rushed through Emelda. She recalled only too well the carnage that had ravaged the Nightguard and the wizard's warning that the destructive force was indiscriminate in its wrath, striking both friend and foe. She tightened her hold on Gustaf and tried to hurry away from the gathering storm.

The black mist hurtled into the mob, slamming into them in a wailing torrent. Men screamed as the spell wracked their bodies. Emelda cried out as she felt phantom claws scratching at her, piercing her flesh to attack her vital spirit. Gustaf thrashed free from her grasp, howling in pain. The agony of the spell snapped him back to awareness. He looked about, frantic for some means of escape.

From the magic Morrvahl had unleashed, it seemed there was no escape. Emelda saw strands of material, like wisps of gossamer, being drawn out of her. She felt it being stolen, drained away by the black mist. All around, the ruffians of the mob were screaming, their own spectral essence seeping out from their skin. To Emelda's eyes, they were diminishing, somehow lessening in a way she couldn't fathom. It was like watching a block of ice melt, but at the same time she knew there was no physical change. What was being taken from them was their essence, the spark of their souls. And she knew the same ghastly thing was happening to her!

'Sigmar guard me!' Gustaf shouted, his hands clasped about the icon he wore. For just an instant the strands being drawn out of him froze, as though his prayer had arrested the power of the spell. Then he crumpled against the ground as the horrible process redoubled itself.

Emelda faltered, slumping to her knees. She couldn't withstand the pain any longer. Around her she saw the mob was faring no better. Men lay curled on the ground, sobbing as Morrvahl's magic afflicted them. Not one of them was still on his feet.

As suddenly as the black mist had been conjured, it was banished.

Emelda gagged as the essence that had been draining out of her abruptly came rushing back. Her head reeled with the swift transition, her body convulsed with agonised spasms. Around her, she could see the ruffians writhing in torment.

'Braskov, Voss!' Morrvahl snarled over the groans and cries of the mob. 'On your feet! Hasten!'

Emelda struggled to rise. She found her sword lying beside her and grabbed it with a hand that felt as though it had been buried in snow. She shook her head, trying to clear the medley of conflicting sensations.

'Hurry,' the wizard enjoined them. His tone was weary and Emelda noted that he was leaning on Gravebloom, using the scythe to keep himself upright.

Gustaf staggered onto his feet and helped Emelda up from the ground. 'Help Morrvahl,' he told her before turning and dashing off. Emelda stumbled through the groaning ruin of the mob. It was an effort not to trip over the writhing figures. At last she reached Morrvahl. The wizard's face was drawn, his beard shot through with grey.

'Magic is a vicious servant and a merciless master,' the wizard said. His body felt almost weightless when he leaned against Emelda's shoulder, as though he were more wraith than flesh. The contact sent a new shudder through her.

'That way,' Morrvahl directed her. He pointed to a section of the wall behind his now overturned chair. 'Before they recover.'

'Then they won't die?' Emelda asked.

'Killing them would have meant killing you,' Morrvahl answered. 'That would interrupt my plans.' A spasm of pain twisted his face. 'Though constraining the soulstorm's hunger may have been injudicious.'

Emelda swung around when she heard someone rushing towards them. She was relieved to see it was Gustaf. The vampire hunter gripped his sword and pistol. 'Couldn't leave these behind,' he said with a smile.

'They're starting to revive,' Emelda warned, nodding at the mob. The spasms of pain were lessening and a few of the men were now sitting up.

Morrvahl gestured with Gravebloom at the wall. 'The sixth stone from the bottom. The one smaller than those around it. Press it, Voss!'

Gustaf did as the wizard bade him. He slapped the indicated stone with the butt of his pistol. Immediately the wall swung back, propelled inwards by some hidden hinge. A filthy stench came rushing into the cellar. Emelda could just make out a dark passageway behind the wall.

'The old sewers,' Morrvahl said. 'They lead under the whole district. That's our way out.'

Gustaf grabbed a lantern off the wall and led the way into the tunnel. Emelda helped Morrvahl through. The brick-lined channel was just wide enough for them all. The ground under their feet, however, was nothing but a crusted mat of filth that cracked and split at their least step, letting fresh vapours add to the loathsome smell.

'Close the door,' Morrvahl told Gustaf. The vampire hunter tried to swing the stone panel back, but it resisted him. The wizard propped himself against the wall and motioned for Emelda to help.

'It won't budge,' Emelda reported when their combined efforts failed to move it. 'The mechanism must be broken.'

Raised voices sounded from the cellar. Among them Emelda could pick out that of Karlion, trying to rally his followers. Even if the mob had been too dazed to see their escape, it wouldn't take them long to figure out where they'd gone.

'We've got to get out of here,' Emelda told her companions. She wasn't sure how rattled Gustaf was from his head wound, but from the look of Morrvahl they couldn't draw on his magic any time soon. 'They'll be after us.'

Morrvahl reached beneath his robes and drew out a small bag. A wicked look wormed its way onto his face. 'If they follow us, they'll regret it.' He looked from Emelda to Gustaf. 'Stay close to me, or you'll have something to regret as well.' He leaned against Emelda for support as the three of them scurried down the tunnel.

'There they are!' Karlion's voice shouted before they'd gone more than a dozen yards. Emelda looked back to see the vigilante and several of his men standing at the secret door, torches and weapons in their hands. The mob surged into the sewer and started after the refugees.

'No,' Morrvahl hissed at her when she reached for her sword. 'We'll let others fight them for us.' His eyes glistened with savage mirth. 'Keep close to me,' he said again. The wizard drew open the bag he carried and hurled its contents towards Karlion's mob.

Emelda saw what looked like a cloud of dust explode from the bag. By the torchlight she could see a shimmering haze settle about the walls and floor, even a few of the men coated in the substance. The mob drew back, shouting in alarm, but when no immediate distress afflicted them, they came running forwards again. Whatever the wizard had intended, Emelda thought it had failed.

Then the rats came. She saw first one then another snout poke up from the filth on the floor. Beady red eyes glimmered in the light, wicked yellow fangs clicked hungrily. She saw whiskers twitching as the vermin smelled the powder Morrvahl had thrown. Whatever abominable sustenance the rats were scavenging for in the sewer, now they'd been enticed from their burrows by a more appealing scent.

At first only a few rats erupted from the floor. Huge and hideous, their bodies distorted by the necrotic rot of the things upon which they fed, the vermin squealed and chittered as they scampered towards the mob. The foremost of the ruffians struck at them with their torches, jeering when their bestial foes were struck down.

It was a momentary triumph. In place of those first few, dozens of rats pawed their way to the surface. From burrows in the ground and holes in the walls they came, spilling into the sewer in their hundreds. Now the jeers of the mob became panicked screams. Emelda watched in disgust as a giant rat threw itself on one man, gnawing at him with its chisel fangs. Overcome by fear and revulsion, the man dropped his torch and tried to tear away his attacker. Instantly a score of the creatures were leaping at him, dragging him down with their weight.

'You can't help him,' Morrvahl told Emelda. Until he spoke she hadn't realised she was trying to pull away. Instinctively she was revolted by such a despicable fate. The wizard drew her attention away from the man's doom. 'It would be fatal to leave me now.'

As he spoke, Emelda realised that the rats weren't just around Karlion's mob. Swarms of the creatures were rushing past them, scurrying through the sewer to join the attack.

'While you stay with me, they won't come near you,' Morrvahl said. He raised his voice to be heard over the screams of Karlion's men. The mob was trying to flee back into the cellar, but the vermin were hot on their heels.

'Afraid of making themselves sick if they eat you?' Emelda countered.

The wizard smiled at her and waved his hand. 'By all means, find your own way out. If you think you can. But if the two of you can abide my company a bit longer, I could lead you to another of my sanctums. You see, I'm much too cautious to maintain only one hideout.'

Morrvahl laughed, a sound that under the circumstances was more monstrous than the snarls of the rats.

'One never knows when unexpected visitors will show up. Or what measures must be taken to dispose of them.'

INTERLUDE 5

The quayside shack was as miserable and dilapidated a bolthole as Karlion could imagine. The smell of dead fish gave it a reek almost as bad as the old sewer he'd so recently escaped. The place was also infested with rats, and the sound of them scampering in the rafters made his skin crawl and sent a chill down his spine. The image of the men dragged down by the sewer vermin was much too vivid in his mind. Only by being faster than his comrades had he avoided sharing their fate. Of the twenty men who'd pursued the wizard and his companions, only five had emerged unscathed. In that regard, Karlion could count himself one of the lucky ones.

He pulled the blanket tighter around himself as the bitter bite of the freezing night snaked through the ramshackle walls. Lucky? Karlion didn't feel particularly lucky. The followers he'd assembled to attack the wizard's hideout were either dead or wanted nothing more to do with him. Loew was of a similar opinion, livid that Karlion had led a mob against Emelda and Gustaf. It was further proof to Karlion that Loew lacked the vision and determination to build a real rebellion against Radukar. He lacked the stomach for the ugly necessities and subterfuge attendant to any chance of success.

Karlion had no such scruples. There wasn't any limit to what he'd do to rid Ulfenkarn of the vampires. But his ruthlessness had backfired on him. First there had been Radukar's brutal retaliation against the area where the murder was staged. That had made the people cower in their homes as much as they could. He'd been warned that the Volkshaufen was looking for him. Somehow his role in the murder of the exciseman, a crime he'd intended to be blamed on Baron Grin, had been discovered. Now Watchmaster Arno was searching the slums for Karlion. Instead of rallying followers to his cause, he'd made himself a target.

The militia was trouble enough, but Karlion knew the slums were teeming with spies ready to report him for a crust of bread. There were few friends he considered close enough to trust not to betray him, and most of them had died in the sewer.

'Quiet! Nagash rot you!' Karlion snarled, throwing an old bottle at the scampering rats. He felt a twinge of contentment when the vermin squeaked in fear and scattered. Then his mind turned back to the fiasco in the wizard's cellar.

Karlion was almost certain Morrvahl and Baron Grin were one and the same. He was less sure if Emelda and Gustaf were his helpers or his dupes, but when he'd led his mob down into the cellar he'd decided it was best to consider them enemies as well. How different things would have been if the fight had turned out in his favour. That mob would have become the core of a movement, a revolution that would cast off the tyranny of Radukar. Instead it had all exploded in his face and he'd been forced to run and hide.

The sound of footsteps outside his hideout snapped Karlion from his reverie. His hand curled around the grip of a dagger and he scrambled behind a broken crate. From this vantage he could watch the only door into the shack.

Three knocks against the wall followed by two against the door itself eased Karlion's anxiety somewhat. It was the signal he'd given to his friend. If he was going to avoid the Volkshaufen and Radukar's spies, he had to stay undercover. To do that he needed a confederate to bring him provisions.

Karlion rapped the side of his knife against the crate twice, giving the counter-signal. He was too wary to lower the weapon or emerge from cover. There was only so much trust he'd put in anyone, even a friend.

The door slowly opened and a figure slipped into the darkened shack. There was enough light in the shadowy hovel for Karlion to note that his visitor's arms were empty. No visible weapons, but no bundles of the expected provisions either.

'Where are you?' a familiar voice whispered.

'Where's the food you were supposed to bring me?' Karlion replied.

The figure turned towards him. He could see the man's head shake from side to side. 'I left it behind,' he answered. 'This place isn't safe for you. A spy told Arno about it. The Volkshaufen will be here soon.'

'Nagash take all traitors,' Karlion hissed, thinking of Witalas and the betrayal of the vigilantes. His eyes narrowed with suspicion. 'How do I know you didn't tell them I was here?'

His confederate laughed. 'Would I risk myself coming to you, or stand back and count my money while the militia did all the work?'

Karlion had to concede the logic. He stepped out from behind cover but kept a firm grip on his dagger. 'Where will I go?'

'I've already arranged something,' his friend assured him. 'Nobody will find you.'

Karlion let his friend lead the way. Cautiously they exited the shack and crept into the icy street. In the distance, they could hear the clatter of armour as a patrol of Ulfenwatch prowled the waterfront. Karlion wondered if the skeletons were coming to surround the shack. It seemed to him the sound of their march was moving away rather than coming closer, but he also knew how deceptive sounds could be in the empty, echoing streets of Ulfenkarn.

His friend urged him down the deserted passageways, moving from streets to alleys and from alleys to narrow runs barely wide enough for a dog. Karlion took comfort in the circuitous, difficult course. It would make tracking him difficult for the Volkshaufen. Then he frowned. The militia might be lost, but their masters had more occult methods of finding their prey.

'This place,' Karlion said. 'Will it be safe from the vampires?'

'As safe as any place in the city can be,' his companion told him. 'Until we're delivered from Radukar's tyranny. But that will demand much blood before it happens.'

Karlion nodded. 'I'm surprised to hear you talk of rebellion. You refused to join Loew's group.'

'Hunting Baron Grin?' The other man sighed. 'A delusion. A distraction from the bigger menace. What consequence are a few lives to free our city from Radukar?'

His friend's words brought a smile to Karlion's face. 'I've been thinking the same thing. For any great good, sacrifices must be made.'

'An appropriate turn of phrase,' the confederate said, an enigmatic edge to his words. He stopped at the end of the narrow run and waved Karlion forwards. 'We're here.'

Karlion pushed past his friend. Ahead of them was a wide avenue lined with dilapidated homes. He could see the glow of rushlights behind some of the shuttered windows. He studied the structures, searching for the hideout he'd been promised.

'Which one is it?'

The answer was a sharp, stabbing pain that erupted between his shoulders. Karlion gasped as he tried to draw breath into his body. Strength fled from his limbs. The knife clattered to the cobblestones as he slumped to his knees.

'I misspoke when I said they wouldn't find you,' the fugitive's attacker declared.

A kick sent Karlion sprawling across the icy cobblestones. His eyes focused on the shadowy figure and the gleaming knife in his hand.

'It's necessary that everyone knows what happened to you,' the murderer announced. He started forwards, the sharp blade descending towards Karlion's face. 'You were only pretending to be Baron Grin.'

The mocking words hissed in Karlion's ear as a hand clamped tight over his mouth and the blade stabbed into his cheek.

'Allow me to demonstrate the proper way to render an offering to the Skull Lord.'

CHAPTER TEN

When he'd taken the Blood Kiss, Arno had imagined his dread of the Ebon Citadel would lessen, but as he was led through its grim halls, he found the fear was still there. Even before the cataclysm overwhelmed Mournhold, the castle had been a shunned and forbidding place. As a child he'd shivered in his bed from the tales told to him by his grandmother of the deathless vampire who dwelled within and fed on the blood of bad little boys. There was enough truth in those stories to preserve his fear when he grew older. Condemned criminals offered up to Radukar, and those who even in those days gave themselves freely to the vampire's deadly kiss. The survival of the city had been maintained by such gory rites long before the Wolf claimed complete dominion over Ulfenkarn's people.

It was only by effort of will that Arno was able to put one foot before the other. Pride and ambition were the things that kept him going. Confidence withered inside him the moment the Nightguard came to escort him to Radukar, when he was marched through the haunted desolation at the centre of Ulfenkarn and beheld up close the horrors that now infested the ruins, scenes beside which his worst nightmares as a mortal were gracious and comforting. No, there was no security in a world where such things could be. There was only the urge to survive, the stubborn persistence to endure and do whatever was needed to prove his value to his master.

The undead ogors plodded through the sombre halls, their footsteps echoing into the distance. Sometimes a fleshless skeleton would cross from one room into another, its bones draped in the mouldering livery of a servant. A beautiful woman wearing a bright red gown drifted into view, her skin as pale and smooth as midnight milk, her hair cascading down her shoulder in a long braid. Arno noted the keen interest glistening in her eyes when she spotted him, but recognised the look for what it was when he saw the gleam of her fangs. He was still too near to his former mortality to be safe from the hunger of other vampires. Sometimes they didn't balk at draining a thrall dry when the mood set upon them. Perhaps such thoughts were in her mind, for she had a petulant scowl when she glanced at the Nightguard and realised he'd been summoned by the Wolf. She did give Arno an inviting smile before vanishing into the shadows. A look that promised him she'd be waiting if he were to gain liberty from his escort.

Down a winding stair the ogors led Arno, deeper and deeper into the earth until he judged they must be well below the spire of rock the citadel was built upon and down in the roots of the city itself. Through the dank and musty passages he was conducted to an iron gate. Two of the Nightguard lumbered forwards and opened the heavy portal. The Watchmaster, feeling small and puny after the ogors' display of strength, followed behind his hulking guides.

Beyond the iron gate were many iron-banded doors of black

wood. Arno could dimly hear moans and wails issuing from the closed rooms, and sometimes the gibbering of a broken mind would scratch at his senses. He did his best to ignore the tortured sounds, reminding himself of the oaths he'd sworn and the lord to whom he'd sworn them.

At last the Nightguard brought him to a sunken room. Arno descended a few steps. One of the ogors followed him, crouching to clear the low ceiling. The Watchmaster heard the dull scrape of the creature's head on the roof and glanced up to see a decayed crust of skin clinging there. The Kosargi itself was oblivious to its injured scalp, and simply lurched onwards.

'You arrive at last.' Radukar's voice echoed through the chamber. The Wolf stood beside a low table or shelf of stone. His white cloak rippled around him as he turned to face Arno. From his left hand, a dark object dropped to the floor. Arno noted with no little fear that it was the messenger bat he'd sent to the Ebon Citadel. The animal had been drained of blood.

'I dislike being kept waiting,' Radukar stated, coming towards Arno.

'The city was… agitated, eminence,' Arno said. He glanced aside at the ogor, hoping for some show of corroboration, but the undead hulk was as oblivious as a lump of lead. 'We… had to… divert where things were too unsettled.' He shuddered at the recollection of a patch of morbid ground that had opened up under one of the Nightguard and sucked it down into its greedy maw.

Radukar made a curt gesture with his hand, dismissing Arno's protest. 'The message you sent stated that the rebel Karlion had been found.' The vampire's lips curled back in a menacing smile. 'But not in circumstances you considered desirable.'

Arno knew there was no value in trying to mitigate his case. To try to hide anything from Radukar was folly. Often with lethal consequences.

'Yes, eminence,' he said.

He gestured to the ogor and the creature set down the burden it carried cradled in the crook of its arm. A human corpse, its head denuded down to a skull.

'There was also this,' Arno said. He reached into the satchel he carried and drew out its ghastly contents. A patch of skin roughly a foot across. He held it up so that it could be seen clearly. 'Baron Grin wanted us to be certain who his victim was. So he cut the face away in one strip and left it behind with the body.'

Radukar took the grisly trophy from Arno. He stared at it a moment, then tossed it aside. 'The murderer appreciated his imitator even less than your Volkshaufen. In his way, Baron Grin is showing us that he wasn't responsible for the last killing. He's proud of his work and that has made him arrogant.'

'Then this is the work of the real killer?' Arno asked.

The vampire drew a deep breath. Disgust flickered over his features. 'I can smell the rancid taint that has corrupted the body. This wasn't a pretender.' His eyes gleamed with a savage glow. 'Of course there's more than one Baron Grin. There's a whole society of them.' He turned and glanced back at the table. 'Isn't that right, poppet?'

As Radukar turned, Arno could see the table better. He saw that there was a kind of box lying on it, a container that looked like nothing so much as a coffin made of glass. It wasn't empty. Inside there lay a pale, bloody, naked thing. Such were the extent of its wounds and the horrible manner in which it was sprawled that it took him some time to realise what he was looking at was human.

'One of our Baron Grin rebels,' Radukar pronounced, gesturing to the captive thing.

Arno stepped closer and got a better look at what was in the glass coffin. He was sickened when he saw the reason for the prisoner's strange outline. The bones had been removed from her arms and legs, leaving each limb a shapeless mass of quivering flesh. She turned an agonised face towards him and he saw that her teeth had been removed. A guarantee, he supposed, that she wouldn't bite off her own tongue to end her suffering.

'Rebels?' Arno muttered, trying to focus on Radukar's words more than his ghoulish handiwork.

'Indeed,' the vampire hissed. 'Their ambition is to end my rule, though they've strayed to a strange path by which to accomplish it.' He thrust a finger at the prisoner, indicating the grotesque mark etched into her scarred skin. 'The mark of Khorne,' he said, naming the obscene sign. 'The cult that is responsible for Baron Grin dedicates each victim as an offering to the Blood God. They think they can invoke the power of Chaos to overthrow me.'

Arno shook his head in disbelief. 'That is madness! The Blood God would destroy everything! No one would be left alive.'

'Those depraved enough to venerate Khorne care little for such things,' Radukar said. 'They only care that there is death and carnage to dedicate to their god.' He smiled as he looked again at the wreck of his prisoner. 'The only thing they fear is the inability to make such an offering. To be rendered so harmless they can't even harm themselves.'

Arno saw the tortured prisoner clench her eyes in despair, her face twisted by misery and shame. For just an instant he felt pity for her.

'You've confirmed this, eminence?' he asked.

Radukar nodded. 'I've had a long talk with her. I caught her before she could finish making a new offering to her god. Karlion's death was twofold. Partly to convey a message, partly to replace the sacrifice I spoiled.' His hand tapped the side of the glass coffin. 'Yes, we had a long talk. At first she had little to say, but soon enough she begged to tell me things I didn't even want to know.'

The Wolf turned from his mutilated prisoner.

'Come, Arno. I've work for you and your Volkshaufen. This wretch has told me all I want to know of her foul cult. I know how many they number, who they are and where they're meeting.' Radukar's eyes blazed with annoyance and he clenched his fist. 'The only thing I don't know is their ultimate plan. The magister who leads them claims everything they do is towards a greater design. But he's not seen fit to divulge what he intends to his deluded followers.'

'What then will you do, eminence?' Arno wondered.

'I know where they're meeting, and when,' Radukar said. 'We will seek them out at this gathering and exterminate them.' He bared his fangs at Arno. 'With better results than you provided at the Kaldgrief refinery. Some of Loew's vigilantes escaped. I'll not suffer any of these cultists to enjoy such good fortune.'

Radukar studied the ruined structure, its remaining walls stabbing up from a weed-choked mound of rubble. The whole place stank of death and blood, an aroma that had persisted long enough to seep into the very stones. Before the destruction of Ulfenkarn it had been an abattoir to which the whales and the great beasts of the sea had been dragged up from the docks to be butchered at leisure. The thrifty owners had harvested every speck of their catches, rendering the least appealing portions into fertiliser for farmers and chum for fishermen. Ink and poison from kraken had been portioned off, and the mighty bones of the leviathans had been pulverised into powder that would eventually become the mortar that maintained the castles of the nobility.

The vampire, however, felt a nagging familiarity for this place. His eyes roved about the vicinity, trying to peel back centuries of construction and picture it as it had been long ago. Over his long life Radukar had forgotten many things, but there was something here that resisted being forgotten. A note of warning that would not relent.

'The guards have been deployed,' Arno reported to Radukar. The thrall bowed his head, but he wasn't able to hide the uneasiness in his voice. He was surrounded by a mixed force of Nightguard and Ulfenwatch, fully aware of the power Radukar's soldiers could unleash on their master's command.

'They understand their orders?' Radukar pressed Arno.

The Watchmaster nodded. 'They've been told, eminence. They are to look and listen, but leave the fighting to the Ulfenwatch.'

'I depend on their vigilance. You've warned them what happens if they fail.' Radukar didn't need to emphasise the threat that hung over each of the Volkshaufen. The militiamen had been divided into groups of three, each with a dozen skeletons. The Ulfenwatch had many advantages over mortals, but wariness wasn't one of them. The men were to keep a careful lookout and raise the alarm if they spotted any of the cultists trying to flee from some hidden door or secret tunnel. The undead would then move in to deal with such fugitives. Radukar wanted the whole cult destroyed this night. Fear would keep the militiamen attentive to their duties.

'We will descend and scorch the dragon in its lair,' Radukar said. He turned from Arno and motioned to the undead around them. Six Nightguard and a score of Ulfenwatch stirred into motion. They entered the ruined abattoir, marching with eerie silence. Deadening spells had been laid upon them to dull any noise they might otherwise make. Radukar knew from his prisoner that the cult depended on the clatter of disturbed debris to warn them if anyone was closing in upon their obscene temple.

The Nightguard lumbered over to the spot where the concealed door was hidden. The captive had told Radukar it would be barred from below when the cult gathered. As the undead ogors worked their glaives under the edges of the sunken panel, the Wolf smiled. However strongly the cult barred the gate, he was confident it wouldn't resist the brawn of six Nightguard. It only needed a moment's exertion for the hulking monsters to prise the door upwards. He could see the torn hinges and shattered bars that clung to the ruined panel. The spell laid upon his minions, however, rendered the violent process completely silent.

The moment the door was broken open, half of the skeletons plunged into the exposed hole. Another enchantment was upon these undead, a spell that made the Ulfenwatch move with the swiftness of an aelf. They charged ahead, swords bared. Radukar caught the smell of tainted blood wafting up from the pit and knew his minions had dealt with the sentinels below.

'Come,' Radukar commanded. At his gesture, three of the Nightguard descended into the pit. The Wolf and Arno followed behind them. The rest of the force brought up the rear. It wasn't long before they found the guards the Ulfenwatch had cut down – three crumpled figures strewn on the floor amid welters of polluted gore. Radukar noted the emblem of Khorne gashed into each of their foreheads.

'It's impossible they could move at liberty like that,' Arno said when he saw the corpses.

'Perhaps that is why they bear the mark of Khorne so brazenly,' Radukar suggested. 'So that they must remain hidden. An effective way for the cult to keep its most fanatical members under control. Don't forget the killer who was murdered because he went too far with his victim. The slaves of the Skull Lord are known for their maniacal excess.'

Radukar paused, his thoughts straying back to a distant time when he'd sailed to Ulfenkarn in the *Impaler's Gift* with his loyal Kosargi, the Blood God's hordes ravaging the city, ready to crush all beneath their barbarian blades. The Wolf was cheered as a liberator, exterminating the Chaos marauders and driving them to ruin. Now these insane fools thought to appeal to Khorne to assume the role of liberator. As though the Blood God cared anything for their petty suffering.

The walls of the underground passage were of ancient stone, caked in a crust of old blood. The floor was given over to a crimson mud through which bloated leeches crawled. Radukar could feel the vileness of corruption all around him, the abominable taint that permeated the air. He wondered how long the cult had thrived to so saturate this place with their stigma. Surely this evil had flourished here long before the fanatics announced themselves with the Baron Grin murders.

The spell that rendered his undead minions noiseless made it easy for Radukar to pick out sounds that should otherwise have been lost to the rattle of armour and the footfalls of ogors. He could hear the scratch of rat claws as vermin crept through their tunnels behind the walls, the drip of moisture as it slithered between the stones to dampen the mucky floor. Faintly, from a great distance, there came the murmur of voices.

'This way,' Radukar directed his followers. The vanguard of animated skeletons started off, their ensorcelled bones yet endowed with fleetness. The Nightguard plodded along, their boots churning the gore-soaked mud. Leeches squirmed over their rotten flesh.

'These must be part of the old sewers,' Arno speculated. He gripped a lantern in his hand and cast its rays upon the vaulted ceiling overhead. 'That explains the... blood. The abattoir drained its vats here when it was still in operation.'

Radukar shook his head. 'This filth can't be called blood. It's been conjured by foul rites, revived from lingering residue and perverted into something that doesn't belong in Shyish. This is a manifestation of Chaos, an echo of Khorne's realm.'

The vampire paused. His eyes narrowed as he considered the magnitude of power displayed around him.

'This shouldn't be possible,' the Wolf declared. 'No pathetic cult of madmen should be able to invoke such power.'

Fright shone in Arno's eyes. 'Eminence, should we turn back? If there's any risk to you...'

Radukar sneered at the vampire's concern. 'I am master of Ulfenkarn. There's nothing in this city that doesn't owe its existence to my forbearance.' Irritated by the thrall's fear, he motioned his troops onwards. The question of what had happened to the tunnels under the abattoir could wait. Attending to the cult was the matter at hand now.

The sound of voices grew more strident as Radukar marched through the grim passageways. Several diversions opened onto the tunnel they followed and at each branch one of the Ulfenwatch was left behind. If any of the cult slipped past the vampire and his Nightguard, they'd have to fight their way through the skeletons and thereby leave a clear record of their escape route. Only two skeletons remained by the time they caught up with the vanguard, who had stopped as they came within sight of the tunnel's ending.

Ahead, the passage opened into a greater space. Radukar could feel the change in the air as it shifted from the close confines of the tunnel to the expanse of an underground chamber. The source of the voices was near enough now to pick out distinct words. The language, however, was no tongue with which the vampire was familiar. That alone was cause enough to denote it as an esoteric language, for in his many centuries Radukar had learned most modes of speech used by man, ogor and duardin.

'Wait here,' Radukar told the undead. With Arno following him, he moved towards the end of the tunnel. 'Douse your light,' he ordered. The lantern was hastily extinguished and they moved onwards towards the red glow that emanated from the chamber before them.

'Now they are mine,' Radukar said as he crouched at the mouth of the tunnel and gazed upon the scene in the chamber. It was an immense hall, twenty feet high and twice again as long. The uneven walls marked it as having been crudely excavated, a primitive expansion to the original sewers. The patina of old blood was even more pronounced here, however. The walls glistened with long strips of clotted gore, like some daemonical moss. The floor was a morass of the same filth, a sanguinary swamp from which crimson mist drifted. Rising from this mire were ledges of rock, islands of solidity amidst the blood bog. Upon the largest of these islands, the cult was gathered.

Radukar reckoned the cult's numbers somewhat beneath two score. They wore a motley assortment of vestments, denoting the varied strata of Ulfenkarn's society they belonged to. Labourers, artisans, fishermen and vagabonds, the highest and lowest of the city's mortals had its representation. They grovelled before an altar built from human skulls, slashing themselves with knives in their deranged worship. Behind the altar, his face hidden behind a hound-like mask of bronze, a priest in scarlet robes cried out the strange litany that whispered into the tunnels.

'They... they defile your name, eminence,' Arno gasped.

The vampire nodded, registering his name wound into the obscene invocation. 'They cry to the Blood God to set his curse upon me,' Radukar snarled. But as he listened, he picked out another name from the strange words. A name he knew from old.

'Slaughn.'

The name dripped from the vampire's fangs like poison. Understanding came to him when he heard the magister speak that name. He knew why the setting of the abattoir seemed familiar to him. It had been built over the very spot where he'd fought Slaughn the Ravener long ago. He gazed up at the roof of the chamber. Yes, this might be under the very place where he'd vanquished the daemon prince, running him through upon his sword. The destruction of Slaughn was the feat that relieved the siege of Mournhold and broke the great Chaos horde.

'So that's what they hope to accomplish,' Radukar said. 'They don't seek to call upon Khorne's power directly. They're trying to conjure Slaughn's spirit back from the Blood God's keeping. To set the daemon prince against me again.'

'Is such a thing possible?' Arno wondered.

Radukar's fangs glistened in a fierce smile. 'These swine won't get the chance to make it possible,' he said. In response to his ire, the skeletons and Nightguard plunged into the room, their decayed limbs enervated by their master's fury.

'Doom is upon you, scum!' Radukar howled as he swept into the chamber, barrow-blade clenched in his fist. 'You've dared defy your master, now suffer the price of your madness.'

The cultists turned from their grisly altar and from them there rose an answering roar. Devotees of the murderous Khorne, these mortals showed no fear before the undead onslaught. They raised ancient axes and swords, bludgeons and flails, weapons left behind by Slaughn's vanquished invaders centuries ago.

'Blood for the Blood God!' the madmen shrieked. 'Skulls for the Skull Throne!'

The enemy surged forwards. The Ulfenwatch, moving faster than the hulking Nightguard, were the first to meet the cult. The armoured skeletons slashed and thrust with their blades, but the cold precision of the undead was unequal to the savage frenzy before them. The berserk cultists clove skulls and severed limbs with their vicious weapons. Ancient mail crumpled under the battering impacts of maces, revitalised bone splintered beneath the sweep of axes. In a matter of heartbeats, six of the skeletons had been destroyed with only a single enemy balanced against them on the scales.

Then Radukar was in the fight. Unlike his mindless minions, his heart pulsed with the ardour of battle. He matched the fury of the cultists and exceeded it with a malice that had endured through many lifetimes. A slash of his sword took the arm of one foeman and sent it spinning through the air in a welter of gore. A downward chop bisected the head of a madwoman and dropped her to the floor in a mash of spilled brains. One enemy he caught by the neck in his other hand, lifting him off the ground as though he weighed nothing. Blood streamed down Radukar's arm as his fingers pierced the throat. His flailing adversary kicked at him with his boots and stabbed at him with the spiked peen of his axe, but to no avail. Against the awesome might of the vampire, his resistance was meaningless. A flick of his wrist and Radukar snapped his neck and threw the quivering body full into the faces of the other cultists.

'Challenge Radukar and die!' he yelled at the enemy.

Now the enormous Nightguard entered the fray. A shrieking cultist was cut in two by the cleaving edge of an ogor glaive. Another ended with his body ground into pulp beneath one of their iron-shod boots. Yet the crazed rebels refused to desist. They swarmed about the monsters like angry ants, ripping at them with their blades. Ribbons of decayed flesh hung in strips from the Nightguard as their foes struggled to bring them down.

'Eminence!' Arno screamed. The Watchmaster threw himself upon a cultist who'd circled around behind his master. The enemy was knocked to the ground and an instant later the thrall pulled the man's throat out, leaving him to writhe in his death throes.

'None will escape us,' the Wolf growled, resuming the attack. Half the cultists were dead or dying, but that meant half the job was yet to be done.

'It's you who shall not escape!' the masked magister screamed. Unlike his mad followers, the leader remained where he'd stood when the undead broke into the hidden temple. His eyes glared balefully from behind the bronze hound-mask. 'Too long has your presence profaned Mournhold! Now you shall answer to the Blood God, Wolf of Nagash!'

Radukar wagged his blade at the magister's mask. 'A dog is a wolf without pride,' he said mockingly. 'A wolf knows no master, but when a dog forgets who its is, death is its measure.'

A clutch of cultists charged at Radukar when they heard him insult their leader. The vampire's barrow-blade ripped open the belly of one, the strike of his hand collapsed the ribs of another. He dealt with two more before he realised the last of the group stood rigid and still, transfixed by a crimson glow. Radukar drew away, sensing the obscene energy that was building inside the man's body.

'Ravening Slaughn, let your presence walk among us!' the magister shouted. 'Manifest your wrath in the body of your disciple that vengeance may be brought against the defiler who dared stand against you!'

Radukar could see bands of red energy pulsing from the altar and seeping into the glowing man. The cultist's skin darkened, becoming the colour of an old scab. His body began to swell and contort, bones elongating and popping as they assumed new dimensions. Hair dropped from the scalp in bloody clumps as the skull curled and flattened into an almost reptilian shape. In the man's pain-wracked eyes, a malignant force blazed. Radukar recognised that hideous presence. It was the fiend he'd vanquished here long ago.

Slaughn the Ravener, daemon prince of Khorne.

Arno cried out in terror, and even the Nightguard were staggered by the ancient evil being drawn down into the chamber. Surviving cultists slashed at themselves in a frenzy of mad adoration, their blood streaming from their wounds.

Radukar alone held his ground. He sneered at the transforming body of the daemon's host and spat at its feet. 'Few are idiot enough to challenge the Wolf twice,' he snarled.

Radukar's face peeled back in a cold smile. The body Slaughn was trying to possess was still changing, but not in any way the magister had intended. The darkened skin was sloughing away, dripping off the stretched bones like melting wax. Those bones in turn were cracking, crumbling into crimson powder. Where a moment before he had been swelling into the semblance of a giant, now the man was disintegrating into gory wreckage.

'Dog of Khorne!' Radukar shouted at the masked magister. 'Your ambition is beyond your ability! Or did you think it such an easy thing to summon Slaughn back from his well-deserved destruction?'

As he jeered, Radukar saw the daemon's presence wink out in the changing eyes. What was left of the possessed cultist toppled forwards, crashing down and sinking into the muck. The Night-guard surged back to the attack, striking the disciples of Khorne before they could recover from their shock.

Only the magister retained any sense of purpose. He spun and dashed away from the altar. Leaping from rock to rock, he sprinted for the tunnel back into the sewers.

Radukar moved to intercept the leader. He struck out, his hand grasping the ear of the mask. It crumpled in his powerful grip, but the magister pulled away. The man ran on, leaving the dog-faced mask in the vampire's hand. Before the Wolf could pursue, three surviving cultists charged him. Though he was swift in annihilating them, the delay was enough to let the magister flee into the tunnel.

Radukar snarled in disgust and began his pursuit. He passed two tunnels where the guarding skeletons had been destroyed. A third lay shattered up ahead of him. He could sense that the fourth was still unchallenged further on. He paused at the mouth of the third opening. It was clear his quarry had chosen this route to make his escape, but why, in his haste, had he rejected the other two? Radukar considered the question, letting it temper the urge of the chase. The cultists might have been fanatics, but their leader had thus far displayed a streak of cunning.

'To me,' Radukar hissed. In response the skeleton guarding the fourth tunnel hastened to its master. He pointed and sent the creature marching into the side passage. He watched as it ambled into the darkness.

'Eminence, all the rebels in the chamber are dead,' Arno reported as he rushed to join Radukar. He glanced at the passageway. 'The leader went this way?'

'Yes,' Radukar said, fangs gleaming. 'I think he expected me to follow.'

The words were no sooner spoken than a tremendous roar shook the tunnel. Out from the darkness a cloud of dust came billowing towards them. The magister had covered his escape using some sort of trap that collapsed the whole passageway when a pursuer reached it.

'Was he killed? Did he escape?' Arno gasped.

'His cult is finished,' Radukar proclaimed. 'They intended to revive Slaughn and use the daemon against me, as though Slaughn would care what they wanted. I forced their hand too soon. They weren't ready.'

'But the leader?' Arno asked again.

Radukar turned the bronze mask over in his fingers. 'He won't elude me for long.'

Arno nodded. 'Then Ulfenkarn is free of Baron Grin. The murders are over.'

The Wolf smiled at Arno. 'Are they?' he hissed.

'If the cult is finished...' Arno started to say.

Radukar waved aside his speech. 'This cult is only one of the groups who dare to oppose me. I will see them all destroyed. I'll crush the last dregs of hope from the hearts of these rebels.' He stared at the mask in his hand. 'Yes, they will all be reminded why they shudder at my name.'

Radukar started down the tunnel to the steps leading back to the abattoir. Arno hurried to keep pace with him.

'What are your orders?' the Watchmaster asked.

'Maintain your patrols,' Radukar told him. 'Act as though tonight never happened.'

'I don't understand,' Arno said.

'You don't need to,' Radukar replied. 'You only need to obey.' He stared again at the bronze mask. 'Do exactly as you've done before. Change nothing.'

'What will you do, eminence?' Arno wondered.

Radukar's visage curled into the semblance of his namesake, all refinement subdued beneath the primordial savagery of the Wolf. His fingers tightened about the mask he held, the bronze groaning as it was twisted out of shape.

'I'm going hunting,' the Wolf growled.

INTERLUDE 6

Regnir Kielholz looked anxiously at the darkened sky as he hurried through the dim alleyways that branched off from the waterfront. It was in this area that the exciseman had fallen to Baron Grin's knife. The killer's readiness to murder an official impressed on Regnir that anyone could become the next victim. Nobody was safe.

The middle-aged whaler had a great fear of running into Baron Grin, but balanced against that fear was ambition. The *Stormchaser* was only two days in port and her crew had been paid their meagre share of the profits. Each sailor's part was just about enough to keep him from starving until the ship set sail again, but Regnir wanted more. So did many of his shipmates. Thus they'd spent most of their time playing cards in the loft above Granny Crowfoot's shop. The stink of boiling shellfish permeated Regnir's clothes and beard, but the discomfort had paid off. Two dozen of his shipmates had joined in the gambling, everyone trying to pad out his low wages with something from the next fellow. For once, it was his turn to be the lucky one. Through the day, hand after hand had favoured him. He'd persisted until he had a purse nearly six times what he'd started with.

Well aware of the jealous, resentful looks the losers had turned his way, Regnir passed on Granny Crowfoot's offer of lodging when the game ran late. At the time it seemed to him that the unknown dangers of Ulfenkarn's benighted streets were better than the covetous glances from the other whalers.

Now Regnir wasn't so keen on the choice he'd made. The rustle of leathery wings told him that blood-bats were prowling the sky. The scurry of clawed feet was a constant reminder that corpse-rats infested the waterfront, feeding off scraps thrown away by fishermen but never above sinking their teeth into a man if they got hungry enough. Once he spotted a gaunt shadow creeping away down an alley and was reminded of stories of ghouls that lurked under the piers and came out at night to steal bodies left in the gutters. He fingered the broad-bladed knife thrust beneath his belt and wondered if he'd get the chance to use it if a ghoul did confront him.

To all these menaces had to be added the depredations of Baron Grin. The *Stormchaser* had been out at sea during much of the killer's rampage, but Granny Crowfoot and others he'd met since returning to port had recited to Regnir the full catalogue of crimes in exacting and gruesome detail. Gutted like a fish and with his face peeled away struck him as a ghastlier death than being caught in the maw of a kharybdis.

Money! Regnir jostled the heavy purse in his hand. The winnings were enough to sustain him until his ship left again. There was enough for him to share with Sofia. He thought his wife still lived in the shack behind the tailor shop. It had been several months since he'd seen her, so he wasn't certain. The last time they hadn't parted on the best of terms. But now he had money, and that would make things different.

Regnir paused as the alley opened out into a broader street. He tried to gauge his bearings. Yes, that was old Mueller the candle-maker there. Now if his memory served, two streets down would be the Black Ship. He smacked his lips when he thought of the tavern. Normally his wages would barely let him crawl into a grog-shop without being thrown out into the street, but with what he had now he could patronise the Black Ship and fill his belly with real drink and not whatever had been squeezed out of a sick dog. He'd be careful this time, not squander everything. Just a few flag-ons of mead, maybe a bottle of wine. There'd be enough left to give something to Sofia. He made himself a promise of that. Of course, it was a promise he'd often made and just as often broken.

The sound of clattering armour sent Regnir scurrying back into the alley. He knew the sound of the Ulfenwatch on patrol. Breaking the nightly curfew was one of the hundreds of laws that could see the violator exsanguinated. He swallowed the knot in his throat when he thought of his blood being drained off by a vampire. Sometimes the vampires destroyed the body after-wards, but just as often they left it for scavengers. Worst of all was when the executed returned to a horrible semblance of life and wandered the streets as a deadwalker.

The whaler clung to the darkness and waited for the Ulfenwatch to pass by. Regnir was focused on the sound of their armour as the skeletons drew ever closer. It was that fixation that caused him to miss the fact that he was no longer alone in the alley until it was too late.

A sense of wrongness, a sudden chill that crept down his spine made Regnir spin around. He gasped in fright when he saw a shadowy figure standing just behind him. A chance beam of light glimmered from the keen edge of the knife in the stranger's hand.

Regnir's first instinct was to reach for his own blade, but even as he started to move, he knew it was too late. The stranger's knife flashed out, striking his gut with such force he thought it must have punched clear through to his spine. He felt his blood gushing onto the cobblestones as he collapsed to his knees. He coughed and more blood bubbled out into his beard. He stared up at the cloaked shape of his killer.

Tomorrow new rumours would race through Ulfenkarn's slums. Baron Grin had killed again. This time the victim was a whaler named Regnir Kielholz. A man whose recent good luck had run out.

CHAPTER ELEVEN

Gustaf could feel little tingles of pain crackling up and down his spine. Maybe he was getting old or maybe he'd just been wounded one too many times over his years as a vampire hunter, but whatever the cause, his body didn't care for the hunched posture he'd adopted as part of his disguise. The junkmen who prowled about Ulfenkarn's slums all had that same, stooped appearance, their bodies bent by lugging away the effects of the recently deceased. There were several unsavoury dealers who acted as collection points for the possessions mourning relatives sold to the junkmen when they made their rounds. A cloth stained with red hanging from a window was the sign that summoned them, but the human vultures weren't above knocking at doors when their carts weren't full enough to unload to the dealers.

Convincing Emelda to adopt such a disreputable mantle had taken more than a little persuasion on Gustaf's part. He'd had to overcome not just the hauteur of her noble upbringing but also her sense of martial honour. But junkmen were too good a disguise to ignore. Because they were largely despised, people tried to avoid them except when their services were needed. Their job was such that it took them into every habitable district, so there wasn't any danger of looking out of place. At least, as long as they looked like junkmen, and didn't arouse suspicion.

That was why Gustaf endured the dull pain that nagged at him. He wasn't going to do anything that might jeopardise their excursion away from Morrvahl's new sanctum. The Volkshaufen were out in force and the daylight patrols of Ulfenwatch had been increased. Baron Grin was killing again and it appeared Radukar was working his minions around the clock to bring the murderer to heel. Gustaf and Emelda had seen for themselves how energetic the militiamen were about stopping anyone who attracted their interest. Neither of them could risk the chance they'd be recognised. After escaping from Radukar himself, they were certain that the vampire was looking for them as keenly as he was Baron Grin.

'You're certain this is necessary?' Emelda asked, not for the first time. Even more than Gustaf, she was unrecognisable under the soiled leather slicker and frumpy hat that formed part of her disguise. For an added effect, she'd worked her hair into a confused tangle and applied dried porridge to her cheeks to simulate one of the grisly skin diseases that often afflicted the scavengers.

Gustaf looked back across the decrepit cart they were moving through the streets, he at the front, pulling, while Emelda pushed from behind. He gave her a dour look.

'It's our best chance for tracking down Baron Grin. We know Radukar is still hunting the killer. It's more important than ever that we find out who it is.'

Even beneath her disguise, Gustaf could see the discomfort Emelda felt. She didn't like the plan, hadn't from the very start. Unmasking Baron Grin – but instead of stopping him, simply sitting back to observe. They'd only act when they were certain they would get Radukar along with Baron Grin.

'What if Karlion was right?' Emelda asked. 'What if the killer is Morrvahl?'

'I don't see how that could be,' Gustaf said. 'I know we've had our suspicions in the past, but after he rescued us, I don't think Morrvahl is Baron Grin. He's exposed himself to Radukar, that means the Wolf is after him as much as he is us. The one way to change that is to lure Radukar into a trap. If the wizard was responsible for these murders, he'd be setting up a trail to lead the vampire some place where we'd have a chance of destroying him.'

Emelda shook her head. 'I'll reserve my own judgement until after we've spoken with your friend.'

Gustaf was more disturbed by her continued suspicion of the wizard than he was ready to admit. Because she just might be right. He hoped they could learn something that would at least ease that worry.

A run-down block of timber-and-plaster houses was around the next corner, most of them pressed in against one another so that there was no space for pathways between them. Gustaf noted the building they were looking for and made a subtle gesture to Emelda to point it out to her.

'So that's where Vladrik secretes himself when he isn't in some unsavoury den,' Emelda commented.

Gustaf motioned her to be quiet and gave the street a wary look. There weren't many people around, but those who were enjoyed his appraising stare. Emelda noted at once his anxiety.

'Something's wrong?' she whispered.

'I'm not sure,' Gustaf said. 'Nothing I'm certain of, but right now every instinct is telling me we're being followed.'

'Radukar's spies?' Emelda wondered. 'Or maybe Karlion's back on our trail.'

'Or Morrvahl, if what you suspect is true.' Gustaf turned that possibility over in his mind. 'He knew the purpose of our leaving the hideout.' His hand slipped down and patted the heavy pistol holstered underneath his slicker. 'We'll circle around the street once and then come back. Keep an eye out for anyone who looks too interested in what we're doing.'

They moved their cart down the length of the street, prowling the side opposite Vladrik's building. Gustaf made a show of examining every building as though he were looking for a hanging flag. He wanted to distract anyone watching them. The more they looked at him, the less likely they were to notice Emelda looking at them. When they reached the end of the block, they turned the cart around the corner.

'Did you see anyone?' Gustaf asked.

'Nobody that seemed interested in us,' Emelda replied. 'Maybe you were wrong this time.'

Gustaf didn't think the suggestion was likely. A vampire hunter didn't last long at his trade unless he developed a knack for recognising the moment he was no longer hunting his prey because it was hunting him.

'We'll come back along the other side of the street. Keep watching. If you see someone we'll just keep going and try to find a place where we can either lose them or deal with them. Otherwise we stop in front of Vladrik's building and head in.'

When they returned to the street, Gustaf felt his instincts fairly screaming at him. It was an effort for him to maintain the illusion of looking for flags in the windows. Every time he turned his head and they pulled the cart a few more yards, his eyes roved across the people on the street. None of them seemed out of place. He caught no furtive movement that might betray an anxious spy. That didn't mean there wasn't one there, only that they were good at shadowing their targets.

'I didn't see anyone,' Emelda reported when they were closing in on Vladrik's. 'Do we stop or keep going?'

The decision wasn't an easy one to make. Time was crucial for them more than ever. Karlion might find them again and bring another mob against them. The threat posed by Radukar was more immediate than it had ever been. Every day risked ruin. Locating Baron Grin, using the killer to draw Radukar into a trap, was the only way Gustaf saw that they might stave off disaster.

'We go in,' the vampire hunter declared. Gustaf let the long poles he was holding rest on the ground. Emelda came around from the back of the cart. Both of them directed a warning look at the people on the street. That, at least, was in keeping with junkmen, an unspoken threat that they'd clout anyone they caught rummaging through their salvage.

Gustaf rapped on the splintered door of the building. Boards and planks had been crudely nailed to it to reinforce it. He couldn't hear any sound from inside, so he knocked again, louder and more impatiently.

'All right! All right! Don't knock the house down!' a voice snapped from inside. A tiny panel was drawn open and a wizened face with a bulbous nose peered out at them. The old woman's eyes narrowed with contempt when she saw Gustaf and Emelda. 'Nobody asked for you scum to be carrying on here! Off with ya, or I'll turn the dogs on you!'

Gustaf returned the landlady's grimace with one of his own. 'Mind your tongue,' he growled. 'We've business here. There's a flag hung from the top window.' He'd estimated from the woman's appearance that the only way she'd leave the building was if she was dragged out of it. Her show of gruff authority was a veneer to cover the constant fright he saw at the corners of her eyes.

'That'd be that Vladrik,' the landlady muttered. 'Maybe he's finally clearing out some of that trash up there.'

The little panel snapped closed again without warning. The sound of bars, bolts and chains being withdrawn came from behind the door. After a minute, the portal swung inwards. Gustaf could see that it had been reinforced on the inside as well.

'You'll find him at the top,' the old woman stated, turning her large nose towards the ceiling. She spun around and stamped her foot when she saw Emelda still on the landing. 'Well, come on! In or out! I haven't all day to waste on the likes of you.'

The instant Emelda was inside, the landlady had the door closed again and hurried to restore its battery of barriers.

'Hold on,' she grumbled when she saw Gustaf start towards the stairs at the back of the hallway. 'I'll show you the way. Don't want you makin' a mistake and botherin' one of my tenants.'

Gustaf and Emelda were obliged to match the old woman's pace as she conducted them up three flights of stairs. For all her rancour towards junkmen, her tongue remained loquacious.

'Vladrik,' she said in a huff. 'Fancies himself some sort of scholar. Has all sorts of peculiar people comin' around all times of the day with books and such what they've found. Don't know how he pays for all of it! Stuffed to the rafters that garret is! Books and scrolls and scrolls and books and maps and underworlds know what else.' She paused and tapped a crooked finger on Gustaf's chest. 'I mean, what good is all of it? Books! Ya can't eat 'em. Can't wear 'em. Can't even make a good fire with 'em, not that he'd let anyone try.'

'Does he have much of a collection?' Emelda dared to ask.

Somehow the landlady managed to twist her face into an even more sour expression. 'He's got a bloomin' library up there! I don't see how the beams can take all the weight. I keep warnin' him to stop bringin' more in here. If that floor gives out, I'll sick my dogs on him, so help me I will!'

The old woman's tirade ended as they reached the uppermost floor. She pointed at the only door that faced the landing. 'That's where he lives,' she said. 'I'm happy he's finally getting rid of some of that trash. If it were up to me, I'd say take it all and you're welcome to it.' She turned and started back down the steps. Gustaf could still hear her complaining to herself as she withdrew down through the house.

'Now I understand why Vladrik goes out,' Emelda said when she was certain the landlady wasn't close enough to hear her.

Gustaf chuckled at the remark. 'The only reason he leaves his rooms is to meet with his contacts and find out if anyone has salvaged some sort of document from the old noble estates.' He straightened up from his disguise, grateful to discard the stoop he'd taken on. He rubbed his hands at the small of his back, trying to ease the pain. 'Vladrik's been pretty successful. As you'll see.'

He knocked at the garret door. Three sharp, two short, and then three sharp again. Gustaf had only used the special signal twice before, usually meeting Vladrik in some public place. When the door was opened, the smell of old books struck his nose. The scholar was framed for just a moment in the doorway, the room beyond lost in darkness. He was heavily bundled in a dark blanket. The contrast of blanket and Vladrik's pallid face was marked, and Gustaf was struck by the change that had come upon the scholar.

'Vladrik, it's us. Gustaf Voss and Emelda Braskov,' the vampire hunter said when he felt the man's hostile gaze.

At once Vladrik's pose became agitated. 'Inside, quick,' he said. He motioned his visitors into the room and slammed the door shut behind them. 'There are some candles over there near the window.' Gustaf could just make out the scholar's finger as he pointed to a heavily curtained alcove.

Emelda navigated her way through the cramped walkway that slithered between stacks of mouldering books piled on the floor. She reached a small table next to a big sealskin chair and recovered a tarnished bronze candlestick with the stumps of five candles protruding from its arms. Gustaf followed her lead and drew from his belt an Aqshian firebrand set in a dragonbone box. After a moment of contact to one of the wicks, the candle flickered into life.

'Only light two, if you please,' Vladrik said. He gestured to his eyes. 'I've been ill and it has made my eyes weak.'

Gustaf did as they were asked. Even in the dim light afforded by two candles they could see the garret was stacked with books. Shelves and racks dominated every wall and stood wherever there was space for them to be crammed. The floor was piled high with mounds of mouldering tomes. The farther reaches of the garret, the other rooms connected to this one, were hidden beyond the candle's light. From previous visits, Gustaf knew there were three in total, all of them in much the same state.

'I've had no word of Darrock,' Vladrik said as he sank into a chair nuzzled between two overstuffed bookcases. With the blanket tucked around him, only his hands and face stood out from the shadows.

'We didn't come to ask about Darrock,' Gustaf said, though he'd dared hope the witch hunter had been located. 'We came to find out what you can tell us about Baron Grin.'

'Oh, so that's what brought you here,' Vladrik said. 'I can only tell you that there have been more murders. Two for certain and a third that might have been Baron Grin's work if he was interrupted before he could strip away the face.' The scholar waved his fingers against his cheek as though doing just that.

'We were hoping your contacts might have learned something,' Emelda said. 'That they might have found out something about Baron Grin.'

Vladrik's eyes glittered in the candlelight. 'If any of them did, I can assure you they'd tell the Volkshaufen, not me. Watchmaster Arno can pay better.' He nodded at the books around him. 'My area of expertise is the past. The history of Mournhold and our people. In more recent matters, I fear I'm not so well versed.'

Gustaf pondered that point for a moment. He knew the value of history and legend when hunting vampires. The same could hold true for mortal killers. 'You've read much about Ulfenkarn,' he said. 'Has there ever been a spree of murders like these before? I mean before the cataclysm.'

'I've never heard of anything like Baron Grin,' Emelda said.

Gustaf turned to her with a look of apology. 'You were born into the nobility and then went straight into the army. You've been insulated from the perspective of the lower rungs of society. You might not know their stories and folk tales.'

Vladrik nodded. 'It is true. The things that interest the nobles and their chroniclers, the matters that concern them, aren't the same as what's important to a charwoman or a fisherman.' His gaze focused on Gustaf. 'You believe there might be some sort of precedent? A precursor to these murders? Even if there were, what would you hope to gain from such knowledge?'

'A clue to who Baron Grin is,' Gustaf said. 'Maybe a hint to motive.'

'If the motive isn't butchery, then what would it be?' Vladrik mulled that over for a moment. 'Mayhem and unrest. The work of rebels trying to rouse the people against Radukar.'

'Something. I can't believe these are just murder for its own sake,' Gustaf explained. 'There's got to be more. A reason why he kills the way he does. If we found that out, we might be able to find him.'

Vladrik leaned back in his chair, the shadows enveloping him so only his hands and eyes were visible. 'What will you do when you find him? Don't think me stupid, I know your ambition is to destroy Radukar. Baron Grin has stirred up the people, forced them into such unrest that even the Wolf can't ignore it.'

Emelda stepped away from the window and held the candles higher so their light fell upon the scholar. 'What are you suggesting?'

Vladrik shielded his eyes against the light. He remained silent until Gustaf drew Emelda back.

'I'm wondering what you intend to do. Avenge the murders, or congratulate the rebel? What are you willing to do to destroy Radukar?'

Gustaf shook his head. 'We haven't decided yet,' he admitted. He felt sick inside to confess that he didn't know if he had any limits. If it came to destroying Radukar, how many lives was he willing to sacrifice?

'Can you help us or not?' Emelda demanded, her voice tense.

'There *are* some contacts I could ask,' Vladrik said. 'A few books I could consult. I'll need time to do both. Say that you return here in two days. By then I should be able to tell you if it looks worth pursuing.'

'Two days,' Emelda agreed. She glanced over at Gustaf. 'You'll have to ask Sigmar to keep us hidden until then.'

'Better to trust Sigmar's providence than Morrvahl's magic,' Gustaf countered. He turned back to Vladrik. 'We'll be back in two days. By the way, the landlady was under the impression we came here to cart away some of your books.'

Vladrik showed him a thin smile. 'On your way out, tell her there was a mistake. Tell her I wanted to buy, not sell.'

The scholar laughed as his guests moved to depart.

'Tell her that. Just be ready to outrun her dogs.'

Loew maintained his vigil outside the house Gustaf and Emelda had gone into. It hadn't been easy to track down the pair after their escape from the cellar. The vigilante had been forced to employ some cunning to find them again. He wasn't likely to forget his first meeting with the vampire hunter in the Black Ship, and that particular memory had offered a clue. The man Gustaf had met that night was the reclusive Vladrik, a person with whom Loew was acquainted. By keeping a close watch on the house, he was prepared when Gustaf paid his visit.

Gloved hands closed about the knife hanging from his belt. Loew had heard all about Karlion's attack on the cellar. Several of the vigilantes who escaped from the refinery had been there. The wizard who was working with Gustaf and Emelda had killed several good men with his foul magic. It was too late to do anything about that, but Loew could make sure their deaths weren't in vain.

The door of the house opened and the shrewish landlady rushed a pair of shabby junkmen from the building. Loew appreciated the effectiveness of the disguises. Until they'd stopped outside the house, he hadn't been sure if they were who he was waiting for. But for just a second he'd spotted the holster of Gustaf's pistol under his slicker when he'd gone inside, removing any doubt he was mistaken.

Loew let the two phoney junkmen start pushing their cart away before he casually strolled towards them. He'd adopted the mantle of a mendicant and made a few whining requests for alms as he approached. He was still about six feet away when Gustaf's eyes widened with recognition and he reached for his pistol.

'I wouldn't do it,' Loew cautioned. 'I've forty men hidden in the neighbourhood. One call from me and they'll be on you like bloodbats on an open vein.'

'Loew!' Emelda gasped. From her reaction, it seemed she hadn't seen through his deception and only recognised him from his voice. Like Gustaf, she started to grab a weapon.

'The same warning goes for you,' Loew said. 'Braskov or no, my men will kill if they have to.'

'Isn't that what you intend to do anyway?' Gustaf asked.

Loew glanced up and down the street. 'Not unless we have to.'

He frowned when he saw that the altercation was drawing attention. 'There's a courtyard in front of what used to be a mansion two blocks down. Head there. I'll be waiting for you.'

'Why should we?' Emelda said.

'Because my men will be watching you,' Loew replied. 'Because if you don't, then they will take action. None of us wants that. We can still be useful to each other.' He was certain that his last words would make enough impact that they'd do what he asked. More than the threat of his men, it would be curiosity over his intentions that would bring them.

Loew reached the courtyard well ahead of Gustaf and Emelda. They were burdened by the cart that was part of their disguise. If they left it behind it would arouse instant suspicion. They might even get accused of being spies for Radukar. He didn't think they'd appreciate the irony in that situation.

The mansion Loew had chosen for their liaison had fallen into disrepair. Wealth and opulence had given way to the tawdry necessities of a ruined city. It was now a tenement, its rooms divided into homes for people who once would have been beaten for even daring to approach the front gate. A study in miniature for how the fortunes of Ulfenkarn had changed. The workers had inherited the splendour of their former bosses only to find that legacy a bitter one. Even if they wanted to, they couldn't rebuild. Not while the tyranny of Radukar was looming over them.

When Gustaf and Emelda arrived, Loew could see their wariness. He could imagine that along the way they'd been trying to spot the forty men he'd claimed were watching them. As they entered the courtyard, he noted that both had hands under their slickers and knew they held weapons. He was sure Gustaf's pistol was aimed at him as the vampire hunter came near the chipped stone bench he sat on.

'That won't be needed,' Loew told Gustaf.

'I'm of a different opinion,' he replied. 'If they know I can shatter your head like a melon with a twitch of my finger, your men will hold back.'

Loew snickered. 'They would,' he said, 'if I had any men out there. Between those I lost at the refinery and the men who went with Karlion, I'd be lucky to scrape together ten men, much less forty.'

Emelda took another step towards him. 'If that's true, why the deception?'

'To ensure you'd come here,' Loew explained. 'Without some manner of threat, you'd have gone away. Perhaps leaving me with a blade in my belly for my trouble.'

'That could still happen,' Emelda said, drawing her sword. 'Your men tried to kill us at Morrvahl's hideout.'

Loew's expression turned grave. 'I wasn't party to that. It was Karlion's idea. After the Kaldgrief refinery, he was worried everything we'd started to build would be lost. He took it on himself to rally new fighters to the society.'

'By pointing the finger at us,' Gustaf said. 'Saying Morrvahl was Baron Grin and that we were helping him.'

'Karlion did worse than that,' Loew confessed. 'He was convinced that we could use Baron Grin to draw people into the greater cause. The cause you yourselves helped inspire. To rally the people to rise up and cast down Radukar.' He paused, trying to work out how he would tell them just how far Karlion had gone. 'When it looked like the murders were over and Baron Grin was dead, he worried the people would become docile again. So he killed an exciseman and made it look like Baron Grin's work. Then he led that mob against you.'

Emelda glared at Loew. 'A fine compatriot you chose for yourself. Where do I find this gallows-bait and thank him for all he's done?'

'When you're in a battle you look for fighters, not saints,' Loew said, irritated by that superior tone that was so characteristic of the old nobility. It was an effort to remind himself that Emelda wasn't like the decadent family whose name she bore. 'You've told me enough about the wizard, I've heard enough about his spells, to know you choose your own compatriots for their utility, not their character.' He pointed at Emelda's sword. 'And whatever you intend to do to him, I assure you worse has already been done. It seems Baron Grin doesn't care for imitators. He killed Karlion two nights ago.'

Loew could see that this bit of news hit Gustaf and Emelda like a brine-leviathan's tail.

'I'm sorry to spoil any plans for retribution,' he added, 'but it's too late for that.'

After a moment, Gustaf posed a question. 'Were there any clues? Any hint who killed him?'

'Aside from Baron Grin's handiwork?' Loew nodded slowly. 'Yes there was. Karlion was in hiding. It seems the Volkshaufen were looking for him. Probably they figured out it was Karlion, not Baron Grin, who murdered the exciseman. Yet for some reason he left his bolthole and went out into the streets at night. I think he was led away. By someone he knew and trusted.'

'That could be the key to finding out who Baron Grin is,' Emelda said. 'You could look into who Karlion's friends were–'

'And see if one of them is the killer,' Loew said, finishing the thought. 'The idea has merit, but before I act on it, I need to know what you would do if you found him. I disagreed with Karlion's methods, but I don't deny that Baron Grin is a useful weapon against Radukar.'

'He'd be even more useful if he could bait the Wolf into a trap,' Gustaf said. 'We know Radukar himself has been drawn away from the Ebon Citadel by these murders. If we knew where to expect to find Baron Grin, we'd be able to anticipate the vampire too.'

'That's also an idea that has merit,' Loew said. 'You're both aware of my cause. I want to see Radukar's tyranny brought down. I'll make enquiries. See what I can learn.' He smiled at them. 'Where can I get word to you if I discover something?'

'I think it better if we meet you,' Emelda told him. 'Just in case the attack on us wasn't just Karlion's idea.'

Loew shook his head. 'I see I'll have to earn your trust all over again. All right. I'll be at the Black Ship each night after eight bells.' He rose from the bench and started back towards the street. 'Until I see you again – be careful. You won't be any help to me if you get caught by Radukar. Even with a wizard's help, it's testing luck too much to expect to escape from him twice.'

INTERLUDE 7

Nadya Jabuik felt strange when she was awakened, as though someone had shouted in her ear to rouse her. There was no sense of fatigue or confusion, as was usual when she rose with the morning to tend her father's poultry in the yard behind their hovel. Her mind was as bright and clear as though she'd slept for a week. She knew that was impossible, but the darkness in her room sent a rush of fear through her. Was it possible she'd slept through the whole day? She knew her father would never have let that happen. Unless it had been his voice calling to her? But no, that couldn't be. Still, what had awoken her? She waited to hear the voice again, but there was nothing. Perhaps it had only been a strange dream.

There was enough starlight sifting through her shuttered window to allow Nadya to make out the clay pitcher beside her bed. Sight of the water made her decide she couldn't have slept the entire day or she'd have been thirsty. This was the same night as when she'd gone to bed, only a few hours from when she'd closed her eyes. How then was it possible she felt so hearty?

Nadya was a young woman, a few months from her third decade. She was counted the prettiest woman in their district. But to entertain a husband would be an imposition on her father, a fact he reminded her of continually. After her mother was killed by deadwalkers, her father had raised Nadya by himself, sacrificing much of his own health and comfort to provide for her. Now, as his decrepitude advanced, he relied on her to do most of the work, to return the support he'd given her. Much as she wanted her own family, Nadya felt obligated to stand by her father.

Yet as she turned and set her feet on the cold floor, all thought and concern for her father receded into the back of her mind. A kind of wonder came over her. Nadya's eyes glistened as she looked about her room. She marvelled at the way the starlight and shadows created strange patterns and fantastical suggestions. This had been her room ever since she left the crib, but tonight it felt as though she were seeing it all for the first time.

Nadya stood and moved towards the window. She drew away the heavy bars and pulled back the shutters. Blood-bats and other prowling creatures had no place in the fascination that now consumed her. She wanted the full glory of starlight to fill her room and make it even more enchanting. The icy breeze that wafted through the open window whipped across her nightgown and sent a cold shudder along her skin. She smiled, delighting in the sensation.

The slums of Ulfenkarn, so shabby and miserable in daylight, now took on an aspect that Nadya found enticing. Much as her room, starlight and shadow wrought their magic across the city. She was seeing it all as though for the first time. In that moment, standing at the window, she knew that standing back and passively observing wasn't enough. She had to be there. She had to experience it.

The climb down from her window was something Nadya had never dared before. One ardent admirer had once tried to climb up to her while her father was asleep, but he'd slipped and broken his leg on the street below. She'd been wary of leaning too far out from the window after that, but tonight the fear of falling was a faraway thing, a concern for someone else, not her. The chill of the wall under her bare feet made her almost giddy with delight. Every sensation that came to her only heightened the dreamy bliss that clung to her, filling her with a sense of rapture.

The cobblestones of the street were rough under her toes, but Nadya felt emboldened by their abrasiveness. Everything only added to the glory of the night. In the distance she heard the howling of wolves, a sound she'd always trembled at before but which now made her heart flutter with anticipation. There was sweetness and comfort in the cries such as she'd never dared to hope she might one day claim for her own.

Nadya glided down the street. She felt impatient now, greedy for the even greater sights that were waiting for her just beyond the next corner. Onward she raced, her pulse quickening with each dancing step. Hurry! Hurry! the blood in her veins cried.

She stopped in a little courtyard beneath the forlorn mass of an old mansion. Nadya knew this place was no longer a home of grand lords and wealthy patrons. Now it was a tenement given over to scores of labourers who occupied its decaying rooms. A squalid finish for a place that had once been so beautiful. But tonight, at least, a remnant of the old glory had been restored. She couldn't see any sign of the commoners who now laid claim to the building. There was only the echo of what had been.

Nadya started when she saw someone move towards her from the shadows. Fleetingly the thought came to her that some ruffian had emerged from the mansion, but as the features of the stranger came clear to her she smiled at such foolishness. There was nothing common about *him*. Of all the marvels she'd seen this night, all paled beside the handsome vision she now gazed upon.

He didn't speak, but Nadya somehow knew he wanted her to come closer. She obeyed without hesitation, her eyes drinking in the invitation she saw on the stranger's face. Closer and closer she moved. Fear, shame, obligation, all of these were gone now. Only desire remained.

Nadya faltered when she saw the knife in the stranger's hand. But it was only for a moment. She wouldn't resist. She couldn't resist the command of those eyes.

After the knife had plunged into her body and she was sprawled on the ground, her life's blood streaming from her torn flesh, Nadya watched her killer as he carefully placed things on the ground around her. She smiled at him and tried to lift her arms when he turned back to her.

So this was Baron Grin. The thought should have terrified her, but she could harbour no grudge against the stranger. Not while those eyes were staring at her. Even the gleam of the knife was feeble beside the glow in those eyes...

CHAPTER TWELVE

Emelda climbed the stairs up from the basement into the gutted remains of what had been a bakery before the cataclysm. There was only so long she could endure being in close proximity to Morrvahl and his outré collection. If anything, the bottled bits and pieces he'd assembled in this reserve sanctum were even more unsettling than those left behind in the old hideout. Morrvahl claimed the specimens could let him gauge how the Shyish Nadir was affecting both the living and the undead in Ulfenkarn. Whatever he hoped to learn, she didn't see any way it could be so vital it justified that morbid assembly of dismembered limbs and pickled organs.

The swordswoman drew back the trapdoor just behind one of the remaining ovens and peered across the desolate room above. Except for a few piles of refuse, the building was barren, looted and ransacked long ago. Anything that was small enough to steal or fragile enough to break apart had been removed, leaving only a few stone ovens and a couple of supporting beams. There was nothing in here to betray the presence of trespassers in the basement. Gustaf was careful to obscure any prints they left in the dust.

But as she emerged from the trapdoor, Emelda became alert. There, on the floor, she could see footprints. Despite Gustaf's caution, there were marks on the floor. Someone had been here, searching the bakery to judge by the way the marks circled around. It was possible some desperate looter had wandered in hoping to find something others had missed, but she didn't think they had the luxury of accepting that idea. The other possibility, that someone had come here looking for them, was too dangerous to ignore.

Emelda turned back towards the trapdoor when she heard movement close beside her. The cold steel of a blade pressed against her side, prodding the slim gap between the sections of her armour. She knew at once from where the antagonist had come. The only place he could have approached to close upon her so quickly. He'd been hiding inside the old oven.

'Don't reach for your sword.' Once again, Emelda was surprised by Loew's voice. She turned her head and saw the vigilante crouched beside the oven, his knife pressing into her skin. She groaned inwardly. They'd been followed on the way back. Despite the circuitous route Gustaf had taken, Loew had managed to shadow them and find their new hideout.

'You're going to kill me anyway when your mob shows up,' Emelda hissed through clenched teeth. 'A unique way of regaining my trust. I have to give you that.'

For the second time, Loew surprised her. He pulled away his knife and tucked it back in its sheath. Emelda didn't wait to give him a chance to surprise her again. Spinning around, she gave him a kick that sent him sprawling in the dust. Before he could even start to rally, her sword was poised at his throat.

'One reason why I shouldn't finish this,' Emelda snarled.

Loew held his hands up. 'I'm alone. There's no one else coming,' he said.

Emelda doubted that. She motioned for Loew to stand. With her sword still pressing his throat, she guided him over to the trapdoor. She stamped her boot on the hatch. Three hard bangs, then she moved away again. The sound would ring through the basement and alert her companions.

'I followed you–' Loew started to speak, but his words were choked off when the trapdoor was flung open. Gustaf sprang up into the bakery, horse pistol clenched in his fist. His eyes fastened on the vigilante and were instantly hostile.

'What's he doing here?' the vampire hunter snapped.

Emelda trained an equally savage look on Loew. 'Trying to find us. This proves Karlion's raid was all his idea. We were fools to listen to him before.'

'You're fools if you don't listen to me now,' Loew insisted.

'Perhaps we should hear him out.' Morrvahl's entrance into the room was less spry than Gustaf's had been, but the thorn-wrapped haft of Gravebloom appeared to frighten Loew far more than the pistol did. 'If you don't like what you hear, we can always kill him later.'

'You heard the wizard, Loew,' Gustaf said. He moved around Emelda and glanced about the rest of the bakery for any other intruders. 'Get talking. It'd better be good.'

'Start with why you followed us,' Emelda demanded. Her hand reached to the knife on his belt and threw it to the floor. She pulled her sword away from Loew's throat but kept the weapon ready. He'd feel freer to speak without a blade at his neck, but she didn't want him to forget that if anything untoward developed, he'd be the first to die.

Loew massaged his neck, obviously relieved to have the sword removed. 'There isn't much time to waste,' he said. 'I followed you because I felt that if I did learn anything we might need to act quickly. Too quickly for me to wait around at the Black Ship for who knows how many days.' He paused and looked around. 'You should be grateful, because something's happened. Something we have to act on right now.'

'Rallied enough thugs to lay a trap for us?' Gustaf suggested.

Loew darted a sullen look at the vampire hunter. 'There's been another murder,' he said. 'Baron Grin's killed again. Only this time the Volkshaufen hasn't found the body.'

'You're certain of this?' Morrvahl asked, stepping towards Loew. 'You're positive this was one of Baron Grin's victims?'

'Yes,' Loew nodded. 'Everything is the same as... as the other body I saw.' He looked sick for a moment but hurried to continue. 'Two of my men are watching the corpse. Nobody has touched it. It's just the way it was found.'

Morrvahl stroked his beard. 'This is interesting. I dare say it might even prove illuminating.' He fastened his eyes upon Loew. 'Where is this victim?'

Emelda noted the uneasy way Loew looked at her and then at Gustaf. 'I swear on my soul it isn't a trap. I'm not trying to trick you.'

'Where'd you find the body?' Emelda sensed the trepidation rolling off Loew.

'The courtyard where we talked,' he answered. 'But I swear to you this isn't a trick! Would I be so stupid as to do something so obvious?'

'You might, if you were desperate,' Gustaf said. The vampire hunter turned and peered out of the doorway into the street. Watching for lurkers.

Emelda shook her head. She gave Loew a half-hearted smile. 'Anybody resourceful enough to lead a vigilante society in the shadow of Radukar's spies wouldn't be this sloppy. No matter how desperate.' She lowered her sword. 'I don't think it's a trick.'

'Thank you for that,' Loew said. 'But we have to hurry if we're going to get there before the Volkshaufen find out.' He looked down at the floor. Emelda motioned that it was okay for him to recover the knife.

'We will have to hurry,' Morrvahl pronounced. He swept between Emelda and Loew, heading for the bakery door. 'But be aware this may yet be a trick.'

'I swear to you, again, that it isn't,' Loew persisted.

Emelda stared at the wizard in confusion. 'If it's a trick, why go?' She backed away from Loew, far enough to be out of reach of his knife.

A grisly laugh rattled up from Morrvahl's chest. 'I didn't say Loew was the trickster. But it would be interesting to discover who is.'

The wizard would say no more but continued on into the street. Emelda turned a bewildered gaze on Gustaf, but the vampire hunter merely shrugged and followed after Morrvahl. She gestured for Loew to precede her before leaving the bakery.

'I hope he isn't right,' she told the vigilante. 'I want to believe there's still courage and honour in the people of Ulfenkarn. Don't betray my hopes, Loew.' She tapped the blade of her sword. 'That would be a costly mistake.'

A crimson twilight swept across the city, the fading sun discoloured by the dark clouds and the malignant influence of the Shyish Nadir. Morrvahl knew his own attunement to the forces of magic rendered such phenomena more distinct, but he could tell from the uneasiness of his companions that they also felt the influence of rampant energies. In time, unless it could be harnessed in a beneficial manner, the nadir would transform all Ulfenkarn into a nightmarish wasteland. All would be consumed.

Gustaf led the way to the courtyard, moving slowly so that he could try to spot any enemies waiting to ambush them. Emelda was guarding Loew, intent on redressing any treachery, though it was obvious to Morrvahl that she didn't believe the vigilante was being duplicitous. He shared her opinion. Only a fanatic would offer himself up as hostage to draw others into a trap. Loew wouldn't do that, not unless it was Radukar he was trying to destroy. By the same count, Emelda and Gustaf would be ready to make the same sacrifice.

Morrvahl's own ambitions weren't so altruistic. Destroying Radukar was only a means to an end for him. With the Wolf gone, he'd be able to study the Shyish Nadir more freely. To do that, of course, he had to outlast the vampire. The others had only dim visions of what would happen after Radukar's demise. For him, it was the whole of his focus.

The streets were rapidly emptying of people as the inhabitants of the slums hastened back to their homes before the curfew fell. Morrvahl wondered if it was fear of the authorities, the creatures slinking in the ruins or the blade of Baron Grin that made them hurry. Each held the promise of death; it was only a question of what kind of death. That, too, was a manifestation of the nadir. Amethyst magic was the essence of death, and in its raw state it suppressed and corroded the material of life. Even the foul perversion of that magic created by Nagash, the black art of necromancy, was inimical to life. It restored husks and shadows, not vibrant, living beings. Even the highest of the undead, the vampire, could perpetuate its semblance of life only by continually replenishing itself with essence stolen from the truly living. For civilisation to thrive in Shyish, the magic of the realm had to be channelled into a positive rather than negative force.

'We're almost there,' Gustaf announced. The vampire hunter moved with a briskness to his step now, trying to strike a balance between the necessary semblance of haste needed to blend in with those around him and the vigilance that would allow him to spot ambushers.

'If only we aren't too late already,' Loew said. He started forwards, compelling Emelda to keep pace with him. 'I don't see any Volkshaufen around. If they'd found the body, they'd have closed off the courtyard.'

Gustaf gave Loew a warning look. It wasn't lost on the vigilante that there was a pistol aimed at him from under the vampire hunter's cloak. He drew back and smiled nervously. Gustaf turned around and headed through the rusted gates into the neglected courtyard. He stood there a moment, studying the scene, then motioned the others forwards.

'Where are your people?' Emelda asked Loew.

'There, behind the bushes,' Loew said, pointing to a tangle of overgrown thorns coated in snow. 'That's where the body is.'

Morrvahl nodded. He could feel the nearness of death, the amethyst magic drawn to the vacuum left by an extinguished life. 'Something's dead over there.' He gave Loew a sharp look. 'If there's a signal you need to give your men, give it.'

Loew put a finger under his lower lip and sounded a curious whistle. A moment later there was an answering note from behind the bushes.

Gustaf kept in the lead as they plunged into the tangle. The instant he was out of sight from the street, the big horse pistol came out from under his cloak. It would make a convincing argument if Loew's men had mischief in mind. Morrvahl let a flicker of power ripple through him, an ember of arcane energy that he could quickly fan into a violent flame if the need developed. He didn't anticipate trouble, but it was wise to be ready for it.

'Sigmar's grace,' Gustaf intoned from up ahead. He stepped aside to allow the others to join him. He didn't train his pistol on the two ashen-faced labourers who stood at the edge of a small clearing surrounded by thorn bushes. Splayed across the open ground at the centre was a woman's body. Immediately the trademark characteristic of Baron Grin was obvious. The victim's face had been flayed to expose the bare skull beneath.

'I told you this was Baron Grin's work,' Loew said. 'You asked me to find a link to the murderer, well here is his handiwork.' The vigilante repressed a shudder as he looked at the corpse.

Emelda walked past him and circled the body. Her eyes were hard as she studied the corpse. She knelt down and examined the wound in the abdomen. 'One powerful thrust,' she observed.

'That fits with the other body I saw,' Loew reminded her.

Morrvahl came forwards and stared down at the cut. 'This was made with a wider blade,' he stated, thinking of what had been revealed to him by his divinations.

Emelda peeled back the torn edges of the nightgown and took a closer look. 'The blow was a powerful one. The blade has pierced clear through and severed the spine.' She let the gory tatters fall back in place. 'Few people can do such havoc with a thrust like this. It would need the strength of a madman... or a monster.'

Gustaf moved to join Emelda and made his own inspection. 'There aren't any marks on her arms or hands. No sign that she tried to defend herself.' He looked up in dismay. 'I've seen this sort of thing before. A victim placed under an enchantment. No will of her own, but utterly submissive to the commands of the bewitching force. She didn't fight back because she wanted to die.'

'You speak of enchantments, but let someone have a look who knows what he's talking about.' Morrvahl loomed over the body. He closed his eyes and let his spirit reach out to the wisps of magic swirling about the body, seeking any residue left behind by a hostile spell. 'Not that I expect you to believe me, but I sense no magical essence clinging to her. If a bewitching spell had been cast, there would surely be some.' He scowled at Gustaf. 'Perhaps a large snake slithered into the courtyard and fascinated her with its gaze.'

Gustaf bristled at the wizard's mockery. He started to say something, but Morrvahl wasn't listening. Instead he was focused on a detail that Emelda hadn't remarked upon. The wizard spun around and snapped a question to Loew.

'How long ago did your men find her?'

'A little less than two hours?' the vigilante said. The two labourers nodded their heads, confirming the estimate.

'This corpse isn't like the others,' Morrvahl said. He pointed down at the wound and the ragged marks about its edges. 'Something has been at the body.'

'We chased away a big corpse-rat when we found it,' one of the labourers offered.

'Is that important?' Emelda asked.

Morrvahl tugged at his tuft of beard. 'The other victims have been befouled in a manner that repulses even the hungriest scavenger.' He gestured with the butt of his staff at dark stains around the body, then at strange marks in the dirt around those stains. 'Bats have been here, lapping up the blood.'

'They never did that before,' Gustaf said. 'At least not with any of the murders that were really done by Baron Grin.' He looked accusingly at Loew. 'What about it? Is this more of your doing? You don't have Karlion around now to do it for you?'

Loew raised his hands in protest. 'I didn't do this. You think I'm mad enough to sink so low? And to what purpose? What reason could I have?'

'If you're ready to think Loew sloppy enough to do this, why not consider that Baron Grin could be sloppy as well?' Morrvahl suggested. 'The other murders might have been carefully plotted before they were executed. This one might have been hasty and the killer unable to invoke the power that repulses even the corpse-rats.'

'He was in a hurry because he's been following us,' Emelda offered. 'He knew we'd been here and wanted to send us a message. A warning.'

'That's possible,' Morrvahl said. 'Baron Grin might know you're looking for him. However, this could also be his way of mocking you. Daring you to catch him.' His eyes fixated on a mark on the ground. He walked over and crouched beside it. His fingers brushed against the dirt and came away dusted in a reddish powder. 'Quick!' he ordered Gustaf. 'Check her feet. See if any of this is on them!' He held out his hand so the vampire hunter could see the strange dust.

'No, nothing like that,' Gustaf reported when he'd made an inspection of the feet.

Morrvahl reached to the small book hanging off his belt from a hook. Nestling Gravebloom in the crook of his arm, he opened the volume and wiped the dust on a blank page. A muttered incantation ensured the substance would adhere to the yellowed parchment.

'Dried blood? Something that the bats missed?' Emelda asked.

'Not this, though there's something of blood about it,' Morrvahl replied. He closed his eyes a moment and pictured the deathly wrongness that saturated the material. 'Yes, blood and something more. It's dirt, of a sort, but it doesn't belong here. And it wasn't brought here by the dead woman.'

'Then it was left by Baron Grin!' Loew exclaimed. He rushed forwards and looked at what was left of the material on the ground. 'This looks like the clay around the blood farms in the western district.'

'Baron Grin was in a hurry and made a mistake,' Gustaf said. 'He left a clue to track him down!'

Loew stood up from the ground, a frustrated look on his face.

'I can't be certain, but it isn't quite right. It looks like the soil at the blood farms, but it's different somehow.'

Morrvahl closed his book and considered the vigilante. 'Different, perhaps, but still a place of blood and slaughter. Just the sort of place one would expect to find Baron Grin.'

The dull red twilight vanished into darkness with an abruptness that stunned Gustaf. He cast his eyes skywards but could see only the faint impression of clouds rolling through the night. A cold wind rustled through the bushes, carrying with it a dank and evil smell.

'Undead are coming,' Morrvahl hissed in warning. Close upon the wizard's words there was the rattle of armour and the creak of fleshless bones from the street.

'Ulfenwatch!' Loew snarled, drawing his knife. The other vigilantes brandished cudgels and looked about anxiously.

Gustaf firmed his hold on the horse pistol and drew his sword. 'You guessed wrong, Loew. Radukar's slaves did find out about this murder.'

Screams rose from the decayed manor as the occupants saw the Ulfenwatch streaming into the courtyard. The sound of slamming doors and closing shutters followed soon after. Gustaf took aim at the pathway between the thorn bushes, ready for the first skeleton that showed itself.

Or so he thought. Without skin to snag on the thorns, the Ulfenwatch plunged straight through the ragged growth. Gustaf twisted around just as an armoured skeleton came crashing through to his right. He levelled the pistol and fired. The report boomed through the courtyard and set icicles falling from the trees. The skull exploded under the impact, fragments flying away as the smoking helm went spinning off into the brush.

'Stand fast!' Loew ordered his men. 'Our only chance is to win through before reinforcements come.' He rushed a second skeleton as it lurched out of the bushes. His knife crackled down across its ribs, breaking two of them. The undead took no notice of the injury, just slashed at the vigilante with its short sword. Loew dodged back just ahead of the rusty blade.

Emelda intervened, her heavier sword striking the exposed bone of the skeleton's leg. Her blow sheared through the limb and sent the thing hurtling to the ground. She grabbed Loew's shoulder and drew him back.

'You won't do much with that,' she said, frowning at his knife.

He nodded and darted forwards to wrest the sword from the fallen skeleton. The undead resisted his pull and clawed at him with its other hand. Loew snarled in rage and kicked his boot into the leering skull, shattering its jaw and fracturing its eye socket. A second kick collapsed the skull entirely and the thing wilted against the ground.

Gustaf reversed his grip on his pistol, employing its plated butt as a club while he slashed at the skeletons with his sword. 'They keep coming!' he shouted to his companions. He downed one enemy by hewing through its pelvis, then cracked the skull of another with a stroke of his pistol. Neither was finished, however, and as they forced their mangled bones back into the fray, more of the fleshless horrors were emerging from the bushes.

'More of them behind us!' one of Loew's men shouted. The two vigilantes plied their clubs against a brace of skeletons attacking from the rear. One of the creatures fell under their frantic blows, but a moment later the Ulfenwatch gained retribution. A corroded spear transfixed one of the men, piercing him in the lung. A ragged cough, speckled with blood, was the last sound he made as his killer ripped the weapon free and went after his comrade.

'Enough of this,' Morrvahl growled. His eyes glowed with a ghostly light. The same light spread across Gravebloom's curved blade. The wizard stepped towards the skeletal spearman. A sweep of the scythe and the creature was ripped asunder, bones and armour parting like butter under the enchanted weapon. He turned and lashed out a second time, this time attacking the undead trying to flank the group. Two more skeletons fell, mutilated by his magic.

'We've got to win through to the street!' Gustaf shouted to the others. He finished one of the skeletons he'd crippled, then smashed the face of another just emerging from the bushes. 'If we stay here, they'll pull us down one by one.'

'I'm with you!' Emelda called back. She rushed in and settled the other skeleton he'd injured, then met the attack of another enemy coming from Gustaf's right. The creature collapsed as her sword smashed through its armour and broke its spine.

Gustaf pressed ahead. He released the pistol and let it hang from the cord around his arm. The next skeleton he attacked, he brought his sword crashing through its wrist. The severed hand fell into the brambles along with the blade it gripped. A second slash cleft its other arm. Closing upon the creature, he reached under its mail shirt and grabbed its spine. Using his grip for leverage, he pitched the thing backwards, using it to block the advance of the undead behind it.

'This way!' he cried.

Emelda was right behind him, keeping the skeletons from flanking him. Loew closed from his left, using the captured sword to cut a path through the thorns. Morrvahl turned and hurried to pursue the others, the glow in his eyes and around Gravebloom's blade starting to fade. The last of the labourers started to run after them, but a skeleton's sword chopped him down. The injured man howled as three more of the undead thrust their blades into his prostrate body.

'Come on!' Gustaf shouted again. He brought the pommel of

his sword smashing into the skull of the skeleton he was pushing and let the dead husk crash to the ground. The open part of the courtyard was rife with more Ulfenwatch, but they'd neglected to block the gates. As the nearest skeleton swung towards him, he shattered its knee with his sword and left it struggling on the ground. 'Hurry! The gate's open!'

Gustaf held his position while the others rushed past him. Emelda paused, intent on helping him, but he waved her on.

'Go! I'll be right behind you,' he assured her. The distant sound of clattering armour told them both that more Ulfenwatch were on the way. They'd have to manage their escape now or never.

Skeletons marched towards Gustaf, trampling the crippled bones of their comrade. More emerged from the bushes, trying to surround him. He knew once they got past him, they'd be after the others. He also knew there were too many to hold by himself.

Backing away, Gustaf sheathed his sword. His hands raced frantically over the powder horn he carried. He opened the cap and poured some of the gunpowder on the ground, then dropped the mostly full horn beside it. Next he drew out the Aqshian firebrand. It was a fabulous instrument, an irreplaceable weapon in the Order of Azyr's arsenal. But he saw no other way.

'That's right, you boneheads, keep coming,' Gustaf said, taunting the skeletons as he continued to back away. When the first of them was right beside the powder horn, he threw the firebrand. The superheated ember from the Realm of Fire clattered across the ground and ignited the spilled gunpowder.

The explosion threw Gustaf through the open gates and into the street. His ears rang with the roar of the detonation, his eyes were dazzled by the flash of flame. When he picked himself up, he saw the courtyard strewn with broken armour and shattered bones. The few skeletons that were still moving were damaged beyond any capacity for pursuit.

'What did you do?' Emelda cried. She hurried to him and helped him off the ground. Loew and Morrvahl stood a few yards farther down the street, both of them looking at him with gaping eyes.

'Squandered my resources,' Gustaf answered. He frowned at his pistol and returned it to its holster. He turned his head. Either his ears were worse than he thought or the Ulfenwatch's reinforcements were much closer than he'd imagined. 'We've got to get going. That was a one-time deal. I can't do that again.'

'We'll never get out of this district,' Loew said. 'They'll close the whole area off.'

Gustaf nodded. Then he smiled. An idea had occurred to him. 'We'll lose them in the alleyways,' he suggested, looking at Loew. 'That is if you know your way around here.'

'That won't help,' Loew objected. 'They'll close in. We can't outrun them forever.'

'We don't have to,' Gustaf promised. 'As soon as we see a break, I know where we can hide.'

From the roof of the dilapidated manor, Radukar watched as his enemies fled into the streets. The vampire's fangs glistened in a predatory smile.

'You're letting them get away, eminence?' The question was posed by the vampire standing beside him. Watchmaster Arno was genuinely confused by his master's tactics.

'They're resourceful,' Radukar commented. 'A Sigmarite fanatic, a rabble-rousing rebel, a potent wizard and the last of the Braskovs. My enemies are an eclectic combination.'

'They've threatened you,' Arno stated. 'It's dangerous to let them get away.'

'Right now, they're trying to find Baron Grin,' Radukar said. 'Whatever their other motives might be, they intend to track the killer back to his lair.' He turned and posed a question to Arno.

'If you thought you knew where Baron Grin was and could trap him, would you show restraint?'

Arno nodded, understanding in his eyes. 'I would bring in every resource available to me, focus everything into catching him.'

'I'm depending on them to do the same.' Radukar stared down at the smoking remains of the Ulfenwatch. 'These mortals are full of surprises, don't you think? They might have other assets I don't know about. Friends as yet unknown to me. Let them find Baron Grin. Let them marshal their full might.'

The Wolf's eyes burned with hunger.

'Yes, Arno. For the moment it is useful to let the hunted believe they are the hunters.'

CHAPTER THIRTEEN

Emelda felt relief when they finally lost their pursuers and could circle around to the refuge Gustaf was leading them towards.

'I'll cover our tracks,' Morrvahl said, motioning for the others to delay. The wizard removed what looked like a handful of dried beetles from a pouch. He crushed the husks between his hands and scattered them across the alleyway.

'I can still see our footprints in the snow,' she told him.

Morrvahl's eyes sparkled with grim amusement. 'The undead won't be able to,' he said. 'I saw no living militiamen with the Ulfenwatch. Had there been, this little conjuration would be worthless.' He waved his hand above the disintegrated insects. They glowed with an eerie light.

'Let's get moving.' Gustaf frowned, clearly unsettled by the wizard's morbid magic. 'Otherwise they won't need to see our tracks, they'll see us.'

Emelda was surprised when, after a few more turns in the maze of alleyways, they came out on a familiar street. Nearby was a familiar building. 'That's where Vladrik lives,' she said.

'And where we're going to hide,' Gustaf replied. He hastened to the door and rapped against the panel. 'Open up! This is the Volkshaufen!' he snarled in his most authoritative tone. The sound of someone moving in the hallway could be faintly heard. More distinct was the barking of several dogs.

'She won't open that door,' Emelda whispered. 'She barely opened it for us during the day, she won't open it at night.'

Loew eased up beside Gustaf. 'Mention the Ulfenwatch. Ever since they expanded their search for Baron Grin, some Volkshaufen have been patrolling with the Ulfenwatch. She might keep that door bolted against a militiaman, but everyone fears antagonising the undead.'

Gustaf seized on the idea. 'Open!' he commanded. 'Open or I'll have the Ulfenwatch break it down!'

The added threat worked, and the viewing panel slid open. Gustaf stepped before it so that he was the only one visible to the landlady. She didn't recognise him without the disguise, but beneath her obvious fright there was a glimmer of suspicion. She turned her head about, trying to peer past the vampire hunter.

'We've no time to waste,' Gustaf snapped, pressing his bluff that he was part of a Volkshaufen patrol. 'If Baron Grin escapes us, you'll be held to account. Radukar will know you helped the killer get away.'

That speech brought a speedy reaction. The landlady didn't even close the panel before she was working the assortment of chains and bolts that secured the door. The instant the portal cracked open, Emelda threw her armoured weight against it. The door was flung wide, and the landlady stumbled back and fell to the floor.

Emelda looked down at the woman for a moment; then the sound of ferocious barking had her staring down the hall. Two enormous mastiffs, sensing the hurt done to their mistress, burst through the weak panels of an inner door. Teeth bared, the dogs fixated on Emelda and came rushing towards her.

Emelda drew her sword. 'Call them off,' she told the landlady. The old woman was too overcome by fright to respond even if she had wanted to.

Before the huge dogs could close upon Emelda, Morrvahl entered the hallway. The mastiffs turned their heads, their attention diverted to the sinister wizard. Fierce barks gave way to anxious whines. The animals backed away, hackles raised. When Morrvahl took a step forwards, they yelped and scrambled back to their room.

'Thanks,' Emelda said. 'You saved me getting bitten. I couldn't fend them both off.'

The wizard shrugged. 'Dogs and cats have a persistent dislike of me,' he replied. 'I decided to put that prejudice to a useful purpose.'

Loew had the door closed and bolted again. Gustaf reached down and lifted the landlady off the floor.

'Now you understand why you shouldn't open the door at night,' he said as he set her on her feet.

Through the woman's fright, a sudden spark of realisation hit her. 'You're the junkman! You were just casin' the house before! Plannin' to rob it!'

'If we meant harm, we wouldn't waste words,' Emelda advised her. She gestured with her sword, making sure the landlady had a good look at it.

'Go back to your room and stay there,' Gustaf ordered the woman. 'Whatever else you might hear tonight, stay in your room.' He pointed to Morrvahl. 'That man is a warlock and he'll know if you start wandering. It'd be better for you if you don't, I can assure you.'

The landlady nodded her head. She stared at Morrvahl for an instant, eyes round with fear. Then she glanced back at Emelda's blade. There wasn't need for any further reminder. Turning about, she hurried down the hall after her dogs.

'Think she'll stay put?' Emelda asked.

Gustaf tilted back his hat and smiled. 'I think it would need Sigmar himself to get her to come out before daybreak now.' He motioned to the stairs. 'Let's go up. I don't know if Vladrik heard anything, but if he didn't, we'll just have to wake him.'

It transpired that the whole house had been wakened by the commotion. While the rooms on the lower floors kept their doors securely locked, the garret was open. A rectangle of blackness was all that could be seen of the room inside.

'He might be waiting to stab whoever goes in there,' Loew whispered. 'Can't see to tell who might be lurking there.'

'Vladrik,' Gustaf called out, raising his voice as much as he dared. 'It's Voss and Braskov, with a few friends. Can we come in?' He waited for some reply, but there was only silence. After a minute he had his pistol in his hand, reversing his hold so he might ply it like a bludgeon. 'This is getting us nothing. I'm going in.'

Emelda held him back. 'No, you're not,' she told him. 'If he's waiting in there with a knife, I'm the one to go in.' She rapped her knuckle against her breastplate. 'My skin's thicker than yours.' She darted a sour look at Loew. 'At least when I'm not taken unawares,' she added.

Gustaf hesitated, not liking the idea but knowing it made more sense. He looked over at Morrvahl, but the wizard shook his head.

'If you don't want this man dead, don't ask me. My magic isn't known for its restraint.'

The vampire hunter nodded. 'Be careful,' he told Emelda.

Emelda smiled and unbuckled the scabbard from her belt. She held it in her left hand. 'If Vladrik wants to fight, I'll try and subdue him with this.' She stared into the darkened garret. The situation reminded her of moments on campaign, when her troops had conquered some marauder tribe. There was always some hut or cave that needed clearing of any lurking enemies. More often than not, she'd taken that hazardous duty as her own. Now she was doing it again.

Across the threshold, the musty smell of salvaged books filled her nose. Her initial momentum was dulled when her shoulder struck a bookcase and sent several volumes crashing to the floor. Emelda tried to recall the layout from their previous visit, the course the narrow pathways took between the stacks. She probed deeper into the room, uncertain if she should call Vladrik's name. Doing so would make the scholar aware of her presence. If he proved antagonistic, that would be a possibly fatal mistake.

As it turned out, he already knew where she was. Emelda swung about when a sudden light rose to her left, ready to lash out with the scabbard, braced to parry a blow with her sword. A thin laugh met her reaction. There, illuminated by the glow of a candle, was Vladrik, bundled much as before and seated in his book-lined alcove.

'Lady Braskov again,' he greeted her, bowing his head. Even with the candle only an arm's reach away, Vladrik was all but lost in the shadows. 'Please, make yourself at home. You do me credit to visit me so soon after our last meeting.'

'Gustaf is here too,' Emelda said, keeping her weapons poised. 'Didn't you hear him?'

'Voss? No, I didn't.' Vladrik sighed. He reached to his face and wiped at his eyes. 'I must have been lost in my thoughts. Ask him in. It's possible I might have something useful to tell you.'

Emelda returned her sword to her scabbard and called to Gustaf. The vampire hunter led Morrvahl and Loew through the clustered books towards Vladrik's light.

'It's late for you to be calling,' Vladrik said. 'I've had no word of Darrock.'

Gustaf shook his head. 'We came here for shelter, not information,' he said.

'Maybe, but I have some information all the same.' Vladrik pointed at the shelf behind where Loew was standing. 'There's a lamp there. Take one of the candles and light it.' He held his hand to his face in a shielding motion. 'Mind my eyes and hold it back. You'll need it, not me.'

Emelda handed a candle to Loew then turned back to Vladrik. 'What did you find out? Something about Baron Grin?'

'Something I'm surprised you didn't know,' Vladrik said, staring at Emelda. 'Gustaf was trained by the Order of Azyr to combat vampires and the undead. Your friends, I don't know, of course. But you, Emelda Braskov, were a soldier on campaign, scourging the land of barbarians.' His hand lighted upon a book resting in his lap. Emelda could see it was bound in black with a grisly icon set into its cover. A chill swept through her as she recognised that symbol.

'Sigmar save us, the arrows of Chaos,' she gasped. It was an emblem she'd seen many times on crusade, cut into the dead flesh of sacrificed victims, carved and tattooed on the living flesh of marauders, embossed on shields and etched into armour. A foul symbol of all the Ruinous Powers.

Vladrik nodded. 'Chaos,' he echoed. His fingers caressed the book. 'This is an ancient tome. Much older than Mournhold. Older than Belvegrod. Perhaps it once rested in the libraries of the Katophranes before they roused the ire of Nagash. In here are recorded worlds that were and worlds that shall never be. The lore of the Dark Gods, their daemons and their disciples.'

Flipping through the book, Vladrik found a page he'd marked with a red ribbon. He proffered it to Emelda. She took it over to Loew and stared at it under the lamplight. The words scrawled on the pages were unlike any characters she'd seen before, but the illustration was clear enough. A body with its face cut away to expose a bare skull. Gouged into the forehead was a symbol she knew even better than the arrows of Chaos. The Skull Rune, the profane emblem of Khorne, Blood God of the marauder hordes.

'Baron Grin makes offerings to Khorne,' Vladrik stated. 'That's the secret of these murders. Each one has been an unholy sacrifice to the Skull Lord.'

'The killer has never made the mark of Khorne,' Emelda objected. The book felt more than heavy in her hands. It felt obscene, like a serpent slithering under her fingers. She was grateful when Gustaf stepped over and took it from her. He looked at it for a moment and then shook his head.

'Would an offering to the Blood God be accepted if the sacrifice wasn't marked?' he asked Vladrik.

'If the killer bore the mark instead,' Vladrik explained. 'That is enough to draw the notice of Khorne. The Blood God is always hungry and eager for offerings. Victim or killer, if one bears the mark and has performed the proper ceremonies, it is enough.'

Gustaf turned back to Emelda. 'By not leaving the Skull Rune on his victims, Baron Grin tried to hide his intentions.' He snapped his fingers. 'That's why nothing would scavenge the bodies, why the bats wouldn't lap up the blood. Everything had been dedicated to Chaos. It was all corrupt.'

'Then the body we found tonight can't be one of Baron Grin's,' Emelda pointed out. 'You found signs that bats and rats had been at it.'

Loew drew back. 'I already said it was Karlion's idea to copy the murders, not mine! You can't think I'd be so daft and clumsy as to lead you back to someone I myself had killed?'

'There might be other possibilities,' Morrvahl suggested. 'You already had a notion the killing was a warning or a challenge. It might be that Baron Grin didn't feel it appropriate to consecrate this death as he had the others. Indeed, it would be in keeping with the mind of a fanatic to draw such a distinction.'

Emelda considered that last point. 'I've seen the slaves of the Dark Gods do many strange things. Things no sane person would do. It's entirely possible.'

'Then that dirt we found might yet lead us back to Baron Grin's lair,' Gustaf declared. 'If he really was there, then it could only have been left by him.'

Vladrik leaned forwards in his chair, his keen eyes glittering in the lamplight. 'What was this evidence you found?'

'A kind of red dirt,' Emelda said. 'It reminded me of the soil at the blood farms.' She looked over at Morrvahl. 'We gathered some of it to compare.'

'Let me see it.' Vladrik's voice was eager.

Morrvahl stepped towards the scholar and held out his book. The pages rustled of their own accord until they settled on the one where he'd deposited the dust. Vladrik peered intently at it.

'This didn't come from the blood farms,' he said at last. His eyes met Emelda's. 'Take the lamp and go into the next room. You'll see a desk, and behind it a map of Ulfenkarn pinned to a frame. Take it down and bring it here.'

Emelda did as the scholar requested, squeezing through the piles of books to reach the inner room. It was crammed with even more shelves than the outer one. It took her some time to finally decide that one massive heap of tomes was in truth the desk, its outlines hidden by the stacked volumes. Behind it, just as he'd said, was a wooden frame with a detailed map of the city burned into a long sheet of vellum.

Vladrik rubbed his hands together excitedly when he saw her return with the map. His eyes roved across it for a few seconds; then he pointed at one particular spot. 'Here,' he said. 'This is where that dirt came from. That was once the largest abattoir in Ulfenkarn. It will take the blood farms years to match the blood that has soaked into that ground. That's where Baron Grin came from. What place would be holier to a disciple of Khorne than a place of slaughter and butchery?'

'I don't know,' Loew said, looking over the map. 'I don't see how Baron Grin could kill in all the places he has and slink back to his lair within the course of a night. This old abattoir is remote, but it isn't so remote that nobody would spot him if he was moving around by day.'

'There's another reason why I know this must be the spot,' Vladrik said. He tapped his finger again on the map. 'It was here, in this very spot, that Radukar slew Slaughn the Ravener in ages past. The taint of the daemon prince has contaminated that ground. A worshipper of Khorne would be drawn to it like a vulture to carrion.' He sank back in his chair. 'More, I know there are tunnels underneath the old abattoir's ruins. Where better for a murderous madman to hide?'

Gustaf took the map, looking it over for himself. 'It's just possible. Baron Grin might have other hideouts he's used before, but I think Vladrik's right. A follower of Khorne would be drawn to such a place. It isn't too far from here, and we know he was there before he killed that woman in the courtyard.'

'Then let's go and settle this murdering fiend,' Emelda said, picturing in her mind all those Baron Grin had killed. 'Once we have him, we can decide how to use him to trap Radukar.'

'You'll need my help to find the tunnels,' Vladrik interjected.

'It'll be too dangerous for you,' Gustaf told him. 'This won't be like one of your books.'

'Just the same, you need me to be your guide,' Vladrik said. 'There isn't much night left to look around.'

Morrvahl shifted Gravebloom from one hand to the other. 'I

shouldn't worry.' He looked over at Emelda and then Gustaf. 'My assets will be able to find any hidden tunnel for us.'

'You don't understand, I have to go,' Vladrik insisted. 'I need to. As you say, Gustaf, this isn't like one of my books. This is real. Something happening to me. I've lived too long in history and legend. It's time I did something of my own. While I can.'

'There'll be fighting,' Emelda warned. 'We might not be able to protect you.'

'It's too late to worry about that,' Vladrik said.

He waved Emelda towards him. The lamplight banished the shadows and revealed the scholar's condition. This wasn't the man she'd met at the leech-parlour. This was a pale, scarecrow of a man, his eyes sunk deep in his sockets, his hair fading into an ashy grey. Veins stood distinct under his parchment-thin skin, like black worms crawling through his flesh.

Vladrik let his visitors drink in the ghastly sight. 'You see, I'm dead already. I was caught by one of Radukar's creatures. It infected me. There's no stopping it. If I'm fortunate, I'll only die and not come back as… something.' He gave Emelda an imploring look. 'This is my last chance to *do* something, to help liberate Ulfen-karn. Please let me.'

Emelda nodded. She looked at her companions. 'It might be the tunnel is hidden too cleverly for Morrvahl's spies. We might need Vladrik to show us the way.'

She turned back to Vladrik.

'I make this promise to you. If you die, we'll ensure you stay that way.'

Loew had seen the old abattoir only at a distance before. He could feel his skin crawl as they entered the ruined ground. There was a sense of hostility that permeated the air, and he did not think it was because of prowling creatures. There'd been a moment as they approached the ruins when a flock of bats started to swoop down, only to peel away when Morrvahl waved his staff at them. The wizard had a malignant presence all of his own.

Morrvahl appeared unfazed by the abattoir's atmosphere, but Loew judged both Emelda and Gustaf weren't so stoic in their feelings. He could see the way their fingers played with the pommels of their swords, anxious to draw them at the first sign of danger. Vladrik was harder to evaluate. The scholar's infection made him almost as cadaverous in appearance as the wizard, and the way he hugged his heavy fur cloak close to his body made all but the most fleeting glimpses of his visage impossible. His step was firm and unerring, however, as he led the way. Loew just hoped the man's confidence was drawn from knowledge rather than delusion.

The piled debris and crumbling walls of the building were looming over them when Vladrik suddenly stopped and pointed to a particular spot.

'There,' he declared. 'That was an old drain leading down into the sewers.' He nodded his head and sighed. 'Much blood flowed through these channels until the ground itself was changed.'

Gustaf stepped forwards and examined the spot. 'There's something here,' he told the rest of them. 'Help me clear the rubble.'

'This can't be the right way,' Loew said as he helped move jagged pieces of masonry. 'If there's a passageway here, Baron Grin couldn't use it. Not with all of this covering it.'

'He might have covered it after he left,' Emelda theorised. She shook her head and looked over at Gustaf. 'That means he won't be in there and if he sees we've moved the rubble, he'll know we were here.'

Gustaf smiled and threw aside the stone he held. 'Baron Grin is craftier than you give him credit for.' He nudged a length of knotted rope that squirmed its way up from the debris. 'The other end of that is down there,' he said. 'So, when the killer comes home, he can tug on the rope and knock over some rubble he's piled up. Covering his tracks. There's a reason this fiend has been able to hide from Radukar. Don't underestimate him.'

A trapdoor was exposed once the snow and debris were cleared. All of them stood back, none moving towards the iron ring set into its surface.

'If he's so clever,' Loew said, 'then he might have rigged something to warn him when that door's opened.' He scowled and looked at the stones they'd moved. 'He might've heard what we were doing. Be waiting down there even now.'

Emelda nodded. 'This is familiar to me,' she told them. 'Campaigning against the barbarians, there were many times the last few survivors had to be hunted down in places like this.' Her eyes became as cold as steel. 'It's dangerous work. Too often soldiers who survived the battle would fall prey to some hidden lurker.' She drew her sword and gestured to Loew. 'Open it. I'll go first.'

Loew frowned at her directions. 'You're more important than I am. The people will rally to the last of the Braskovs far more readily than they will to someone who came from their own ranks.'

He frowned at that sentiment, but he knew it was true. The people of Ulfenkarn had been conditioned to look up to the nobility, to almost venerate them. Even the cataclysm and the tyranny of Radukar hadn't changed that. Those who despised the nobility were often those most in awe of their status. They might reject that authority, but they knew its hold over the public.

'Besides,' Loew added, 'when it comes to a fight, you're still more valuable than me. If one of us has to trigger a trap, let it be the most expendable.' He was touched by the hesitance he saw on Emelda's face. It didn't sit right with her to let him take the risks. Loew smiled. If the people of Ulfenkarn were to be led by a noble, let it be a noble like Emelda Braskov.

'He's not wrong,' Gustaf stated. 'In a standing fight, you're the best among us.' He slapped his holstered pistol. 'My equaliser doesn't count for much after we escaped the courtyard.'

Emelda stepped back but kept her sword ready. 'The important thing is to know when to be careful and when to be quick,' she told Loew. 'If something looks wrong, it probably is.'

'Hold out your knife,' Morrvahl said. When Loew complied, the wizard laid his hand on the bared blade. His eyes flickered with an eerie light. The same ghostly radiance spread down onto the blade. 'For a small time, this will serve as a light to guide you and an enchantment to strengthen your blows. You may have cause for both.'

Loew felt uneasy accepting the wizard's gift, but he knew there was wisdom in his course. He'd seen for himself the efficacy of that same spell when applied to Morrvahl's scythe. Baron Grin had every advantage; maybe a bit of magic would give Loew some slight edge.

His hand curled about the iron ring. 'Here's to luck,' Loew said as he wrenched the door open. It resisted for a moment, but then creaked upwards. Below was a darkened pit that led into a tunnel.

'Keep to the main channel,' Vladrik said. 'Don't divert into any of the side passages. You might get lost in the sewers and never find your way out.'

To all the other fears boiling in his belly, the scholar had to give Loew still another to think about. He focused upon the greater scale of things. He was fighting for more than just himself. He was trying to lift his people out of the squalor and degradation to which Radukar had condemned them. Against that lofty ambition, his own life mattered little.

The air in the pit was noxious. However long the abattoir had been gone, the tunnel was rank with the smell of blood. The light from his knife lent everything a strange colour, a deep purple shade that was uncomfortable to the eye, but which drew out details in stark relief. He could see the old brickwork of the sewer, the many holes gnawed into the walls by rats and moles. The ground under his feet was dry and crusty. He was grateful the light didn't draw out its natural hue, because he didn't need his suspicions of what it was confirmed.

Loew looked for anything out of the ordinary, any sign that might betray some trap laid by Baron Grin. He could see nothing. He wondered if Emelda would have been better, if her experienced eyes would have seen something that he'd missed. There was no use in such questions, however. The die was cast. The choice was made. Now it was left to him to do all that he could to ensure the others came to no harm.

He was about a dozen yards into the tunnel when he first heard the noises. Loew's skin crawled at the sound and his mind raced to try to identify the source. There was a nagging familiarity to it, yet it was distorted as well into something still more horrible. It seemed to come from all around him. A scratchy, scrabbling sound, like crabs trying to climb out of a pot.

Then he saw a brown head pop out from one of the holes in the wall to his left. Had it been closer, Loew would have struck at the thing. It was a verminous muzzle, foul with necrotic decay. Beady eyes gleamed from above chisel teeth. A corpse-rat, corroded by the undead flesh it had consumed. The animal lunged into the tunnel, its naked tail lashing behind it in the dust. From the other holes, more of the rodents appeared. Before Loew could even move, a dozen of them were ranged against him. Yet still the sound of scrabbling claws continued. Increasing!

With a sense of mounting dread, he looked to the right. Ahead there was a dark opening, one of the side passages Vladrik had warned him against. There the noise was growing into a cacophonous din. To his horror, a swarm of rats surged up from the passageway, hundreds strong.

The vermin gazed at him with their hungry eyes. For a moment there was silence, a hideous tableau of man against animal. Then the stand-off shattered. One of the rats sprang at Loew. His knife flashed out, cutting the creature in two. The smell of its filthy blood agitated the rest of them, snapping whatever strange restraint had held them in check. Squeaking in rage, the animals rushed forwards. Some ravaged the body of the dead rat, but most made straight for Loew.

Again, the knife slashed out. Another rat fell, but now there were far too many for Loew to contend with. One leaped up and landed on his shoulder. He could feel its claws scrabbling for purchase even as its fangs ripped into his tunic. Other rats charged up his legs, tearing at his trousers and cutting into the flesh beneath. Loew used one hand to grab at the rats, but for each he pulled free two more took its place. His knife struck out wildly, trying to fend off the creatures rather than deliver any killing blows.

Loew's mind thundered with the loathsomeness of what he knew must be his death. He'd stood against the Volkshaufen and the Ulfenwatch, faced Radukar and lived to speak of it, yet here he was in a sewer being devoured by corpse-rats!

Just as Loew's resolve was collapsing into despair, a ghoulish light exploded within the tunnel. The beady eyes of the vermin, a moment before a hellish crimson, now turned to a pallid yellow. They squeaked, but now in terror rather than rage. A scampering horde turned tail and retreated in a frantic rout, scrabbling back to their holes and into the passageway. Those clinging to Loew were the last to run. The vigilante took savage satisfaction in lurching after them and splitting two of them with his knife.

'You should have cried out,' Morrvahl chided Loew as he strode towards him. The wizard's staff shimmered with residual energies left by his conjuration. 'Until I saw your peril, I thought you'd merely agitated the rats. I didn't know they'd decided to make a meal of you.'

'I thought you were the one who could control the vermin,' Emelda said, scowling. She moved around Morrvahl to inspect Loew's injuries.

'A specimen here and there I can make into my agent,' Morrvahl explained. 'But I'm hardly the godbeast of rats. You should be grateful I was able to frighten the horde before they chewed Loew down to the bone.'

Emelda threw the statement back at Morrvahl as she looked at Loew's bleeding legs. 'They've nearly done just that,' she snapped.

Loew smiled and pushed her hands away. 'It isn't that bad,' he assured her, biting against the pain he was actually feeling. He looked over at Morrvahl. 'My thanks for saving me. I'm in your debt.'

The wizard chuckled and stroked his beard. 'Indeed? One should be careful to whom one is indebted, friend Loew.' The thorns wrapped about Morrvahl's staff writhed suddenly, as though sharing some grim mirth with its owner.

'Can you go on?' Gustaf asked. The vampire hunter and Vladrik were just behind Morrvahl. 'We grew worried when the glow of your light couldn't be seen from above, so we followed you down.'

'If you need to go back, none will think you a coward,' Emelda said, still frowning at his torn legs.

Loew shook his head. 'Just give me a moment to bind my cuts,' he said. 'I'll be ready to press on then.' He smiled. 'It'll take more than rats to finish somebody who's stood up to Radukar.'

The bravado impressed Gustaf and won a nod of approval from Emelda. Vladrik, however, had other concerns.

'Yes, bind his wounds. And quickly,' Vladrik admonished them. He looked around at the walls and ceiling, at the floor and the rat carcasses littering it. 'This is a dangerous place to shed blood. A daemon prince doesn't die the way a mortal does. Its essence lingers where it was vanquished, tainting the place of its seeming destruction. Biding its time until it can return.'

Gustaf turned to the scholar wearing an expression redolent of horror. 'Is *that* what Baron Grin hopes to accomplish? He's trying to resurrect Slaughn?'

The question sent raw terror pulsing through Loew's veins. He could see that Emelda felt the same. All their lives they'd been told the stories of Mournhold's darkest days, when the Chaos fleet of Slaughn the Ravener had descended upon their city. How the daemon prince had butchered his way through the heroic defenders, unstoppable as a typhoon. It had taken a monster like Radukar and his Kosargi ogors to defeat Slaughn and end the daemon's evil.

'Perhaps Baron Grin believes it is better to destroy the city and all who live in it than leave the place to Radukar and his vampires,' Vladrik said.

'Then he's more than desperate,' Loew retorted. 'He's completely mad.'

'It's like Baron Grin's trying to turn back time,' Emelda said. 'As though he could change things so Slaughn's horde took Mournhold instead of Radukar saving it from Chaos.'

Vladrik only smiled at her remark. 'If the Wolf suspects such intentions, then you understand why he's involved himself personally in the hunt for Baron Grin. Even Radukar has no desire to contend with Slaughn again.'

Gustaf gripped the icon of Sigmar he wore. 'If any of this is true, then it's doubly vital we stop Baron Grin. Not just to use him as bait for Radukar, but to stop his insane plans.'

They pressed deeper into the tunnel. The stench of blood intensified, bringing with it an increase in that atmosphere of hostility. Loew thought about what Vladrik had said. The daemon prince Slaughn, his essence corrupting the place of his destruction. Baron Grin, appealing to the Blood God. Had he managed to rouse that malefic spirit? Stirred the residue of Slaughn from the dust of oblivion?

Ahead the tunnel opened into a great chamber lit by flickering torches. Loew was sickened by the sight, for the floor was covered in streams of blood. It was a bog of gore from which little islands of stone rose. Upon one of these stood a grisly altar built of bones, the icon Loew now knew as the Skull Rune impressed upon it in bronze. The sight sent a flush of rage pulsing through him, as though Khorne were crying out to all the anger in his soul, urging him to lose himself in a frenzy of slaughter.

Loew resisted the urging with difficulty. He only broke free when he heard Emelda shudder beside him.

'Which one is Baron Grin?'

He turned his head and saw that there were dozens of people standing on the stone spires. They made a grisly scene, their bodies painted in blood, their arms raised in adoration towards the altar.

'They all are,' Gustaf hissed. 'An entire cult of Khorne worshippers under the very streets of Ulfenkarn. By Sigmar, they're an abomination!'

The moment the vampire hunter invoked the God-King's name, the cultists turned around. They lowered their arms and stared at the intruders with vacant eyes. Loew noted the grievous wounds that marred their bodies, horrible cuts that no one could survive.

'They're undead,' he gasped. 'Deadwalkers!'

The zombies dropped down from their perches and into the slush of blood that filled the chamber. Slowly they advanced upon the group. Others, much nearer, reared up from beneath the mire of gore. They lunged at the heroes with clawed hands, trying to rip and tear at living flesh. Emelda dropped one with a sweep of her sword that cut its head from its body. Gustaf met the attack of another by caving in its head with the butt of his horse pistol. Morrvahl struck out with his staff, the briars wound about it entwining one of the deadwalkers. The creature visibly withered as Morrvahl drew its sustaining magic from the husk.

Loew plunged his knife again and again into the zombie that

came for him. It fell under his attack. The lingering enchantment on his blade let it punch through flesh and bone like it was cream. A mush of blood and brains bubbled away from the creature as he held it beneath the surface of the bog.

'They die easy enough!' Loew felt exultation as the deadwalker fell limp.

'Their threat lies in their numbers,' Emelda warned. More of the zombies were already closing upon them, advancing with the same mindless malice, taking no notice of their casualties.

'We can win this!' Loew shouted. Then a peal of laughter froze him where he stood. Confidence drained out of him, replaced with icy fear.

'There is no victory for you here, only death.' The words echoed through the chamber. It was a voice none who heard it could ever forget.

The voice of Radukar.

The vampire appeared upon the island of stone where the altar of bones stood. He gazed disdainfully at it. A swing of his barrow-blade obliterated the structure and sent skulls plopping down into the blood bog.

'You sought to use the Khorne cult to trap me, but instead it is you who are trapped.' Radukar directed a lupine smile at his enemies. 'Though I must confess I expected more of you. Had I known you were so few, I'd not have gone to all this trouble.' His laughter rang out once more, echoing off the walls.

'Butcher! Monster!' Loew shrieked at the gloating vampire. 'You'll answer for what you've done to my people!'

Radukar fixed Loew with his fiery gaze. 'Little man,' he snarled, 'I've not even started with your people.'

He extended his arm, and from behind the largest of the stone spires three Nightguard lumbered into view. Loew felt his heart sicken with dread.

'I am, however,' the vampire continued, 'almost finished with you.'

CHAPTER FOURTEEN

Gustaf gripped his Sigmarite hammer so tightly that it dug into his palm and cut the skin. Dread pulsed through him. Radukar! Here! The vampire was right to gloat. They weren't ready for this. Their one hope was that they might still escape. Get back down the tunnel before the Wolf and his Nightguard could come to grips with them. He whispered a prayer.

'Sigmar, preserve us in our moment of calamity.'

It wasn't the God-King who answered Gustaf, but the cold voice of Morrvahl.

'Stand back,' the wizard warned them. 'Be ready to lend me strength,' he added, his eyes dropping to Gravebloom and the thorns wound about the staff. Gustaf understood the meaning. Morrvahl would use his magic, but there would be a cost.

'Let me show you real magic,' Morrvahl growled at Radukar. His eyes took on a ghostly light. All the colour drained from his face and his dark beard turned silvery grey. A nimbus of power swirled about Gravebloom and, at the same time, the shadows in the chamber darkened. Morrvahl strode forwards, heedless of the advancing zombies and undead ogors. His eyes were locked upon Radukar, and for just an instant there was a flicker of uncertainty in his pose.

Suddenly Morrvahl made a chopping motion with the scythe. The lengthening darkness came rushing in, now a spectral wave of shrieking energy. Gustaf could see the wispy suggestion of lost souls in that malignant tide, the dread essence of amethyst magic. The deathly power of Shyish itself. That unleashed energy poured down upon the undead, vengefully penetrating them to draw out the polluted magic that sustained them. One after another the deadwalkers collapsed, their morbid frames shrivelled by Morrvahl's spell. They pitched forwards to splash into the mire of rancid blood, some of them crumbling into pieces as their falls broke the last threads of necromancy holding them together.

For a minute the occult tempest raged, and with each heartbeat it seemed Morrvahl became weaker and more wizened. At last he could sustain the effort no longer. Like a candle being snuffed out, his spell evaporated. The storm was over, and Gustaf stared across the aftermath. Only a few deadwalkers endured; most had been destroyed utterly. The Nightguard were still standing, but their rotten flesh looked leathery and brittle, and when they moved their steps were slow and shambling. Not enough to destroy them, the spell had at least weakened the ogors.

Then Gustaf lifted his gaze to the spire of rock where Radukar stood. The vampire had drawn his fur cloak around himself during the arcane onslaught. Now he flung back the covering, like a bat throwing open its wings. Whether Morrvahl's spell wasn't enough to harm him or he had protections of his own, the Wolf was unhurt. His eyes blazed with a mix of mockery and rage as he glared down at his enemies.

'Morrvahl's spent!' cried Emelda. It was obvious to anyone who looked his way that the wizard had exhausted himself with his conjuration. He leaned wearily against his staff, barely able to keep himself standing.

'We can't win this,' Gustaf declared. Slow as they were, the Nightguard and remaining deadwalkers were still advancing towards them. Even if they could hold their own against the undead, the creatures had a powerful reserve in the person of Radukar himself. The vampire had yet to commit himself to the fray, content to leave the fighting to his slaves.

'We've got to run,' Loew agreed. He rushed over to help Morrvahl. The moment he came close, however, the thorns around Gravebloom sprang at him. He shouted in panic as they dug into his skin. Blood dribbled from his cuts, but it was something else that was being drawn from him and siphoned into the wizard. A spectral transfusion of energy that had the vigilante writhing in pain.

Gustaf hesitated to help Loew, wary lest he too be caught by the thorns. Emelda allowed herself no such hesitation. She dashed over and began unwinding the tendrils coiled about him. They scratched and tore at her as she removed them and from her, too, energy was being drawn out and fed into the wizard.

Radukar's sneering howl drew Gustaf's eyes from the grim tableau. The Wolf glowered down at them from his perch.

'You think to escape? There is no escape, fools! I stayed my hand this long because I thought you'd bring other fools into my trap. Instead, all you've brought is your own destruction!'

The vampire gestured imperiously with an outstretched finger. Gustaf heard a moan of agony sound from behind him. He spun about and watched as Vladrik fell to his knees. He'd forgotten about the scholar in the midst of battle. Now he was given ghastly cause to repent that mistake. The dark robes were tearing apart as Vladrik's body swelled beneath them, flesh and bone expanding rapidly into some new and hideous shape. The wasting infection, so obvious before, had been but a symptom of a far more complete corruption.

'Sorry, my friend,' Gustaf said as he lunged at Vladrik. They'd promised to ensure the scholar was truly dead. He intended to keep that promise by ramming his blade into the man's heart before his obscene transformation could be completed.

Instead the vampire hunter's sword was caught in a clawed fist. Flesh bubbled and steamed as it reacted to the silvered steel and Sigmarite blessings, but Vladrik kept his hold. Gustaf tried to rip the weapon free, but his efforts were futile. He watched on as the scholar continued to change. The frail body was now a misshapen hulk with broad shoulders and corded muscles. Grey hair sprouted from the naked flesh. Vladrik turned a tortured face towards Gustaf, an anguished appeal in his eyes. Then the human visage collapsed entirely. Intelligence fled from the eyes, replaced by bestial hunger. The forehead drew back into a longer and flatter skull. The face bulged outwards, lengthening into a fanged muzzle.

'Vargskyr!' Gustaf named the horror before him. He sickened at the enormity of Radukar's cruelty. The Wolf belonged to the all but extinct Vyrkos bloodline, a breed of vampire known for their lupine characteristics. Not all who were bestowed the Blood Kiss to join that foul assembly became true vampires. Many became bestial monsters, the ferocious vargskyr. Such was Radukar's power that he'd deliberately inflicted the curse upon Vladrik, letting it lurk inside him until the Wolf should call it forth.

Radukar's mockery rolled through the chamber once more. 'You sought Baron Grin, but I found the truth first. There was no Baron Grin, only a shabby little cult. So I took their leader and decided to make him the monster he pretended to be.'

The beast that had been Vladrik threw back his head and howled, an intonation at once mournful and malignant. Gustaf looked in horror on the thing that had been the scholar, the man who'd led the Khornate cult. He berated himself for not guessing at Vladrik's heresy before. Who but a man of his education and resources could have found the secret of this place, or known the profane rites by which the Blood God's favour could be earned? When he'd described the intentions of Baron Grin, Vladrik had been relating his own ambitions before he fell under Radukar's shadow.

Gustaf ripped the hammer from around his neck and cast it into the vargskyr's face. The icon struck it below the eye, but instead of falling to the ground, it stuck to the creature. The sickly smell of burning flesh filled the air as the icon sizzled against the monster's unclean skin. Gustaf was dragged forwards as the beast reeled back in pain. Vladrik raised his other claw to rip the holy talisman away. As he did, for a moment, his grip on Gustaf's sword weakened.

'For your victims!' Gustaf snarled as he pulled his sword free. The silvered edge sliced across the vargskyr's fingers, severing two of them and leaving the others mangled. There was no pity in him for either the beast or the man he'd once been. Vladrik *had* been the mind behind Baron Grin and the Khornate cult. A traitor and manipulator who'd tried to use Gustaf and his allies the way they'd intended to use Baron Grin.

'For Sigmar!' Gustaf shouted, and drove home his attack. The sword slashed across the vargskyr's chest and left a wound that smoked and bubbled.

Before he could strike again, the huge beast swatted him with the back of his hand. The impact drove all the breath from his lungs and sent him careening through the air. He slammed against one of the rocky projections and splashed into the blood bog.

Gustaf tried to rally, forcing himself to move despite the tingling numbness that crackled through his body. Before he could, he was pushed beneath the surface by a powerful weight. Red agony pulsed through him as the crushing mass threatened to flatten him against the bottom. His head beneath the mire of blood, he could only dimly make out a tremendous shape looming over him. He knew at once what it must be.

One of the Nightguard had its foot on him! Whether it intended to smash him or drown him was of little concern to Gustaf. He'd be dead either way and there was nothing he could do to stop it.

Emelda gnashed her teeth against the pain that rippled through her body. The thorns from Gravebloom dug into her flesh, unerringly seeking out even the smallest gap in her armour. She could feel blood trickling across her arms, but she knew it was the least harm the wizard's staff was inflicting on her. She thought of the mad wretch lying upon the cellar table, and how Morrvahl had drained the man's vitality to replenish his own. Then the wizard had been aware of what his staff was doing; now he appeared too weak to prevent it from acting on its own.

It took more will than she knew she possessed to lift her sword and bring it chopping down at the grotesque tendril. Emelda had resisted doing so before, uncertain how such an attack would affect Morrvahl, but now she felt there was no choice. Gravebloom could drain both her and Loew to shivering husks, helpless before the advance of Radukar's forces. They had to be free or all of them would die.

When the blade slammed into the thorny vine the impact shook through Emelda's bones. It was like striking a wall of stone, such was the resistance the tendril presented. She retained her grip on the sword only by a miracle; for her fingers were numb with the shock. How much strength it would need to cleave through the sucking coil she couldn't imagine. Yet she was determined to try. She raised her sword to strike a second blow.

That blow never fell. Emelda was stunned to see the thorns pluck themselves from her skin. The entire vine snaked away, whipping back around the staff. Those entwined about Loew likewise retreated, leaving the vigilante exhausted but still standing. Morrvahl, on the other hand, was much recovered, though his beard was still shot through with grey amid the black and his face still bore a haggard look. He stared at Emelda with an expression that was the last one she ever expected to see him wear – apologetic.

'Too much,' the wizard muttered. 'Gravebloom took too much.'

Emelda had no time to judge whether Morrvahl's contrition was genuine. A flash of motion caught her eye and she spotted Gustaf as he was thrown across the chamber. She saw him crash against one of the stone slabs and sink into the pooled blood beneath it. She wasn't the only one to spot his distress. One of the Nightguard lurched towards the stricken vampire hunter.

'Gustaf!' Emelda shouted. Even if he heard her, there was no time for him to react. The undead ogor had reached him and stamped its foot down, plunging him under the sanguinary surface.

Emotion took over. The very thing she'd always warned her soldiers against now overwhelmed Emelda's brain. She charged out into the gory mire; her only thought was to save Gustaf. How she'd accomplish such a feat was a problem she couldn't think about. She only knew she had to try. As she reached the Nightguard, a familiar glow suffused her sword. She smiled. Morrvahl had recovered enough to conjure at least some of his spells. This was one she knew how to put to good use.

Emelda lunged at the ogor. The enchantment around her blade magnified her power beyond that of a mortal human. The sword crunched into the back of the Nightguard's knee and exploded outwards from the kneecap. Shards of flesh, bone and armour went spraying in every direction when she wrenched her weapon free. The rotten hulk toppled, crashing down into the bog, its lower leg shorn away.

'Back to the underworlds with you!' Emelda yelled. She sprang onto the ogor's back and brought her sword swinging downwards. This time her target was the thick, bull-like neck. A headsman's axe would have barely cut the skin, but her magically augmented sword bit clean through. The brute's head sloughed away, rolling through the mire like a grotesque barrel.

She looked around. Gustaf was back on his feet, covered from head to toe in rancid gore. How much of the blood was his and how much was from the bog, she didn't know, but she could tell he was gravely injured by his twisted posture.

'Get away,' Gustaf said. 'Before it's too late.' He crouched down and retrieved his sword from where it had fallen in the mire. 'We can't win this.'

Emelda felt hot fury well up inside her. They'd risked so much, endured so much. It couldn't end this way. The Wolf was here! If they all tried… But she knew it was futile. The dweomer was fading from her sword, Morrvahl's spell worn through. She'd finished one Nightguard, but two others were closing upon them, along with the last few deadwalkers.

'The vargskyr… Vladrik,' Gustaf said. He pointed to the tunnel. Emelda gasped when she saw the beast and recognised the tattered robe stretched across its monstrous body. The thing was pacing back and forth, cutting off their retreat. 'You'll have to win through. Get the others out. Live to fight another day.'

'And what will you do?' Emelda demanded, upset by the fatalism she heard in Gustaf's words.

The vampire hunter reached to his belt and withdrew a small vial. Emelda's eyes went wide when she saw it with its stopper fashioned in the shape of Dracothion. She'd heard of the concoction before, a distillation of Stardrake blood. It could endow a warrior with prodigious strength, render him insensible to pain. It was also a deadly poison, killing even the heartiest hero within a few hours. A dreadful tool. A weapon of last resort.

'I'll keep Radukar busy,' Gustaf said. 'Give him something to worry about.' A smile flickered on his face; then his expression grew solemn. 'Get out, Emelda. Live. Your city needs you.'

'You will be remembered,' Emelda vowed. She fought back the urge to slap the vial from his hand as he brought it to his lips. She knew he was right. This was the way it had to be.

Emelda turned and dashed towards the tunnel. One of the dead-walkers tried to intercept her, but she cut it down on the run. The zombie thrashed in the mire, struggling to rise with both its arms broken by the swordswoman. Morrvahl and Loew were facing the vargskyr, scythe and knife at the ready. The pair were ready to meet the beast's charge, unaware that it had been told to guard the way out, not join the attack.

'We've got to fight our way past that thing!' Emelda told the two.

'But… that's Vladrik,' Loew stammered.

'It was,' Emelda hissed. 'Now it's just another of Radukar's monsters.' She met the vargskyr's savage gaze with an equally vicious glower. 'It's in our way.'

'What about Gustaf?' Loew said.

Morrvahl understood the severity of Emelda's expression. 'He's staying to buy us time.' His hands tightened about Gravebloom. 'Let's not waste what he's given us.'

Emelda nodded. 'We attack it together. A vargskyr is stronger and faster than we are, but it has the brain of a beast. That's the advantage we have to exploit.'

'I might have what we need,' Morrvahl said. He drew a packet from beneath his robe. It was similar to the one Emelda had seen him use against Karlion's mob. He glanced from Emelda to Loew. 'You need to distract the vargskyr so I can be certain of hitting it with the powder.'

The image of what had befallen Karlion's men in the sewer set Emelda's stomach churning, but she knew they couldn't afford such qualms. However dastardly the wizard's methods were, they had to use every resource they had.

'You'll get your distraction,' Emelda promised. 'Just see to it the vargskyr's the only thing you send your *assets* to attack.' She shuddered at the thin smile Morrvahl gave her. She knew too well the wizard's callousness. If it was a choice between escape and risking the lives of his companions, she knew what he would choose.

She also knew it was their only chance.

Gustaf's veins throbbed with hot, invigorating power. The hurts that only a moment before had threatened to cripple him now faded into a dull and indifferent sensation. He felt more alive than he'd ever known, his every sense quickened to a degree he hadn't thought possible. Colours and odours, even the feel of his clothes against his skin, were heightened to an intensity of experience he'd never known. He might have been blind and insensate before, so marked was the contrast.

The thrill surging through him was interwoven with a bitter irony. He felt alive, but he was in truth dying. The human body couldn't endure the wyrmbrew. The same potency that empowered him was also consuming him. The moment he imbibed the draught, he was a dead man, trading his allotment of years for the brief resilience fuelled by the elixir. Once its energy was spent, so too was his life.

'So, don't squander it.' Gustaf scolded himself for allowing the power to intoxicate him even for a few heartbeats. He was trying to buy time for Emelda and the others. He had to make sure they escaped, or his would be a wasted sacrifice.

Gustaf rushed towards the island of stone where Radukar stood. The remaining Nightguard moved to intercept him. Their heavy glaives, capable of splitting a horse in half, swung at him. The wyrmbrew coursing through his body enabled him to dodge past the cumbersome weapons. He didn't pause to challenge the ogors but circled around them. A leap and a scramble and he'd reached the top of the rocky spire. He kicked aside one of the bleached skulls from the shattered altar and faced the Wolf.

A contemptuous curl twisted Radukar's lip as the vampire regarded the foe who now confronted him. 'I was content to let my slaves attend to you,' he said. 'You'll regret demanding my notice, Sigmarite. If I must sully my hands dealing with you, I shall expect satisfaction.'

'Expect destruction instead,' Gustaf snarled. 'Make what peace you can with your master, Nagash.' He sprang at the vampire, his silvered blade flashing out in a deadly arc.

The speed of his attack caught Radukar by surprise. Narrowly the Wolf avoided the blessed blade, whipping his cloak around and letting the enfolding mantle intercept the blow. When he dodged back, a great tatter of shredded fur spilled from the rent garment. Radukar whipped the torn cloak from his shoulders and coiled it around his left hand. The other reached to the sword on his belt and pulled it free.

'So, there's more to you than I expected, Sigmarite,' the Wolf said. 'This may even prove more amusing than tedious.' The vampire's eyes blazed with anger. 'But I promise you'll learn one thing before I let you die. Radukar answers to no master!'

Gustaf dashed in to resume the attack. As he did, Radukar cast the torn cloak full into his face. The vampire hunter stumbled back, taken by surprise. Radukar's fearsome barrow-blade lashed out in a sideways sweep. Gustaf managed to parry it, swatting it aside before it could gash his ribs. Even with his empowered muscles, he felt the ponderous strength behind the Wolf's attack and his sword was nearly ripped from his grasp.

'Prolong it all you like, your death is inevitable,' Radukar snapped. The vampire swung his sword once more. This time Gustaf couldn't drive the attack aside. He blocked the blow with his own blade, the two weapons grinding against one another as the enemies strained to break free.

'My death *is* inevitable,' Gustaf barked back, 'but when I go to my grave, I'll not go alone!' Focusing his determination into a single effort, he broke away from Radukar's assault. The two combatants lurched away from each other.

'Grave? Your carcass will know no grave!' Radukar promised.

The Wolf lunged back at his foe. He unleashed a flurry of thrusts with his sword, shifting tactics from overwhelming force to deadly rapidity. Gustaf wasn't able to match the vampire's speed even with his own reflexes quickened by the elixir. One of the thrusts stabbed true, skewering his shoulder. Spitted on the point of Radukar's blade, Gustaf was flung aside and sent careening down into the mire.

'Your flesh will be the fodder of crabs and eels,' the vampire hissed. 'Your corpse will fill the bellies of vermin.' He strode to the edge of the slab and glared at Gustaf as he lay in the rancid blood. The Nightguard were already moving towards the prone warrior.

Gustaf could see the horrible wound he'd been dealt. Bone showed through the wet, mangled flesh. There was no sensation of pain, however, and there was no agony in his tone when he jeered at the vampire, 'I've fought grots who hit harder than that.'

Radukar's face contorted with outrage at the insult. That instant of anger gave Gustaf an opportunity. Beneath the blood, his hand found one of the fragmented skulls from the Khornate altar. His fingers gripped it by the sockets and whipped it upwards, hurling it at the vampire's face.

Radukar's reaction came in a blur of steel. Exhibiting the super-human deftness of the vampire, he intercepted the crude missile. The skull exploded into shards of bone, slashing in every direction. Radukar howled as his face was sliced by the flying debris.

Gustaf rolled aside as one of the ogors chopped at him with its glaive. He sprang to his feet as the second moved to attack. Its swing missed him, but in avoiding it he found himself within reach of the other Nightguard. Before the mutilating edge of the monster's weapon could hit him, the hulking brute froze in place.

'Back!' Radukar roared at his minions. Pale treacle seeped from the cuts on his face, the putrid ichor that flowed inside a vampire and which could only be revitalised with the blood of a mortal. He wiped the back of his hand across his forehead to clear away the filth. His malignant eyes bore down on Gustaf, transfixing him with an unspeakable hate. 'This one,' he hissed, 'this one belongs to *me*.'

Like his namesake, the Wolf pounced from atop the stone slab. His sword came ripping down, and this time Gustaf wasn't able to twist away. The blade clove through his left arm, shattering the bone and all but severing the limb.

'Has a grot ever–'

Radukar's taunt ended in a snarl of pain. Despite the mutilating blow, the wyrmbrew flowing through Gustaf kept him on his feet. Instead of wilting in pain as the Wolf expected, he lashed out with his blessed sword. It raked across the vampire's hand, splitting it and sending a plume of foul smoke bubbling from the wound. The sting knocked Radukar's barrow-blade from his stunned fingers.

'Sigmar's wrath is upon you!' Gustaf shouted. The next moment he was knocked back by the impact of the vampire's fist against his chest. He could feel ribs snap under the blow.

'With my bare hands, then,' Radukar bellowed. He left the barrow-blade lying where it had fallen and charged at Gustaf once more. His steaming hand closed on the vampire hunter's mangled arm. Before the blessed blade could be brought to bear, the Wolf tightened his hold and pulverised Gustaf's forearm.

Again, the vampire expected his enemy to be overwhelmed by pain. Too late did he see Gustaf's sword come stabbing down. The point pierced Radukar's leg, but before it could be driven any deeper the Wolf smashed the hand that gripped the weapon, shattering every finger. A kick sent Gustaf sprawling back into the mire.

From where he'd fallen, Gustaf watched as Radukar wrenched the sword free. Smoke sizzled up from the wound as undead flesh reacted to the silver. Too enraged to care about the injury, the vampire took the blade and snapped it across his knee. Gustaf could see the blistered skin where it had come into contact with the blessed weapon.

For a moment, Radukar glared into Gustaf's eyes. Then he looked up and a vicious smile crept onto his face. He was looking past the vampire hunter. Towards the tunnel. Towards where Emelda and the others were trying to make their escape.

'So, that was your plan,' Radukar sneered. His gaze turned back to Gustaf. 'You tried to buy them time. Well, let this thought go with you into the underworlds – you suffered all this for nothing. They will not escape me.'

Gustaf struggled to make use of his broken limbs, but the strength and immunity to pain endowed by the wyrmbrew couldn't compensate for shattered bones. He could only watch helplessly as the vampire came for him and pray to Sigmar that Radukar's words were wrong.

The vargskyr slashed at Emelda with its long claws. She ducked the vicious swing and slashed at the beast with her sword. It was agile, dancing aside as her blade narrowly missed it. In doing so, however, it put itself within reach of Loew's knife. The vigilante gashed it across its hairy flank. A broth of foul ichor jetted from a severed vein. The monster spun around and snapped at him with its jaws. Loew dodged the bite and replied to it by raking his steel down the creature's face, cutting it from its lupine muzzle to its fanged mouth.

'Keep it busy,' Emelda yelled. She put action to words, thrusting the point of her blade into the vargskyr's shoulder. She could feel the sword glance off bone but was relieved by the stream of loathsome fluid that gushed from the injury.

The monster snarled and spun once more. This time Emelda wasn't as fortunate in avoiding its assault. The claws raked across her armour, drawing sparks as it gouged the steel. The force of the blow knocked her sprawling. The vargskyr howled in predatory victory and would have pounced on her had Loew not intervened. The vigilante's knife ripped into the brute's head, piercing its eye.

'Over here, you cur!' Loew spat at the wolfish beast. The vargskyr sprang at him, bowling him over. One of the claws flashed down. Loew screamed as his back was opened up by the fiend.

Emelda recovered her sword and rushed back to the attack. She was desperate to get the vargskyr away from Loew. Not simply because of the monster's savagery, but because Morrvahl was ready to cast the horrible dust over the brute. Death from the monster was better than dying the way the wizard was planning.

Yet Emelda was risking that horrible destruction herself by closing on the vargskyr and trying to pull it off Loew. A dread such as she'd never felt before gnawed at her gut when she slashed the beast's ribs and succeeded in focusing its attention back onto herself. Its lips curled back in an angry growl. She retreated before it, luring it away from Loew. She was careful to keep close enough that the vargskyr didn't turn back, yet far enough that she was just out of reach of its claws.

'Now, Morrvahl! Now!' Her tone was almost pleading as she shouted at the wizard. Every step she expected the vargskyr to lunge at her, to seize her in its claws and bite her with its fangs. Then, while it held her, the powder would settle over them both and she'd feel the gnawing bite of very different fangs.

Morrvahl took a few steps forwards with what, for the still-weary wizard, amounted to haste. The packet was open now and a quick toss sent its contents billowing outwards. Emelda jumped back, trying to put even more distance between herself and Morrvahl's target. The vargskyr started after her, but not soon enough to escape a heavy dusting.

There ensued a hideous scene. Emelda continued to engage the vargskyr, fending it off with swings of her sword. Every heartbeat seemed as though it were an eternity to her. She kept listening, straining to hear the faintest sound from the tunnel, the first indication that verminous destruction was rushing out from the sewers. Thoughts of the wizard's magic distracted her, made it impossible to concentrate on the deadly foe before her. Twice she felt the vargskyr's claws rake against her armour, and once the beast's snapping jaws came within an inch of her face. The longer their fight persisted, the more frustrated the brute became and the more frenzied its attacks.

'They're coming,' Morrvahl called to her. The wizard stood over Loew, ministering to the vigilante's wounds. His eyes were focused past the melee and into the depths of the tunnel.

Emelda heard the scrabble of claws and the agitated squeaks. A heavy, musky odour slammed into her senses. The vargskyr turned its head, its bestial instincts warning it of a new threat.

But warned or not, the monster was unable to stop that verminous tide. Up from the darkness a flood of corpse-rats converged upon the vargskyr. Berserk with hunger, provoked to madness by the scent of Morrvahl's powder, they didn't pause for an instant but swept over the vargskyr. It howled in defiance, swatting and ripping at the rodents, flinging their bodies in every direction. At last, however, it was covered entirely, smothered beneath a horde of gnashing fangs.

Emelda turned from the horrible sight and ran over to help Morrvahl with Loew. She brushed the wizard's hands aside as she examined the vigilante's wounds. Her eyes darted to Gravebloom and the vitality-sucking thorns wound about it.

'He's bad,' Morrvahl said. 'He can't make it.' The wizard had noticed the direction Emelda's gaze had been drawn.

'We'll get you out of here,' Emelda assured Loew, defying Morrvahl's prognostication. Her conscience was already wracked by letting Gustaf sacrifice himself. She wasn't going to leave another comrade behind.

Loew was more pragmatic about his chances. 'You can't save everyone,' he coughed, blood trickling from his mouth. He took her hand in his, his fingers closing tight. 'Liberate our people, Lady Braskov. Free them of Radukar. Do that and my spirit will rest easy.'

'By the last drop of my noble blood, I swear it,' Emelda vowed. She had to raise her voice as the sounds of the corpse-rats intensified.

'Ulfenkarn will be free,' Loew said. For a moment his expression was peaceful; then his eyes took on a frantic expression. 'The beast!'

Emelda and Morrvahl looked up just in time to see the vargskyr stumbling towards them. From head to foot it was enveloped in squirming, gnawing rats, yet the creature refused to lie down and die. Part of its lupine face protruded from the furry swarm. Ripped and bloodied, bone showing through its torn skin, the vargskyr glared at them with its remaining eye. Brute though it was, the monster seemed to sense who was responsible for its dilemma. Uttering a fierce growl, the beast lunged at Morrvahl.

Emelda tried to intercede but was knocked flat by the vargskyr's charge. So too was Morrvahl. The beast loomed over him, ready to bury its fangs in his throat.

Just as it was about to attack, the vargskyr twisted around. Loew's knife impaled its foot, pinning it to the ground. Enraged by the sudden attack, the beast now turned its ire upon the vigilante.

Loew shrieked as the beast's jaws snapped around his head and crushed his skull.

'No!' Emelda raged. She leapt from the ground and fell upon the monster. Heedless of the frenzied rats squirming all across its body, she swung at the vargskyr. Her sword crunched into its side, slashing through rats and chewed flesh to split the creature's bones.

The vargskyr spun around, Loew's decapitated head clenched in its jaws. It swung at her with one of its claws, but before the blow could fall, the limb was struck by Morrvahl's scythe. Severed claws flew from the hand. The wizard glowered at the beast.

'I'm much too busy to be killed by a failed vampire.'

The monster's attention shifted back to Morrvahl. Emelda struck while it was distracted. She thrust her sword into the flesh exposed by the earlier slash. Her intention was to pierce the vargskyr's heart, but in this she was thwarted. Her reach wasn't enough. The lupine beast turned back to her and pounced.

Emelda pitched backwards, the hulking vargskyr above her. It clenched its jaws, crunching what remained of Loew's head. She was showered by the hideous debris. Before it could snap at her, she swung her sword. The angle was bad, and she only managed to scrape the already chewed muzzle. The beast's eye gleamed hungrily as it started forwards.

Before the fangs could close about her own head, the vargskyr collapsed onto its side. Emelda watched it writhe, unable to account for its distress. Then she saw the wound she'd dealt and then expanded. Her sword had been unable to reach the heart, but she'd opened a route for the rats. The vermin were scrambling into the gap, chewing their way to the monster's organs. Like a true vampire, the vargskyr couldn't survive destruction of its heart, whether that destruction was wrought by a stake of Aqshian fyrewood or the ravenous fangs of a hundred rats.

'It almost worked.'

Emelda spun around at the sound of Radukar's voice. The last vestiges of hope died inside her. The Wolf was walking towards them through the streams of rancid blood. Dangling from his fist was Gustaf's battered body.

'Look,' the vampire hissed, drawing Gustaf's head back so he was looking at Emelda. There was still a flicker of life in him. 'They almost got away.' Radukar's smile was filled with cruelty. His fangs glistened as he added a final insult. 'If you'd fought harder, Sigmarite, they would have escaped.'

A sharp crack echoed through the chamber as Radukar broke Gustaf's neck with a twist of his hand. He flung the body at Emelda. It crashed almost at her very feet, quivering as the last threads of life fled from it.

'Bastard!' Emelda snarled at the vampire.

Radukar merely smiled at her. 'Worry about yourself, *hero*. Worry if your death will be quick or slow.' He strode forwards, hunger in his eyes. 'No, I think it will be slow. Killing the Sigmarite was thirsty work.'

The Wolf savoured Emelda's anger. In all the little group of rebels, she was the one who posed the biggest threat to his plans for Ulfenkarn. Last of the Braskovs. The scum would rally to her. She could give them hope. At least, she could if she was alive.

Emelda stepped away from Gustaf's body, her fingers tight about the grip of her sword. Radukar could tell she wanted nothing more than to bury the blade in his flesh. But she was too wary for that, refusing to give in to her wrath, despite his goading of her. She was trying to use strategy and calculate a way to win.

'I'll have to be careful,' Radukar said. 'After I kill you, I'll want to show your carcass to the people. Your face will have to be recognisable to them. The rest, however...' He made a dismissive wave of his hand.

'Come and try it,' Emelda goaded him, gesturing with her sword.

Radukar laughed. 'Your bravado is absurdity itself. Surely you know none of you are leaving here alive?'

'If I'm to die, I'll not die alone.' The words came from the wizard. He stood a little away from Emelda on the other side of Vladrik's dead bulk.

'That's the second time I've been told that tonight,' the Wolf said. He nodded towards Gustaf's body.

'Then what you heard was a prophecy,' Morrvahl retorted. 'Run while I've still a mind to let you.'

The vampire's harsh laughter echoed through the chamber. 'I can tell you've run out of tricks, warlock. If you'd any command left over that vermin, you'd have set them on me already.' He pointed to the dead vargskyr. 'I saw for myself the toll your first conjuration took on you. Impressive, but I don't think you've anything that powerful left in you.'

Radukar snapped his fingers and the last of his Nightguard lumbered forwards.

'I need to make an example of Braskov,' he said. 'But I don't need you at all.' He waved the ogors forwards. 'Kill him.'

'Yes,' Morrvahl said, clutching his staff tight. 'Kill him.' The wizard's eyes shone with a ghastly light. At first it was a greenish glow, but then it rolled into a dull crimson. A baleful energy exploded from his staff, surging through the chamber.

Radukar felt the change at once. The atmosphere of carnage and wrath that lingered in the temple of Khorne was now magnified, swelling into a palpable aura of bloodshed. Dimly sensed before, forces long ago drawn by the cult's sacrifices now manifested themselves. Red shadows leapt from the walls and dripped from the ceiling. Twisted, inhuman shapes that struggled for some foothold in reality.

Radukar focused his own powers against that phantasmal host.

He drew upon his command of occult energies to counter the horde evoked by Morrvahl's spell. Dimly he was aware of the wizard, comatose on the ground, helpless against the least attack. Yet to deal with him would be to ignore the threat he'd summoned.

Vladrik and his foul cult had fixated upon reviving Slaughn. They'd ignored the other hungry things that would be drawn by their rituals. Daemons of the Blood God, sniffing at the periphery of Shyish, needing only the right key to break through to a place steeped in the malice of Khorne. Morrvahl had turned that key and thrown wide the door.

The things struggling to manifest weren't daemons, or rather they were as much of daemons as the profane temple's power could sustain. One, perhaps two could have materialised fully, but this horde dispersed the energies too greatly amongst themselves. They were naught but shadows, suggestions of bloodlust and havoc. Yet where they lacked form and strength, they possessed other qualities.

The phantasms swirled around Radukar. He could feel them clawing at him, trying to force their way into his body and claim a vessel for themselves. His will was stronger, easily capable of fending off their attentions. Wail and rage as they might, the daemons had no chance to possess him.

Not so with the other undead. Little more than husks animated by a kernel of black magic, the Nightguard and zombies were far more vulnerable than Radukar. He saw one of the deadwalkers fall only to lift itself again, a vicious awareness now glowing in its eyes. More of the phantasms strove to claim a hold upon the mighty ogors. The two Nightguard were wrapped about in bands of red shadows as the daemons fought against each other to claim one for their own.

'Back to your infernal realms!' Radukar howled at the phantasms. He plunged into the red shadows and reached the closer of the two ogres. His hands stabbed into the Nightguard's chest, piercing mail and bone to crush its heart between his fingers. The sustaining essence evaporated and the undead slammed back into the mire, now an immobile hulk, useless to the daemons. The swirling shadows converged upon Radukar, clawing at him with their wispy talons. The vampire ignored their ineffectual malice and turned to the other ogre.

He knew at once he was too late. No storm of red shadows surged about the Nightguard now. Instead it stood there, fingering its glaive and glaring at him with fiery eyes. Radukar knew he looked into the eyes of a daemon.

'I denied you Ulfenkarn once,' the vampire snarled. 'I do so again!'

The daemon's reply was an inarticulate bellow. The ogre charged at Radukar, moving with far more agility than even a living Kosargi had shown. The Wolf darted aside as the glaive came cleaving downwards and sent a curtain of rancid blood exploding from the mire. The possessed creature spun about and thrust at him. Fast as it was, Radukar was faster. He brought his hand chopping against the weapon, breaking its haft and sending its head splashing into the gory muck.

'Ulfenkarn is mine!' Radukar raged. He dived at the ogre, but his attack was blunted by the sweep of the glaive's haft. He was thrown back by his enemy, tumbling across the chamber. When he rose from his fall, the possessed brute was charging after him.

Nearby was the carcass of the Nightguard the swordswoman had decapitated. Radukar leapt from the onrushing daemon's path and threw himself towards the dead ogre. He reached under the gory mire until his hands closed around what he was looking for.

The daemon's eyes blazed with immortal wrath. The possessed hulk charged at Radukar once more. The Wolf didn't try to leap clear. Instead, in a show of superhuman strength, he dragged up from the blood the glaive wielded by the dead ogor. He set his foot against it as though it were a pike and braced himself for the attack.

Daemon or not, the ogor couldn't arrest its momentum. It drove itself upon the glaive, the head crunching through its armour and rotted body. The impact bore the weapon clear through the decayed flesh until it erupted out from the brute's back.

Even Radukar's strength was unequal to retaining his hold. The glaive was ripped free from his hands as the impaled ogor staggered away. The daemon possessing it wrenched the weapon free, casting aside the one Radukar had broken. It glowered at him for a moment; then an expression of alarm pulled at the ogor's rotten features. Flesh began sloughing away, dripping from the bones like melting wax. The disintegration spread. The newly won glaive spilled from hands no longer capable of gripping it.

'Did you think you could last long in a dead body?' Radukar laughed at the daemon. Raw hate shone back at him, but already the infernal awareness was fading, drawn back beyond the boundaries of Shyish. Across the forsaken temple, the red shadows were dissipating. The possessed deadwalkers were crumbling, no more capable of sustaining a daemon than the ogor had been. In a short time, the last of the phantasms was gone and all but the smallest trace of the murderous atmosphere was extinguished.

Radukar turned back to the tunnel. He wasn't surprised to see that Braskov was gone. She'd used the distraction to make good her escape. She'd even taken the wizard with her.

'We'll meet again,' Radukar vowed. His eyes shone with pitiless malevolence. 'Ulfenkarn is mine,' the vampire said as he withdrew from the hidden temple. 'And so are all those within its walls.'

EPILOGUE

Awareness returned slowly to Emelda. Unfortunately for her, the first thing she was aware of was pain. The back of her head felt like an orruk had been bouncing it off its foot. The rest of her body was no better. Like one big bruise.

It took a moment for her eyes to adjust to what little light was around her. She could see that it came from torches set into sconces on a stone wall. Between her and the light was an obstruction. A series of iron bars.

Memories swirled through her brain. The final, terrible spell Morrvahl had conjured to cover their escape from Radukar. The effort had stunned the wizard, leaving him insensible. Emelda had carried him away from the Khornate temple while Radukar fought the gruesome apparitions. He was still in a stupor when she brought him back to the surface and headed into the streets. It was there they'd been caught. A company of Volkshaufen lurking in the area had set upon them. It was a hopeless struggle. When she was finally beaten down by the cudgels of the militia, she'd thought it was the end.

Instead it appeared she'd been captured. Emelda looked aside and felt relief when she saw the unconscious figure of Morrvahl lying on the straw-strewn floor. She didn't like the wizard any better, but she'd been responsible for him when they ran into the militia. She'd have felt guilty if he'd been killed.

'So, you're awake.'

Until he spoke, Emelda was unaware that there was someone else in the cell. She could make out a man leaning against the wall. Average build and height. From what she could see, he had a hawkish profile and a certain arrogance in his eyes. She judged him to be just ahead of his fourth decade, though there was a hardness to his features that told of a rough and unforgiving life.

'Arno's troops brought you in here hours ago,' the man continued. 'I thought maybe they'd beaten you past the point of no return.' He nodded at Morrvahl. 'He hasn't so much as groaned once. An old man like that should have sense enough to keep clear of the undead.'

'Are you saying I'm too foolish to have any sense?' Emelda prodded him.

The man stepped away and turned towards the bars. 'I'm saying you look like trouble. I might be a stranger in Ulfenkarn, but even I've heard people whispering that the last of the Braskovs is back.'

Emelda slowly gained her feet. It irked her to talk while he was standing above her. 'What is this place?' She moved to the bars and stared out into the chamber beyond. It was a far from pleasant sight. A central room adorned with every implement of torture she could name, and several she couldn't. Along the walls were more cells, many of them with prisoners of their own. She noted most were humans, but there was a shifty-eyed duardin staring out from one and the sleeping bulk of an ogor filled another.

'You might call this Radukar's menagerie,' the man said. 'A collection point for troublemakers interesting enough to be sent to the Ebon Citadel.' He shrugged. 'The place is a bit more full than usual since Radukar's been busy with Baron Grin.'

Emelda shook her head. 'The Wolf won't be busy any more. Once he learns we're here, he'll have plenty of time for us.'

'I don't plan to be here when that happens,' the man said. 'I intend to escape. Want to help?'

Emelda smiled. She'd managed to elude Radukar himself three times now. She wasn't about to let this gaol get the best of her.

'Try to stop me.' She extended her hand. 'Emelda Braskov.'

The man grasped her hand in his own. 'I'm happy for your help,' he said. 'I'm Jelsen Darrock.'

The introduction was bitter to Emelda. 'Our paths should have crossed long before this,' she said, regret in her voice. 'I knew a friend of yours. Gustaf Voss.'

'Knew?' Jelsen asked, obviously disturbed by the choice of that word.

'He's dead,' Emelda told him. 'He died so I might get another chance at destroying Radukar. When we get out of here, Jelsen, I intend to continue our fight. I'll not rest until Ulfenkarn is free and I hold the Wolf's heart in my hand.'

From one of the other cells, the sound of a song reached Emelda. A childish rhyme recited by a captive whose sanity had been broken by the horror around them.

> 'When ye hear the scrape, scrape, scraping of Old Gorslav on his walk,
> The only sound he ever makes, for he ain't one for talk.
> Flee then, fool, and hide away, and hope he don't come take,
> And bind your arms and drag ye off to bury ye awake.'

It sent a cold shudder through her and she wondered if her bold words were anything but empty bravado. If there was anything that could draw Ulfenkarn back from the shadows.

ABOUT THE AUTHOR

C L **Werner**'s Black Library credits include the Age of Sigmar novels *Overlords of the Iron Dragon*, *Profit's Ruin*, *The Tainted Heart* and *Beastgrave*, the novella *Scion of the Storm* in *Hammers of Sigmar*, and the Warhammer Horror novel *Castle of Blood*. For Warhammer he has written the novels *Deathblade*, *Mathias Thulmann: Witch Hunter*, *Runefang* and *Brunner the Bounty Hunter*, the Thanquol and Boneripper series and Warhammer Chronicles: The Black Plague series. For Warhammer 40,000 he has written the Space Marine Battles novel *The Siege of Castellax*. Currently living in the American southwest, he continues to write stories of mayhem and madness set in the Warhammer worlds.

YOUR
NEXT READ

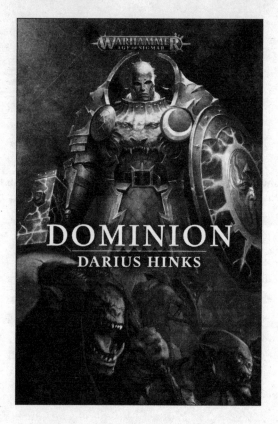

DOMINION
by Darius Hinks

Witness the destructive forces that are on the rise in the Realm of Beasts first-hand,
and see the indomitable defences of Excelsis tested like never before.
